Prologue
The Chained God Unchained

As soon as she sensed what was happening, Slya Fireheart fled. She seldom did much actual thinking, but her survival instincts kicked in when the Chained God Unchained began sucking her essence from her.

Golden Amortis laughed at the big red god, bold and clumsy, as destructive in her affection as she was in her anger, laughed as she watched Slya go running off, laughed because she thought she'd won the little war for the attentions of the Chained God Unchained.

It was much later, almost too late, when she realized just what it was she had won.

Amortis wrenched loose and fled, a pale wrinkled remnant of herself, managing to escape because he was no longer interested in the dregs she offered.

The Chained God Unchained settled on a mountaintop to digest what he'd acquired through the Talisman BinYAHtii and to consider his lifepath. He was mobile now, his existence no longer threatened by decay, but the memory of his near extinction annoyed him. "Hmp," he said. "That was good, but what do I do now?" He scratched a living metal finger along the smooth line of his jaw; pinglows glinted in his eyes, glows like the lights and diodes that flickered across his control panels when he came alive inside the starship computer, part circuitry, part vegetable matter with a heavy dose of the unformed magic force that floated everywhere in this miniature universe. He flexed his hands, watching the metal shift like flesh. " 'S good, I like this, No going back, no way, never again. Hmp. Make sure of that. Make sure. . . ."

Natural forces could no longer touch him. Dismiss those.

Individual gods, even the great ones, couldn't harm him. BinYAHtii would suck in everything thrown at him and feed it to him in usable gulps. Nonetheless . . . there was something nibbling at him . . . keeping him weaker than his potential . . . weaker than whatever it was eating at him . . . something so intangible he could never visualize it . . . draining off his force . . . like the two or three times that shorts drained power from the computer.

The Great Gods? Were they banding together to strike at him? Unlikely. He'd watched them for millennia. They walked their separate paths; if they came too close, they quarreled with varying degrees of bitterness and fury and burst apart again.

Tungjii? He didn't want anything to do with Tungjii. A little god, disgusting in hisser habits, but there was something about himmer that warned against attack.

He considered Perran-a-Perran the god paramount, a diffuse and elusive god, but immensely powerful, more powerful than all the gods combined . . . or was he? If Perran-a-Perran were afraid . . . "AFRAID OF ME?" His sculpted mouth spread in a broad grin and the pinlights danced faster in his eyes. "Afraid of me, isn't that a kick." His brows came down. "I've got to stop that drain. To be safe, I've got to be stronger, strong as he is." He lowered the lids over his glinting eyes. Deep within, in his secret core, he thought: I've got to BE him.

He needed more power. To survive while he acquired it, he had to start small and build. Small gods. Local gods, demiurges, tutelaries, naiads, sylphs and dryads and whatever else lived by and through the Power that filled this Universe.

He rose from his mountaintop and began eating gods.

Chapter 1
A Walk Along the Shore

If they flew across land or sea, they did not know it,
east, west, north or south, they didn't know where they
were being swept, they
> could neither escape the vortex nor change
> direction. Round and round, endlessly
> wheeling through a roaring chaos,
> Navarre, Faan, Desantro
> and Kitya,
> round and round,
> facing each other
> with their backs
> to the howling
> gyrating
> gray wind. . . .

which set them down on a bleak and barren shore,
icy spray lashing them, sand driven by the north wind
scouring their faces.

They had nothing but the clothes on their bodies—
except for Kitya who had her belt pouch with its small
treasures, her skinning knife and the lethal hairpins
Navarre had crafted for her.

Curling her arm across her brow to keep her hair out
of her eyes, Faan turned a half circle, inspecting first
the ragged chalk cliffs with the straggling patches of
wiry grass like fringe along the flat tops, then the sea-

shore and the sea. For an instant she thought someone was watching her, but the feeling blew away before it was more than a shiver in the spine.

Fire burned through her body, heels to head, but she ignored it, using her free hand to haul up the overlong skirt as she kicked at the sand, sending a small crab into a desperate scuttle for shelter. "Gonna gonna kick and scratch," she sang. "An't gonna catch me ee." When she saw the tan grains flashed to glass by the heat in her toes, she changed the words. "Gonna gonna kick and burn. An't gonna put their hands on me."

Her voice was lost in the wind, so she let the song die and went back to looking around. Out in the tossed gray water she thought she saw the flukes of a jade green fishtail. The Godalau? She jumped back, caught her foot in the dress and nearly fell. "Potz!" She hauled up the heavy blue velvet, twisted around so she could see down her back, straightened with a little bounce. "Kitya, loan me your knife, huh? I'm going to break my neck if I don't get rid of this extra cloth."

Kitya raised her thin brows, pinched her mouth together. Silently she handed over the knife, then dug in her pouch for a comb and began dressing her long black hair into its travel knot.

Faan wrinkled her nose, popped her lips in a mock kiss at the woman's back. *You put it on me, it wasn't my choice.* She slashed at the skirt of the dress, shortening it to mid-calf so she could walk without tripping.

Ailiki the mahsar appeared on the beach south of them and came picking her way fastidiously along the shore, avoiding the fingers of the advancing tide, the dead fish and sprawled sea weed. "Aili my Liki," Faan called, sudden happiness bubbling up through her as she saw the one creature who'd been with her all her life, the one who'd never gone away for more than a little while. "My wandering sister, welcome back."

Ailiki sat up, waved her pawhands, then returned to her leisurely stroll.

Holding her hair again, kicking the ragged circle of blue velvet away from her, Faan ran along the sand to meet the mahsar.

Navarre scowled at the sea, rubbing a finger along the crease by his nose. "There's something . . . I almost remember something. . . ."

Kitya squatted beside him, waiting, relaxed as a cat between pounces.

Desantro dug into a pocket and pulled out a handful of crushed bone and raveled cord. She swore, turned to Kitya.

Kitya blinked her dark crimson eyes at the mess, then managed a shrug without losing her balance. "Sorry, Desa. I couldn't raise a dead man's ghost. No houseplace, no bone, no fire, no nothing."

Navarre looked down. "What's that?"

"Kech. Gave a line on Desa's brother. Gone bust." Kitya got to her feet with an easy flow, put her hand on Navarre's arm. "Can't make another unless I have a homeplace where my feet tie to the earth, even if it's only for a day or two."

The corner of his mouth hooked up. "Or in my presence, hmm?"

"That, too."

Faan cooed to Ailiki, scratched behind the delicate ears and under the chin, laughed as the mahsar's purr vibrated through her. After a minute, though, Ailiki stiffened, then wriggled vigorously, her nails biting through the thin blue velvet of the dress. When Faan let her go, she jumped to the sand, sat a moment on her hind legs staring at the top of the chalk cliffs, then she began to fade. Before Faan could scoop her up again, she'd vanished completely.

"Liki, my Liki, Aili Ailiki," Faan cried, anguish shaking her voice. "Where are you, don't play with me like this. Ailiki!"

There was no answer, not a hair of the mahsar left behind.

"Mamay," she whispered. "I need you. . . ." She flung around, came running along the shore, fighting back tears, knots twisting and untwisting inside her.

When she reached Navarre, she caught him by the arm. Her hand was glowing red hot and she felt him wince, but she didn't turn him loose, just walked as fast as she could. "Listen, you keep saying there's some god protecting me, so use it. Find Rakil, you can do it, find him and take us to him, or bring him here, you can do it, you know you can." She shook his arm. "Listen to me, Magus, you want to, I can feel it, do it, don't jegg me you don't. Do it!"

He pulled his arm free, stepped back. "Sorcerie, control! You've learned that, at least. Look at yourself. You're burning up."

Faan glanced at her hands, pushed them behind her, wound her fingers together, tightening them till it hurt. Hair blowing about her face, she glared at him, words collecting in her throat, choking her because she couldn't get them out fast enough. "Do it!" she managed finally. "Coward. Do it!"

He went white with anger, ice not fire. "I cannot," he said softly. "I will not. Listen to me, brat. I curse the day I met you, I curse the softness that made me listen to you. I've lost my home, my friends, my life—and you call me coward?" His voice went so quiet she almost couldn't hear him. "Do you have any idea what could happen if I did what you wanted, if I woke the Wrystrike to fullness? Listen to me, Sorcerie, and be shamed if you are capable of it. I had a wife once, her name was Medora and I did adore her. I had a son once, his name was Bravallan and he was the light of my

eyes. I was searching then, trying to understand what
had happened to me. I went apart to a tower by the
shore, but Bravallan was as full of curiosity as a durran
is filled with seed and one day he followed me. Look at
that sea, Sorcerie, look at it heave, gray and icy. My
tower was beside a sea like that. Medora came to me
and stood with her shoulders slumped, her brown eyes
swimming with the tears she refused to let drop. She
said to me, 'Bravallan my baby, Bravee my son, do you
know what you have done to him?' And she pointed out
to sea where a baby dolphin swam, crying out his fear
and his loneliness. 'I could kill you,' she said to me.
'But I won't. He's a baby, he needs someone to look after him, hear how he cries. Change me.' And I did,
Sorcerie, knowing I could destroy him and her completely this time. I was desperate and flung the Strike
aside and killed a town for her, but she lived. I stood on
a beach like this and watched her swim away with him,
the blood of a hundred innocents on my soul. And you
ask me to chance that again, you ask me to risk Kitya
for a stupid brat I don't know and don't want to know?"

Fire flared along her arms, her hair spread out from
her face, crackling with worms of tiny lightning as
power drained off it. "I don't care about your stinking
stories, I NEED my mother free. Find him. . . ."

Before she could say anything more, Kitya moved
between them. She took hold of Faan's hands, winced.
"Saaa, you're hot. Stop this, Fa! Listen to me, you need
us, think, child, think baby, you'll kill us all if you go
on, think. . . ." She made a lulling croon of the words,
nodding encouragement as awareness returned to the bicolored eyes.

Faan gasped, pulled free, and fled to crouch beside
the incoming tide, her body shuddering with the sobs
that tore through her.

*   *   *

Kitya turned as soon as Faan ran, reached up and stroked her sore fingertips along Navarre's face, the heat bleeding from them into his icy skin. "V'ret, she's just a child and hurting," she murmured. She stepped back, spoke with a touch of acerbity in her voice. "Go find some people for us or shelter or something. From the feel of this wind and the look of those clouds, it's going to be a cold, wet night and I've no desire to spend it outside."

He gazed at her, the years of memories she didn't share like glass between them. Without speaking he walked away, heading for the rugged spike of rock that rose twice as high as the chalk cliffs.

Desantro ran a hand through her damp, tangled hair. "Nu," she said, "it's going to be a rough ride.

"My mama says if there's a wrong way to do anything, folk will find it. Desa, give me what's left of that kech, will you? I'm going to see if Faan can use it."

"Dropped it round here somewhere, ah!" Desantro scraped up the remnants of bone and herb, passed them to Kitya. "You think she's got anything left after all that?"

"All I know is, if we're going to get out of this mess, Fa and V'ret are going to have to get along. It'll be a start on that if she can come up with something. If she can't, nu, we haven't lost anything, have we? Do you think you could hunt up a nice shiny shell?"

Searching for the concentration she needed, Faan gazed at the mother-of-pearl that lined the curved inner surface of the shell; it shimmered, loopy pastel pink lines chasing pale blue ones, as the gray light fluctuated through clouds flowing past overhead and the air gelled about her.

The wind whined in her ears: NO NO NO NOOOOOOO.

The broken kech rattled by her knee, fragments of it blew away.

Her arms were weighted, moving them was pushing against a current. She fought that, too. There was heat in her, the ashes of anger at everything that had wrenched and torn her life from what it should have been, at all the beings who tried to control her. She looked up, scowled. "Eyes . . ."

Desantro got to her feet, scanned the top of the white chalk cliffs. "Nayo nay," she said, "there's no one watching."

"I know, but . . ." Faan hunched her shoulders and fixed her gaze once more on the shimmering interior of the shell, fighting to find focus.

The heat and turmoil grew stronger. The resistance grew with it, as if even the sand she knelt on worked against her. And the eyes . . . the eyes . . . that no one could see . . . she knew they were there . . . hating her, watching . . . willing her to fail. . . .

Kitya knelt beside her, curled a hand about the nape of her neck. "Faan, listen, my mama said what you can't win by beating on, you can wheedle."

Faan started, nearly dropped the shell. She swallowed a yelp, clamped her teeth on her lower lip. *I'm sick of hearing about her jeggin mamay!* She didn't say it; if she said anything, it'd all start up again and she didn't think she could stand that.

Kitya began stroking the curve of Faan's nape. "Be quiet," she murmured, added a gentle incantation in her birthtongue, "Niya naluk niya paluk niya naluk niya. . . ." Over and over she said the words until they flowed into Faan's blood.

Faan lingered a moment in that centered serenity, in memories of the warmth and love she'd had from her Salagaum Mamay, then she sighed and gathered herself. This time she felt calm and competent; the forces in her fingers flowed to her beat. Earth and air fought her, but she brushed them off and whispered the focal words that should have brought the mirror gleaming between her palms.

It didn't happen. Instead a little glass fish floated there, a tiny limber fish filled with sunfire, its body flexing gracefully as if it swam in waters she couldn't see. She blinked.

Kitya's breath tickled her ear. "Say his name."

"Rakil," Faan said, raised her brows as the fish turned through a quarter arc and pointed north. Kitya rising with her, she got to her feet and turned to face north along the shore.

The fish quivered, but didn't change its point.

Navarre came back.

The fish vanished as he reached them.

"Sorry," he said. "What was that?"

Faan wiped her hands down her sides; it was a minute before she could look up at him. "I don't know," she murmured. "At a guess, it's the ghost of the kech." She blinked. "Whatever, it was telling us that Rakil's somewhere to the north of here."

"Hmm. Kat, the kech, what direction did it point before?"

"West and a hair south."

"Then we're south and west of Valdamaz across sea water, which means that . . ." he waved at the heaving gray water, "what we're looking at out there is the channel called The Sodé and this is the island Kaerubulan—that is, if your brother hasn't shifted his location since you pointed him."

Kitya spread her hands. "Who can say?"

"Kaerubulan," Faan said. She got to her feet, too tired to fight any longer. "So what's Kaerubulan that you know it so quickly?"

Though he avoided looking at her, Navarre responded easily enough, "It rates a listing in Lexicons and Transactions; the folk here are . . . interesting. Shape shifters with an allergy to magic."

"Allergy?"

"It's said to poison them. That's all I know. They're a secret people."

"I see." Faan dug her toes into the sand, remembering too clearly the bitter arguments she'd had with Reyna, the pain she'd given her adopted Mamay. She wasn't bothered by any pain she'd given Navarre, but Reyna would be shamed to see his daughter acting like a Jang-bred saisai. Tears gathered again, but she fought them back. Even if Reyna were here, he wouldn't know her or remember what he'd taught her. *I remember, I'm the only one who does.* "Navarre, I'm sorry," she said. "I'll tell you why if you want to hear it, but that's not important. I'll . . . I'll watch my temper and . . ." Her control frayed by his cold face and lack of response, she clamped her teeth together to keep the rush of hurt and fury from spilling out again.

Kitya pinched Navarre's arm. "Say something, you!"

"What?"

"Ooyik."

"Labi labba, if you wish. Faan, the fault was mine as much as yours."

It was a grudging acknowledgment, but it was obviously all she was going to get. She looked away from him, saw Desantro mouth the word *Men!* and roll her eyes; it started a quiet giggle in her that went away when she looked down and saw her hands shining against the blue velvet. "Magus, help me," she said. "I'm hanging by my fingernails, and I don't know how much longer I can do that."

"May I touch you?"

"Tja."

He laid his hand on her brow; she could feel him flinch at the heat in her, but he didn't pull the hand back until he had what he needed. He moved away a few steps, and stood gazing out at the sea, muscles jumping now and then about his mouth.

He's searching for a tactful way to say it. Give it up, Magus. There's not much difference between tact and lies and I need the truth.

Without looking at her, he said, "There's nothing I can do to help you, Sorcerie. Not until we're off Kaerubulan. You've been taught disciplines. Practice them."

Faan twisted her face into a clown's grimace, the way the Salagaum Jea used to when he had a date he didn't think he'd like. "No magic at all?"

He looked round at her, a smile startled out of him. "This far from everything? As long as there's no one around, why not."

It was getting easier. Pretending to laugh seemed to make her feel like laughing. "I know what you want. Hot meal in your belly and fresh water to drink."

"And you don't, Sorcerie? Nu, Kat, I saw a house with a pier we can reach before sundown if we start now. You're right about the storm, we'll need shelter." He tucked his arm in Kitya's. "Shall we go?"

Chapter 2
Storms Present and Coming

The Karascapa tavern in the waterfront district of Tempatoug was a big rambling place, dark, smoky and hot despite the sleet driving down outside. In a booth against the back wall Rakil listened to the wind howl and shivered; after so many years in southern lands he'd lost whatever love he'd had for winter storms, especially those that came out of their time, late in Kaerubulan's brief bright Spring. Silently cursing the whim mixed with greed that brought Purb to this ungodded island with its twisting Shifters and bitter storms, he sipped at his hot wine and made forgettable small talk with the Trader Jatjin who was sitting at the table with him.

Rakil looked very much like the sister he hadn't seen in decades, the same beaky nose and high cheekbones, the same brown eyes with green flecks near the pupil; he was thinner, more than a head taller. With the tavern's murky light smoothing away the finer wrinkles from his face and blurring the cynicism in his eyes, he might have been Desantro's son rather than her younger brother.

The bonedancer on the drum in the center of the room was drawing booms and clatters from the broad resilient surface with its inset stone and shell while two Shifters with exaggerated female forms swayed and shimmied through a complex dance that had a clump of dockers hooting and snapping their fingers, some of them leaning over the groaning copper rail to grab at the dancers who avoided the hands with the ease of much practice, flicking silken scarves over wrists as they did so without breaking their wide-eyed, ecstatic bond with the beat.

Rakil banged his mug on the table, then raised it high. The potgirl caught his signal and rattled her cart over to him; she was dark and squat, aggressively bonetype, staring at the world through a fringe of coarse black hair. Rumor was she was deaf and blind in one eye, probably because she ignored equally praise and insult, smiles and frowns. She plucked the mug from his hand, brought it under the barrel's spigot and had it on the table again in one smooth motion; at the same time she was agitating her pokers in their bed of coals. She thrust one of them into the wine. As it sizzled and added a tang to the stale air, she raised a brow at Jatjin; when he shook his head, she collected a pring for the drink and a cob for the poker, then rattled her cart to the next table.

Jatjin's eyes narrowed to slits to keep out the curls of steam as he gulped down a draft of his wisuk, smacked his lips afterward; he leaned back so his face dissolved into the shadow beyond the feeble light from the candle stub guttering out its final minutes in the center of the table. "This is being the last batch I am bringing in," he said. "Baik a baik, we are making a good thing out of it, but is coming the Noses. The jellies is getting nervy, winding up t' a fight, ia? Better we are going somewhere else while they be shaking down, ia?"

"Where there's need the price goes up, ia?"

"Bem. Till you be doing the paying and in blood not gold." He took another mouthful of the cooling wisuk, patted his straggly mustache with the back of his hand. Mouth twisting in a smile half pride, half deprecation, he reached up, plucked a hair from his head and held it close to the candle where it glittered like silver wire. "White hair," he said. "Is not being every man who lives to have 'em, ia? Me, I am living till I be bald and toothless."

Rakil chuckled. "With seven times seven wives and enough children to people a city."

"That I am having already. Why I am spending so much time at sea, ia? Is being quieter in middle of typhoon, ia?" Jatjin leaned closer, his beady eyes glinting under the hedge of his brows. "You be listening to me, Rak. I am thinking ol' Flea's head gone soft this time, else he is being out of here a month ago, ia? Not staying around while the jellies run amok. And not just staying, sinking his feet in it. I am liking you, Rak. You are being twistier than a jelly in a fit, a good thing in a trader, ia? I am saying ship out with me and give the jelly wars a miss."

"The Flea's a bad enemy, Jatjin, and he's a man to spend a handful of gold to get a copper back." *And, Old Man, I'd only be trading one master for another. Hunh, more than one. Every man's the master of a runaway slave.*

"Is being a waste if you are getting chopped. . . ." Jatjin stopped talking as he caught sight of a small dark man threading through the tables, coming toward them. "Sa sa, 'tis done. We be talking of other things round Oglan, but there is being a place open for you should you be coming away from here, Rak." He paused, frowned. "Should you be coming alone."

Rakil pulled his scarf higher on his face and plunged head down into the storm that blew along the straight-ruled streets of Tempatoug, streets with never a single bend to break the flow of the wind and the rush of the sleet. With their undulant bodies and fluid minds the Shifters were drawn to the simplest and harshest of forms, the line and the square; even triangles were suspect, though they did concede that rain and snow slid easiest off a slanted roof. That shape-hunger was why some of them had a desperate need for those they called bonemen, the unchanging strangers they brought in to do heavy lifting. It was why Humarie had let him give her a bone name. Humarie. He wanted to see her, wanted to sink into that yielding, infinitely responsive flesh, but this wasn't his day with her and Purb the Flea was waiting for him, his temper chancy.

Ghosts blew past like patches of fog, their scratchy cries drowned by the wind; he never knew what they were saying, so he was grateful for that at least. Because the Shifters couldn't see or hear them, they wouldn't let ghostmen onto the island to lay the earth souls of the dead. The city swarmed with ghosts, from the newest and strongest to the worn out wisps of decades-dead grandfathers, all of them yammering yammering yammering about their wrongs and miseries and curling themselves about people, trying to get them to listen or do something, no one knew what. He usually felt nervous about walking through them, but tonight it was hard to tell them from the rain and sleet and, in any case, he was too distracted to care.

Rakil turned into a sideway that was little more than a crack between the concrete walls of two of the rigidly square blocks that the Shifters called buildings. The wind was gone, suddenly, but sleet was hitting one of the roofs, bouncing and running down the slope, cascading to the ground in a mix of ice and water, chasing away the ghosts that usually hung about up near the eaves. Cursing under his breath, he hunched his shoulders and waded through the slush until he reached a gate in the wall that extended from the back of the north building to the next street over.

The gateway was plugged with ghosts.

He pushed into them and huddled as much of himself as he could under the lintel while he fumbled for the key and let himself into the minute garden with a few pale green spears half drowned in mud and naked trees with ghosts caught in their branches like tent-caterpillar webs. He hurried along the walk, feeling in his pocket for the housekey, but Purb had the door open before he reached it.

The Flea slammed it shut as soon as Rakil was in, hauled the bar down and turned. "Well?" Purb the Flea's voice was high and squeaky when he was excited, though that wasn't what earned him his nickname; he'd gotten the Flea from his habit of leaving on the hop most of the places he'd lived in.

"Not a whisper of trouble." Rakil unwound the scarf, hung it over a peg, began loosening the lacings of his cloak. "The exchange was made two hours ago. The Browneyes were satisfied with the swords and spearpoints and they got them loaded on their ponies along with the barrels of oil-gel without any interruption from Yelloweye patrols. The essences they passed over were what they'd promised, no scanting in quality or volume. Jatjin's messenger was slow because his mount stepped in a hole and broke a leg so he had to walk part of the way. That's why I'm later than we expected." He hung the cloak on another peg and stood hunched over and dripping on the entranceway flags. "Baik a baik, it all went very well."

"The suap?"

Rakil reached inside his shirt, brought out two heavy leather purses. "Jatjin and Browneye, no argument either side. Haven't counted it yet, but the weight feels right."

"They're wet." Purb stepped back. "You're dripping on me. Put that in the study, then go get yourself cleaned up." His voice had dropped to its usual growl. "Don't take forever. I'm getting together a dinner, I want to tell you how to set it up and what you should order for it."

"I hear," Rakil said, the words as neutral as he could

make them. He went sloshing off, the icewater in his boots no colder than his distaste for what he was going to have do.

Purb bustled about the table rechecking everything Tamtim the Cook had done. His best place settings were out, the Shiro-ware white, gleaming, without a crack or a flaw—the Flea's personal taste was more elaborate, tending to gold with lots of curly engraving, but the Shifters wouldn't allow bonemen to use the high metals. The center of the table was a riot of blooms from the most expensive of the forcing houses, great sprawling arrangements of purple and orange with explosions of fern and trailing vines that threatened to get into the food. The white linen mats at each place were stiff with white-on-white embroidery in the elaborate geometrics of Shifter design, the milkglass eating sticks had a matching design pressed into them, the soup spoons were molded tortoiseshell with white ceramic handles, the paired straws at each place were etched crystal— and, as a compliment to the guests, had the signifier of the subDuke Browneye Snarl at the center of the design—rather, a boneman's approximation of the complex sign the Shifters used for their ruler; Rakil had been astonished to find that the Shifters had no written language. When he asked Humarie about it, she said, "If we want half-truth, we send a boneman; if we want a lie, we write it."

Purb the Flea had gone as far as he could, walking the dangerous line between honoring his guests and exceeding his station. He stepped back, viewed the effect of the wall lamps. "I still think we should have light at the table, even if it's only candles. I need to see their faces."

Rakil sighed. They'd had this argument with each dinner Purb had arranged for his Shifter contacts. "If you don't feel like listening to me, Janguan Purb, re-

member what TwoFinger EarTwitch said when he was
teaching you the jellydeal. Shifters don't like light in
their eyes. If you want to irritate them, sa sa, but think
about it."

Purb pushed his lips out and looked stubborn, but he
dropped the matter. "You'll stand behind me and translate; keep it smooth and keep it fast. This is important,
Rak; I want them sweet when they leave."

Rakil pressed his lips together. Despite their need for
them—or perhaps because of it—Shifters despised
bonemen, considered them little better than workbeasts;
even the obsessives who hung about bonelife because
they needed to, even they had no respect for what they
desired, loathing themselves for their indulgences. Purb
was blundering ahead as usual, seeking to force those
around him to accept his vision of himself. It wouldn't
work this time. "You haven't told me yet who they are,
Janguan Purb. I'd better know how to speak them."

"Baik a baik, Rak. Come." He led Rakil into his
study, sat down behind his desk and folded his hands on
the mat. "Anyone could walk in there any minute.
They're all spies for Earwaggle SnakeTongue, you
know it as well as I do. Sit, man, you make me nervous
standing there like that."

"Kanga berk, Janguan Purb."

Purb the Flea unwound his hands and began tapping
his fingers on the mat, small thuds like the rain hitting
the shutters, the last sputters of the storm that had hung
over the city for days now. "They aren't going to be using their right names or their right faces. B'ja, you don't
need to know those, just what to call them. The most
important one will be PointedEar NoseWaggle, the
other, Redhair EyeTwitch. They know trade sign well
enough, and I wouldn't be surprised if they actually can
understand speech, so keep that in mind in your translations. We will be negotiating a Futures Contract. I want
an exclusive concession on blueflower essence, that's

the most important thing, after that, appointment as Harbormaster's Deputy, and last, anything else we can squeeze out of them that might be useful—but no pushing. And remember, the end of the meal is the end of the deal, so watch sharp, Rak."

"Ia sim, Janguan Purb."

"Make sure the best towels are in the dressing room, new slippers, anything they'll need if it's still raining, tell the maids to get their cloaks and boots dry, and if they don't do it right, they'll get the whip. I want everything perfect, Rak, perfect!" He coughed. "You can go now, you've got a lot to do."

"Ia sim, Janguan Purb." He stood, bowed and went out.

If I was a freeman, I'd 've done better to go with Jatjin, he thought as he hurried for the kitchen. The Old Man was right, what a nose he's got . . . still, the Flea's survived before, and he might wake up this time and dive for cover . . . if I ran, he'd have my skin . . . no doubt about that . . . I've seen him. . . . He shivered. Vindictive little sod . . . gods! Not time yet . . . ride it out a while longer . . . I can always run . . . Humarie . . . she won't come . . . won't leave her people . . . besides . . . the old idiot . . . he's almost family . . . don't want those bastard jellies taking him down. . . .

He slowed, smoothed his hair back, straightened his tunic, then walked into the kitchen. "Tamtim," he told the cook, "he likes the table. Good work. Sperrow, where are you? Ah. You've got the dry room hot? Good. Get Birri and Tigla in here, I want . . ."

It was too easy, he thought as he escorted the Shifters from the house after the dinner was finished and the accords signed.

He stood watching them walk along the narrow way, heading inland away from the bonequarter, envying them a little as he watched the ghosts cringe away from them, plastering their insubstantial forms against the walls. The rain had stopped completely and the clouds were breaking up; in the intermittent moonlight he could follow the shift and slide of those mutable bodies, even something of the flow of change that was the part of their speech only Shifters could manage. He couldn't read what they were saying, but had a strong suspicion they were laughing at Purb for thinking that bargains with bonemen meant anything once the pressures were off. They didn't bargain hard, he thought, because they're damn sure they're not going to have to pay off. I'd better start setting up get-outs. If Purb comes round, we'll hop together, if not. . . . He sighed, pulled the gate shut, locked it, and started inside. If he gets chopped, I want to be away from here. A long way away. Guffrakin . . . ia sim, the Owl to get the brand off my butt. Stinking jellies. . . .

He walked slowly back into the house, stopped in the kitchen.

The cook looked up from the bird he was carving. His broad red face was slick with sweat. "He happy?"

"Bubbling. They lapped it up, Tam, like they hadn't seen food in a month. You all did good."

Tamtim grunted, pleased. "Pull up a chair. From what Birri and Tigla says, you didn't get a mouthful."

He was too annoyed to be hungry, but it was better to keep Fat Tam sweet. "Can't. Have to go listen to him eat it over again, you know the ritual. Save me a plate, I'll be by for it later."

He left the kitchen and walked slowly to the study where Purb was waiting for him. Not the Flea now, he thought, the Blind Mole pushing his little pink snout into a trap. Gods! It wasn't something he admitted much, even to himself, but he had a reluctant fondness for the old twister, grown up somehow beside repeated bursts of anger and frustration. How long has it been?

Twenty-five years. A quarter of a century. Baik a baik, that's a long time. A long time. . . .

He knocked at the door, went in without waiting for a summons.

Purb was sitting at his worktable, going over a sheet of parchment covered with black ink scrawls, seals affixed along one side. He looked up, grinned at Rakil, moved his hand so the sheet snapped into a tight roll. "Hoo hoo," he chortled, "All we got to do is wait, Rak, then we're set."

Rakil smiled, set his hands palm to palm and bowed over them. *They'll burn their copies the moment they get to some safe place and if you try to use yours, you're dead.* He couldn't resist a small nay-say, though he knew it would anger the Flea. "If the Browneyes win this time."

Purb whinnied, not angry but amused. "They will, old son, they will. A ragged granny whispered in my ear."

Rakil managed a sour smile. *Ghosts now, is it? Fool!*

Purb pushed the roll aside. "Baik a baik, we've got a godon full of legal essence it's time to move out. Who's in port now?"

"Traders Orn, Gaaf ni Secorro, Orao Kotkal, a few more who can take the leftover odds and ends. Hairim Zadem and the *Wave Jumper,* he's heading out before the end of the week, bound for Bandrabahr. He should be good for a consignment if we can't get the right price here. Kinok Assach and the *Dark Moon,* just got here, bound for Savvalis after this, then back along the coast all the way to Silili with a stopover at Kukurul. It's a long route, but he usually keeps clear of pirates and the like and he's no cod at bargaining. There are four, five more, but to speak frankly I wouldn't trust any of them with yesterday's bran mush."

Purb pulled at his nose, frowned. "Secorro's a pij would rob the coppers from his mama's eyes. Last time we . . . baik a baik, forget that. And him. Start working Orn and Kotkal, then Zadem and maybe Kinok, though a year's a long time to wait for a profit." He got to his feet, grunting with the effort of shifting his weight. "Get started tomorrow morning, see what they want, then I'll finish the deal."

Rakil couldn't sleep.

Purb had stopped locking him in years ago, just told him to be back by breakfast or he'd get a dozen cuts to teach him the value of what he'd wasted; his time belonged to his owner which made him a thief if he took it for himself. He was late just once. Purb did the job with his own hands, then had a healwoman in to take care of the bloody meat he'd made of Rakil's back.

He rolled out of bed and went to the window. The Wounded Moon was gibbous waxing, floating in a hole in the clouds near the undulant hilltops beyond the city, their terraces filled with plants in bud, though he couldn't see them now, only the pale river of ghost stuff that came out of all the nooks and crannies of the city to moonbathe in those perfumed gardens. He stood resting his elbows on the tile sill, trying to ignore the cold that was striking up through the sleeves of his nightshirt.

If he went to see Humarie, he'd have to watch men climbing the stairs, coming down with that blind sated look that he knew was on his own face when it was his turn. He hated knowing that. Almost as much as he hated knowing it was only her madness that gave him even the little bit of her that she chose to grant him. If she didn't have the bonesickness on her . . .

He thought about leaving. He could go home. Back to Whenapoyr. Home? He was four when the raiders came. Sometimes he dreamed about trees, huge trees with roots bigger than he was. There wasn't much else. Except his sisters. For the first time in years he thought about his sisters and wondered vaguely what had happened to them. Tariko was two years younger, just a baby; it was a long time before he forgot how she cried and cried in that stinking hold. Desantro was older, ten years between her and him. She took care of them both, fought the other slaves to get food for them. Got beat for it, too, with wide soft straps so they wouldn't break her skin. She was the first one sold. One day she was there, the next, she was gone.

The ground under his feet was turning treacherous, sliding away, chasms opening. He cursed Purb for his stupidity, his greed, his blindness, banging his fist on the sill as futility and helplessness flowed over him, threatening to drown him.

Shivering with cold, he crawled back into bed and after a long struggle finally dropped into a restless, dream-ridden sleep.

Chapter 3
Turn and Turn Again

Judging by the animal droppings, bits of leaf, webs and dust laminated on floors and walls, the house had been abandoned for years, probably since the stream that ran along beside it went dry, taking out the fishers' water supply. Even the ghosts were gone, worn by time to frazzled nothing.

The walls were a rough gray concrete, the outside surfaces pasted with shells in interlocking squares; though these decorations were broken and falling off and the concrete was cracked and crumbling in a few places, the structure seemed fundamentally intact. The roof was glazed tile, black and deeply ridged; it, too, seemed intact despite repeated hammering from storms like the one that was sweeping south along the coast, storms that had eaten away large chunks of the chalk cliffs rising above the house. The Shifters built well.

Inside, they found three small rooms and an attic, no furniture except an old copper gallon-pot with holes in the bottom.

Navarre stood in the doorway smiling affectionately as he watched Kitya survey the debris. The smile vanished when he glanced over his shoulder at the clouds boiling toward them, black and heavy with rain. "I'll see what wood I can collect." He drew the knuckle of his forefinger along Kitya's face. "And leave you to get on with it, nu?" He laughed and went out.

Kitya sighed. "It's a herd I need for this den. So . . ."

Desantro backed toward the door. "We'll want something to eat," she said, "I'll go dig some clams and stuff." She left hastily, almost before she'd finished announcing her intentions.

Kitya snorted. "No taste for cleaning, that one."

"Me either, Kat." Faan grinned at her, then lifted the pot, screwing up her mouth as she shook out the bones and dried skin of a long dead rat. "This shouldn't be too hard to fix. Sibyl had me making holes and closing them up forever, or at least it felt like that. And I'll turn some seawater for us. I'm getting thirsty."

Kitya nodded absently. "Do it outside, hmm? Mix and match magical turns won't work too well anywhere and here, it could be worse. That's what it feels like, anyway."

"So I noticed." Faan waved her free hand. "Like Desa, I go."

Light glittering off the knife-edged facets of his golden face, the Chained God Unchained glared from the godspace at the Four as they walked along the beach. They'd caught his roving eye when Meggzatevoc flung them out of his Land and he'd recognized a danger in them; he didn't know how that could be or why such puny creatures rang warning bells in his head, but he was clanging like a Gerngesse dinner call. Part of the nibbling that wouldn't let him alone? No. Nibbling to come. Plotting against him. He knew it. All the time they were milling about on that beach he'd tried to reach down and squash them. It should have been easy, but he couldn't touch them. Something stopped him, something he couldn't see or feel—as if a pane of glass harder than steel stood between him and them. Perran-a-Perran, he was sure of it now,

though why the God Paramount was bother-
ing with such puny mortals was something he
didn't understand. And that bothered him, too.

He whipped up the storm, tried to blow
them back out into the water and drown them
there, but the wind slipped from his hand, the
storm slowed and didn't touch them. He nodded his great head, filling the space around
him with golden light that might have cut like
knives, if there'd been anything in there close
enough to him. "That makes one thing clear,
my pets. But there's nothing to say someone
or something else can't do the job for me."

He probed the island's coast till he found a
band of Shifters searching for smuggler
traces, sent a wind to whisper in the leader's
ear that four deadly magicians had invaded
their land, then he patted chaos into a pillow
shape, settled himself more comfortably, taking time from his god-grazing to watch with
satisfaction as the riders raced along the
coast, tethered their mounts out of sight, and
flowed into their wolfhound form so they could
spy on the incomers without being discovered.

Faan wrinkled her nose, primmed her lips. The wind
rumbling ahead of the storm was damp and cold, digging up wet sand and driving it into her; the sun was a
gray blur behind the clouds—but she had one dress and
no immediate prospect of replacing it, so she pulled it
over her head, folded it neatly and set it on one of the
mottled gray and white boulders that lay in a fan-
shaped fall across the beach.

"Brrr!" She stamp-danced across the sand, slapping
at the copper pot ... tunk tank tunk tank, stomp and
stomp. "Wow-ow-ow!" she squealed as the icy sea wa-

ter began curling about her ankles, creeping up her legs as she waded cautiously deeper into the surge.

Kneeling, she sloshed the pot in the sea, scooped up handfuls of sand and scoured it as clean as she could get it, the sand scratching through what seemed decades of tarnish and crust. "Kitya's ma isn't the only one with aphorisms," she told herself with a forced cheeriness that the Sibyl would have punctured fast; she knew that, but she didn't want to think about her yearning for her mother . . . for someone who cared about her. It was too hard and too distracting. "Old Sibyl had a bunch." She sloshed water about in the pot, inspected it, and scrubbed some more. "Spells work best when you keep them simple, she kept telling me, surfaces meld or melt better when they're clean. It only takes a little care to make things ready and it can save you a lot of bother later."

She sloshed the sand around, dumped it out, dipped up more water and dumped it again and again until all the sand was gone. "I suppose that's as good as it gets." When she stood, her feet burned and went numb; it took concentration to get herself and the pot back up on the beach.

She settled herself on a boulder beside the one where she'd left her dress, pulled the pot onto her knees, the heavy wind whipping her hair about her face until she could hardly see. She shifted around so she was half facing it, curled her toes against the cold, and frowned into the cavity; the copper was wrinkled and dented, still discolored, though there were striations of brightness where the sand had cut through the tarnish. One of the holes was a ragged circle she could put her fist through, the other was a long narrow slit with curled lips as if someone had thrust a knife through the metal, jerked it out again.

I did say easy, didn't I. She looked up, scowling at the line of the cliff. "Eyes," she said aloud. She cupped her hands about her mouth and shouted, "Go away, I'm going to work. I don't want to hurt you. Go away!"

A huge dog, or maybe it was a wolf, looked over the edge of the cliff, then pulled back. She heard yips that faded into the howl of the wind. "Sucks to you," she yelled. "Go eat your tail, mawb!"

She shivered, so suddenly alone, in a way she hadn't been before. Mamay, ah ma ma. . . . Her lips moved in the child's word which, with her name, was all she brought with her from her mother's arms. And Ailiki, of course, but Ailiki was gone. . . .

"I need something . . . a shell, bone, something. . . ." She set the pot down and kicked through the weed and debris until she found an abalone shell and another she didn't recognize, long and narrow with a rough top. She took them back, settled on the rock again, gazing away from the pot, out over the metallic gray water, watching it lift and fall as if the sea were breathing, watching it surge and roll, wash in, retreat. Her own breathing slowed, matched itself to the sea. Once again she felt air and earth pushing at her, trying to deny her; once again they were too feeble to stop her.

Copper fires danced along her arms, flickered over the pot. Inside the hollow the shell blurred, took color from the fires and flowed across the hole. There was a lurch at the base of her stomach, then there was a patch of shiny new copper, grooved and pitted like the shell that was. "Whoops! Gotcha!" She touched the patch, stroked her fingers across it, pleased with what she'd made. It was good. She felt good. With a sigh, she turned back to the sea.

Breath in breath out, let the transform slide, send the fires home, breath in breath out. . . .

The wind howled, the air went stiff as setting gelatin, her breathing was labored, her movements sluggish. The land itself was trying to smother her, but she wasn't going to let that happen.

When she was ready, she reached into the pot and smoothed the second shell along the narrow hole; copper flowed under the ball of her thumb and the slit melted together, made-copper bonding to smelted-copper.

The heat flowed away from her hand and she was shivering again. The sea hissed. The wind hissed and screamed. Sand scoured along her arms and legs, whipped into her face, missing her eyes only because she got her hand up. She could taste the hate around her, cold as the wind, impersonal as the stone.

Eyes.

The wolf again? Nayo, it had a different feel, like acid dripping. Something was hating her, wishing her harm.

Snatching up the dress, she held it against her. "What kind of pervert are you?" she yelled at the cliffs, "Peepjan peering at a girl getting dressed? Get outta here!"

She pulled the dress over her head, thrust her arms through the sleeves. "Jeggin bastards, mushguts, hiding behind a rock." She picked up the pot and started trudging back to the house, searching as she walked for whoever or whatever was overlooking her, heat rising in her as she burned through the resistance around her.

Nothing.

Navarre, diyo, he was half a mile away down the beach, she could feel him teasing something toward him, sense the delicate tugs, the sea-deep patience in him. *Fishing for dinner. We're gonna get awful tired of fish.*

Kitya was in the center of a whirl of housemagic. Faan only brushed at her, not wanting to disrupt her work.

Desantro was digging, annoyed at the cold, immersed in what she was doing—with the behind-thought always of worry about her brother.

Nothing else. . . .

Nu, the wolf was back . . . he'd brought his pack
with him . . . they were atop the chalk cliffs, looking
down at her. Black wolves and brindle . . . more than a
mile off, watching her, terrified . . . diyo. . . .

Plague carrier. Yeuch!

She scratched her fingers along the rim of the pot.
"Water next." She twisted around. "K'lann! talking
about water." She scowled at the clouds streaming toward them, the line of rain marching along the land.
"That's going to be drowning us soon. Time to get inside. I'll fill the pot and Navarre can fetch it in."

The storm dropped on them with the sunset, rain
drumming on the tiles, pouring from the ceramic gut-
ters; very little got in, especially in the kitchen where
they were spending the night. The roof was tight, the
walls intact.

At first Faan slept heavily; her stomach was comfortably full and she felt safe, the forces that tugged at her
gone for the moment.

Around the heart of the night, she began to dream.

*Bathed in an angular golden light, a horned
beast chased her endlessly, never stopping, never
letting her rest, it was terror with razor hooves
and a rack of antlers whose points threatened to
rip her flesh from her bones.*

She groaned in her sleep, her hands groped, fell
limp.

*A golden statue of a man stood with his feet
planted in mist, his arms crossed, his eyes black,
sucking holes that frightened her. His lips moved
in a short word, a simple one; she couldn't hear
him speak, but she knew what he said. DIE. Over
and over, he said it. DIE DIE DIE. . . .*

Faan moaned, reached out for Ailiki, but the mahsar

was gone; whimpering softly, she folded her arms across her beasts, hugging herself in the dream. Mourning the loss of the mamay she could remember, Reyna who might as well be dead, he'd forgotten her with the turn of the dance. She saw it as abandonment, she couldn't help it. Struggling to remember the mother she hadn't seen since she was three, aching, yearning, nothing there, nothing but need. . . .

The wolf pack came into the kitchen, trotting erratically about, sniffing at the sleepers, pawing them, great shaggy beasts with hard yellow eyes. They touched noses and went away, it was as if they melted through the walls, but they left behind a smell of fear and rage. . . .

Faan drew her legs up, bent her head to touch her knees. "Mamay," she moaned in her sleep, the words mumbled and indistinct. "Mamay, come back. I'm afraid, Reyna, don't go. I should've gone with you. Why didn't I go . . . why didn't I go?"

She fought to wake, but she couldn't. She was lost in the dream and couldn't escape it.

Clear images vanished and all that was left was a sense of slithering *things* crawling over them, crawling through trails of bitter yellow smoke that drifted in through the door and collected over her and the others.

Everything faded and she dropped deep into a drugged sleep.

A sudden pain in her side woke her. Her head stuffed, an evil taste in her mouth, she pried her eyelids open and found herself nose to toes with glossy black boots, damp sand caked between the soles and uppers, dark blue trousers stuffed into them, flopping over the tops. When she turned her head to look up at the man standing ominously silent beside her, she felt a pressure against her neck. She lifted her hands, touched smooth, segmented shell. "What . . ."

The man bent, wrapped a hand in her hair, jerked her to her feet.

Anger burned through her; she started to call flame, felt a sudden burn on her neck and tumbled into blackness.

The Chained God Unchained twisted the wind to howl at them, "Kill her, kill them all." But they didn't hear him, perhaps they couldn't since they were inside, perhaps they simply didn't want to. He couldn't speak directly unless he wanted them messily dead. He was tempted, but he restrained himself and settled back to watch.

When Faan woke again, she was confused for several moments until her nose and finally her eyes told her she had been thrown across the back of a horse. Tied there like a sack of grain, head on one side, legs on the other. How . . . ?

Her memories were blurred, uncertain and she set them aside, tugged at her wrists. *Rope. Braided leather ropes. I won't let you make me a slave. I won't. . . .* She forced concentration and started to call fire to burn herself free.

When she woke again, her neck felt raw, her confusion was worse, but this time she managed to remember enough to realize her captors had done something to her so whenever she tried to use her Talent, she was knocked out.

The torque. That shell thing around her neck.

She wriggled and yanked angrily at the ties, cursing in the Edge talk she'd learned as child, fighting the terror she didn't want to admit to, her stomach revolting, bile burning in her throat.

She twisted her head so she could look ahead and

back. *Diyo, they got us all. Ailiki . . . what . . . ?* She couldn't see the mahsar, couldn't feel her around, then she remembered. Ailiki was gone. *K'lann! Tungjii, where are you when I need you? It's not fair!*

She yelped as a ghost of a horned beast brushed against her, then trotted beside the horse. It looked at her with knowing eyes. *Shape Shifter.* "Peepjan, jeggin ro, what do you want?"

It tossed its head, seemed to laugh at her, then galloped off, vanishing into a herd of beasts much like it, but gray and brown and solid with life.

The rocking sway and jar went on and on. After a while she slept.

They traveled inland for three days, moving from the straggly brush and thin patchy grass of the chalk cliffs into a rolling savannah with herds of stocky horned beasts and the occasional predator who might be a born beast or a Shifter out on a raiding run. Faan found that she couldn't tell the difference, even when she saw the beast up close, not unless it stopped to twitch and sign with her silent captors. Or maybe they were all Shifters, the superior predator having killed all the lesser ones.

She was riding now with a thin pancake of a saddle and no stirrups, a hobble running from ankle to ankle beneath the belly of the horse, other hobbles binding her hands to a ring between her thighs. Navarre was on the horse ahead of her, Kitya and Desantro followed behind her. The Shifters rode in a ragged circle around them.

The ghosts of dead Shifters came in teams to mock at the Four. She thought at first that their captors were ignoring the visitations, but after a while she was convinced they saw nothing. There were people like that, the Sibyl said. It's a kind of protection they have. Nothing dead can reach them.

Abeyhamal's Gift was giving her fits as the translator

crafted in her brain struggled with the complex sign language of the Shifters; it kept trying to make her body shift and flow with the fluid ease of the talkers and giving her blinding headaches when the stubborn flesh refused. Despite this, she was beginning to be able to read them—though what she learned gave her no comfort. Now and then she wondered why the Gift didn't trigger the shell creature's poison, but she couldn't dredge up any explanation that even halfway convinced her. It was as disturbing as Navarre's assertion that the gods had chosen her for some purpose and were protecting her until it was accomplished.

Whatever the truth was, she could do nothing about either puzzle except ignore them and concentrate on surviving this mess. In Zam Fadogurum they said *Never trust a Mal,* meaning people with power will act how they please. With gods, it was even worse. *The dome over the island, god-garbage, that's what it is. Used and thrown away.* She closed her hands over the pommel, dug her nails into the leather. *God-garbage. . . .*

The rolling plain began to rise into low rounded hills; trees multiplied, broom and brush replaced the grass and broadleafed creepers.

When they came to a river, narrow and busy with white water, boiling over and curling around wet black boulders, the Shifters relaxed and began joking with each other, pleased with themselves now that they were in home ground, bringing in a fine haul of neutered magicians.

The walls of the river canyon grew gradually higher and steeper until they were riding in shadow, the remnants of the storm blowing past overhead, blocking any sunlight that might have managed to struggle down to the water.

A whistle nothing like a birdcall dropped delicately into the echoing roar of the water.

The Shifters kept moving, but the point rider threw

his head back and answered the call, surprising Faan who'd decided that they didn't speak because they couldn't. Apparently they preferred the twitching gesture talk, no doubt because they assumed their captives couldn't understand them. She smiled at the thought, pleased despite her aching head, and decided to keep quiet about her ability to read their signing.

Five hours later the canyon opened into a valley wide and deep, with rich green fields and a small lake at one end. There was an island in the center of the lake, and on the island, a structure like a castle built of a child's toy blocks enormously enlarged. There wasn't a curved line anywhere and the only acute angles were in the spiky roof of the central bulk and those of the half dozen towers placed symmetrically about it.

There was a small neat village on the far side of the lake and people out working in the fields—men, women and children; some of the children seemed barely large enough to walk but were set to pulling weeds, which they did with a grave care that astonished Faan—and when she thought about it, angered her. She'd trotted around after Reyna when she was about that size, pretending she was helping, but only because she adored being with her adopted mamay, not because she had to.

They were chatting, singing while they worked. It only took one glance to see that they weren't Shifters. *Slaves on a tether. Like us as long as we have these mutes round our necks. Jauks. At least we're not jeggin happy about it.*

The workers in the fields whispered to each other, the children swirled into clumps beside the road, stared at them as they rode past, then eddied into new clumps, whispering, hitting at each other for emphasis, breaking apart, coming together again.

The clouds were broken here, the sun hot on the back of her neck; the wind swooping down from the north had a chill bite, but its strength was greatly lessened. In-

stead of mold and damp, she could smell the fresh
turned earth and the flowers like small pink trumpets
nodding from vines that grew in green luxuriance on the
banks of the ditches that flanked the road. The medley
of green smells brought back memories of another
green and gentle place, a place she'd only seen in
dreams and through a crystal shield. Her shoulders
slumped a moment, then she straightened, jerked her
head up. *If I have to fight every jeggin god there is...*
"Gonna kick and scratch," she sang; when Navarre
turned to frown at her, she glared back but let the song
fade. "There's stupid and there's stupid, horse." She
turned laughter into a snort that started her mount's ears
flicking. "Tja, horse," she murmured, "cases like this,
declare war, but keep it quiet. Quiet like a creepin
mouse, sneak up and bite 'em. Gonna gonna kick and
scratch," she whispered, her voice lost in the shuffle of
the hooves; the last time she lost her temper and yelled
at the Shifters, they beat her with a long limber cane
that stung worse than nettles and left red rash lines
where it touched her. Riding was a pain after that. "An't
gonna get me eee ... an't gonna get me eee...."

As they came off the bridge, the leader held up his
hand, stopping them, then leading them off the road to
wait on the grassy verge for a procession to move past,
a double dozen androgenous figures in hooded robes
woven from silk ribbons, the ends left loose to flutter in
what breeze there was, pastel ribbons, pinks and laven-
ders and soft pale greens. Six carried a bier with a body
laid out on it, naked and stiff, flesh like milky quartz, a
forked radish with no sex at all. The rest walked in two
lines behind the bier.

Dead Shifter? Party games for the morbid. Hunh.
Faan leaned forward, so interested in what she was seeing that she forgot the guards. A stinging cut from one
of the burnsticks reminded her where she was. She

straightened, sat rubbing at the red mark on her arm and waiting for the order to move on.

It didn't come.

The funeral procession stopped on a paved square with a large stone block in the center; it was gray and opaque, the top excavated in a long hollow. Near one end there was a box carved from what looked like black jade, square and topless and empty.

With slow, angular movements the hooded Shifters lifted the dead one from the bier to the stone, fitting it into the hollow. Hands writhing in a silent chant, they circled the stone; round and round they went, pausing at intervals to empty over the corpse the contents of vials they fetched from inside their robes. Round and round they went, until an opalescent liquid filled the cavity.

They stopped, lifted their arms high, the sleeves of the robes falling away to the elbow, male arms, the muscles and tendons showing through the hairless white skin, the long bony fingers changing, writhing, melding, breaking apart, a rhythmic soundless gestured chant that made Faan's head ache again.

Abruptly all but the leader reached inside their robes and brought out small round pots glazed white as their skin.

Faan pressed her hand across her mouth to keep in the giggles. *They must have a pantry hooked to the ends of those ribbons. Wonder what else is in there?*

While the leader continued the writhing sign-song, the others tipped the tiny pots over and poured hot coals into the liquid.

Translucent blue flames shot man-high, dancing in time with the gestures of the leader.

The corpse melted. The flames died.

The leader took a tube from within his robes and siphoned the liquid into the jade box.

It shivered. There was a high thin sound.

Four of the robes lifted the box, tilted it on its side and struck their fists against the bottom.

A crystal brick popped out, four others lifted it onto the bier again and the procession started off.

Faan rubbed at her throat, tired of sitting and watching activity whose reason and purpose she couldn't know. *Let's get on with this, you jeggin sarks. I'm bored. You know that? B O R E D, bored.* "Gonna gonna ..." Another sting from the guard beside her. *You like doing that, don't you, creep? Huh. Enough's enough, girl. Let it lay.*

The lead captor lifted his hand again and they started off.

When they got close to the palace or whatever it was, Faan glanced at the nearest wall, then swallowed hard and repeatedly, bit her lip till she was close to drawing blood. The crystal bricks it was made of were exactly like the one she'd just seen formed from the body of a Shifter. *Living inside the bodies of the dead. Gods, I don't understand these people.*

Faan shuffled into the tall angular room, looked around as their captors halted them in front of a dais with a throne chair on it, the leader hurrying away through a door beside the dais. The unvarying symmetry of the design was ugly to her eyes. Not a curve anywhere—and if there was any wood in the construction of this interior, they didn't let the grain show. Every surface had a raised or incised design and it was all painted, mostly in shades of blue. The paint had been applied with great care, sanded and reapplied until the color seemed to ooze across the walls. Even the massive throne chair was painted that oppressive blue. There was a blue velvet cushion in the seat with silver piping; it looked as hard and angular as everything else in the room. *One thing about all this paint, those crys-*

tal bricks are out of sight. Yeuch. A place this big, how many dead did it take to build it?

The square lamps had acid-opaqued white glass held in place by strips of silver and gold so only the glow from the flame showed through. Flames had curves and dancing irregularities no matter how still the air.

The Four were ordered by sign and silent threat to stand still and say nothing; a tap on the cheek with one of the burnsticks warned Faan to stop gawking.

Faan pulled the corners of her mouth down. If she'd had room to run, she'd have thrown a tauntdance and a namechant at these pompous would-be Mals, ought to see old Amrapake, they want to know what a real tyrant's like, a tauntdance like she and Dossan and Ma'teesee used to do in the Edge. "We are the Wascra girls," she muttered under her breath, "paste the ponkers, waste the wonkers, Wascra Wascra Wascra we." All this dignity and solemnity were getting to her. Didn't matter they'd take burnsticks to her, at least they'd know what she thought of them. She caught Navarre's minatory eye, sighed and subsided as she had before. *Vema, vema, Magus. I'll be good. For the moment.* She brushed at her buttocks where one of the Shifter guards had swatted her with his burnstick. *Let me get shut of this stupid neck thing, and you're gonna dance like there's no tomorrow.*

A cortege entered at the far end of the room.

The Shifter stalking a half-step in front of the leader of the snatch band was huge—two men wide and half again as tall as any of the others, none of it fat. He looked powerful and dangerous and Faan had a strong feeling it wasn't just facade.

He was dressed in a dark blue robe with white fur and silver lacings, wide cuffs elaborately embroidered in interlocking squares and had a silver chain about his neck set with square cut sapphires.

A white-haired old man in an unpressed, oatmeal

shirt and trousers of rough weave shuffled after him, face sagging into fold upon fold, eyes fixed on the floor.

Flanking the old man were two guards with triple stringed crossbows and eyes that glinted in the lamplight as they flicked about the room, never still, always measuring.

Tsah! Scared of us? Sucks to you, fool. You better be scared.

The big man climbed the dais steps, settled into the chair, and scowled at Faan and the others. A gesture brought the old man to stand on the bottom stair, turned so he could see the Shifter in the chair and the captives at the same time.

"I am the Speaker to the Bonemen," the old one said slowly, his hands moving in quick round gestures.

Sign-pidgin, Faan thought.

Abeyhamal's Gift relaxed. She could almost feel it sigh with relief. Her fingers twitched, but she shoved her hands into her sleeves and hugged her arms against her body.

"When you speak to me, you will call me Gichador. There are some things that must be made clear to you. You are magic-makers. You will not be permitted to do that here. Be still! You can ask questions later. It does not matter why you came to Kaerubulan. You are here and must bear the consequences of that. You wear the surdosh about your neck. It is a freshwater worm with a plating of shell. You will have noticed that it has a certain property and you will discover that its strength grows in proportion to the time it lives on you. You have worn it for slightly more than three days; your hands have been hobbled and kept away from your necks. These restraints will be maintained for another two days. After that, the surdosh will have sunk its fibers deep into your flesh; if you try to tear it loose, it will be as if you slashed your own throat."

He paused to let them absorb what he'd just said, his pale blue eyes hooded by wrinkled lids.

"During these two days you will be taught the patto—the signs I am making now—so you will be able to understand the kaerame. You will find the Kaer easy masters as long as you do what is required of you, but they have little tolerance for troublemakers. Now," his tongue flicked out, ran over his thin blue lips, "I am going to pass to you the questions of the subDuke Yelloweye. The women will remain silent. The man will answer quickly, completely, and in tones of respect." He turned his head, watched the subDuke sign, turned back. "Why did you come here and who brought you?"

A muscle twitched at the corner of Navarre's eye, but he bowed slightly and when he spoke his voice was mild. "We did not come here deliberately. We were wrecked on your shores. Look at us. We have nothing. Less than nothing now that you've taken our gifts from us."

Gichador turned away, signed rapidly, waited as the subDuke's face twitched and shifted, his hands flowed in swift angry curves.

Faan watched, head aching again. Gichador's translation had been reasonably accurate and without added comment; it seemed to her quite likely that the Shifter knew exactly what had been said, just didn't want to bother with bonespeech. From the look of him, he was annoyed, skeptical, half-inclined to have them all strangled to save himself the trouble of waiting for the surdosh to take root. *I take it back, Amrapake's got nothing on you, kumber. Walk small a while, Fa.*

Gichador bowed and waited.

The subDuke leaned back in the chair, one hand spread across the lower part of his face as he contemplated the ragged lot his men had brought him.

After a long silence, a finger waggled bonelessly, his other hand swooped through a meld of signs that said as much. He scowled at Navarre a while, then demanded names and histories of all of them, and if they were related, how.

When Gichador finished passing on the questions, Navarre bowed again, spoke in the same slow mild way. "The tall one is my wife, the girl my student, the other her companion. We were traveling south from Savvalis when our ship was attacked and sunk. It happened during the night and we were all asleep. There was just time to get away. . . ."

The questioning went on for nearly an hour with Faan fidgeting toward the end, distracted by the pressure in her bladder, too stressed to admire any longer Navarre's deft footwork as he blended a pinch of truth with a quart of lies.

Faan pressed her thighs together and thought dry thoughts until at last they were led away and shut into separate cells.

Chapter 4
In the Labyrinth

Rakil lay in a tangle of sheets soft and slippery as Humarie's skin and watched her move through the leaf shadow dappling the room; the strung-bead blinds had been looped back from the balcony's glass doors to let in the afternoon sun after it filtered through the new green leaves on the mendreyki trees in the garden beyond. The beads were rounds of silver filigree alternating with fired clay pellets glazed with that bright purplish blue the Shifters seemed addicted to, strung on delicate silver chains; the lengths that hung loose clicked in the breeze blowing lazily over the garden walls.

The same breeze brought drifts of incense from the burners to tickle his nose. Humarie always had incense burning when he was with her; he asked her to do it because it kept out the ghosts who drifted through the garden and got caught in the tangle of tiny branches that grew along the major limbs of the mendreykies.

Humarie stretched, her flesh rippling sensuously on whatever she had instead of bones; she turned her head, smiled over her shoulder at him, then strolled to the chair where she'd tossed her wrap. "Lazy man," she said. Her voice had odd overtones, as if it came from multiple throats. "Out of bed, you. It's story time."

As he watched her pull the pale blue Lewinkob silk about her and tie the belt, he lay thinking about all the times he'd been with her. When they made love, she

wanted to be on top, in control. He closed his eyes, remembered her breasts bobbing gently as she worked,
her face changing to his face, reflecting what she saw,
his face coming down to kiss and nibble him. *I wonder,* he thought, *are you a woman or only the semblance
of one? I know so little about you Shifters. Do you even
have male and female? For all I know, you bud and
drop off like those mendreyki trees outside. And what
does it matter? I know what I see, what I want to see.
And I'll pay whatever it takes for my time with you.* He
sat up, slid his legs off the side of the bed. "Bath first.
By the time you're set up down in the garden . . . it is
the garden, isn't it?"

She nodded and took a step toward the door. "Do
you want some cakes today or only buttered toast?"

"Toast will do me fine."

"Do hurry, will you, Raki? You know how I adore
your stories."

"I know."

Rakil slid the glass door back and stepped onto the
balcony. The breeze up here still had a bite in it, but the
sun was hot; the storm had blown south and there
wasn't a cloud visible in the sky, though drifts of ghost-
stuff eddied through the bushes and vineplants.
Mendreyki leaves brushing against his shoulder, he
leaned on the rail and looked down into the garden. The
maid was setting the ritual tea on a small table beside
the fountain. Humarie was lying in a long chair, ankles
crossed, bright silk pillows piled around her.

He stood a moment watching her, then went down
the steps, crossed the small patch of grass and settled
beside one of the smooth square stone blocks arranged
symmetrically about the angular sculpture dark with
trickling water. Dishes of incense placed on the rim of
the fountain sent up trails of white smoke, the pungent,

green aroma drifting around him, driving off the bother-some ghosts.

"Sa sa, what will it be today?" he said, leaning toward her, thin brown brows lifting to underline the question.

"Something sad," she murmured, the humming overtones intensified by her eagerness. "Sad and filled with color."

He thought a moment, then nodded. "I remember a story . . . I actually saw part of it and heard the rest one night when I was serving dinner and Purb's guests were talking about it.

•••

There was a thief called Davindolillah. I say a thief because he belonged to the Guild of Thieves—ia sim, even the thieves have a Guild in Kukurul.

Davindolillah was a youth whose dreams were bigger than his gifts. He was astute enough to know this and drew to himself two others who made up his lacks, a brown-eyed girl who was as clever as she was pretty and an elf of a boy with hands light and agile as mayflies.

Once we were settled in, Purb was busy with visits so I had the afternoon free and went out to see Kukurul—this was the first time we'd been there, though I'd heard of it for years.

Kukurul. The pivot of the four winds, the pearl of five seas. Expensive, gaudy, secretive and corrupt. You can buy anything there and I do mean anything . . . birth, death, pleasure, profit . . . anything. There's a broad avenue that leads from the harbor to the great Market, the Ihman Katt. Along it you'll find brothels catering to every taste, from well trained beasts to frightened children. There are the Assassins Guild Houses that advertise men of the knife, men of the ga-

rotte, women of the poison trade. There's the biggest
slave market in the Two Continents. And—more important to Davindolillah's story—halfway along the Katt
there's a narrow black building. The Black House. It
sells death and torture. You can watch it done or do it
yourself. I shivered when I walked past that. I didn't
hear anything or see anything, the ghosts were exor-
cised as soon as they were made, so there were none of
them hanging about, but there was a chill on my neck
and the hair on my arms stood up.

I hurried on and lost the chill in the heat and smells
of the Great Market. It's a paved square two miles on a
side where you can buy a meat roll or a jewel the size
of your fist and only heat, sweat and stench are free.
There are trained dog packs for nervous merchants or
lordlings who don't enjoy personal popularity with family or folk; rare ornamental birds and beasts; honey-
comb tanks of bright colored fighting fish, other tanks
of ancient carp, chameleon seahorses, snails of marvelous color and convolution; fine cloth and rare leathers;
blown glass of every shape, color, and use, including
the finest mirrors in the world; gold, silver, copper-
smiths sitting among their wares; cuttlers and sword-
smiths; jewelers with fantastic wealth displayed about
them; spice merchants; sellers of rare orchids—I
couldn't begin to name them all. And winding through
the cluttered ways, there are water sellers, pancake
women, piemen, meat roll venders, their shops on their
backs or rolling before them. Noise is a solid thing,
Shifters would be right at home because signing has become a minor art there.

I wandered through the pressing crowds, gawking at
everything around me. I was very young then, that time
between boy and man, and I'd never seen anything like
this.

I saw Davindolillah swaggering along one of the
lanes between open-face shops selling silks and linens

and printed cotton fabrics. He was a handsome youth, gleaming in a coat of sweat and not much else, with eyes like bits of jet and skin the color of caramel over coal. Around his neck he wore a fine iron chain and the spread hand of the Thieves Guild.

He was strutting and cavorting for a brown-eyed girl; she was pretty and sweet and even those preoccupied with buying and selling spared a brief smile as the boy and the girl took their romance past them.

A Black House man with a space all round him came hurrying by, his eyes on the ground. It seemed he brushed against the brown-eyed girl. She screamed and fell limp at his feet. The boy yelled with rage and flung himself at the man.

The Black House was tolerated as long as those inside paid their fees and bought their merchandise at the slave market—or at least, kept their raids discreet and left the powerful alone. No one liked them. The merchants were ready to cheer the boy on and as word passed, more and more people moved between me and the fighters. Because I wanted to see the outcome but all I could see was men's backs, I jigged around, hunting for an open space, working my way from the cloth-sellers row to the jeweler's row. As I got there, I saw a little gray figure snatch half a dozen gems from several jewelers' tables and fade into the crowd when some one spotted him and yelled for the guards that had hurried off to quell what they thought was a riot.

I learned later Davindolillah broke off the fight, grabbed the girl and went running with her, the merchants opening a path for him, respecting his grief and his urgency. They laughed at themselves later— somewhat grudgingly, but also in admiration—as they learned that they'd been had. The Black House man was an actor hired for the afternoon who knew nothing about the plot, the brown-eyed girl was an apprentice in the Thieves Guild and the little figure I'd seen snatching the jewels was the third in the conspiracy. It was a clever plan and the three of them got a very good price selling the jewels back to the merchants who'd lost them in the first place.

But Black House was annoyed and Black House held long grudges.

The brown-eyed girl disappeared a week later, on a night when the Wounded Moon was new and never a sliver showed. No one but Davindolillah fussed about that, not even the Thieves Guild. These things happened all the time. She was a pretty girl and clever. No doubt she'd found herself a patron and sailed away to temporary luxury. She'd show up again if she chose to return—or not. No one cared but the young thief, no one listened to him, or answered his questions. 'Forget her,' people said, 'a girl's a girl. You can find a hundred more if you reach out your hand. Cleverer girls and prettier girls.'

On the night of the next new moon, a man came up to Davindolillah outside the tavern where he'd been drowning his anger in sour wine; the man handed him a small carved box and vanished into the dark. The elf child took it from him before he could open it and got them both to the nearest Diviner.

The Diviner held the box, then pushed it away with a shiver and a frown. "There's no danger here," she said, "only sorrow. Take it away. You will not open it here. I will not have that. Go."

The elf child took it before Davindolillah could and tolled him back to their quarters in the Guild Hall. When they were there, Davindolillah opened the box.

From a bed of crumpled white silk two brown eyes looked up at him.

Seven days later the Black House burned to the ground; it took half a dozen other Houses with it and ate out a good part of the slave market. The Council's Seer needed about two seconds to know what had happened and the enforcers went looking for Davindolillah. He was gone, the elf child with him.

This what the mirrors showed: Davindolillah dug out a drunken sorcerer who was too far gone to fear the magic behind the Council but together enough to pop the smallest of salamanders through for him and contain it in a spelled wax cage; the young thief took the cage into the Black House and left it. Then he and the elf child caught the first ship out and were two days at sea before the spell wore off and the salamander flamed. For some reason, no one had a guess what it was, the Council couldn't find them and no one heard from them again."

•••

Rakil sipped at the cold tea and watched Humarie emerge from her dreams. It was the stories more than the money that bought his time with her; they were a drug she couldn't get enough of. She would have listened for days on end if he had the repertoire and the endurance, but it was his life he was expending on her and there were limits to that.

When the haze had cleared from her amber eyes, he set the cup aside. "You should travel and see for yourself, sweet Humarie."

"De nai," she said, the humming overtones so strong they nearly drowned the sense. "The part can never leave the whole. We are bound, bonelover, I told you that, I told you true."

At the door to the House, Humarie put a hand on his arm, stopped him as he was about to leave. "Everyone knows what he's doing. Warn him that the . . ." she made the complex sign that meant her folk, a flutter of the face and a swift double curve of her hand, "they're getting angry and soon there'll be trouble. I say this because I have a fondness for you, boneman. There's no one can tell stories as you do. If he will not listen, then go yourself before you find yourself fertilizing the flowers beside him."

Rakil walked down Godon Way without seeing it, for once not hearing the yammer of the ghosts. His head and body were in a roar of contradictions. He was extravagantly elated that Humarie cared enough to risk punishment to warn him and sick with fear/anger/frustration. When he nearly stepped under the hooves of a team of oxen, he pulled himself together and went to take a look at how the loading was going on the *Wave Jumper*. Zadem was taking two hundred jars of assorted essences on consignment.

Wreathed in clouds of cheap incense, the Harbormaster's Deputy was inspecting each of the jars, stamping the Kaeru seal in the soft wax his assistant splashed onto the corks. Zadem's cargo chief was hovering over the ladesmen as they lifted the sealed jars and set them in their nests of straw and twisted more straw around them.

The ladesmen knew what they were doing and used to nervous merchants; they worked with the economical speed that years of practice had packed into bone and muscle, weaving the nests, twisting the straw into caps; they fitted a pressboard square into the crate and built a new layer of nests and set in the next dozen jars as the Deputy finished with them.

The trader Orao Kotkal was sitting on a stool in a corner, chewing on a balsam pachastick, watching the work and waiting for the Deputy to get to his jars, two dozen from the last of Purb's legal blueflower; Orao had bought holdspace and passage on the *Wave Jumper,* the first step on his way home to Kukurul and the Market where he expected to pull in triple his costs. He nodded a greeting as Rakil threaded through the small crowd of workers and officials and came to squat beside him.

"This the last?" Rakil said, a flip of his hand taking in the small cluster of jars.

"Ia sim." He tapped the stick against his teeth as he stared out the open double doors of the godon. "*Jumper* sails next tide."

"Hmm. Any problems?"

"De nai. Same suap's usual." He moved his head casually, his small shrewd eyes darting from shadow to shadow. "Favor for favor. Be on her, eh?"

"Rumors?"

"Flea's head gone soft, 'f what I hear's true."

"K'berk, friend." Rakil flared his nostrils and pulled his wide mouth into a brief inverted arc. "He's always pulled it off before."

"Ia sim, but this lot . . ." Kotkal went back to chewing the stick, his eyes half-closed, his face gone blank.

Rakil stayed where he was a while longer, watching the ladesmen nail the crate shut. As the Deputy and his trailing aides came toward Kotkal, he stood. "Owe you one," he murmured, added in louder tones, "Any difficulty, send to the Janguan Purb, I'm sure your path can be smoothed without any fuss."

Rakil sat on the bitt looking out over water bright and jagged as broken glass. He didn't know what to do. After so many years of keeping track of Purb's moods, he didn't have to guess about how the Flea would react to these warnings, no matter how many directions they came from. He could even understand a little of what was eating at the man. Purb was feeling his age. He was nearing seventy and that was a long time to stay on the hop, no matter how clever the flea. They'd been here five years now, the longest they'd stayed anywhere; it looked like he was trying to scratch out a nest for him-

self here, a place where he could finally stop watching
his back.

Gods, if he'd only stay away from plots and
schemes, he might even have his safe retirement, if not
here, somewhere. *Trouble is,* Rakil thought, *he can't
keep his fingers clean. He's drawn to conspiracy. . . .* He
smiled, rubbed his thumb across his fingers. *Say Tungjii
to a wine cellar. Hmm.*

He glanced over his shoulder at the sun. It was half
below the roof line, less than an hour from setting. Purb
would be waiting for his report. *There must be some
way I can slide in a warning without getting his back
up. Some way. . . .*

"The *Wave Jumper*'s leaving with the tide tonight.
Assach will be another three days in port. Janguan
Purb . . ."

"What's this, what's this?" Purb scowled at him,
hands closed into fists. "If it's the same glop you've
been shoving in my ears for weeks now, forget it."

"Just wanted to say be careful. The whole district is
antsy. Everyone seems to know what's happening. If
you're counting on secrecy, that's gone."

"Tell me how, hunh, hunh, you just tell me how."

"If you mean it's me spreading rumor, de nai, O
Janguan. Have I ever babbled your business? You know
I haven't."

Purb fiddled with a hangnail, swore as he jerked too
hard and drew blood. He glared past Rakil, licking the
blood off his finger. After a moment he slapped his
hand down. "Nai de nai de nai, I don't care! They
aren't going to snatch this from me."

Rakil said nothing.

"Ride it out," Purb went on more calmly. "That's
what I'll do, it doesn't matter, things always get bumpy
before the ends are tied up." His eyes narrowed, fixed

on Rakil's face. "You're not thinking of running out on me, eh?"

Rakil said nothing, kept his face blank.

Purb sighed. "One more year and you'll have your papers and the brand canceled. I swear it, Raki. One more year. I need someone I can trust." He hesitated as if he were going to force a promise, then let it drop. "Chur! Nosewaggle sent one of his boneserfs while you were out. He wants more of that oil-gel. . . ." He grinned suddenly, snickered. "Jellies want gel, hee hee, jelly gel, haaaaw." He sobered, looking sourly at Rakil who hadn't even cracked a smile. "That's the way you want it, huh? B'ja, who can we get to do it?"

"Assach's bound for Silili, be over a year before he's back, if he does come back. From what I hear, he's about had it with the suaps he has to pass out to everyone and his dog. The essences make it worthwhile, but only just. Zadem's by-the-book, you know that, he wouldn't come within smelling distance of smuggling. Horst the Hennerman operates a slaveship with a little cargo on the side; he won't touch anything that might put off his best customers. Biljart shuttles between here and Savvalis. His *Klauseely's* the only ship I'd set foot on, the rest of the so-called masters would strip you and dump you overboard first chance they got. It'll have to be someone in port at Savvalis, maybe Korder or Gritch."

"Savvalis. Hmm. Have to send someone, wouldn't I. Someone who knew the scene." He lowered his wrinkled lids, rubbed his thumbs together. "Sa sa, Rakil my man . . . MY man . . . pack my gear, make arrangements with Biljart. I'm going myself, you'll stay here and watch the business."

"Ia sim, Janguan Purb."

Five days later Rakil stood on the wharf watching the *Klauseely* creep toward the mouth of the bay. *I fum-*

bled that, he thought. *I shouldn't have said anything, I knew how he'd take it.* He turned, frowning. If Purb comes to his senses in Savvalis, he won't be back. He'll send word I should close things up and do a flit. Done it before. "Chur!" he muttered and began walking toward Godon Way. *Purb said it might take a month, I'll wait a month and if I haven't heard by then ...* He shook his head and turned into the alley that led to Purb's rented house, batting absently at ghosts that swooped down to chitter at him.

Chapter 5
War Games

FAAN

Faan sat in a square uncomfortable chair, her wrists manacled to the arms, the edge of the seat cutting into her bare legs; the tunic she'd been given to wear came only to mid thigh and was so skimpy it hiked up when she sat. There were no ghosts in here, which she found odd because this place was built from the bodies of the dead. *Maybe that ceremony does the same thing as a ghostlayer. These people are pe-cul-yar.*

Gichador stood at a lectern, a stylus in his hand and several tablets of wet clay ready for making. "I am going to ask you questions," he said in his mild tenor. His lack of emphasis was, in the circumstances, more effective than a shout. "Answer fully and truthfully. Lies always discover themselves."

Potz! A load of it. Still, he has got a point, he compares our answers and comes back on contradictions and gets corrections one way or another. I suppose that could get painful. Riverman said you want to lie, keep it simple, keep it quick, and don't volunteer. Vema, let's do it.

She folded her hands in her lap and fixed her eyes on him, saying nothing.

He stared at her a moment longer, waiting for her to speak, then ran the stylus in a stamping dance across the wet clay. He wiped the wedge-shaped end on a small square cloth he took from a pile of cloths at the right of the tablet. "Name."

"Faan Hasmara."

"Two names, mmm. Which is the family designation?"

"Neither. The first is given, the second taken. It is a description."

"And it means . . ."

"Twice-abandoned."

He stared at her again, but let it be. "Your homeland?"

"I was reared in Zam Fadogurum, which is on the eastern rim of the South Continent."

The stylus danced. He was aware of her equivocation, but let that be also. "What gifts, talents, or training would give you value to the subDuke?"

"None that you're willing to use. I am a sorcerer in bud, just beginning my training. I can't cook and I'm not good at cleaning; plants die when I touch them, sooner or later anyway. I can read and write, but only Fadogur. I suppose I could learn what you're doing quickly enough, I'm reasonably clever."

"How long have you been the man's student?"

"Not long. Less than a year."

"Describe his gifts."

"He is not a sorcerer, he's a Magus. I know little about him except he is a scholar and able to teach what he doesn't do. That is for me the paramount gift of a Magus."

"Surely you know more than that."

"He's a good man and he can teach. What more do I need to know?"

"How does a sorcerer differ from a mage?"

"That's the same question. I'm not interested in that, I've got enough to learn with my own Talent."

"Describe that Talent."

"Some sorcerers are bound to air, some to earth,

some to water. I burn within and without. It is necessary to contain this fire; this is what he teaches me."

"What effect will the surdosh have on your fire?"

"I don't know. Nu, Gichador, I'm only fifteen, I have scarcely begun to train." She'd shaved a couple years off her age, knowing she looked younger than she was; let him misjudge her capabilities.

"The woman with the spots on her face, what gifts does she have and why does she travel with you?"

"She has no magic, though she's very skilled when it comes to tending plants. She is my companion, friend, and protector. I have no family. A girl alone attracts a great deal more attention than she wants, most of it hurtful."

"Where were you going when you were cast into the sea?"

"The Magus said it was necessary to continue my training in greater solitude. Valdamaz had too much to burn." Good, she thought, they bought Navarre's little tale.

"The wife of the Magus, what are her gifts?"

"She holds household well and she has a small talent for finding things. I have spent little time with her. She seems pleasant enough and makes life easier for us all."

"She is not like the rest of you, she has scales like a serpent. Why?"

"You'd best ask her. I don't know and I don't care."

"You seem to have no interest in anything but yourself."

"So? I've got problems. I don't have time for other things. Or I didn't. Now . . ." She shrugged.

The questions went on and on, but she'd built a persona for herself of an arrogant, incurious, self-involved child and simply answered within the limitations of that child. She couldn't know what Navarre and the others would say, or had said, and she wasn't about to guess; what she wanted was to keep information about them to a minimum without alerting Gichador to what she was doing. On and on, question, answer, stylus jumping, turning, in a swift and endless dance across tablet after tablet.

The Chained God Unchained glanced at the scene in the interrogation room. "Idiots!" He listened to the girl's lies, sighed with impatience—and a reluctant touch of admiration. "Clever little Sorcerie. Ahhh, I wish you were dead! Interference?" His elegant nose twitched, twitched again as he snuffled about, smelling for godstuff rubbed off on her. Nothing there, but the quick, efficient slaughter of the Four which he'd envisioned when he'd set the searchers on them had been deflected somehow. "Hmp. Leave you to the Shifters, they seem to have a firm hand round your throats." He bent over, guffawing at his joke, straightened, still chuckling. "You sure aren't going anywhere soon. Back to the pastures for me."

Eyes sparking with anticipation, the Chained God Unchained returned his attention to Chaggar the Green Man, Land God of Gallindar, leaned over him and drew power from him, sucking it in, burping with pleasure as it filled him.

On the morning of the third day after the interrogation, a warder came for Faan and took her to the Great Hall where they'd been brought the first time. Navarre was there already, kept separated from Kitya and Desantro; Faan was taken to join the women.

The subDuke Yelloweye Clawwag was seated in his

thronechair, flanked by his guards, with Speaker Gichador standing as before on the end of a step where he could see Yelloweye without having to turn his head.

The subDuke signed with an angry force.

Gichador translated, his voice unintrusive, almost no hesitation between phrases, so that it was as if the signs themselves spoke. "We do not like people who play with magic; we pull them up like weeds when they try seeding themselves here. Were circumstances usual, I would have the lot of you strangled, your bodies burned for fertilizer."

He paused, eyes on the SubDuke's hands; the Shifter had dropped them, left them resting on his knees while he glared at the intruders, the pause meant, no doubt, to impress on them the vigor of his displeasure. Faan kept her face and body still, but under her breath she chanted, "Paste the ponkers, waste the wonkers . . ."

"You are fortunate that you come now. We have a use for you. The three women will be held as hostages and you, Magus, you are going to be a weapon. The Browneye Faction, that mob of stinking ferrets, they're attacking the Premier Duke Yelloweye Longtooth. They have been conspiring with ungrateful worms among the bonemen merchants to smuggle in weapons and corrosives. You were captured by a search band hunting these sneaking aberrants and intent on immolating them in their own firegel. You, Magus, will be taken to Browneye Snarl's miserable domain. You will be loosed there to destroy what you can; if you survive until the Browneyes are whipped as they deserve, you will be allowed to take ship out, as long as you agree not to return again. Your women will be brought to you. If you attempt to avoid attacking the Browneyes or try turning your magic on us, one of the women will be killed, then another, if necessary. You will be watched. Be silent. We do not wish the intrusion of your stupid voices. We do not need your agreement, nor will we haggle in any way."

After a last series of emphatic signs which apparently contained instructions to their warders, since Gichador didn't bother translating them, Clawwag stomped out.

When Faan woke, she found herself once more belly-down across the back of a horse, hearing the thud/whump/blow of the horse ahead of her and the several more behind her, all of them moving along this narrow path through scattered trees growing on the side of a hill; over the acrid reek of the horse she could smell generic mountain odor compounded of fine dust, damp, rotted wood, lichens, and a thousand sorts of green.

Shadows were thickening about them, details getting lost as the light faded; Shifter ghosts ran by her head and jeered at her, their silent laughter harsh as nettles across her nerves.

Sly, aren't you, you twitchy jinks. And I'm a fool for drinking that tea. She tugged tentatively at her hands, then sighed. *Potz. Stuck in a rut. Hmm ... the Mezh would make this look sick ... no magic, so no shamans ... still, there's this jeggin torc thing ... there has to be a way to get rid of it. ...*

The sun was coming up when they reached the end of the journey. Faan had managed a few hours of nightmare masquerading as sleep after her warders had refused to let her ride rather than be hauled along like a sack of grain. The sleep hadn't helped much, her head was throbbing and her body ached as if the arms she stretched in dream toward a woman with no face were still straining to grasp the mother she couldn't remember.

The Shifters dismounted, led their horses around a

fall of scree, stopped in front of a ragged opening in the slope, a dark mouth choked with ghost stuff; the Shifter earth souls came rushing out like bats at sundown, whirled around over them, ignored by the guards who didn't seem to see them. One of the Shifters cut her loose, caught her as she started to slide and eased her onto the stony ground. He knotted a rope around her wristbonds, dragged her arms down, threw a half-hitch about her ankles and tied the loose end to an iron ring set into a heavy boulder, left her crouched there and went to join the other who was unloading the packponies.

The packs were bulky and heavy; the Shifters went shorter and thicker so they could handle them, and even then they sagged under the weight. Watching them, she understood why they kept bonemen serfs to do the heavy work.

Four of the packs were filled with bricks which they piled up beside the cave mouth, a fifth with a gray-white dust which they emptied into a wooden tub. One of them took a sack into the cave and came out with it bulging and dripping. He emptied the water into the dust and went back for more, while the second began stirring the mix in the tub.

The morning was bright and cold, the dew on the sparse grass was chilling her toes and striking up through the thin shift, but that wasn't what made Faan shiver. She felt fire begin to seethe under her skin, re-pressed it fast; if the surdosh knocked her out again, it'd just make it easier for them. She brought her knees up tight against her torso, slid her hands down so she got a few inches of slack in the rope and began loosening the half-hitch.

Ignoring the ghosts that ran at her, angry and hissing as they struggled desperately to distract her and prevent her from freeing herself, watching the Shifters with

quick sideways glances, she got the tether rope off her
ankles and worked the ties loose, freeing her feet. When
she was finished with them, she began working on her
hand ties, using her teeth on the knots. Give me a minute, she prayed, Tungjii Luck, one minute, that's all.
K'lann! The rope tasted foul and the prickly fibers
rasped her lips, but the knots weren't complicated, she
was getting it. One minute, oh please, one minute
more. . . .

One of the Shifters looked round and swore. They
rushed at her, caught her by the shoulders and ankles.
She struggled, but they ignored that; they might not
have the bone to lift heavy objects but their tensile
strength was enormous. They dumped her in the cave
and one of them sat on her while the other pressed his
thumb into her neck until she slid the long slide into
nothing.

She woke as they were setting in the last of the
bricks. She was lying on a blanket with a second pulled
over her and a third folded into a pad under her head.
There was a pack leaning against the cave wall, the
rope ends cut from her hands and feet flung down beside it. "Jeggin sarks," she screamed at them as she
scrambled up, the blanket falling away. "I'll twist your
m'rijes into ropes to hang you."

They ignored her, slapped on the mortar and
slammed the bricks in place, holding one until the mixture set, moving on to the next.

She threw herself against the wall and achieved only
bruises. She tried to push the new bricks out, but they
held them against her until the mortar went solid with a
faint squeal.

The last brick went home and the light was gone.
She was alone, not even a hostile ghost to keep her
company.

NAVARRE

As the saddle tilted under him, Navarre shifted to keep his balance; he drew in a long breath, then swore and spat out the fold of thick black cloth he'd sucked into his mouth. He'd ridden for three days with that sack over his head, with little rest and almost no food. Once a day the Shifters forced him onto his knees and rolled up the bottom of the sack; with him crouching like a suppliant with his hands tied behind him, they fed him strips of meat and nuggets of rolled oats and crushed nuts baked in honey, then made him lap water from a bowl, water drugged to keep him too hazy to do think or act. He was furious, a cold anger, hard and slippery; he cherished it and waited. They had to remove the surdosh, and when they did. . . .

They went north for three days, then west up a steep, winding trail.

They'd been riding more or less on a level since sunup, moving slowly, the sounds of the horses' iron shod feet rebounding from the cliffs on both sides.

He shifted again as the trail slanted more steeply and wondered just how far this other domain was from Yelloweye Clawwag's land. Which reminded him about Kitya. She was a freeranger, too long a captivity would kill her. Faan could take care of herself—or the gods would take care of her, didn't matter which. Desantro he didn't know, pleasant enough woman, but nothing to him. Kitya . . . Kat . . . he'd laughed at her little magics and taken her tending without thanks or even acknowledging it . . . not till now. . . . Hang on, Kat, I swear I'll come for you. I swear. . . .

When they stopped, Navarre could smell trees around him, hear the bustle of a small stream. They left him sitting on the horse until the camp was ready, then one of them cut the hobbles on his ankles and tapped him on the thigh with the burnrod, the Shifter way of telling the Magus to swing down however he could.

When he was seated, his ankles tied and the other end of the rope looped round a tree, the hood was jerked all the way off. He sat blinking at the fire and the shadowy figures around it, the ghosts howling in the treetops so loudly he could barely hear himself think. The others were deaf to the clamor, without magic, cut off from their dead in a way he could not conceive.

It was a boneman who'd taken his hood off, a boy of thirteen or fourteen; he stopped a few paces off, stood holding the handful of black cloth, waiting for what came next.

One of the Shifters walked round the fire and stopped beside the boy. He signed and the boy translated.

"When we leave, go straight west and begin your work. Do not attempt to bargain with the Browneyes. They won't listen and we'll know what you're trying. One of your women will die for it. Kneel now, bend your head down to give us the best access to the surdosh; if the removal is not done properly, it will kill you."

As Navarre followed instructions, he saw the Shifter take a glass vial from a pouch on his belt and an iron needle the length of his thumb. The Shifter dug out the wax capping the vial, dipped the needle into it and came toward him.

Hands were on his shoulders, holding him still.

Something touched the surdosh; he felt it like a jolt through his body.

Then there was pain, enormous, brutal pain. . . .

When he woke, he tensed, sense memory invading him . . . but the pain was gone and so was everyone else—the Shifters and the boneboy were gone, the ghosts gone with them; they'd taken the ropes off him, left him nothing . . . no, that wasn't quite true, they left two pieces of dried meat and a handful of those grain nuggets.

He got to his feet. The Wounded Moon had set and darkness pressed in on him like a pillow on the face, no wind, a thick, oppressive stillness. His neck itched. He rubbed it, felt skin and no barrier and gave a shout of wild joy. Free. His soul, which had been as cramped as his limbs, expanded as he flung out his arms. Free. Then he scratched the rash where the surdosh had been and squatted to eat the unappetizing meal they'd left him. Not really free. Not as long as they had Kat. And the others.

Shivering with cold and semistarvation, he started down the mountain an hour later when dawn was pinking the horizon behind him.

Chapter 6
The Flea's Hop

Rakil opened the cashbox, wrinkled his nose at the scattering of coins inside. *Good thing Purb's due back soon,* he thought, *household cash is getting low.* "Chur, I thought there was more than that," he said aloud, "just like the old chapadot to leave me short."

He slid open the door-window and stepped into the greening garden to check the sun. "Almost noon. She doesn't like it when I'm late. Sa!" He'd have to go into his stash for the coin to pay Humarie's sharikin. *Bem, no problem, I have to wash up and change my clothes anyway. Tsa! it's going to be a pij in the butt getting that back from the Flea, he squeals like he's losing blood when he has to pay out coin. Ah la, there's an argument in there somewhere, maybe a golden lever will pry him loose. . . .*

With this last consignment gone, the godon was nearly cleared out; they could skip with most of their profits, not like the last time when all they saved was their skin. Bem, and a few household goods, including Purb's emergency stash and his. If he could persuade the old man to leave. He pulled the door-window shut, turned the lever over to lock it, and left the office.

In his bedroom he kept an old seachest, battered and ugly with its lock broken. It had a water-tight sidron lining which was the visible excuse he had for lugging it around. It also had a tricky secret pocket which no one had located yet—and they'd tried; big thieves had little thieves like dogs had fleas. He lifted out his spare tunics, set them on the bed, thumped his fingers over the pressure points on the left end. A door popped open showing a narrow cavity with a curl of paper in it and nothing more.

Not one of his two hundred gold pieces left, not one, nothing but air and dust.

He swore, snatched up the paper. It had Purb's seal on it in whitish wax with candle soot mixed in and three lines of his crabbed writing, freeing Rakil and at the same time declining any responsibility for him hereafter.

The Flea had hopped again and this time he'd hopped alone.

Blood roaring in his ears, throat swollen. As he took in the enormity of the betrayal, Rakil kicked the chest against the wall, went plunging around and around the room in a blind rage, slamming his fists into the walls, cursing hoarsely. Finally he flung himself into a chair and sat with his head in his hands. "I'll kill him," he groaned, "I'll strip his skin and make him eat it."

Ash pale, he wiped the sweat from his face, dropped his hands between his thighs and sat hunched over, staring at the floor. "Sentimental swill," he muttered. "Surrogate father, aaaah gods! Dumping me, leaving me anchored here by ... Say it, man, anchored by your rahos. Ragwhipped by a whore you don't even know's a woman."

While he'd been drifting in a dream, Purb had used him as a screen so he could set up a safe way of hauling ass out of the mess he'd gotten himself into.

"I was too thick to see it. What a fool, what a stinking fool."

He tipped the chest upright, set the shirts back in it, and closed the top. There was no point changing clothes now, he couldn't afford to cross Humarie's doorstep, let alone climb the stairs with her. He pressed his head against the wall, opened and closed his hands behind his back while he fought back images of other men climbing those stairs, other men enveloped in that warm shuddering flesh. He sank his teeth into his lip to keep the howl inside. He'd made too much noise already. All it would take was one snooping servant and one quick report, then Snakeeye would be here to see what was up, with questions Rakil couldn't possibly answer.

There were clothes hanging on hooks in the wardrobe, Purb's best outfit, the one he wore at his dinner parties. Which was like saying to the maid who came in to dust: I've just stepped out a while, I'll be back before you notice I'm gone.

His rings were gone. All of them. There were a few gilded bronze ear studs left to look good to ignorant eyes and deceive ignorant minds. *Cool now, Rak, cool and careful. You know the Flea. Step by step. You're ahead of him now. He expects a month's start, but he's only got a week. You can catch him. Step by step and you'll get him. Squeeze your money out of him and show him ... and show him. ...* He closed his eyes a moment, then went back to his inspection.

The stash was a padded, pocketed belt with a waterproof lining that Purb kept in the flowerbox outside his window. It was most definitely gone; a few of the flowers were showing the strain of hasty replanting.

Rakil searched the room, hunting for the idiotic screeds those Shifters had put their seals to; they'd guarantee a fast trip to the strangling post if Snakeeye got a look at them.

He stopped, gripping the bedpost so hard the wood creaked. "De nai, not here. Calm, Rak. Step by step. My room."

He went slowly and sedately downstairs; his tunic was clinging to his back, soaked with sweat, salt sweat stinging his eyes, but he kept his face smooth, pasted on a faint smile—until he had his bedroom door closed behind him.

He found the treaties rolled into tight spills and **pushed** into the curtain rods.

He stared down at them, his hands shaking. *Twenty-five years. I've served him twenty-five years, saved his skin I don't know how many times, wormed round people for him, cheated and lied for him.*

It was obvious now. The Flea had planned this months ago. Made everyone believe he was gone over the edge. Kept the Shifters sweet because they thought they had him hooked. *He fooled them all and he used me to do it. He threw me away. Like I was garbage. Worth less than these. . . .* He twisted the parchment sheets in his hands until they squeaked protest then tore in half. He stared at them a moment longer, then threw the pieces in the basin on the bed stand and went to fetch a candle. Once they were burned he was a little bit safer. A breath or two, that was all he'd be buying, but he needed that breath. *Cool and calm. Step by step. You'll get him, ia sim, you will. And you'll make him sorry. . . .*

When the treaties were reduced to greasy black ash, he took the ash outside and scattered it over several flowerbeds, ignoring the ghosts that dropped down to watch him. The Planner was in charge now, the part of him Purb had polished into a tool that he'd used before now with consummate skill. Rakil was feeling nothing any more. There was only determination left, an ice hard drive that nothing was going to deflect.

One bit of luck, there's no mages to backtime a fragment and fetch the whole, no Diviners to touch and read. Eyes and memories are all I'll have to worry about and with a little luck I'll be long gone before

those memories surface. Hmm. Assach's Dark Moon
leaves on the next high tide, which is. . . .

He dredged into memory, digging out bits of over-
heard comment, absently brushing his hand through an
overly intrusive ghost, ignoring its indignant chitter.

*Which is an hour before midnight tonight. Assach'll
be taking on the pilot about then, casting off and letting
the outflow carry him from the bay. Tricky business, all
too easy to get stuck in the sandbars round the mouth
and the* Dark Moon's *a big ship, one of the biggest to
call at this port. If I can get onboard and hidden, master and crew will be far too busy to search out stow-
aways until they're safely into The Sodé. On the way to
Savvalis. Which is, thank Tungjii the Blesséd, only three
days' sail, perhaps less in a ship like the* Dark Moon.
*With a water skin and a few precautions—and some
luck—I can do that on my head.*

*Bem. Now I have to keep things cool for a few more
hours. First step, Humarie.* He went back into the office, nodding to a maid who slipped past him in the hall
as he reached the office.

Spy. That's one thing the Flea had right.

He wrote a note to Humarie saying he'd have to miss
this week, some business had come up and he couldn't
get free in time to see her. That had happened several
times before, so the note wouldn't raise the alarms his
unexplained absence might. He gave the note with a
coin to the kitchen boy and told him not to wait for an
answer. He stayed a moment exchanging jokes with fat
Tam, warning him he wouldn't be home for dinner, then
he strolled back to his rooms and laid out his best
clothes. The Planner tightened its hold, there was nothing in him now, no thought of revenge or hurt, nothing
but getting through the next minute, then the minute after that, and so on, minute by minute.

He had his bath; the water had cooled more than he
liked, but there wasn't time to heat it again; he shaved,

brushed his hair, touched it with just a hint of blueflower. When he left the house, he grinned amiably at the houseman washing the entrance walls and strolled out into the street. As far as the household was concerned, he was on his way to Humarie.

In the sack he dangled so carelessly from his right hand was every cent left in the household coffers, plus anything else he could find that was small and salable, even the gilded bronze ear studs. There wasn't much. He couldn't cart around china and glassware, too bulky and too breakable. There was also a change of clothing, two pairs of razors, some soap and a brush that would do for his clothes as well as his hair. A good appearance saved a lot of harassment; that was something else he'd learned from the Flea.

He could feel a muscle jump beside his eye, the tic that came on him when he was angry but couldn't show it. The Planner ignored the body's small rebellion; the tic didn't interfere with what had to be done, so there was no point wasting energy trying to smooth it out. There was a pain in his gut, a cramp. That, too, was merely something he had to live with. Anger exudate, like the sweat that eased a fever. It would go away when he found Purb. When he got his money back. Two hundred gold pieces, collected over a quarter of a century. Not wealth, but enough to keep him from starving when he was too old to work. *What a miserable worm Purb is,* he thought with distant disapproval, *stealing a slave's pittance. I'll have that back if I have to chase you to the antipodes, old man. And if you're dead, I'll render it from your lard.*

The godon was deserted and almost empty when he got there, the packers gone for the day though the incense pastilles they burned to chase the ghosts away were still sending up threads of smoke. There were a hundred or so jars of essence left that nobody had

wanted, a few empty crates, a messy pile of discarded
packing straw. He took off his good clothes, changed
into working gear he kept in a closet in the godon office, and began packing those last jars. They had no
seals, but he wasn't worried; once they were in the crate
no one could tell that anyway and he knew a few bent
traders who worked out of Savvalis, so he'd have no
trouble fencing the jars though he'd have to take a tenth
of what they were worth. Better than nothing. Besides,
the crate was his ticket on board the *Dark Moon* and his
survival pack. If he worked things right. If Assach had
a little space left in his hold. Assach was a tight man
and emptiness was waste.

It took Rakil most of the afternoon to get the jars in
clean and buffered properly so they wouldn't break in
transit. It looked so easy when the ladesmen did it, but
his fingers stumbled over each other and the straw fell
apart uselessly time after time until he finally found the
right twist. On the top layer he set a blanket from the
watchman's cot, a filled water skin, a packet of bread
and meat, and the rest of his gear.

When he knocked in the last nail on the crate lid, he
closed his eyes, weary beyond anything he could remember; after a moment, though, he scraped the sweat
from his face and patted the crate as if it were a pet
he'd been playing with whose eccentricities had taken
his mind off his troubles for several hours.

He washed up, put on his good clothes and went
hunting for Assach.

Karascapa Tavern was throbbing with noise and heat
when Rakil went in. Assach's bald head glistened as if
he'd oiled it; he was sitting at a small table close to the
drum, leaning back in his chair, sipping at a pot of hot
miuz, watching the dancers and stroking his long black
beard with his free hand. He was Phrasi so it was
braided into dozens of thin, glistening plaits.

Rakil wove through the tables, stopped beside Assach. "Can we talk?" he yelled, raising his voice to cut through the noise.

Assach ran his tongue along his teeth, bulging out his lips. After a minute he nodded at the second chair, took a long pull at the miuz, set the pot on the table and leaned forward. "What?"

Rakil sat, put weight on his elbows so his face was close to the shipmaster's. "I picked up a deal this afternoon. Crate of essences with a bonus if I can get them to Savvalis in three days. You have any room left in your hold?"

"Just one crate?"

"Cleans us out."

"Bem. We can tuck it in. How soon can you get it to us?"

"Round an hour. How much?"

"Mm. One crate, just to Savvalis. Tell you what, we'll make it a pring and call it even."

"I'm sure you would. Ha! Five cobs. I'll have to hire porters for the job, your men will be scattered over the district celebrating their last night here. It's easy money, Assach, all you have to do is unload the crate and leave it on the dock at Savvalis, that's the bargain. I'll get the price before I bring it on board; once it's in the hold my worries are over."

"Hmm! The Flea's tighter than a lemon pucker. Five cobs it is. Got a bit of paper?"

Rakil made a pretense of searching through his pockets, came up with a wrinkled piece of wrapping. He smoothed it out, held it still as Assach dripped wax on it from the candle stub in the center of the table and thumped his signet in it when it was stiff enough

"Give that to Jerass with the fivebit. He'll show you where to put the thing."

"Bem." Rakil shoved his chair back and stood. "Good sailing, Assach. See you some other time."

Assach nodded at him, then banged on the table to get the potgirl's notice. His miuz had chilled, he wanted a poker in it.

In the hold of the *Dark Moon,* Rakil fussed with the crate until he heard the whistle from the pilot who wanted to come on board. He sent the ladesmen after Jerass, started to follow them up the ladder, then dropped lightly back and found a place among some bales wrapped in several layers of tightly woven canvas. He stretched out on them and waited, listening to the hubbub and confusion as the crew returned and the pilot fussed about.

The *Dark Moon* swayed free of the wharf and began turning. The pilot boat bumped against the ship's side not far from where he lay, dull thuds muted by the rope fenders. He could hear the thump of feet, shouts, the chaotic, controlled confusion of departure as the ship creaked around him, dipped and rose in long graceful arcs.

Half an hour later the pilot went overside and his rowers took him back to the wharves. The *Dark Moon* seemed to shake herself, free her elbows from her sides, then she really began moving. They were in The Sodé now, running before the wind.

Rakil shuddered as his rage came back to him now that the immediate danger was past. He lay gasping, opening and closing his fists until sheer exhaustion forced him into an uneasy sleep.

Chapter 7
The Joys of War

The Chained God Unchained looked down at the crouching withered god, nudged him with a golden toe. "Nice nutty flavor. Might be back when you've had some time to plump out again. Think about that." He smiled, burped, and ambled lazily away from the drained Chaggar, sliding through god space, measuring the Land Gods who came under him like a man cruising a smorgasbord, searching for delicacies to tempt a failing appetite.

Sarimbara, Land God of Jhakki Sarise, stirred beneath Dil Jorpashil, sending tremors through the earth and cracks through walls. The Serpent drew back his thorny, horny head and hissed, then tried to screw his coils deeper into the earth. It was useless, the Chained God Unchained reached down and stroked the curve of Sarimbara's neck, teasing lines of force out of the Serpent, reeling them slowly, indolently into himself, the Talisman BinYAHtii the focus and feed-point.

As he sipped at the Serpent's tangy essence, he turned his head, glanced down at the Four and smiled, contented for the moment to see this potential set of gnatbites controlled so closely. "I'd prefer them dead," he murmured to the arched and shivering Serpent, "but you-know-who still has a mind to preserve them. Aaah, you're a delicious morsel, O my sweet Sarimbara. I'd be enjoying my graze even if it weren't so necessary. Yesss, does that feel good? Think of all the years you can rest in the dark earth replenishing yourself, dreaming long slow dreams."

NAVARRE

With a prickle on his neck that told him he was being watched, Navarre reached the foothills before the day heated up; whoever it was stayed a long way off, afraid of being poisoned by the mage's magic. *Walking plague center, huh! That's what they want. Gods! I have to figure out what to do. And how to do it without getting chopped by both sides. And the Wrystrike.* His stomach churned when he thought what the Wrystrike would do to people so vulnerable to anything magic. *I have to . . . Kat. . . .*

He walked through scattered trees, circled rock piles nestled in patches of brush as if the hills were insects and laid their eggs that way, jumped ravines when he could, went round when he had to. Out near the horizon patches of white smoke ran on four feet or two, their eyes like wounds watching him. Ghosts. Wasted deaths, bodies left to rot, earth souls to haunt the land.

The boneboy said go west and keep going, so he did, resenting the eyes, coldly furious at the strings on him.

The sun climbed, there was no wind, and the heat was stifling; as he slogged along, he cursed them over and over for not leaving him any water. He found a pebble, sucked on it and tried not to think of rivers and tea and cold white wine and all the other liquids that had graced his life.

As he emerged from the hills, he came on a small farm village nestling in a hollow.

Dead Shifters were melting in the heat, their ghosts writhing and howling wordlessly, the agony of their deaths compressed into that punishing sound. He slapped his hands over his ears and struggled forward through a stench different but as revolting as that from the boneman corpses, the dead horses and cattle.

Half the buildings in the village were burned to the ground, mere patches of ash. Others stood like snaggle teeth, walls charred, roofs fallen in or burned off.

He found a well in the court of the largest house, the one most nearly intact. When he cranked the bucket up, the water was clean and cold; he drank some, poured the rest over his head.

Go west, they said. Murdering skem!

He brought up more water and once again drank from the bucket. This time he didn't stop until he couldn't force down another sip.

With angry, suffering ghosts yammering and hammering futilely at him, trying to drive him out, he wrenched open the half-fallen door and began searching the house for anything he could use. He didn't expect to find food, but a water skin would be useful, a bit of rope, a blanket even. The ghosts followed for a few moments, then went gliding away; they could sense the magic in him and it sickened them.

Navarre came back to the kitchen because he felt closer to Kitya there; it was a smallish room at the rear of the house with a fireplace, a broken table, and little else. He sat cross-legged on the dusty tiles and relaxed into his center; his breathing slowed, his eyes glazed over. After several deep slow breaths, he lifted his hands from his thighs, cupping them as if he held a disc between the palms.

The mirror shimmered alive.

> *Kitya crouched in a small dark place, an iron chain about one ankle. She had two of the links in her hands; slowly, patiently she was rubbing one against the other.*

She looked better than she had when they took her away from the garden, probably because she was working on escape and had hope again; already she'd rubbed a shiny groove into one of the links, a few more days and she'd be able to twist it open. He watched her a moment longer, smiling fondly. *Hard to keep the woman down.* He expanded the image and shifted viewpoint.

They'd put Kitya in a small stone building, a cube with no windows and a single door barred on the outside. Not far from the cell there was a three-sided shelter made of poles and thatching. Two Shifter guards sat in its shade, playing a gambling game with stone cubes and a grid drawn in the dirt.

Show me Faan.

The mirror was suddenly black from edge to edge. He muttered, concentrated; the blackness faded to a muted gray.

> *Faan was feeling her way about a cavern (as far as he could tell there was no light at all). She had dirty streaks across her face and arms from the damp and slimy moss on the cavern walls. She stumbled into a pool, swore and backed out again, groping her way to a crumpled pile of blankets. She managed to get one of them folded and sat on it, pulled another about her shoulders. She was shivering with cold, but her face was flushed and the surdosh was shifting uneasily, its shell plates clicking together.*

Even through the mirror he could feel the heat building in her and remembered uneasily what he felt when he touched her back there on the beach, the sense of immense power, controlled at that moment, but only barely.

His fingertips started to burn.

Hastily he shifted viewpoint and expanded the field.

There was a bricked-up cave mouth, another of the three-sided shelters, two more guards, one sleeping, the other throwing a small knife at a knot in a length of firewood, retrieving it and throwing it again. And again and again and again.

He shut off the scene, set the search for Desantro. He didn't know her as well as the others, had no strong feelings about her, but according to Faan she was a catalyst like Kitya and for the moment he had no reason to dispute that.

Chained at the ankles, Desantro crouched against a stone wall, rubbing a link against the crack between the stones, wearing away the iron and the stone at the same time. A sliver of stone like a knifeblade cracked free of the wall and fell beside her foot. She tucked it in her shirt and went on working.

That is one practical woman, he thought. No wasting time deciding what to do first. She does both.

He moved the viewpoint as before. Desantro was in a stone cube like Kitya, there was the same sort of pole shelter and again two guards doing whatever they could to break the tedium.

Whispering the incantation that would start the mapping of the locations, he focused mind and body on the mirror. Mapping came close to the boundary of the Wrystrike. He had to be sure he didn't go over because he needed truth without distortion.

Clawwag's Vale was a long oval with mountain ranges on both sides; the short axis was close to fifty miles, the long nearly two hundred. Kitya's cell was near the northern end, Desantro's nearly thirty miles off in the foothills near where they came into the valley. Faan was the closest; her cave was northeast of him, less than twenty miles away. He swore when he saw how scattered they were; the image wrinkled and shivered till he got himself in hand, then he switched to the Browneye domain and located Snarl's Citadel, a bright, irregular patch a hundred and fifty miles southwest of this desolation he sat in. "Labi labba, that's that." Scowling at his hands, he let the map fade and the mirror wink away.

Clawwag and his lot might be ignorant, but they weren't fools. Even if the Wrystrike would let him jump without dangerously damaging the landscape and putting the lives of the women at risk, he wouldn't dare try it. The Shifters had some means of long distance communication that he couldn't pick up and so couldn't block; what he'd seen on the trip from the coast and after made that quite clear. Break one of the women loose and the guards would set on the others, kill them before he could reach them. *Except . . . we're here because Faan needs us. . . . Neka, I can't chance it. She's the one the gods are protecting, not me or Kat or even Desantro. If I become a danger to her, I'm history.*

He grimaced, got to his feet, sick at the thought of his actions killing an indeterminate number of Browneye Shifters—males, females, and children—anyone who was near him when he worked. "Nu, if I'm going to be a plague spreader, let's spread it among the right people."

He folded his arms, focused on the idea of oil-gel, then slid swiftly between the realms, heading for the Browneye Citadel and the weaponstores there, a perilous breath ahead of Wrystrike fury, holding both of them insulated from the ordinary folk of that domain so he could keep damage to a minimum.

FAAN

Faan huddled the blanket around her, teeth chattering from her plunge into the pool. "Pichads! Jeggin sarks! You'll be sorry. . . ." She was cold and hot at the same time, fire souls ran like worms under her skin, the water dripping from her hair sizzled and steamed.

The surdosh felt them, too; it was stirring, pressing one part of itself then another against her neck, exuding an acid that burned her and peeled off large pieces of skin. It wasn't fully roused, but the moment she moved to control the fire, it would act.

She rubbed at her feet, cursing the god Meggzatevoc as an interfering maggot for tossing her out of his country barefoot and destitute; she rubbed and rubbed and slowly, slowly she got warm again—but not comfortable. The darkness pressed down on her, made it hard to breathe, as if her nose were connected to her eyes. *Midsummer's Eve.* The words burned in her head. *I'll have everything I need by then, Tungjii promised. Need. . . .* The need for her mother was growing in her like the fire, stronger and more compelling with every breath she took.

She brooded.

The pressure built beneath her skin.

Under the surdosh her neck was rasped raw.

The fire moved back and forth, up and down her body, round and round, the surdosh tightened on her neck, trembling and oozing acid.

She wove her fingers together and squeezed until her knuckles went white, ground her teeth, hunched her shoulders and tried to hold on. . . .

The fire exploded out of her.

The instant before it was crisped, the surdosh struck. . . .

* * *

When she woke, her clothes and the blankets were gone and every hair was burnt off her body. Fire-demons were circling angrily about the cave, swooping over her, raking their claws along her body.

Head throbbing, she forced herself up, ignoring the demons. If they could hurt her, she'd already be ash. She pressed her hands against her eyes. The surdosh was dead and the raw ring on her neck had healed while she was out, but she was still sealed in this miserable black hole.

After several deep breaths she wiggled her fingers, then drew her legs up, folded her hands, and rested them on her knees. She sucked in another breath and stared down at her thumbnails; they caught the flickering red light of the angry demons and shone pale pink in the light from the circling demons.

The Sibyl had taught her how to dismiss fire elementals, not full flaming demons. Still, the demons were fire, too, maybe. . . .

They were chittering with rage, demanding that she let them out, let them burn and burn, it was their nature to burn, it was horror to be stuck in this wet dark place with its stubborn unburnable stone.

She focused more tightly on the shimmer in her thumbnails and brought up the series of grotesque words she'd found to trigger the Firedismiss.

She felt the resistance again, grunted, and pushed. . . .

Her talent flared suddenly; she nearly lost her grip, but recovered and SHOUTED the DISMISS at the fire-demons.

They fought her, like the little elemental fires had fought her the first time she killed a man, but in the end they popped out, flung home across the countless levels to the fire worlds where they were spawned.

Trembling with weariness and the dregs of fear, she knelt beside the pool, scooped up icy water, and drank until her stomach cramped with the cold. She stayed on her knees, crafted a willo for light and looked deep into the black water, searching in it as if it were a mirror.

And found Desantro.

And found Kitya.

"Jegging sarks, scattering us all over the place. Tsah!" She got to her feet and looked around. Everything that could burn in that pocket of a cave had burned. She rubbed her hands along her sides, then circled the pool and inspected the end of the cave.

There wasn't even a crack in the stone, but that didn't matter now.

She spread her hands, flattened them against the back wall and concentrated, muttering the focal words, melting the stone into air.

When Faan came round the side of the mountain, she saw the pole shelter and the two horses tethered to the stone ring they tied her to; one was nibbling at the sparse grass, the other had his nose in a small stone trough; he lifted his head, looked round at her, then went back to his drinking. She bit her lip, then circled cautiously around them.

The Shifters were crumpled on their ground, eyes open and glassy, skin covered with patches of blue-gray mold or eaten away in huge nauseating ulcers. They weren't dead yet, but it wouldn't be long. The stench was appalling.

Faan gagged, backed away, dismayed by the reality of what had just been words a short time before. Magic poison. "I did it. Me and the fire-demons. Mamay. . . ." The last word was a long gasp, a reaching toward . . . what? Reyna who raised her? Kori who bore her? She gasped again, pressed her hands against her eyes and willed the thought of both to the back of her head. Horror at what she'd done would have to wait on survival.

And her heart's need would wait until ... *nayo, no time for that.*

Breathing shallowly, she edged past them into the shelter; she had to get out of here and fast. The dead men would have blankets and food, gear for the horses and maybe, with a little luck, a spare shirt or two. She didn't much fancy riding about the countryside naked as a skinned rabbit, not even eyebrows left.

An hour later, she was heading steadily north, chewing on nuggets of honey, grain, and crushed nuts, the second horse on a long lead behind her. Kitya first, because she was closest, then Desantro, then maybe Navarre would know and come to them. *Midsummer Eve. Tungjii promised. Midsummer Eve and the dome would come down and she'd stand in front of her mother. Midsummer Eve. Not quite two months ... travel time....* She fought down an urge to knee the horse into a full-stretching gallop, cursed Sibyl and Navarre because they hadn't taught her to jump like she knew Sorcerers could do, like Navarre himself could do, and she started singing one of the Kalele songs, using the noise to drown the clamor in her head, "Ooh zing zul...."

NAVARRE

The Wrystrike roaring about him, Navarre phased into the present, fell with a faint thud onto the floor of a huge warehouse with bins of iron points and spear shafts against the walls, barrels of oil-gel oozing and stinking around him.

The Strike hit.

The barrels exploded.

Desperately he jumped again, riding the waves of heat and force, cursing the miscalculation that had trapped him, fighting to get into the *elsewhen* so he could run the timelines out of there.

Mistake! Stupid mistake! The words throbbed in his head, crippling his concentration. *Stupid to waste time and strength on this nonsense, I should have. . . .*

An image burned into his mind, Kitya swinging a loop of the chain about her leg, trying to drive off a howling Shifter who was lunging at her with a knife.

"Kat," he groaned, "Ah, Gods. . . ." Grimly suppressing the panic starting to bloom in him, he sought focus and intensity. Breathing slowly, ignoring the buffets of his tumbling body, the hiss of the Strike, he struck at the chains tethering her, tried to draw her to him.

He felt her strong, slender body briefly in his hands, heard in his mind her shout of delight: Navarre!

Then she was gone, torn from him by the maelstrom that had him trapped.

"Kat," he cried. "Kitya. Answer me! Where are you?"

But there was no answer except the silent glee of the Wrystrike as it whirled him away he didn't know where.

Chapter 8
On the Money Trail

The *Dark Moon*'s motion changed.

The creak and squeal of ropes, the muffled thunder of orders, and the thud-thud of hurrying feet dropped through the deck to Rakil's ears as sails came down and a pilot was brought on board.

Filthy and sore, his stomach rolling queasily (it'd been a rough passage), he crept from his hiding place. Working by feel, he levered up the lid on his crate of essences, shoved his gear onto the top layer of straw and used the heel of his boot to knock the nails back down. Then he crept through the narrow trails between the bales, barrels, and crates and crouched behind the ladder to wait for the hatchcovers to be undogged.

Morning light poured in.

Eyes watering, Rakil darted from his ambush, leapt for the ladder and was up it before the crewmen working on a bale could do more than yell. He burst through a group of men standing by the hatch, plunged for the side with more yells following him, swung over the rail, and dropped into the water.

He went deep, swam underwater until he crossed into shadow, then kicked up and emerged beneath a wharf. He clung to a pile, gasping and sputtering, then paddled along until he reached a ladder.

* * *

"Come on, Ziraf, come on, come on." Rakil knocked again, a quick rat-tat of his knuckles on the peeling veneer of the back door. Cold greasy water dripped down his neck from the sodden hair pasted to his skull, one more sin he laid on the balance to weigh against Purb.

There was a scrabbling sound, like rats running across planks in the hold, then the door opened a crack and a rheumy blue eye peered out at him. "Hanh?"

"Rakil, Z'raf. Come on, let me in, I've got something for you."

The eye blinked slowly several times, then Ziraf shuffled back, opening the door just wide enough to let Rakil slide in. "Flea was in town a week ago," he muttered. "Nu, what's doin', Rak? Dievshat, you a mess."

"Things got a bit sticky," Rakil said, "I had to jump faster than we expected. You gonna leave me dripping here?"

Ziraf worked his mouth back and forth, the rattail mustaches that drooped on each side of it wiggling like snakes. He looked to the right, to the left, as if he were searching for something that wasn't there, then he nodded and shuffled off along the dingy little passageway.

Rakil sighed, set his mug beside his plate. "It's good to be clean again. I owe you, Z'raf. There's a crate of Kaeru essences on the dock, no seals, but genuine for all that. You want a piece?"

Ziraf tossed back his kijis, thumped the small thick glass on the table. "How come no seals?"

"Left too fast."

"Tja, and too sneaky, hanh?"

Rakil waggled his hand. "So, you want that piece?"

Ziraf pursed his lips, then nodded.

"Nu, get a couple ladesmen, send them to *Dark Moon*'s wharf. Name painted on the crate's Garlacig. Give you 'n extra jar t' cover expenses."

"Three."

"Two."

"Done."

Rakil reached for the teapot, poured a dollop of the turgid liquid into his mug. "You know what ship the Flea took south?"

Ziraf blinked at him, nostrils twitching. "He didn't leave word?"

Rakil snorted. "Not him. I'm expected to read his twisted little mind and sweep up behind him, then figure out where he's gone to earth. Isn't the first time, won't be the last."

Ziraf relaxed, nodded. "Tja, that's him all right. He kept his head down, didn't stay more'n a night, left with the tide on Pistaar's *Tochshidayan.* Bound for Bandrabahr, if he don't do another leap."

Rakil lowered his eyes and sipped at the bitter tea until he had hold of himself again. "So, better get started on selling those jars. Flea will have my skin, I keep him waiting too long."

"Nu, can't do nothing for a couple days, not till the Svintey's finished."

"What's that?"

"Celebration. Paranasvinte, when they swear in the new Augstadievon, Ledus Druz it's gonna be, soldier man, not so smart, but at least he's honest. Been a bloody mess the past some months, bunch of plotters trying to take over, Candidates murdered, thugs in the streets," he grimaced, "and speeches all over the place; foreigners like us they can't vote, but they sure better be polite and listen. And come dark moon we got to close shop and pass out coins like we the state treasury to every beggar bumps up against us. Nu, things will settle down after a while, but there's gonna be no ships leaving port until the Swearing's over."

Rakil stepped from the sideway onto Tirdza Street, elbowed his way into the celebrating crowd.

Tonight the Caretaker would go back to the temple and Druz of the Ledus family would take over as the new Augstadievon. And tomorrow it was back to work as usual, but now the city was having one last party—according to Ziraf, the wildest of the lot. There were clowns in the street everywhere, mute and dancing, swinging bladders, shaking rattles, whirling bullroarers when there was room, their painted grins thrust in the faces of the passersby. Holy dancers in thin linen shifts pranced in irregular circles, waving wide satin ribbons of many colors, a color for each of the gods, the wide gold ones for Meggzatevoc the local Land God. Diviners sat on high stools, islands of stillness in the chaos, touching the cheek of the questor with one hand, a curved mirror in the other, answering one question for each, often with a single word.

A snaking line of postpubescent boys in red tabards with lizards rampant came dancing from one of the sideways, stamping and leaning first to one side, then the other, shouting, "Ledus. Ledus. Ledus." The crowd opened before them, clapping hands, joining the chant: "Cadet cadet Ledus Ledus."

Impatient at the celebration around him, Rakil fought through the crowds until he reached the shop front, then edged sideways along it until he reached the sideway he was looking for. He wriggled through the people plugging the mouth and brushed himself off as he walked toward the inn where a shipmaster was supposed to be taking on new crew.

Siffaram was a lean man with hooded eyes, his long Phrasi beard twisted into greasy corkscrews, his mustache a bush that concealed his mouth.

The Planner at work again, Rakil slipped on his blandest face. He knew what he was looking at, a slippery man, a cheat, but probably not dangerous if you never went to sleep around him. In ordinary times he'd stay the length of the port from this one, but he didn't have any choice. He had to work his way south and the longer he had to wait in Savvalis, the bigger the start Purb would have on him. Bem, one thing he'd learned from Flea was smarm. Smooth it on, Rak. The sweeter he is, the softer you land.

He bowed and stood with eyes down and hands folded. "Honored sir," he murmured, "it is said that you desire men to work your ship."

Siffaram ran muddy brown eyes over him, sniffed, one nostril flaring, a corner of his mouth curling up in a contemptuous sneer. "What can you do," he paused for emphasis, "old man?"

"Read and write in seven tongues, cipher, cook, handle rope, mend sail. You tell me what you need, I'll tell you 'f I can do it."

"Why's a paragon like you running round loose?"

Rakil looked furtive, his mouth stretching in an uneasy, mirthless smile. "Business went belly up, I'm out on my ear. Owner's got kin to take him in, not me. Besides, I'm tired of heavy winters." He let his eyes skitter uneasily about; he knew what the Phrasi wanted, a shady character with a murky background, a slider, not a fighter. "I want to go south where I don't freeze my arse off half the year."

Siffaram scratched at the jutting bridge of his hawk nose. "Workin your way, not buying?"

"Clerking's steady work, but you don't get rich." Rakil allowed himself a faint smirk, banished it as soon as Siffaram caught it.

"You a writing man?"

Rakil pursed his lips. "So so."

"Bills of lading?"

"Show me an example, I can make you a nice copy."

Siffaram stroked his hand down his beard. "Cargo-master. Start you five chelks the month and found, you provide your own ink and paper and a suit of good clothes for port."

"Agreed. When you want me on board?"

"Tomorrow morning, dawn. We leaving on tide, that'll be third daywatch. Ask for Hadsar, he'll show you where to stow your duff."

Smiling with satisfaction, Rakil fought his way back down Tirdza Street to the teahouse he'd passed on his way to the inn.

He settled over a steaming cup and spent the next hour brooding over all complications in catching up with Purb and wringing his savings from the old man's blood and bone.

Chapter 9
Scattershots

The Chained God Unchained glanced down at Kaerubulan and saw the Girl riding free. "Nibbling," he raged. "Nibbled to death." He flung away the trembling husk of the Serpent and strode closer, his driving pace waking wisps of hot orange and tongues of red in the stuff of godspace. "Pleestin infant gnat! If I could just get you under my thumb, then you could bare your tiny teeth and threaten all you want as I squashed you to a smear! Wait. Just wait. When I'm strong enough. . . ."

He sniffed in annoyance, slapped godstuff into a chair and sat scanning the island, looking for the others. "Yesss, go to it, you plaas," he murmured, the pinlights whirling in his eyes as he saw Desantro struggling for her life against a pair of Shifters determined to kill her. "Yes, good. Only a matter of time and you're dead. Dead and gone. Nothing." The Magus was gone, thrown so far from the scene the Chained God Unchained couldn't get a smell of him; the snake witch was gone with him. That was good, it meant they were both out of the reckoning. "Perran-a-Perran, you've lost your pawns." He rocked on his cushion, his laughter dancing like small black gnats in the glow that surrounded him. "You

could make a song of that. A triumph." His
mouth turned down and he lost his joy as he
caught sight of the Girl again. Her! A bite.
With a vast sigh, he began searching for sur-
rogates who might be able to do what he
could not. "With a little bit of Luck. . . ." He
thought of Tungjii Luck and scowled, slapped
his hand on his thigh, producing a loud clank,
then went back to his search.

FAAN

The horse stumbled, nearly went down, then braced its
front legs and stood shivering, its sides working like a
bellows; the other horse, the one on the lead, shook its
head, started cropping at the grass at the side of the narrow lane.

"K'lann!" Faan slid from the saddle, pulled the kerchief from her naked head and scrubbed it across her
face. She stared at the crumpled cloth for a moment
then tied it on her head. *No time for grizzling. Twenty
minutes and I'll have Kitya loose, then we'll both go for
Desantro. Twenty jeggin minutes. If the Shifters find out
what happened. . . .*

Fingers made clumsy by the need for hurry, she
tugged the end of the cinchstrap loose and began struggling with the rings. She had to get the saddle on the
other horse and start on again. Had to. If Kitya and
Desantro were killed, she was alone. There'd be no one
left who knew her. Even Ailiki was gone. . . . With
small gasping sounds she blinked away the tears that
made her angry. She didn't want to cry, but she couldn't
help it; she was frightened by the chance she might be
abandoned all over again, dumped in this wholly hostile
place, alone. . . .

Around her in the fields the bonemen serfs had

stopped working. They were staring at her. One of them took a hesitant step toward her. Then another.

"Nayo!" Faan set her back against the horse, lifted her hands. "Stay away," she howled. "I don't want to hurt you, but I will."

They stopped and she went back to fighting tears and frustration—and changing the saddle.

Half an hour later, she slid from the back of the second horse and walked through ash and char to a small square cell. The stones were blackened on the outside, but the inside was relatively untouched. Short sections of chain dangled from two staples, the last link on each melted to a dribble of iron. On the stone floor she saw two crystallized smears, all that was left of a pair of Shifters. *Kitya's guards, no doubt . . . two for each of us. Navarre? Diyo, who else . . . what was he . . . Desa?*

She wheeled and ran for the horse, more desperate than before, Kitya was gone. There was only Desantro. . . .

Faan rode from the foothills at a walk. At times her breath came in short gasps and her stomach knotted with fear and frustration until she was almost vomiting, but she needed the horse; she couldn't afford to exhaust herself, if she lost hold of the fire and started burning, the whole land would go, boneman and Shifter alike . . . if she could just jump like Navarre . . . if, if, a dozen ifs. . . .

In the south the lake around the Citadel was a faint blue mist and the Citadel itself a blurred glitter on the horizon as its crystal bricks caught the sunlight coming through the scattered clouds. *Stay in there, you stupid jeggers, leave me alone.*

She grimaced at the twitching ears of her mount, slapped at a stingfly buzzing at her arm. She wouldn't mirror Desantro because the memory of the dreadfully dying guards churned her stomach and the chance of doing that to other Shifters woke a profound resistance in her despite her need for reassurance. All she could do was hope and ride. Desa was tough, she knew how to bend if she had to, fight when she had to, all those years being a slave, at least they taught her that.

The land flattened quickly, grew fences of split saplings and a grid of deep narrow canals. Ghosts drifting unheeded about them, the boneserfs working in the fields watched Faan as she passed, their songs and laughter stopping as if she rode in a rolling sphere of silence.

Shuffle plod whumpf umpf ... slow, slow, intolerably slow ...

The horse's hooves kicked up dust that eddied round his knees ... the saddle creaked, a tiny rhythmic noise ... the erratic wind struck her face and fell away and struck again ... her insistent unhappy thoughts caught those rhythms and flowed on ... endlessly ... futilely. ...

Navarre. He doesn't want anything to do with me. He liked vegetating in that smithy; weren't for me, him and Kitya they'd still be there. Look at me, I've lost everything I had. Even my hair's gone. I had pretty hair. Reyna used to brush it and brush it when I was little. Reyna .. NAYO!

She passed through a village gone silent, the street emptying before her, the children snatched into houses—a reminder she didn't need of how alone and vulnerable she was.

How long before the subDuke gets the news and sends his guards for me? I can't use the Fire here. I CAN'T! But if it gets away from me ... like it did ... would the Shifters rather burn or rot? K'lann! what can I ... there must be no Land God here ... a god is magic from core to skin ... they'd all be dead if they had a god ... what do I know about gods except it's best to avoid them? Ailiki ... she's all magic ... is that

*why she went off and left me? Everyone's leaving
me. . . .*

She stopped at the well in the village, filled the
trough for the horse, pulled the kerchief off again, and
splashed water over her head and shoulders. She could
feel eyes watching her, hating her. Waiting. *K'lann!
doesn't it ever stop?*

She scratched the horse behind his ear, then pulled
herself into the saddle. "Vema," she shouted, "I'm going. Keep your hair on." She grinned briefly, unhappily,
then dug her heels in and started the horse walking.
"Not fast," she cried, "but I'll get there." She waved the
wrinkled, sodden kerchief, then tied it on and settled in
the saddle, watching the horse's head bob, holding onto
the fireworms running under her skin, worrying about
Desantro, wondering what Navarre had done, what it
meant, what all this meant, worrying until she was sick
of it.

"Gonna gonna kick and scratch," she sang defiantly,
"Gonna gonna be freeee." The heavy silence sucked at
her voice, trying to draw the strength from it. "Gonna
gonna kick n' scratch," she sang, insisting on the
sound, shouting down the hate. "An't gonna catch me
ee. Gonna gonna kick n' scratch, an't gonna catch me
ee. An't gonna catch me ee. Gonna see gonna see ee.
Gonna be free. Free ee Free ee Free ee." She roared at
them, her voice hoarse with anger and defiance, then
started another of the songs from the Jang, the songs
she'd sung and danced to when she still had a family
and friends and a home. "Doin me BA A AD, strippin
m' PR I IDE, suckin m' LI I IFE, makin me MA A AD,
hey ey I SA A AY, kiss m' ba ACK SI IDE, hey ey I
SA A AY, suck m' kni I I IFE, hey ey I SA A AY, doin
me BA A AD, doin me BAD."

The wind blowing dust in her face dropped for a moment and she saw riders, half a hundred at least, packed

into a clot on the narrow road, still two or three miles away.

No, no, don't do this.

She twisted her face into a grimace as she remembered the rotting corpses of her guards. After edging the horse to the verge where he cropped contentedly at the tender grass, she sat with fingers curling and uncurling, staring at the oncomers.

I hate . . . I loathe . . . detest . . . the idea of poison . . . the gods don't care how many die . . . Abeyhamal made me dance those poor women into maenads who tore their men apart . . . what'd SHE care how they felt about it? I'm better than that. I have to be.

She looked down at hands straining into fists.

I have to be.

The band of fifty men were bunched up along the road, intermittently visible between puffs of dust. The leader was twice as big as the others. "Yelloweye Clawwag," she muttered. "Kuch." He had a tall, white stallion with a long silky mane and tail, its forefeet weighted, snapping high, its neck held by a checkrein in an exaggerated curve.

Clawwag threw up a hand; the others stopped a little over a mile off and he came on, his prisoned, contorted mount playing out his pride.

She brushed impatiently at her eyes, narrowed them so the red wouldn't show. Kitya's mama's dictum: Don't let the bastards see you cry.

The subDuke pulled the horse to a prancing walk, his face grim under the bronze helm.

Faan sat straighter. He was afraid of her; she could see that in the set of his head, the stiffness of his body. But he came on anyway. He might be a total loss as a person, but he did have courage.

He stopped in front of her. "What do you intend?" His voice was like leaves rustling in a wind; his hands worked and his flesh flowed in jerky twitches, half-aborted signs that echoed his slow words.

Faan's head throbbed briefly, then the pain went away—perhaps because the Shifter spoke as well as signed, perhaps because Abeyhamal's Gift was tired of its futile efforts to compel her flesh into those impossible flows. "To leave," she said.

The subDuke's face glistened in the shadow of the helm as if the top layer of his skin were turning to gel. "We have dead to avenge."

"Then you should contrive to avoid more being killed." She kept her voice cool and carrying, her words crisp. *Don't let the bastards see you cry.*

"And if I order my archers to shoot?" The subDuke pointed at the Shifter guard, then brought his hand down, clawed fingers jerking. "We'll chance the poison if it means you're dead."

"I could burn them to ash the minute the first string twanged." She stretched her mouth in a bitter curve that was nothing like a smile. "Who the fire didn't kill, the magic would."

The subDuke chewed his lip. "Why talk then?"

"I don't go about slaughtering folk unless I'm forced into it. It's a matter of ethics, which may be something you don't understand." The Fire was stirring in her again, as if the Shifters attracted it; perhaps they did.

Come on, Yelloweye, accept you can't win this. Nayo nay, that's not right, we both win if we go off from here alive. Accept it, accept it, gods, let's get it over with.

She closed her eyes and whispered the calming mantra the Sibyl had forged with her.

"You say leave," the subDuke said, the words garbled as his face flowed and contorted. "I don't believe you. What do you want?"

"Believe?" Faan's eyes popped open. "You don't have to believe anything. Watch and see." She leaned over, ran her hand along the horse's neck, patting him, scratching gently into his mane. "If you want to get rid of me faster, provide fresh mounts and food and . . ." She frowned. "And bring my companion to me, Desantro I mean, then warn your folk to stay out of our way. If we're not attacked, I'll take care to use no magic near any of you."

The subDuke fixed his hot, buttery gaze on her for a long moment. Without another word, he jerked the horse around and rode at a high-kicking trot back to his forces.

The fireworms moved restlessly under her skin, trying to escape, to fling themselves at the Shifter; she fought them down, though she could smell threads from her shirt charring in the heat. "K'lann! I'm going to fry the horse and me, too . . . ah, grand! he's not stupid." She slumped in the saddle, almost sick with relief.

Three of the Shifters had dismounted. They tied the reins to a section of fence, mounted behind three others. A moment later the whole lot of them were riding off.

Faan slid from the saddle, tugged at the reins, began walking the weary beast down the road. "They're going to do it," she said, "they're going to bring her, I know it. I'll turn you loose, poor old horse, you've done the job. If you knew what I was saying, I think you'd be grinning, hunh! I would. This place, this stinking place. If I were only free of it."

The next village was emptied of people, but a blanket roll, two sacks of honey nuggets and two of dried meat were waiting for her, along with a limp water skin she was meant to fill from the well in the center of the commons. She tied the supplies on the spare horses, stood a moment with her hands on her hips. "My companion," she shouted. "If I don't see her soon, I'll go looking and you don't want that."

* * *

The Shifters left Desantro beside the river they'd followed into the Vale when they were prisoners; she was crouching on a small square of canvas and tethered to a pair of boulders so she couldn't move from the spot.

She was a bundle of pain, suffering from thirst, hunger, infection, and helpless rage. When Faan cut her loose, she couldn't speak for several minutes, could barely manage to straighten her cramped legs and arms. Faan knelt beside her, feeding her dribbles of water and using the abused kerchief to sponge off her face.

"Wha . . ." It was a faint croak Faan had to strain to hear.

"You mean what happened?" Faan let her take the kerchief. "I don't know exactly. I suppose it's as much my fault as anyone's. Fire got away from me." She passed a hand over her naked head. "Burned everything, even my hair. Killed the guards. Not the fire. Poison from the magic." She grimaced. "Horrible. I'd 've thrown up last year's lunches if I could."

"Good." Desantro pushed up, groaning as her stiff sore muscles protested. "That they're dead, the whaurangs." She scrubbed at her face, then gulped water from the skin Faan handed her. "Guards tried to kill me." Her voice was rough and filled with anger. "They came rushing in like they were crazy, I caught one longside the head with a loop of chain, it was a lucky hit, put him out, t'other one I got with a sliver of stone I chipped from the wall, but not before he kicked the potz out of me." She rubbed at her throat with its black and purple ligature marks. "'Twas when he stopped kicking and started strangling me, he got close enough, I shoved the sliver in his throat and killed the huzun. Gods! his hands froze on my neck and he almost finished me off after he was dead." She sat bathing her bruises with the ragged kerchief, scowling at her toes, then she said, "Navarre, Kat, what happened to them?"

Faan settled herself on one of the boulders. "I don't

know. I went for Kitya first, she was closest." She lifted a hand, let it fall. "The cell was empty, chains melted, guards dead. That's all there was."

"Wrystrike?"

"Maybe. Nu, you think you can ride?"

"I can do anything it takes to get away from here."

NAVARRE

Navarre howled as Kitya whirled away from him, howled as he tumbled endlessly through a churning void. . . .

The tumbling smoothed out and he glided from the fog to land feather light on a dusty, dim red-brown plain that stretched endlessly on every side until it melted into a pale gray sky. He stood flat-footed and empty for a time, drained of everything including thought. No grief was possible here. No rage or anguish. This was the still point, the place where agitation ceased.

After a while he turned in a slow circle, his boot soles scraping softly over the substance on which he stood. "I remember," he said aloud, his voice falling dead inches from his face. "I remember this place."

He started walking.

Each step seemed to be miles long. The dull surface fled beneath him.

He walked on and on.

After an indeterminate time, he saw a dark lump ahead of him.

A few steps and he reached it.

He edged around it, found himself almost to the horizon beyond it. He had to back and fill for a frustrating time before he was actually standing before the silent sitter. This, too, he remembered.

The Sibyl lifted her head and looked at him, a big woman with an ancient wrinkled face, iron black and collapsed on the bone; the smell of age hung about her, musty and intimidating.

Why? he said.

She laughed silently, the wrinkles shifting, her lively black eyes narrowed to slits, but she said nothing.

You are Sibyl, he said. You were created for giving answers. Answer me.

I am only compelled to answer questions, she said. Asked or implied. That is no question.

He frowned at her. Because I know the answer? Then tell me this, where is Kitya?

Elsewhere.

Is she well?

Well enough.

How can I reach her?

Ride the Wrystrike. Her eyes opened wider and wider, immense pools of black, drawing him in, drawing him before he realized what was happening. . . .

He fell into the Sibyl's eyes and went tumbling again into confusion. . . .

When he could see what was beyond his nose, he found himself in a place of . . . what? Streams of light, painted light as if it had passed through a stained-glass window, rays crossing and mingling with each other, color melting into color, emerging pure again. Nothing solid there but him. He looked down at hands like pinkish-brown glass and lost even the certainty of his own weight.

"I remember this," he shouted, "why am I here?" And saw his words stream away, little shimmers of black-edged gold . . . little shimmers . . . his words were diminished here to fleas running through the light lattice.

Light flickered around him; the beams shifted, changed, became a hand so huge the fingers were longer than rivers, the thumb a tower. . . with him a little dark beetle in the center. . . .

He screamed as the thumb came down on him . . . screamed again as it flicked him away like a man flicking away a beetle.

KITYA

Sliding from gray chaos half a dozen feet above a cracked and weathered stretch of flat rock at the top of an immense, deeply weathered cliff, Kitya landed hard, a grunt forced from her. She stumbled toward the cliff edge, grabbed at the nearest of the two trees growing by the brink.

And nearly fell over the edge when the smooth silky bark went suddenly warm and alive under her hand, then started changing shape.

Kitya teetered, arms wheeling, scrambled for balance and stood panting a moment later, watching in astonishment as the tree collapsed into a semitranslucent green chrysalis.

The chrysalis lay quiet a moment, then shivered, rocking back and forth, working toward the cliff edge.

Without stopping to think, Kitya reached for it, but before she touched it, the crysalis split with a sharp dry crack and a figure began unfolding, a small woman with olive green skin and long russet hair, dressed in a worn black tunic and trousers pushed into black boots.

Tugging her tunic down, the woman turned; her orange-amber eyes flicked across Kitya, head to foot, stopped on her face. "I thank you," she said. Her voice was a deep contralto, startling from that slight body. "A tree's a splendid form to rest in, but two centuries' sleep is long enough."

"What?"

"No matter. My name is Serroi. Who are you and how came you here?"

"I am Kitya of the Moug'aikkin." She stood rubbing her wrists, the right, then the left where the iron cuffs had been; her body was dragging in a way she didn't understand, as if she had weights tied to her everywhere and when she looked into the valley beyond, she winced. "I have no idea where here is."

"Incomer. I thought so." Serroi turned around, stood looking down at the confusion below, her hands clasped behind her. "Damn. Coyote's Incomers have really been busy while I was dreaming up here."

Among the old stone buildings a forest of tall, angular, weblike structures hummed in the wind, their stay cables singing. There were odd constructions on the roofs, plates slanted to the south, covered in shining black squares that seemed to swallow the sunlight. Among the buildings, on patches of green lawn, there were groups of young people sitting, talking, eating, pairs intent on each other, individuals reading, sleeping, stretched out and staring into the sky, young people everywhere. No children, very few adults visible. In the valley beyond, a yellow dust haze hung over a checkerboard of fields. On roads between the fields enclosed carts like black water beetles darted about, more of the light collectors pasted over their bodies. Carts of a different shape moved methodically through the fields, the men in them plowing and otherwise working the crops.

It was a busy, peaceful scene and very strange. Kitya glanced at Serroi and saw the wonder she was feeling reflected in the little woman's face. A thousand questions piled up in the back of her throat, but she couldn't think of any way to ask them without poking her nose in where it could get snapped off. *Mama says when you're somewhere you don't know, best way is a shut mouth and open eyes.* She glanced at the sun, glanced again. It looked different here, greener. Where it was, though, meant that the afternoon was more than half gone. "How can we get down from here? I don't fancy spending the night curled up by that tree." She flicked a finger up then curled it back in a Moug'aikkin point at the rugged conifer growing at the edge of the cliff. "Besides, I'm getting hungry."

Serroi scratched beside the oval green spot between her brows. "There used to be a path of sorts. Over here," she nodded to the left, started picking her way across the cracks in the stone and the weeds growing in them.

Kitya followed her a few steps, then swung round as she heard a loud swishing behind her.

The conifer was shuddering and agitated, roaring in a wind she couldn't feel; she took a step toward the tree, her arm lifting. . . .

A thin green hand closed hard on her wrist. "No!" Serroi was sudenly in front of her, blocking her. "Kitya of the Moug'aikkin, don't listen to that one; stop your ears and mind your soul. He'll swallow you in a gulp if you let him and you'll loose a great evil on this world."

"What?"

"Come, better to leave quickly. He'll creep through the tiniest crack given time enough." As Kitya moved her wrist, meaning to free it from the little woman's grip, Serroi stopped her. "No, let me hold you as long as I can. It's safer, I promise you."

The path was in adequate shape, weeded sometime in the fairly recent past and edged with small bits of stone; it wavered back and forth across the weathered cliff, made descending more tedious than risky, but by the time they reached the valley floor, Kitya was shaking with weariness, her knees aching, her eyes blurring.

Serroi stood with her hands clasped behind her, staring at the wall that marched across the valley. It was massive, impressive until Kitya rubbed the sweat from her eyes and looked more closely at it. The merlons were crumbling like a mouthful of rotted teeth, there were cracks in the massive stones of the facade, moss and weeds eroding holes deeper with every season, trees and brush growing up close, their roots attacking the base. *Generations of peace, that's what that means. And miles of walking for us. Okanakura bless, I'm tired, I haven't been this tired ever, not to remember anyway.* "How far is that gate?"

"An hour's quick march."

Kitya looked at her feet. "Quick? I think I can manage a crawl."

Serroi's mouth twitched into a brief half-smile. "This world is heavier than yours, Incomer, it pulls on you, but you'll be used to the weight soon enough."

"You're a demon? This is one of the demon worlds?"

"Hardly. Though I don't know what you mean by demon, probably not what we think here." She started walking slowly along the wall. "No, it's simply a different ... um ... universe, what Julia Dukstra told me once a long time ago. She was another Incomer. She said universes were like the layers of twisted onions, touching everywhere, intersecting nowhere."

Kitya snorted, distracted for the moment from her laboring body. "Sounds like Navarre at his most convoluted. I don't understand a word of it."

"Navarre?"

"A Magus with a curse—may the Wrystrike swallow itself and die of confusion." She turned her head and spat to set the curse on the Curse. "My companion and love, for my sins one might say. A good man with a great bag of bad luck."

"Magus. A man of magic?"

"Yes. And a man of his hands. He's a smith as well and it's a good thing because he'd starve orwise as Desantro would say."

"Was it he who sent you here?"

"Not he. Only a Sorcerer can dip into the demon

worlds. Or a god. No, it was his Curse not him that did it." Kitya ran her tongue across dry lips. "Okanakura's bright eyes, I'm dry. No water, I suppose, till we get past the gate? Right." She was starting to feel light-headed; she knew the reason, it was lack of food and rest that was draining her, taking her back to the time when she was a wild girl running from the A'tuayon, the time when Navarre had stepped between her and death by iron and fire.

"Then you'd better set your mind to living here. The only one in this world who could possibly send you home probably won't."

"I don't know. There's always Faan; if she decides she needs me, she'll manage it somehow." Kitya grimaced. "Anevah, how she'd find me here, I don't know."

"Whatever comes, right now do me a favor, hmm?"

"Of course. What?"

"Forget the name Serroi." She smoothed her thumb over the dark green oval between her brows and looked embarassed. "It's likely I'm ... mmm ... what you might say, a legend. There's no one alive who knows me but. . . ." She shrugged. "As you see, my appearance is distinctive; if I'm recognized, it will be difficult for both of us. If you don't mind, we'll be cousins, hmm?"

"Ah kun, Serroi. I'll give you one of my mother's names, she's a woman of power and strong character. Toyuna. Kitya and Toyuna, it has a beguiling sound, don't you think?"

Serroi laughed, set her fingertips briefly on Kitya's arm. "Indeed it does, cousin. Indeed it does."

FAAN

The first morning they were out of the valley, Faan caught glimpses of movement along the rim of the ravine and knew that just beyond the poison-limit Shifters were watching them, that they'd be there day and night from now on, with the patience of hunting cats waiting for the slightest opening. It was all they could do; with their vulnerabilities they couldn't get any closer.

It was a hot day and dry.

They left the river behind shortly after noon and angled more directly north, heading for Tempatoug, moving through dead brush and desiccated grass, kicking up gouts of hot white dust that blew into their faces and slithered through every crack in their clothing. It caked the horses' nostrils, those they rode and those they led, and muddied their sweat-streaked hair.

Faan mopped at her face with her headcloth, black biters droning from brush and clumps of grass to suck at the drops of sweat on her scalp, darting away too fast for her to swat them. Ahead of her Desantro was riding hunched over, her body drawn into a knot of pain. Faan kneed her mount into a faster walk, clucked to the lead horse, and caught up with the older woman. "You want to stop a while, Desa?"

Desantro shook her head. After a long moment, she said, "When the Mals took my first baby and gave it away, I wanted to die." Her voice was hoarse, her words bunched with the horse's stride. "But I kept on." She turned her head; her face was hard, drawn. "Do you think I'm going to let this stop me?"

The land changed.

The dry, deserted scrub was suddenly furnished with little patches of bloom and narrow, tiled canals filled with clean, sparkling water. Terraces with neat stone walls rose up the hillsides. Plants and bushes, small trees, vines, every conceivable variation of petal producers grew in the plots and terraces; these were the fields that produced the raw material for Kaerubulan's famous essences. Everything but blueflower. That grew somewhere inland that only Shifters knew about.

There were hordes of bonechildren in these patches, pulling weeds, guiding threads of water to roots, laying down feed, pinching off dead leaves, tending the plants with a narrow care. Bonemen trod waterwheels to fill the canals and the buckets, overseers stood on wooden platforms in the corners of the plots, scolding when necessary, putting out flutterets of praise when the notion struck them.

Overseers, watermen, and children ignored the two women—ignored them with an intensity that was loud as a shout.

Faan rubbed her hand across the stubble on her head; according to Desantro, her new hair was coming in iron gray instead of the black she was born with. *Old lady gray before I make eighteen. K'lann, someone or something owes me a debt I'm gonna collect. Some day.*

Desantro drew her sleeves across her face. "How long," she called ahead to Faan, "till we get to . . . what did Navarre call it . . . Tempatoug?"

Faan shrugged, patted at her face with the kerchief. "I don't know. From the look of things, it shouldn't be long." She tied the kerchief about the saddle horn, frowned at her hands. The bones were momentarily visible as dark shadows beneath the amber skin. *Potz! If it were dark, I'd be flashing on and off like a lightning bug. It's getting worse. I'm scared, gods! I'm scared. Mamay . . . nayo, I won't, I won't, I won't think. . . .* She dug at her palm with her thumbnail, scratching convulsively until she was on the point of drawing blood. The glow died and the hands were familiar again, bitten fingernails, scars and smears.

With a long wavering sigh, she bent forward, stroked the horse's neck. *Nu, old fellow, we're not a conflagration, not yet.*

* * *

At the edge of the city, an old boneman stood in the middle of the road with his arms outstretched; as soon as he decided they were in earshot, he started making urgent gestures for them to stop where they were and not come any closer.

"What do you want, O Sanggairs?" he called.

Faan's nostrils flared. "You know. Why pretend you don't?"

Gray replaced the ruddiness of the old man's face as Faan's flesh went translucent and she shone like a minor sun. He tapped a penta across his torso and glanced over his shoulder at the shimmering city, at the dark clad bonefolk moving quickly, silently between mother-of-pearl walls of buildings like children's playing blocks, busy about their ordinary work, ostentatiously ignoring the ragged pair on the coast road. Ghosts oozed up from the streets and clustered over the roofs, giving the city a death shroud; they stayed back, though, frightened of the magic-makers.

Faan waited a beat longer, then she said, "If you must have it in words, we want to talk to someone with authority. Someone who can arrange passage out of here and provide compensation for the injuries done our persons and our liberty."

He was sweating though the day wasn't all that warm; the wind off The Sodé had a sharp-toothed nip in it. "Mutay mutay," he said, his voice rising till the last eee would cut glass. "I'll go talk to the Zondreish. Stay here, you will stay here, won't you?"

Faan pointed at the sun, swung her hand up till her finger pointed to zenith. "Until noon," she said. "Not an instant longer."

There were two of them, both Shifters, large male shapes, midsize between commonfolk and the subDukes, riding neck-curbed, high-kicking beasts, the first on a red and white piebald, the second on a tall sorrel. Capes fluttering about broad shoulders, the sun glittering on bronze helms, they stopped a dozen yards from Faan and Desantro. The leader gestured and the second Shifter rode forward until he was half a length ahead.

There was a sound like dead leaves blowing, then the second Shifter spoke, signing as he did so, translating for the other. "In tradespeak I am called Earwaggle Snaketongue. I am . . ." his arms rippled and his hands changed form, then returned to their massive fists, "Holder of Security of the Zons of Tempatoug. I interpret for the Zondreish." Another complex sign which he didn't bother to translate. "You want compensation?" His eyes were long and narrow, in color a kind of tweed, green with orange flecks; they had all the warmth of the serpent he was named for. "You came on your own, we didn't bring you here. One of your lot has condemned a number of our people to an appalling death and you threaten worse. Why should we pay for that?"

Faan folded her arms across her breasts; she was not nearly as big and broad as they were, but she could kill both of them with the flick of a finger and they knew it "Anything that has happened to yours, you've brought on yourselves," she said firmly. "We were harming no one and intended to leave as soon as we could. You took us prisoners, made hostages of us, used my teacher as a weapon to spread disease and death among your enemies. You owe us and you know it." She smiled, not pleasantly.

"You threaten us."

"De nai, only warn. Treat us well and silk will be no smoother than our slide through your town."

"How much?"

Faan looked down at her hands.

Not even a pretense of consulting. They worked all this out before. Snaketongue is saving face for the

Zondreish, that's all. Gods, I wish I were out of here.
"Two hundred gold. Local coin or trade gold, part of it
can be the equivalent in silver. Passage on a ship bound
south—you find the ship and pay for the two of us. Information about a boneman named Rakil; we've been
told he lives in Tempatoug. He could be a slave. If so,
we expect you to purchase his freedom and bring him
to us. Once this is done, the gold, the passage, the
boneman, then we're gone and we won't be back."

Snaketongue's mount sidled uneasily. Faan got the
feeling he was surprised, that he'd expected her to twist
until she drew blood. "There were two more of you.
What of them?"

"What of them? They've gone where they've gone.
If they come back, then you bargain again. That has
nothing to do with us."

The Zondreish had been watching Snaketongue's
translations; he reached out, closed his hand on the security chief's arm, then started signing furiously. It was
an odd and disturbing thing to watch, this argument so
rapid and violent and at the same time wholly silent.

Head throbbing, muscles in her face and arms twitching painfully, Faan kept her eyes fixed on the pair as
Snaketongue argued down his superior. The Zondreish
was offended in every cell of his malleable body; he
couldn't stand the thought of bowing to boneman de-
mands, poisoners or not. He wanted to use Rakil as a
lever to pry them out without having to part with the
gold. Snaketongue told him not to be a fool, they had
no choice; whatever the poisoners wanted, they'd get;
they were fortunate the girl demanded so little. Besides,
he knew the boneman they were asking for and there
was no chance they'd get their hands on him, he'd fled
the city three days ago, following his master who'd got
himself involved in the Browneye rebellion and left
town only a week or so before he was to be arrested.
The Zondreish nearly exploded at that, but Snaketongue

reminded him this wasn't the time or the place for such discussions, and if he had complaints he'd better lodge them with the Premier Duke Yelloweye Longtooth because he was the one who'd given the orders Snaketongue was operating under.

Leaving the Zondreish silenced and simmering, Snaketongue turned back to Faan. "We agree to your terms, but it will take time. There's a place where you can stay, it is called House Humarie. I'll send someone to show you where it is."

He swung his horse around, waited for the Zondreish to give up his glowering and take the lead, then the two of them trotted off.

Faan watched them disappear around a corner. "It just trickles on and on."

"Mh." Desantro straightened her shoulder. "You did good, Fa. Might've been Penhari sitting there. Mal arrogance and absolute assurance. They don't know what hit them."

Faan managed a smile. "Lovely," she said. "I hate to think what this is doing to my character." She sighed. "Dressed in the rags of a power we can't use, we march like conquering heroes into Tempatoug. March, hah! Shuf-shuf-shuffling along. Let's shuffle, Desa."

NAVARRE

He landed heavily, went down on his knees and stayed there, shaking his head in a futile attempt to clear out the confusion roaring from ear to ear.

He was in an agreeable, meadowish place, blue sky overhead, with cottony cloud puffs chasing across it, around him the faint, pleasant smell from new green leaves and patches of white and yellow flowers scattered through the grass. Beside a small, noisy brook, there was a table with a crisp white linen cloth draped over it, laden with piles of buttery toast cut in triangles with the crusts trimmed off, crystal bowls of red and orange preserves, three steaming bone china teapots spaced along the middle, bone china cups and saucers set in front of a dozen chairs.

Only three of them were occupied.

There was a little wizened man with a huge hat and a stiff collar that rose up past his jaw, a wide soft bow tie. "No room," he growled.

There was a large rabbit with a similar collar and tie, a maroon velvet jacket and a ridiculous little skullcap between his huge ears. He held a teacup in one paw and was glaring from red eyes at a small blonde girl. "No room," he squeaked.

The third had his face in a plate of buttered toast and was snoring placidly. He was a small furry creature with delicate pink ears and a red velvet coat with lace dripping from the sleeves.

The girl stamped her foot. "There's plenty of room," she said and plopped down in the armchair at the end of the table. She busied herself with the nearest teapot, edged a plate of toast and a bowl of preserves within easy reach.

The rabbit watched this with a dour scowl. "You aren't very nice, are you? Pushing in where you're not wanted and haven't been invited."

"If you don't want company, why such a large table?" She bit down on the toast with a decisive crunch, then sipped daintily from her cup.

Navarre slid a dry tongue across dry lips; he got to his feet and took a step toward the table.

His foot came down in an extra-dark patch of shadow and kept going ... down and down and down he tumbled in a mist of sparkling gray. . . .

And landed with stinging feet in an immense cavern lit by glowbulbs.

A young woman with short brown hair gasped and

jumped back from him, a tall creature with the face and teeth of a lion and the body of a man roared with rage and leapt at him.

He recoiled, stepped into darkness and tumbled down and down. . . .

And landed on a city street paved with a smooth black substance wet from a rain that was trickling to an end, glistening in yellow streetlights that turned flesh green and lips a purplish black.

Lights came toward him riding on waves of ear-numbing cacophony, blinding lights, behind them distorted shadows of . . . something.

A reddish streak swept past the lights, scooped him up, and desposited him on a walkway that reflected wetly the colored lightsigns above the storefronts. The streak slowed, coalesced into a man in a sculpted red suit with tiny wings over the knobs where his ears should be and a mask that covered half his face. "Something wrong?" It was a pleasant baritone with a touch of impatience.

Navarre barely heard him. The lights had swung round, come back and stopped, pinning him with their beams. He could see behind them now, could see men like insects with polished ball heads and huge glittering goggles; these creatures straddled two-wheeled vehicles that belched smoke and roar, almost seemed poised to spring at him.

With an exasperated exclamation the red man leapt away from Navarre, increased speed enormously until he was visible only as a red streak that wove among the insectiles and sent them flying.

Wary and more than a little disoriented, Navarre took a step backward and tumbled down and down. . . .

And landed kneedeep in reeds and mud beside a river in spate, brown water thick as pudding and streaked with foam, carrying with it whole trees, bits of houses, broken carts, drowned carcasses of horses and other beasts, now and then a face or a hand emerging from that powerful, imperious current. Even among the reeds he could feel the tug of the river, as it sucked the mud from beneath his feet.

He churned up the shallow slope and hauled himself onto sandstone scree at the base of a cliff about fifty feet high—and became conscious for the first time of the commotion on the far side of the river, a booming so regular it had seemed part of the flood noise. He glanced across the water, got an impression of movement obscured in smoke and whirls of dust, then turned back to the cliff. There was a ledge about fifteen feet up which looked large enough to house him; if he were up there, he could see what was happening and be reasonably well hidden from premature discovery.

"Do your worst," he muttered at the Wrystrike and tried to snap himself onto the ledge.

Nothing happened. If there was any magic in this world, it was so locked up he couldn't draw enough power to light a match; cursing under his breath he scrambled up the shifting, crumbling rocks, began climbing cautiously up the weathered face.

As he reached the ledge, he heard voices dropping from the top of the cliff; hastily he hauled himself over the lip, crouched with his back against the stone; the ledge was more than a yard wide, but the cliff bulged out above it so that anyone looking down would see nothing. He folded his arms on his knees and examined the scene laid out before him.

The river curved in a wide bend, the two arms spreading to the north and south of him; in that lune among trenches and long mounds of earth thrown up in three concentric semicircles, there was an army of men in bright uniforms and turbans, thousands of them, thousands of horses; long black tubes spat fire and more solid missiles that crashed into the distant arc of another army. Missiles came back at them, bursting high above them or thudding in front of the earthworks, casting up gouts of red dust as they exploded.

In the midst of all this a band was playing. Through clouds of black smoke that swirled over the army Navarre could see the horns and cymbals glinting a brassy yellow, drums gleaming gold and red, their white heads shining; the music came in pulses, loud and rousing.

The tubes stopped belching and the smoke blew away.

In the far army trumpets blared.

Disciplined and orderly, a line of red-coated riders came forward, flags flying. On either side of the riders hundreds of men with high fur hats and wide white belts marched in rigid lines, the afternoon sun glinting from the knives set at the end of odd shaped sticks. They came forward at a steady walk, maintaining an even front, a mass of bright color, feet moving in unison, the trumpet calls seeming to urge them on, making this world's kind of magic.

The river force's tubes began booming again, the explosions coming almost continuously. Before the clouds of smoke and dust dropped over them again, Navarre saw the advancing men waver, recover their unity and come on. At the extreme right of the lune a great body of horsemen galloped in a wide circle toward the flank of the marching army, but the attackers' tubes began sounding, their missiles landed among the riders, exploding with much noise and horrible effect as the fragments sliced through the horses' bodies and legs. The charge dissolved.

Navarre shuddered at the horrible wounds of horses and men. He had no idea what the battle was about or why they were so determined to slaughter each other. All he could think of was the waste of it, the piteous waste. It was worse than what had happened in Snarlykeep because there were so many more people in-

volved, and it wasn't just a hard death these men faced,
but maiming, mutilation, a slow, agonizing leaking
away of life. He couldn't watch them any longer, shifted his gaze to the river, and saw a group of men standing beside a great bridge of boats held together by
massive chains with planks laid across them to make a
flat surface they could have driven an elephant across.

Several of the men were watching the attack with
spyglasses, others consulted with the messengers who
ran back and forth between them and the defenders of
the lune. There were tall bearded fighters gathered
around them, shouting things Navarre couldn't make
out, waving sabers and dancing some kind of martial
jig, either part of their magic or an exuberant joy in
slaughter they couldn't suppress as the attack failed and
the attackers retreated in reasonably good order to their
own trenches and earthworks.

As he watched the group, frowning, wondering if he
should or could do something about them and in that
way stop the slaughter, one of the men fidgeting around
the outside of the group took advantage of the preoccu-
pation of the others, edged away a few steps, wheeled,
and went racing for the river, his long legs taking
mighty bites of the distance between him and the bank.
With a last great bound he hurled himself into the water
and began swimming downstream, struggling to stay in
the middle of the river where he obviously expected the
current to carry him away from the battle faster than
any horse.

The configuration of the river and the cross currents
developed by the flood defeated him, drove him to the
northern bank; unless he felt like drowning, he was going to have to take to land again.

Navarre smiled at the coincidence. The man was
coming ashore almost exactly where he himself had
landed on this stop in the world to world tour the
Wrystrike was sending him on.

The fugitive struggled into the reeds, wriggled through the mud with a passionate desperation that carried him along far faster than Navarre had managed; he popped his head up once, but men were talking excitedly up above.

From the fragments Navarre heard, they were cheering on their side in the battle and hadn't seen him at all, but the escapee went back to his mud like a turtle into his shell. He reached the end of the reeds, scrambled up the scree, and threw himself at the cliff face.

KITYA

The double gates were huge, built for defense, but both sets were laid back against the stone and the gatehouse was empty and crumbling like the rest of the wall. Despite her aching exhaustion, Kitya crossed to one of the gates and smoothed her hand along the wood, then stepped back and stood, hands on hips, marveling at the hardness and polish of the massive timbers.

A shrill horn blatted behind her. She jumped, flattened herself against the gate as one of the mechanical carts flashed past, the driver shaking a raised finger at her in a sign she recognized as an insult. He was past before she could respond.

"Ooyik!" She pressed her back against the gate and slid down, sighing as she saw Serroi grin at her. "This must've taken one onga'n effort to build. Why did you need it? Don't your gods protect you?"

"War, lady, and they were in it, heels to hair." Serroi came round a gnarled bush and sat cross-legged beside Kitya. "Let's bide a while before we go on. I'm tired, too, trees don't do that much walkabout."

Legs drawn up and out of the way, they sat in silence for some time, watching the busy carts zip in and out. The road through the gate was paved, but it was not in very good repair considering the hard usage it was getting. There were networks of cracks, half a dozen potholes in eyeshot, and some crude patches of tar and gravel that didn't look like they'd outlast the day.

Serroi wrinkled her nose. "The Janja said magic was fading, a new age was being born. Looks to me like the old age had its good points, at least the roads were safer. Tell me about your gods."

Kitya closed her eyes, wiped the dust from her face as another cart went whizzing by. "Nu, the world is divided into . . . um . . . I suppose you could call them domains." Her nose twitched as a gnat landed on it; she snorted, brushed at it. "Moug'aikkin lands was one, our Land God is Moon Daughter Okanakura the Wise. SHE likes animals better than people, so mostly she doesn't interfere whatever we do to each other. Next land westway they were Ushturaktim and when I was three and riding on my own for the first time, the Khan Ushtur started sniffing round some of our best pasture. I remember the stories, there were a lot of them round then, the clan attoys make up songs about it they traded at breed meets, Okanakura turned every Ushturak who crossed the line to stoats. My mother made a lesson of it for me. She said, 'you want to keep hide and hair intact, you don't mess with a god's landhold.' " She blinked, startled, as a small furry creature came from behind a bush and settled itself at her feet, staring with obvious interest first at her, then at Serroi.

Serroi leaned forward. "Haes angeleh, Shuri. Fare you and yours well these day?"

"Hasna angelta, Meie. Well enough, though to the hills we keep, not ours this new age is."

"Nor mine, I think."

"But now of interest more." It rose on its hind feet, bowed and vanished into the greenery.

Kitya drew her knees up, rested her arms on them. "What was that about?"

"Memory. Old ties being acknowledged. Never mind. Go on about your gods. Every domain has its own god?"

"It's more complicated than that. Every domain's different, some by a lot, some by a little, different rules, different problems. That's one of the things a Magus is good with, like Navarre, he knows everything about all of them, or close to it."

"So you don't have any wars?"

"Hunh! Plenty of blood, slave raids, fighting, long as it's just people, gods don't care. It's only when land's involved they get up on their hind legs and do something. So there're no big wars, domain against domain. One thing we learn early, Serroi . . . Toyuna . . . don't bother the gods, they find enough excuses to meddle without your helping them." She broke off as a cart stopped just inside the gate and a tall woman unfolded from the driver's seat, her weaponbelt clanking against the doorpost.

Serroi got to her feet. "Looks like we'll be getting a ride, Kitya." She extended a hand to help Kitya to her feet. "Say as little as possible, but be polite. This is a meie and she's apt to be a trifle abrupt if she's provoked."

FAAN

Humarie poured the tea, straightened, and examined Desantro's face. "You're kin to him, aren't you." She sang choruses when she spoke as if the sound came from multiple throats.

Clean and dressed in the new shirts and trousers they found in their rooms after they got back from the bathhouse, Faan and Desantro were seated in white wicker chairs pulled up to a white ceramic table in a walled garden with an angular fountain burbling gently beside them. Pastilles of incense burned in shallow dishes resting on the steps of an outside staircase leading down from a second-floor balcony. Ceramic windchimes hanging from the lower limbs of the trees sang sweet cascades of pure notes whenever the erratic breeze picked up enough to set them knocking into each other. There were songbirds flitting about the trees and bushes, hopping across the lawn hunting for grubs in the grass and a few ghosts drifting round the periphery. The serenity of the place was almost soporific.

Desantro blinked. "My brother," she said.

"He was one of my lovers," Humarie said. "I was fond of him. He told marvelous stories."

Desantro leaned forward, suddenly tense. "Was?"

Humarie set the pot down and gave them a slow, sleepy smile. "De nai, he's perfectly healthy, I imagine. He always was, healthy, I mean. Never even caught colds except once when I had to send him home so I wouldn't take it from him." Her eyes were continually turning to Faan as she spoke, as if the Sorcerie with the not so subtle danger flaring off and on beneath her skin was a fascination she couldn't escape. "All I mean is he's gone. Hopped. One day here, the next swish-na-na. Just as well, Snaketongue was about to land on him because his master was fooling round with the Browneyes. Smuggling, you know. Oil-gel and spearpoints. Like that. He's really gone, I mean. Not stuffed in one of the Snake's holes."

Desantro scowled at her teacup, uneasy for reasons she couldn't have explained, even to herself. "Why? I mean, what'd you see in him? What's he like?"

With another of her sensuous sleepy smiles Humarie inspected Desantro's face, then went on with her pseudo-artless babble, ignoring the questions as if they hadn't been asked. "I know that because he came after me, the Snake did. Squeezed like he didn't believe I didn't know what Raki was up to, which of course I didn't; he was too smart to tell me that kind of thing because of course I'd tell the Snake soon's I could get to him and even the Snake knew that so he let me go."

Faan watched the byplay with impatience. When that multiple voice trailed off, she said abruptly, "Where does the Snake think the man went?"

Humarie blinked at her. 'Baik a baik, the Snake doesn't talk to me."

"Tja and I'm your heart's desire. Be yourself, Shifter. If you can."

Humarie stroked a creamy finger down the soft curve of her cheek. "Mutay mutay, if that's what you want. De nai, I don't know from the Snake, but from a client of mine I hear that Raki had a crate put on Assach's *Dark Moon,* for carrying to Savvalis. Nine chances out of ten he went with it. Ten chances out of ten, maybe, since Purb the Flea left for Savvalis two weeks ago. That really got to Snake, he was sure that little slime would be back, seeing he left Raki behind, the house, all his goods. So by now they're together and on their way south, laughing their heads off at the stupid jellies. Sa sa, maybe not Raki, but the Flea for sure."

Desantro drank her tea and frowned at the jumping water in the fountain; she was tense again, angry. "Answer me," she said. "Tell me about him."

Humarie shrugged. "There's little to tell. He's a man like most bonemen, cleverer than some, a fool at times, tricky, blind, stubborn, sentimental, sometimes generous. A man of rancor who feels a strong need to punish insults whether they're imagined or not. A slave who has to please a master, which makes him demanding on those who have to please him." She moved her eyes slowly over Desantro's face and torso, the look an insult only partially concealed. "Much younger than you, of course, though you share a strong resemblance. Is that sufficient?"

"Tell me about the war," Faan said, breaking the tension building between the two women. "Do you know what they made the Magus do?"

"Ia sim." Humarie shuddered, flesh on her face and arms rippling uneasily until she regained control of her body. When she spoke, her expression was subtly harder, her chorus somber, her language more formal. "There is no war. Not now. Half of Snarlykeep burned to the ground and what's left . . . the streets are piled with rotting dead with no one left to sing them into crystal. Poison death, ring on ring of it. Snarl is dead, his family, his connections, as it were, his army; the Browneye clan has been reduced to those who happened to be out of reach that day. It could be the Magus has done us a favor, because it'll be fifty years or more before anyone challenges the Premier Duke again." She whispered like a tree speaking, her head down, eyes on hands linked together on the table top. "Perhaps you have not. The Yelloweyes have created a hatred that will destroy them . . . us . . . will grind us into the ground until there's nothing left but gristle." She lifted her head and opened her eyes wide. Faan saw for the first time they were a clear pale yellow. "When the Snake told me to house you, I was angry, Sorcerie, but when I thought about it, I wanted to see you. I wanted to see Death." She got to her feet. "May you gain your wish and leave soon. I won't see you again."

Faan watched her glide out. "Uh!" she said. "That's a stinking load of guilt she's trying to pile on us."

Desantro jumped to her feet and began prowling about, so full of anger and tension she flung it out like a muskcat's spray. "Bitch!" She repeated the word and added others, spitting vowels and glottal stops.

Faan lifted a cream bun, contemplated it. "At least we've got enough food and clean clothes." She sank her teeth into the bun, sighed with pleasure as the rich sweet cream slid along her tongue. "Come on, Desa.

You can't do anything about this, so you might's well sit down and eat. These are good."

Desantro twisted her face into a wry grimace. "You're young yet." She pulled out a chair and reached for a bun. "But I suppose you're right."

Faan wiped cream off her mouth. "How long do you think it'll be?"

"Tonight, if they had their way. Tomorrow. Next day. I don't know. I suppose it depends on who's in port. I wish. . . ."

Faan grinned at her, mometarily amused. "I know what you wish. You want Yohaen Pok. Vema, why not? He's smart and a better man than most. You should've stayed with him, Desa."

"Family comes first, you should know that, little Sorcerie." Desantro sighed, leaned back watching the water jump and flow. "I'll tell you true, Fa, after this is over, I'm going to find him and see if that offer's still open." She pulled a sad face. "I probably missed my chance, you know. Tungjii kisses you once on the mouth and if you send him off, that's all there is."

Chapter 10
On the Long Chase

Injil-mae, Heyjokkan

Siffaram frowned at Rakil. "You'll get your pay when we leave, not before."

"You thinking I'll run out on you? In this dump? I'm not such a fool."

"After. We leave with the morning tide." He went stumping off.

Rakil watched him vanish behind the barrels lashed down on the foredeck. "And when we leave, he'll be too busy," he muttered and kicked a battered onion into a crate where it splatted and dropped in pieces to the planks, releasing a monumental stench as it fell. Grumbling under his breath, he threaded through the leaking bales and scatters of rotting garbage on the run-down wharf, working along the waterfront to the tavern he'd spotted as he'd supervised the cargo exchanges.

Injil-mae was a small, sleepy port city, the only harbor on Heyjokkan's rugged coast that was sheltered from the storms that roared south along The Sodé. Because Heyjokkan was a poor land and too close to Savvalis to be a stopover port, any long-route traders who put in there were diving for cover until a storm passed by; there was nothing to draw them otherwise. Rakil didn't expect to get any news of Purb, but he had dice in his pocket and meant to add a few coins to his slender stash with scams he'd picked up on his wanderings.

Late that night when the lampstink was thick enough to cut and fumes were eddying like fog around the tables, a man thumped the door open and stood peering through the murk, a big man with a broad, scarred face, meaty shoulders, and fists like mauls. He spotted Rakil sitting alone at a corner table counting his winnings and stomped across to him.

"Eh, Rak, how come you not with the Flea?" He dragged a chair out, lowered himself with exaggerated caution, having learned that even the sturdiest chair could have hidden weaknesses and give way under his weight. "Saw 'im in Jert t'other day, skitterin' round like he knew what he was doin'."

Rakil swept the last of the coppers into his sac, shoved it down his shirt. "Jimmon. Been a long time." He grimaced, told the tale again. "Flea fiddled himself into a mess and had to hop, left me behind to clean up after. Not the first time, won't be the last. He getting into more dirt when you saw him? And how long ago was that?"

"Nah. 'Bout a week." Jimmon leaned back, the chair creaking ominously. He waved a huge arm at the bargirl drowsing on a stool. "Hoy, zassy get your chel over here, I got a thirst won't quit."

Rakil patted a yawn. "Want to roll for it?"

Jimmon grinned lazily at him. "Not with you, shrak."

"Then I'll buy this'n, you can get the next." He dug out the sac. "What you wanting, Jimmo?"

Rakil took a drink of the ale, shuddered. "It doesn't get any better. What you doing in this dump and where you heading, if you don't mind my asking?"

"No big deal. There's a war brewing in Eyoktyr, someone offed the Orzel and her daughters are scrappin' over the seat. Word is they both need sappers and engineers. I'm loose right now, thought I'd drop over and take a look, hire out to whoever pays the most. 'S the easiest way in, through here, no noses, 'f you know what I mean. Don't like noses."

Rakil grunted, drank some more of the ale, bought refills he couldn't afford and spent another hour trading stories with Jimmon. Finally he staggered back to the ship, fell into his hammock and slept like he was dead until the mate booted him out to help with the departure.

Kuloleg, Kalyen (The Mouth of The Sodé)

Rakil passed a narrow slit between two massive godons, heard a soft scuff behind him and hit the cobbles; there was a soft whupping as the missile zipped by, close enough to stir his hair, a thud as it hit the cobbles. A shoulderflip and he was on his feet again, facing his backtrail, bootknife in his hand.

There were three of them, little dark men like blots of shadow gliding from the alley; they hesitated and then spread out, trying to bracket him, slings whirring soft as owl wings over their heads.

He saw the snap of a sling, hit the ground again, the knife flying as his wrist smacked against a broken cobble. One of the lead missiles slammed into his thigh, but he ignored both pains, scythed his leg against the knees of the middle attacker, rolled up, grunting as a second missile grazed his head, grabbed an arm and leg of the down man and threw him at the second mini-thug, flung himself aside and down again, pivoting on his hip (trousers tearing on the rough cobbles), driving a toe at the knee of the third. He didn't connect, but the thug's effort at avoiding the foot sent him staggering back.

Sling jerking erratically, arms waving, the little man

was ludicrously open as Rakil whipped up, lunged and kicked again, this time homing on the groin and hitting the target solidly. Mouth open in a feral grin at the high-pitched whimpers from the dark knot behind him, he went for the others.

The one he'd thrown had his head at a sharp angle to his shoulders; he wasn't going to attack any more transient strangers. The other was still wriggling from under his confederate. With a whinny of fear this one dived into the alley and scurried away, the faint scuffs of his feet vanishing after a few minutes.

Rakil found his knife, stuck it back in his boot, collected a sling and the sacks of lead missiles the two thugs wore looped to their belts. There were a few coppers in their pockets, nothing more; he didn't take them. The left sandal on the dead one had a flap of loose sole, it was the noise from that which had warned him. He wrinkled his nose. A sorry lot, even poorer in brain than they were in coin. He was tempted to toss them a silver bit from pity, but restrained himself and got away from there before someone more efficient took over—or the local law showed up. Strangers never got a fair deal in circumstances like these, especially in ratty thiefholes like Kuloleg.

Besides, he couldn't afford to be searched or questioned. The manumit paper with its scrawl and seal that Purb had left him, that was a joke. A male slave wore an iron stud riveted into the left ear with his owner's sigil graved into the black metal. He'd gotten rid of that. The brand on his buttock was something else; if he were strip-searched, the least the locals would do was resell him. The worst he didn't want to think about.

The body of Guffrakin the Owl lived in a smelly hutch built onto the back of a tavern. Where his mind lived, no one was ever sure, only that it must be weird beyond description. The Owl was a small dark creature, the only excess on his skeletal form the crepey wrinkles in his face and the wattles that swung when he talked. He never opened his door before moonset or left the place in daylight, but he managed somehow to survive, probably because he was a finder without peer, sometimes an oracle, sometimes he did *things* people needed done. He never lied, never asked embarrassing questions, and never explained what he told his clients, but if they figured out what he was saying, they invariably profited from it.

Rakil wiped his hands on his sides, wrinkled his nose at the tears in his trousers. "What we've got," he muttered and knocked on the door. "At least I'm the only one tonight."

He waited. The last time, he'd been in the middle of a long line and didn't get in before sunup which meant he had to come back the next night; even then he'd had to wait over an hour before he saw the Owl. The trampled mud around the hutch was supposed to be some sort of truce ground, but he'd never seen that put to the test and he didn't fancy trying it this night. One mugging was more than enough.

The door opened.

Rakil stepped in and started taking shallow breaths through his mouth; the stench was four years older and at some point in that period had gone beyond anything describable.

Behind him the door closed by itself and the dark inside the hutch thickened; the stub of candle in the center of the small table where Guffrakin was sitting produced more shadow than light. The Owl's eyes shone palely, his wrinkles glistened; his little paws were resting on the table, curved slightly, long fingernails like claws catching glimmers of light.

Rakil dropped a silver piece beside the candle, sat on the stool Guffrakin kept for his clients and put his hands on the table, palms down. "I want a brand canceled," he said. "Will you do it?"

The Owl blinked slowly, his pupils expanded until the iris was a silver ring about the black. The candle flickered with the slow pulses of his breath.

Rakil waited tensely, then jumped as he felt a searing pain in his buttock; it peaked and he ground his teeth, then it subsided to a dull ache. He started to get up, stopped in a half-crouch as the Owl started speaking.

"The Flea's hopping home," Owl said. His voice was so deep that it seemed to be coming from somewhere else since it was impossible that such a meager body could contain it. "Home to a spray of islands round the far bend of the world. Fear and weariness fill him. Hop hop he goes, but he won't get home. There's a neckring waiting and leaches to suck his blood away and when he's dry he's dead. Go to Bandrabahr, that's where you'll sniff out his trail. It's where you're bound to go."

He stopped talking and closed his eyes.

The door swung open.

Rakil winced as he straightened, then limped out— wondering as he went why the Owl had chosen to give him the answer to a question he hadn't asked. He shrugged as the door chunked home behind him. Owl did what Owl wanted and explaining wasn't one of his pleasures.

Bandrabahr. Hunh. Bless Tungjii, I've got friends there. Purb, watch your back, I'm coming. Neckring? Old Purb a slave? Funny if it's me going to put the ring on him. Twenty-five years. That's a long time.

On Siffaram's *Shagourag,* one day out of Dirge Arsuid

Rakil came yawning up the ladder, crossbow slung over one shoulder, the quiver full of bolts knocking against his leg. It was a bright warm morning with a strong following wind and a sky empty of clouds. The swells were long and high; a storm had blown out before them. This was usually a busy route, Rakil could remember a trip when the ship they were on blew hails every few hours on the Greeting Horn. Today, though, the bright blue water was empty from horizon to horizon. The pirates were bad, they said in Dirge Arsuid. Like locusts, eating everything that came along.

They were nervous in Dirge Arsuid, looking over their shoulders, sucking in their guts—and they stayed away from the fountain islands and the canals as if they expected something to come crawling from the water and start eating them. He didn't ask questions; it wasn't safe to ask questions in Dirge Arsuid.

He tapped the mate's shoulder and took his place on the quarterdeck. There was a sailor aloft, sitting in a sling, a glass to his eyes; the *Shagourag* was a tub, capacious but slow, without a hope of outracing a pirate galley. All they could do was remain alert and be ready to fight. He watched the horizon and thought about Dirge Arsuid.

The water in the canals was turgid and filthy, mildew grew in greenish-black stipples on the mortar, and the tiles had a sticky film that made Rakil feel like scrubbing his hand when he accidentally touched it. The city seemed to be rotting, on the verge of returning to the mud and reeds on which it had been built.

It was a city of silences and shadows, of walls and towers. The last time he was there it smelled like clove carnations; they grew in the walls, red and white carnations, they floated in the water, clean water, bobbing past him as he moved along the roughened tiles on the walk beside the canal, red and white carnations with white orchids and a rose or two, swirling round the narrow black boats poling along the canals. Red and white. The whole city was red and white. Every wall was faced with glossy red and white tiles, panels of red tiles, columns of white tiles, patterns of cut tile, red and white swirling together, sweeping along in dizzying flows. The pointed roofs were black tile, shiny black. It rained most days from two till four, thunderstorms that dumped an inch or more into the grooves that ran in spirals from the roof peaks and dropped into channels that fed the glossy black gargoyles that spewed the rainwater in arching cataracts that splattered in the canals.

The Arsuiders wore halfmasks that were stylized serpent snouts, a custom, he'd been told, that they'd adopted from an ancient insult. One hand was always gloved, the other heavy with rings; the whisper was that one or more of those rings were loaded with a poison so powerful a prick was death. They took pride in the outrageousness of their costumes; he'd seen creations in pink lace, feathers, gauze, others in swirling greens and yellows with triangular accents of blood red, still others in blue and purple, red and green, no two alike.

Something was definitely wrong. He'd only seen a few of them where usually there were swarms, and these wrapped themselves in dull black cloaks and the eyes in the holes of the serpent masks were feverish and afraid. He thought about talking with Siffaram but decided he'd better not. He'd get no answers and a rebirth of suspicion from that wary man. Siffaram did not like curiosity even when it was directed elsewhere.

The sea stayed empty as the sun climbed. A little before noon Siffaram came on deck as the *Shagourag* nosed through some debris, a sail, and several barrels.

"That's one gone," Rakil said.

Siffaram glared at him, went down the ladder and paced the length of the ship with long nervous strides, cursing the jumpy sailors, weaving in and out of the deck cargo, bales and barrels with the heavy nets pulled over them and tied to bronze eyelets in the deck.

The wind blew strong behind them, driving them steadily eastward, the *Shagourag* making the best time she ever had. A sailor dropped a belaying pin, nearly got his head taken off by his mates.

And the sea stayed empty.

The wind never changed or dropped; it was like a mage wind, blowing them ahead as fast as the *Shagourag* could lumber. The crew grew more nervous as the days passed and avoided Rakil, having decided some god or other had chosen to favor him. They knew it couldn't be them and he was the only stranger around.

He remembered the Owl's words: *Go to Bandrabahr, that's where you'll sniff out his trail. It's where you're bound to go. Mutay, mutay,* he thought, *as long as it gets me past the pirates.*

Chapter 11
Struggles

The Chained God Unchained laced his golden metallic fingers together and rested his sculpted chin on them, a chin that was losing its clean lines to rounded bulges of stored energy. He pulled his legs up and after a momentary difficulty (his knees had pads of excess flesh and creaked under the load he was forcing on them), arranged them in a loose cross as he contemplated the Girl and the woman Desantro who wasn't dead after all as they escaped untouched from the island and every trap he'd tried to close on them.

"Tsaaaa," he breathed. "Again! Clang clang, the warning's stronger. She's dangerous, that Sorcerie. Who is she? Where did she come from? Curséd Interferer, that Perran-a-Perran. Where did he get her? And why? He's plotting something, I know it. But how's he doing it? I can't see any strings on her. No smell of him on her. Coincidence? Never! What end is Old Pikeface aiming at? He ran his tongue over his teeth, grunted as he leaned over the solid belly that grew with every god he drained, and gazed into the images that flowed across the polished metal of his palms, reading them like the Sorcerie read her mirrors. "Ah. The next intersect.

Gallindar," he said. "Hmp. Green Man. I'll have to stir him up. Megg coped with the Girl well enough, maybe Chaggar can do the same."

He went sweeping across the godspace, reached down. The rag that was Chaggar Land God of Gallindar winced away from him, whimpering with fear.

"Come little sweeting, there's no need for that. I've got some juice for you, Wayyan Dun, and when you've plumped out a bit, there's something I want you to do for me."

FAAN
On the ship, in The Sodé

As the light-tower on the Legar Yayu Spit sank beneath the horizon, Faan turned and leaned her elbows on the rail, watching white water curl from the bow. She was tired, so tired it was hard to keep her eyes open, relief hitting her, she knew that, no more fear she'd poison half the land if she hiccuped at the wrong time. The Zondreish had pulled every string he had available, and even then (seemed like they all had news of Meggzatevoc's Ban) there was only one ship he could get to take her and Desantro, the *Halljinna* of Horst the Hennerman who did a little bit of everything, but mostly hauled slaves. The Zondreish threatened to bar Horst from Tempatoug which was one of his best markets, so the Hennerman gave way and here they were.

Hennerman. Desantro had gone so pale when she saw Horst, her freckles seemed to float free. She had to force herself to walk up the gangplank, her whole body stiff with protest.

Faan looked from Desantro to Horst and back, moved closer to the woman. "Was it him?" she whispered. "Was he with them when . . ." There were too many ears around, so she didn't go on.

Desantro shook her head, said nothing, just kept moving with her eyes fixed on the planks ahead of her feet. Faan admired her silence and her determination. Desa had no choice if she wanted to get off the island and go on searching for her brother, but she managed to wring a kind of dignity out of her compliance.

Faan grimaced, remembering her first glance into the ship's only cabin, that crawling coffin that smelled like every crewman went there to break wind. "No," she said firmly, fixing her bicolored eyes on Horst's bloody browns, suppressing a smile as he noticed them for the first time and began to look worried. "Not a chance." She caught hold of Desantro's wrist and marched into the bow where they'd be out of the way (hoping fiercely that Horst wouldn't challenge her because she simply couldn't stand the thought of anyone dying a horrible death to save her a bit of discomfort).

She saw Horst glance at the pilot, a wiry, little boneman with a face like a rat. The rat's nose was twitching and his dark, beady eyes were wet with anticipation, so the Hennerman just shrugged and went about the business of getting ready to sail.

Desantro looked darkly after him, muttering under her breath.

"Don't fuss, Desa," Faan murmured, "we'll change ships the minute we get a chance."

"If we get a chance." Desa dropped to a squat, wrapped her arms about her legs. "Hennerman!" The whispered word was sharp with venom.

"Tja, but keep it quiet, Desa. Until we get a mile or so offshore. Give me that time, then I'll singe his ambitions."

* * *

As she watched the bow cleave the water, Faan
smiled. When they were far enough out so she wouldn't
poison half the city, she dealt with that miserable cabin.
Horst turned a sickly green with a patina of greasy
sweat when he saw the pale fire leap from her hands
and flash through the room, killing the insect life and
searing away the filth. She was a little surprised how
easy it was, what delicate control she had over these
minor fires; when she'd done much the same thing
years ago, cleaning paint off herself, Ma'teesee and
Dossan, she'd been exhausted when she finished. Now
she wasn't even breathing hard. Maybe it was handling
the fire demons that did it. Sibyl kept telling her to
practice her lessons; the more she did, the stronger
she'd get. Seemed like that was true. Jeggin Navarre, if
he'd just tried teaching her a little. . . .

Desantro was in the cabin, curled up in the lower
bunk, her face to the wall. Gonna stay in here till we
get off this ship, she said. There was a pause before
ship, as if she'd searched her head for more appropriate
words and found none strong enough. Can't stand to
look at his ugly face, she said, and closed her eyes.

Ailiki materialized, balanced on the rail, squeaking
an excited greeting.

Faan stared, her insides melting with sudden joy. She
laughed and scooped the mahsar up, hugging the small
warm creature to her. "Aili my Liki," she murmured, "I
thought you'd left me. I thought you'd gone like all the
rest." She stood a moment feeling the mahsar's purr
shuddering into her body, so happy for the moment she
was shaking and close to crying.

Ailiki wriggled loose and jumped down; she went
trotting off to explore the ship with her inquisitive nose
and her agile black hands.

Faan leaned against the rail, watching her as she appeared and disappeared among the barrels and bales, ran up stays and along ratlines. "If this is an omen," she murmured, "then maybe . . . Midsummer Eve . . . there's just time to reach Jal Virri if we don't have to chase Rakil too far. . . ."

She wrinkled her nose, scratched her nails across the worn wood of the rail. "Nu, might's well try it." She settled onto the deck and sat looking out over the middle rail, past the figurehead, trying to ignore the dip, roll, and rise of the ship, using the swell of the sea to focus her concentration and bring her into the search trance, murmuring over and over the WORDS she'd found with the Sibyl's help, the sound triggers that one day would be all she needed.

The limber glass fish flickered into being, swimming with undulant grace in the forces between Faan's curved fingers.

"Rakil," Faan murmured. "Find."

The fish flipped its tail and turned slightly, pointing a few degrees east of the *Halljinna*'s course.

Faan contemplated the fish a moment longer, then SPOKE again, forcing it to spread and change form until she held floating between her palms a curved mirror as fragile as a soapbubble.

Rakil. Show me.

Rakil stood in the bow of a heavily laden broad-bellied ship, looking into a littered harbor at a skim of low, dark buildings. There were a few smaller ships tied up at crumbling wharves, some open fishing boats, men lounging against the thick walls of godons, waiting for the work an incoming ship might mean, other men fishing with a patience that was ill-rewarded from the meager catch in the buckets beside them, women walking restlessly back and forth, waiting to offer themselves to the crew.

The mirror popped! and vanished, jolting Faan from her trance.

The smells of the ship were suddenly around her, wet wood and dry rot, the stench from the hold that seemed to ooze between the planks, and the bracing salt reek of the wind.

She rubbed her hand over the gray stubble on her head, trembling slightly. The man was Rakil, that was certain; he couldn't look more like Desantro if they were twins instead of ten years apart. "Nu, there's a comfort; at least we're going the right way and that looks like one of the grungy little ports we put into when we came north, so we can't be too far behind him."

She got to her feet, headed for the cabin, relishing the fearful glances from the crew.

"Gonna gonna kick and scratch," she sang under her breath and threw a few dance steps into her strut. She liked feeling in charge again.

Another little jab to keep you honest, you potzheads. Circle wide round me or you'll get your nuh'm's singed.

She pulled the door shut. "Desa, wake up. Some good news for a change."

Desantro shivered, didn't move at first, but before Faan's impatience increased to annoyance, she turned on her back and opened her eyes. "What?"

"I made the fish." Faan grinned, snapped her fingers. "We're going the right way. And I finally managed a mirror. I saw him. On a ship somewhere south of us. Not that far, I think." Faan jigged a few steps, bent quickly, tapped her fingers against Desantro's cheek, straightened and danced away. "It was your brother all right, he matches you freckle for freckle."

Desantro brushed at her face where Faan had touched her, looked at her hands; there was no joy in her, even now. "How long do we have to stay on this

... this ... Fa, I can't ... You said we could find another one."

Faan sighed. "Horst contracted to carry us to his homeport, Desa. We need to get our money's worth from him."

"Jinjavi! Neka, Faan, that's the biggest slave market west of Kukurul, we can't go there. You scare the potz out of him, get a rebate."

"Slaveport. Ah hah, no wonder he gave in. Vema, I'll do it, but it won't be soon, you know that, Desa. Malang is the first chance we'll have to switch, remember what it was like coming north?"

Desantro grunted, turned on her side again, facing the wall, her eyes firmly shut.

Faan shrugged and went out.

NAVARRE

The fugitive got his elbow on the ledge; he levered himself up a few more inches, found a foothold and groped for a crack or knob of stone that would let him pull himself onto the flat.

He saw the Magus. Face congested with rage and terror, he hurled himself over the edge, leapt between Navarre and the cliff, gave a powerful thrust with his shoulder, and sent the Magus flying.

Navarre flailed at the air, managed to get his feet under him; as he fell, he caught a glimpse of the fugitive's red face with its luxurious mustaches and glaring eyes. The red was rapidly receding; when pellets from the men at the top of the cliff began pinging off the rocks around Navarre, his attacker smiled with satisfaction and withdrew into the shelter of the ledge.

A pellet burned a groove in Navarre's arm as he hit the scree. He swore and scrambled down the unstable rocks, threw himself into the reeds. A second pellet clipped the top of his ear. He plowed into the mud and it opened beneath him.

Wet and filthy, bleeding from ear and arm, he fell down and down. . . .

And landed on a floor tiled in black and white squares. He was in a long narrow room with walls of iron. He became aware of a noise, a throbbing that came up through his feet; when he touched the curved wall, it trembled under his fingers. There were several men at the far end of the room, standing near what looked like the keyboard of an organ. One had a tight shirt striped blue and white and tight blue trousers that belled out at the bottom, the others wore form-fitting black coats that came down to their knees, black trousers and boots and peculiar hats like narrow brimmed chimney pots.

On either side of them, there were two great oval windows. Glass. "What!" A school of bright colored fish swam past, a mound of coral moved into view and slid out again. "This thing is moving. It's under water."

His first word had brought the men wheeling around. The one in the striped shirt bounded at him.

Battered from his tumble down the cliff, filthy and exhausted, hungry, angry, confused, Navarre didn't feel like dealing with another man who hit before he talked; he stepped back, his foot coming down on one of the black squares, he fell into it, tumbled down and down. . . .

Onto a stage with lights that seared his eyes and a band playing exuberant overheated music. A curly headed man was walking toward half a hundred people seated in lines of chairs rising on a slant. The man turned, grimaced at him, started toward him.

Navarre sighed, stepped back and plunged again into the 'tween world darkness. . . .

And landed on a rocky knoll beside a horse grazing on the short sweet blades that grew close to the roots of the taller grasses. A man sat beneath the single gnarled tree growing at the peak of the knoll, his knees hugged in his arms, a large hat on the ground beside him. He was long and lean with a wild air to him.

The horse lifted his head as Navarre appeared, snorted softly. The man was instantly on his feet, a weapon in his hand.

Navarre spread his arms to show his hands to show they were empty. "No problem," he said.

The man nodded, slipped the weapon under his coat. "You look thirsty, stranger." He stooped over the gear piled neatly beside the tree, brought up a canteen, unscrewed the lid, and held it out.

Navarre drank, sighed, drank again. "Thanks," he said and handed the canteen back. "My name's Navarre."

"Jim." The tall man screwed the lid back on, set the canteen down and dropped onto his heels, looking out across the prairie once again. "Lost your horse?" he said without turning his head.

"No." Navarre squatted beside Jim, blinked at the grass fire stretching from horizon to horizon. "Saaa."

There was a single rider out there. As the Magus noticed him, the rider looked over his shoulder and saw the fire, stretched out along his mount, urging him into a gallop. For a moment it seemed he was going to escape easily enough because the horse was faster than the fire, then the little mustang went down, sent its rider spinning head over heels. The horse tried to rise, but its foreleg was broken. It lurched and fell back, lurched again, screaming its fear.

The man lay still, facedown.

Jim swore, swung onto the bare back of the golden chestnut; the stallion moved with slow care as he negotiated the treacherous, rocky slope of the knoll, but once he had good footing under his hooves he went like a yellow streak.

Navarre watched Jim shoot the struggling mustang, scoop up the recumbent man and come racing back. The Magus coughed as a sudden gust of wind brought a gout of smoke rushing over him; throat sore, eyes stinging, he bent, groped for the canteen, reached down and down and was falling again. . . .

And landed on his knees in the mouth of a littered, stinking alley, colored lights blinking on and off, reflected in the murky fluid stagnating in the nearest gutter. There was a tearing roar. A vehicle squealed round a corner, a man running after it, a huge man with weapons in each hand, weapons that belched repeatedly, blowing out chunks of buildings and the vehicle ahead of him.

The man saw Navarre, turned one of the weapons on him. Navarre flung himself back, fragments of the wall spattering over him as the weapon roared. He fell into stinking black sacks of garbage, fell through them, down and down. . . .

Into another alley. A man with a pair of knives was attacking a . . . creature, a figure in black and blue, a stiff cowl that masked half his face, a cape with a scalloped lower edge that shifted about the strange form with every move it made.

There was a loud bang behind Navarre, a burning in his injured ear. He flung himself aside and fell down and down, scattering drops of blood through the whirling chaos . . . the Curse was starting to tire . . . Ride the Wrystrike, the Sibyl said . . . no sign of Kitya yet . . . he could almost hear it panting . . . it was tiring, but it wouldn't let him go. . . .

And landed in a long, badly lit corridor with a worn rug running down the middle of it. Down near the far end a door slid back, revealing a brightly lit room the size of a closet, slid closed again after a tall, dark-haired man stumbled out of it. He lurched along the corridor with one hand on the wall, leaving smears of blood on the pale plaster; he fell to his knees, groaned and struggled to his feet, fighting his way forward.

Behind him the door slid open again and this time three small, dark men emerged.

He heard the swish, forced himself around to face his pursuers, a weapon in one trembling hand. He tried to hold it steady, but he couldn't. He went down on his knees again.

One of the pursuers lifted his weapon. There was a sharp crack; the kneeling man jerked, fell over, and lay on his side in a fetal position.

The shooter aimed again.

"No!"

The three small men looked around, startled, then moved closer to their injured quarry.

An eerie mocking laugh whispered down the corridor. A great black shape seemed to rise out of the floor and rush toward them.

Navarre sighed. Another weird one. He looked round, saw a door open a crack and stepped toward it, wanting nothing to do with what was happening out here, stepped and went tumbling again ... down and down ... forever ... the Wrystrike was laboring ... down and down ...

KITYA

"The big moon, that's Nijilic Thedom. The three running ahead of Thedom, they're the Dancers."

Kitya started as Serroi's voice sounded behind her. She glanced over her shoulder, then went back to staring at the moons. "I didn't really believe it till now," she said.

The night was clear and warm, but not quiet. There was music playing somewhere, voices, the blaats and whinnies of livestock and a low pervasive hum from bugs too small to see in the silvery moonlight with its confusion of shadows. Kitya sat on the rim of a fountain where the water played softly over a statue carved from greenstone, the body of a woman stretched in a taut arch, hair streaming, arms straining upward, her legs and lower body already transformed into the trunk and roots of a tree.

"I couldn't sleep," Kitya said. "Too much happening." She nodded at the statue. "That supposed to be. . . ."

"Probably."

Kitya's nose twitched. The subject was closed. That was obvious. "We only have one moon," she said. "The Wounded Moon we call it because there's a piece out of it near the top." She frowned at Thedom. "It's bigger than that, by half, I'd say." She was silent a moment, then said, "When the Wounded Moon was whole. We all say it. Means a long, loooong time ago."

"A long, looong time. . . ." Serroi sighed. "It's as strange to me here as your world would be, Kat. Maybe more. All those questions, no pen and paper to take down the answers, just buttons and letters that go like water across the face of that screen. And did you hear those young people talking this evening when we went to get something to eat? I don't know half the words and the rest seem to have picked up new meanings. This is no place for me."

They sat in gloomy silence, contemplating a future without definition.

"Gods!" Kitya muttered. "Count on them to mess up your life."

"Mm. This Faan you mentioned, she'll be looking for you?"

Kitya bit at her fingers; that was one of the things that'd kept her awake, worrying. "Not without Navarre pushing her. And Navarre . . . I don't know where he is."

"You said she needed you."

"Hai-yah, I was kidding myself; she doesn't need anyone."

"Mm. Your friend Navarre, could he be here, too?"

Kitya looked up, startled. "I hadn't thought of that." Energy flooded her; she jumped up, started pacing back and forth across the short lush grass. "Why not? When the Wrystrike flung me here, Navarre had hold of me for a minute. Why wouldn't he be dragged along?" She turned eagerly to Serroi. "Do you have farseers here? How can I find out? What do I have to do . . . ?"

Serroi ran a hand across her face as if she brushed cobwebs from it. "In the morning," she said. "We can't do anything now."

"You do have . . . ?"

"I don't know." There was impatience and a trace of desperation in Serroi's voice. "I told you, it's a strange place now. In the morning I'll see if there's still a Prieti meien and we'll ask if the Shawar will read for us. If there are still Shawar."

"Hai-yah," Kitya breathed, suddenly chastened. "That'll tear the mask, won't it."

Serroi stood, stretched. "It had to happen sometime, it's just a little sooner than I expected. Oh, the Prieti meien and the Shawar will keep silence if I ask it, but. . . ."

"Yes." Kitya moved to stand beside the small woman. "My mother says rumor seeps through solid stone." She hesitated. "Maybe someone else?"

"None I'd trust. Well, we'll see what happens. At least these people owe me, they owe me big and I'm calling the debt." She started walking toward the Guesthouse. "We'd better get some sleep, Kat. Tomorrow will be difficult."

FAAN
Mulang, Pajan—one of the twin cities at the Gate of
the Notoea Tha

Sitting on the rim of the huge sunken bath, wreathed in
steam and delicate herbal scents from the leaves and
petals steeping in the water, Desantro was washing her
hair, the foaming soap flowing over her hands as she
massaged her scalp. Faan sculled about the bath, enjoying the flow of the hot water along her body; she
bumped into the wall, turned over, and caught hold of
the rail that ran along three sides of the bath. "That
looks like it feels good."

"Mmmm," Desantro said. "Good isn't the word.
Wonnnderful's more like it."

"Nu, now that I've finally got more than stubble,
Desa, will you . . . ?"

"Diyo, bébé." Desantro chuckled. "You look like a
plucked pigeon, Fa."

"Old lady, you mean. Grizzled and grumpy."

"Tsa! A babe pretending to be her own granma."

"Babe, hah! I'm almost eighteen."

"Old lady, yeh."

They were alone in the womanside of the inn's bathhouse; it was late, a little after moonrise, the Wounded
Moon a thin crescent with the tip broken.

Desantro slipped into the water, ducked under and
shook her head, her curly brown hair shedding foam,
unknotting and spreading about her like fine weed; she
came exploding up, rolled over and swam to the edge of
the pool. She levered herself up and shook her head.
"Aaaaan, tja, that's good. Up up, Fa, pull over here and
let me do you."

Faan rolled out of the pool, knelt beside Desantro
and sighed with pleasure as the woman began rubbing
the herb-scented liquid soap into her inch-long hair.

"Old Horst really squealed when you got the refund out of him," Desantro said. Her fingers dug harder.

Faan wriggled, settled down when Desantro slapped her shoulder. "Got him where it hurts." She giggled. "I enjoyed that."

"Hennermen, fgh! They should be piled in a heap and burned to ash."

"Potz, Desa, ease off, that's my head you're kneading. Forget about that jegger, we're done with him. Just think how fast we're closing on your brother. Cuiller's *Mollinya* is the fastest ship on the coast." She grinned. "He told me so himself. So it won't be long before you're holding hands with Rakil and trading stories. And according to Tungjii, I'll be close to greeting my mother. Midsummer's Eve, Desa. We'll be clear of all this by Midsummer's Eve."

"Maybe so." Desantro sank onto her heels, used the back of her hand to push the hair off her face. "That's enough of that. Hop in the water, Fa, and wash out those suds."

Faan scrambled to her feet, eyes closed to keep out the soap. She felt for the rim with her toes, then flung herself into the bath, throwing up a mighty splash. She scratched vigorously through her hair, surfaced, plunged again, came up shaking her head over and over. "Rakil, here we come."

NAVARRE

Forces tugged at him, twisted him, all the sorrows of his life played out before him silent in the gray chaos as if he tumbled through the darkness of his own mind. Down and down. . . .

He flashed through a white room with a strange pedestal in the center of it, a column in the center of the pedestal rising and falling with an eerie grinding noise. He looked into the startled eyes of a man with exuberantly curly hair and a long nose; a girl stood beside him, her hand on his arm. . . .

An instant later Navarre was back in chaos, falling. . . .

Until he staggered onto a patch of pink sand surrounded by clumps of dark yellow grass, its paler plumes rustling softly in a wind that barely stirred the stiff blades. There were huge boulders scattered about with patches of lichen patterning the surface. In the distance, thrusting up against a sky like a blush wine, he could see bluish-green growths that might have been trees though they were like no trees he'd ever seen. It was a curiously silent place, not even the hum of insects to break the sterility of its peace. "It's like a painted garden," he said aloud, wincing as his voice was lost in the soft sigh of the wind.

Then he heard other voices. He found a shallow vertical groove in one of the boulders, stepped into it as three men strolled around a rockpile a little more than a hundred yards off, a blond man who took the lead, a black-haired man with a yellowish tinge to his skin as if he were cousin to the Hina, a brown-haired man with a lined face, some years older than the other two. The fair man and the Hina's cousin wore bright amber tunics, the third wore blue; the tunics fit tight to the body as if they were knitted on very fine needles. The men were looking at a box one of them held, apparently some kind of pointing device like one of Kitya's keches. Their voices came to him on the wind, but not the words. He could hear anxiety in the tones; they were alert, bodies ready to act.

They stopped.

A young woman had appeared from the air, dark-haired and lovely as any man might dream of, dressed in loose brown trousers and a sketch of a top trimmed in silver braid. Her eyes glittered in a stylized pattern of silvered blue paint. She spoke. Her voice was music, though again Navarre couldn't make out the words.

He thought about going closer so he could hear what was being said, but there was no cover and the tension between the woman and the men was so strong he could almost smell it.

She lifted an arm, reached toward the blond man, but the other two interposed their bodies between her and him, blocking every attempt she made at touching him.

She lowered her arm, uncertainty in her lovely face, and sadness. There was more talk, then she vanished and the men began walking again, watching that box.

Navarre dragged his hand across his mouth. His lips were cracking and his throat burned with thirst. Danger or not, those men were alive, solid. They'd have to have water, or know where to get it. He left the niche in the rock and started across the patch of sand, expecting any moment to be jerked away from here, almost hoping for that too familiar fall. This was a desert, a painted place with nothing for him.

The sand tugged at his feet, his head throbbed, and he'd gone beyond hunger into that numbness where the thought of food was repulsive. Water, though. . . .

The three men were talking again, somewhere out of sight. Weary but stubborn he slogged along, trying to get to them.

And stepped into a patch of thick shadow near a squat blue bush and tumbled once more into the chaos between worlds . . . Ride the Wrystrike, the Sibyl said . . . he tumbled and worried . . . the Curse was losing its drive . . . one of these times it might drop him in one of these crazy worlds and leave him. . . .

KITYA

Serroi kept turning her head and frowning as she led Kitya through the confusing maze of buildings and arcades, looking for marks to help her through what had been built since she'd last walked these grounds, making her way finally to a moderately high wall with corbel-supported walkways extending out from the top. Windows in buildings rising behind the wall winked cheerfully in the morning sun.

She went through a pointed archway and around the end of a baffle.

In a corral attached to a long low stable a thin, blonde woman and two grave-faced young girls were sponging down a beast that started Kitya blinking fast, a claw-footed, warty creature with a lizard's head and staring white eyes. "Macai," Serroi said. "Riding beast."

Kitya snorted. "Ugly."

"Better than a horse. It won't break down on you."

They moved into a covered way, came out near one end of a courtyard. At the other end three girls in light smocks and loose trousers were standing in front of a short, stocky woman. The girls repeated over and over a series of four poses, moving smoothly from one to the other as the woman called the numbers.

Another court. Under a bright striped awning a small dark woman sat at a loom, her feet busy at the pedals, her shuttle doing a flickering dance among the threads. On a pillow by her feet a girl worked awkwardly with a spindle, trying to twist an even thread from wool in a squashed sack beside her. The slap-thump of the loom, the soft spin-song of the girl, the other small noises made a serene music that filled Kitya with a sense of peace, reminding her of her mother's toopa and her mother bending over a pot on the fire. There was an ache under her heart and she was suddenly sick with longing for her home.

In another court a woman bent over a potter's wheel shaping a broad flat bowl while a girl knelt beside her, pounding vigorously at a lump of moist clay.

In another there were more dancers, older than the first group, moving to a complex rhythm plucked for them from the round-bellied lute in the lap of a gentle-faced woman.

When they reached the keep, Serroi turned down a broad hall that crossed the one they were in, shoved open a door at the end of it with a touch too much force. It crashed inward against the stop and rebounded. She caught it, pushed it back with more restraint, and stepped into the long narrow room with tall windows marching along one wall and a wooden backless bench pushed against the other.

A young woman sitting at a desk beside the door at the far end ignored them and continued working a button board, her eyes fixed on a screen.

Serroi stalked down the long room and stood with fingers drumming on the desk, eyes fixed on the girl until she flushed and looked up.

"Yes? May I help you?" The words were polite, the girl's smile practiced, but her eyes were cold.

"I wish to see the Prieti meien."

"Have you an appointment?"

"No. Give me a bit of paper, please."

"Why?"

Serroi folded her arms. "As a courtesy I ask, may I have a bit of paper, please."

For an instant the girl thought she was going to be angry, then she shriveled under the force of those orange eyes. "Very well," she said, her voice shrill with the effort she made to keep it steady. She reached into a drawer, slapped a sheet of paper on the desk beside the button pad, threw a stylo down beside it. "Much good it'll do you," she muttered and went back to her tapping.

Serroi thought a moment, then began writing rapidly in a small block at the center of the sheet. When she finished, she folded the paper with quick nervous fingers, producing through complicated pleating a packet slightly smaller than her palm. "Take this to the Prieti meien. Hop it. Unless you want me to take it myself. Believe me, what I say, I can do."

The Prieti meien was a harried woman with gray hair drawn so tightly back into a braided bun that her eyes were pulled up at the corners. Her face was square, heavy in the jaw, her nose long and thin. Her only charm was a remarkable voice, deep, almost baritone, flexible and lovely. "This is astonishing," she said. "Do you expect me to believe it?"

"Go see if the lacewood grows yet on the cliff."

The Prieti meien tapped short square nails on the paper. "Why come so secretly?"

"I was supposed to announce myself to your guardian chini?"

Laughter surfaced briefly in the Prieti meien's narrow gray eyes, then drowned in rue. "She's the daughter of a councillor, one of our dwindling number of supporters, meie. When he asked me to employ her, how could I refuse?"

"Dwindling. The Biserica echoes it's so empty. What happened?"

"They say we're archaic. That we've lost our value. The value they mean is this valley. The land's still ours, but if the meien go, then it's a question of who grabs first." She shrugged. "They say we debauch girls, encourage them to wildness and rebellion, interfere with parents' rights."

"That at least hasn't changed. The girls still come?"

"Oh, yes. There are more than you saw. Not the

numbers Yael-mri had, but I'm no Yael-mri and girls have more choices these days. We could use you, meie. A legend to push back the dark."

"Let me think about it. As a favor, leave it like it is?"

"So be it. Why did you come, meie?"

"To see the Shawar, if that's possible. My companion has a need to ask a question. I owe her, it's her touch that woke me."

The Prieti meien looked fully at Kitya for the first time, raised her thin gray brows.

"An Incomer," Serroi said.

"I see."

"This is our second day, Prieti meien."

"My name is Nischal Tay, meie. Meet me at the Name Hall when quinchalea rings, we'll dine together, the three of us. Perhaps I'll be able to take you to the Shawar afterward. If not, I'll declare you guests of the Biserica and make you free of the valley."

"Better not," Serroi said. "We can camp in the hills. The fewer explanations needed, the happier I'll be."

"As you wish." Nischal Tay sighed. "You'd better take your note with you, Krisda reads anything she gets her hands on and reports to someone, I doubt it's her father. What things have come to." She shook her head, then ushered them out. "Krisda," she told the girl, "I'll be away from the varou for about an hour. Have visitors write down what they need and leave the list on my desk."

When the Prieti meien took the blindfold off, Kitya looked anxiously around. Serroi was beside her, Nischal Tay a half step behind them. They were in a shadowy, vaulted, hexagonal chamber deep in the earth beneath the Biserica. No glowbulbs here, the light in the room, such as it was, came from half a dozen oil lamps set on poles arranged in a semicircle behind six ghostly figures who sat on chairs at the rim of a circular pit, leaving open the arc facing the visitors where a narrow flight of stairs led down to a stone bench in the center of the pit.

Without speaking, Nischal Tay bowed to the Shawar, turned to Kitya and Serroi, gestured at the steps, then went quietly out, the door closing behind her with a dull boom that had a feel of finality to it.

Serroi ran down the steps, waited for Kitya to join her, then settled herself on the bench.

They waited.

The ensuing silence was curiously relaxing. Kitya felt her anxieties and needs slipping away. When she was so relaxed that she was nearly asleep, one of the veiled women spoke.

"Ask."

Serroi pinched Kitya's arm and she started awake. "Is Navarre here?" she said. "In this world. The Magus." She would have gone on trying to explain who he was, but Serroi pinched her again. She laced her fingers together and waited.

"Not at the moment," the first voice answered, then a second spoke, all the voices soft and deep, earth voices, comforting. "Do you understand why you are here?" the second said.

"Chance."

A third spoke. "Yes and no."

"Ah."

A fourth spoke. "One force flung you out, the other guided you here, Incomer. Yours is the gift of patterns, you are here for the enhancing of that gift. Even now you draw strength into yourself."

A fifth spoke. "Rejoice and be blesséd, Incomer. She who Guides and Cherishes has put her hand on you."

A sixth spoke. "You will be called home, Incomer. Do not fear you will be abandoned here."

The first spoke. "The Honeymaid is wild power,

walking the knife blade between control and destruction."

The second spoke. "You will pattern the power for her; you are the base, the foundation of what will be."

The third spoke. "The Magus is the driver, through the Wrystrike he will direct the power and it will strike at your enemy from an unexpected place because of the Wrystrike's misthrow, and coming unexpected, its force will be enhanced."

Kitya broke into the chant, aware of danger and discourtesy but unable to sit still any longer. "The enemy. Who is the enemy?"

The first spoke. "There is a god in your world, Incomer, who is much like one we dealt with here."

The second spoke. "There was death and sorrow, starvation and torment. The meie Serroi can tell you of that. Through her we won free."

The third spoke. "As ours did, your god wants change to end, he wants no surprises, he wants to extirpate every possible danger to his existence."

The fourth spoke. "In the end the only way to achieve total safety is to destroy everything that lives. He does not know it, but that is where he aims."

The fifth spoke. "You see how far you must reach, how important an end you work toward. With your companions, Incomer, you may save your world. May save it. Nothing is certain."

The sixth spoke. "Your Magus is not here yet, but he will be. We don't know when, but we smell him coming."

The first spoke. "When he comes, he will come in your footsteps, Incomer. He will stand beside the tree on the cliff. He must not touch it."

The second spoke. "You must go this day and camp beside the tree. You must be there when he comes."

The third spoke. "You must not let him touch it."

The fourth spoke. "If he does, he frees a hate that will sweep like fire across the world."

The fifth spoke. "He will walk in your dreams, Incomer. He will whisper to you and try to turn you to him."

The sixth spoke. "You can resist him, Incomer. There is a goodness in you and a strength. We feel it. We bathe in its warmth."

The first spoke. "When the Magus comes, he comes quickly. Wrap your arms about him, because he will not stay long. Do you understand?"

"I understand, O Shawar."

The first spoke. "Ask, Serroi."

"Why was I wakened? Was it Chance or was there a purpose in it?"

The first spoke. "We have thought much on that, meie Serroi, but we have no answer for you. There is only confusion in us. Where a matter touches us in our persons, it is more difficult to discern clearly. And it seems this does."

The second spoke. "We sense purpose, but whether it is yours or the Incomer's we cannot say. Likely it's both. The confusion suggests that."

The third spoke. "Be patient, meie. Time will clear the pool."

Serroi stood. "Then I will stay with Kitya until her Magus comes."

The fourth spoke. "No. The danger. . . ."

The fifth spoke. "You know the subtlety of the Noris. You know your weakness for him."

The sixth spoke. "You are right, Serroi. I feel it now, strong as the river of life. I feel it. Go, the two of you, the Maiden's blessing go with you."

The door clicked and swung open. Hand on Kitya's arm, Serroi led her from the pit and out the door. The Prieti meien was waiting in the anteroom beyond. Before Kitya could speak, Nischal Tay touched a finger to her lips, then lifted the folded cloth and tied it over Kitya's eyes.

FAAN

Malang to Daveree. Daveree to Sked. Sked to Kanzeer. Kanzeer to Bebek. Bebek to Jedeti. Port hopping they went along the South Coast, two days sail, stop, three days, stop, two again, on and on. . . .

Faan tracked Rakil with fish and mirror, Desantro watching eagerly for each glimpse of her brother. He was well though worried, Desa could tell that, though she couldn't know why. *We're getting closer,* she said, *one port or another, we're going to catch him. He was in Dirge Arsuid the day they reached Jedeti—and when they left to cross the Tha to the North Coast, heading for Arsuid, he was still there.*

Cuiller drove his men on that leg of his route; he kept a watcher on the mainmast day and night, scanning the sea for the pirates that had thickened like fleas in the Pilgrim season and threatened every merchanter that sailed that stretch of water.

The sea stayed empty for the three days it took to cross the Tha.

Dirge Arsuid

Rakil was gone.

One day before they tied up at the godon wharf of Masna Noordin, the *Shagourag* put to sea, heading east as fast as that lumbering tub could move. Siffaram was as nervous as Cuiller, zigging and zagging like a sidewinder with hiccups—if the twitches of the pointing fish were any indication.

Faan sat in the bow with Ailiki in her lap and

watched Desantro chatting with ladesmen on the wharf
as Cuiller argued with their gowyll over the wages he
was willing to pay. When they'd come through Arsuid
on their way north she'd enjoyed the oddities and brilliance of the place. The brilliance was gone, greyed
down like a handful of royal gems covered with mud.
Even the air smelled of rot.

Desantro laughed, that sensual, deep-throated
chuckle which seemed to weave a spell around every
man who heard it. They clustered around her now like
humming birds about a moonvine in full bloom. She
didn't seem to notice the rot. All she was interested in
was her brother.

Faan felt a sharp stab of annoyance. *Serve her right
if I said t' Jann with it all. I don't have to do this. . . .
Diyo, I do. I NEED family. I NEED my mother.* She
watched the fireworms crawling about beneath her skin,
tears burning behind her eyes, the ache in her middle as
hot and hurting as the worms. *Maybe she didn't want
me, maybe she didn't care, but she's my mother, she's
the only one left who's GOT to take me in. The only one
left I belong to . . . get this over with, you stupid man,
unload your miserable cargo and let's get out of here.
This place makes me sick. And midsummer's coming
closer and closer. . . .*

On the Notoea Tha

"Black sails. Nor' by nor' east, coming on the wind.
Black sails. Nor' by nor' east. . . ." Repeated over and
over, the watch's shout rang across the ship.

In the bow where she spent most days when they
were at sea, Faan frowned at the surging water as
Cuiller crowded on all the sail the ship could hold and
turned her until she was racing east instead of northeast.

Desantro slipped down beside her, breathing fast, her

eyes glittering with excitement. "You better be ready to burn, Fa. Torkel says those black galleys can outrun a thought. And if they have a weather wizard with them, he'll steal our wind and leave us foundering."

"That why we're not running for South Coast?"

Desantro nodded. "Torkel says Cuiller's a canny old bat. The *Mollinya*'s some slower, but she can sail closer to the wind. He's gonna try to outmaneuver 'em. It's worked before, depends on how hungry those bewies are."

The next hours were a mixture of confusion and excruciating tedium. Ailiki pressed up close to Faan's middle as the watchman shouted periodic reports, Cuiller roared his orders, the sailors hauled and tied off, trotted here, there, as disciplined and drilled as any marching troop. Faan watched them, fascinated, remembering the defense of the Low City; there was the same briskness, efficiency, the same sense of tension without panic, the same underlying uncertainty that none of them allowed to surface.

Late in the afternoon the *Mollinya*'s flight failed; half a dozen narrow black ships were closing on them like wolves on a fat elk.

Cuiller brought the *Mollinya* around and set her racing toward the wolf pack. At the last moment he turned her a few degrees south—south because he wasn't going to let them drive him against the coast visible as a faint blue line on the horizon. The pirates got off a few shots with a ballista but most missed or bounced off the ship's side and fell into the water. Desantro's friend Torkel doused the side with several buckets of seawater and the sullen creeping fire from the oil-gel slid down and quenched in the sea. A sailor swept a more accurate shot overside, catching it with a loop of rope before it hit the deck and burst open. Another did fall onto the planks, but its shell was too thick and the deck was tilted at the moment of impact so the hit was glancing;

it rolled through the rail, the only damage it left behind a slight dent. Then the *Mollinya* was out of range and turning east again, running from the pack.

Turning, twisting, feinting to ram, Cuiller fought off the attack, eluding every attempt the pirates made to close with him.

When the sun was sitting on the horizon, Torkel came to Faan and Desantro.

"Master says go below. There's gonna be fightin and he don't want you in the way."

Faan rose to her feet, stood with her back against the rail. "He's been doing well enough till now, maybe they'll quit with the dark."

Torkel shook his head. "Never thought they'd hang on this long. Usz'ly they break off after 'n hour or two. Dark comes, though, it's their game, jinda. So come you, it's down below till this be over."

"Fa . . ." Desantro touched Faan's arm. "You better . . ."

Faan made a face, nodded. "Vema vema."

"Nu, get at it while there's still some light." Desantro nudged Torkel. "Listen to her. Now her back's to it, Sorcerie'll ash that scum down to the waterline."

Torkel's eyes widened. He looked nervously at Faan. "I better go tell Master what comes, migi miga."

Desantro grinned as he went trotting off.

Faan looked at her, shook her head. "It's going to mean trouble, Desa."

"Better a little foofaw than being dead. 'Cause for sure I'm not going as slave again."

"K'lann!" Faan caught hold of the rail and leaned over it, searching the sea for the wolf pack.

The pirate ships were behind and to the south, very hard to see, their black sails merging with the gathering dusk.

"Keep everyone off my back, Desa. I need to concentrate." Faan began the subaudible chant; the fire-worms under her skin who'd been quiescent for days now writhed and struggled, fighting against her control—but that was a minor distraction, chased away by the cool flow through Ailiki as the mahsar leaned against her legs; something else was leaning toward her, something wild and hot as the sun. There was a membrane between her and this thing, stretchy but tough, like the uncured airsac of the gulpers that Funda fishers caught in the Koo Bikiyar. That unexpected, pleasantly ordinary image caught from her past steadied her and a memory that had been closed to her opened suddenly. She saw what she'd done in the cave. So simple. . . .

She reached through the membrane, caught hold of the demon surging about behind it and brought him sweeping through; holding the wriggling, complaining salamander in her mind's strong hands, she continued the arc, sent him brushing against the six black ships. Whatever he touched burst into white fire, she could hear the screams of the few men who managed to leap into the water, she brought the protesting salamander down to the water it hated, brushed the swimmers to ash like the ships, then flung him back into his own PLACE. . . .

And collapsed, exhausted, to the deck.

Chapter 12
In Bandrabahr

Rakil sat in the corner of the coffeehouse listening to the talk swirl around him and brooding over all it was he didn't know. No one had seen the Flea. He'd been careful to keep his head low, but he'd tapped every source he could think of and come up empty. What t' pich is going on?

Two shabby but self-important men sat at the table next to him, out where they could be seen smoothing their beards and looking wisely cynical, one of them talking, the other nodding at appropriate intervals.

Ten coppers for a wrinkled yam, would you believe it? And the Ijar raised the rent again. Two coppers, would you believe it? I ask myself, who's getting all this? I ask myself why don't I get some of it? Cha, the answer's plain enough, no patron, no patronage. Amortis curse my father's souls to Pran's deepest hell, may he suffer thirst without water and boils without cease, for gambling away the family Mirs and Barr. Let me buy you another there, might's well spend the little I got and get some joy of it, it's la'n-sure not enough to live on.

Rakil was afraid he knew exactly what happened. Siffaram had jogged all over the Shakkar Gulf following some system of his own, one he refused to talk about, retreating to his cabin every few hours, emerging after a few minutes to order a new course.

Whatever he did in there, it worked. They'd sailed through a lot of garbage from wrecked ships but never saw a black sail coming after them. If Siffaram had some way to keep track of raiders, the number of changes he made had to mean the Gulf was infested worse than Rakil had ever seen it in the two decades he and Purb had passed back and forth along the Notoea Tha.

A prosperous silk merchant sipped at his coffee and smiled at the two men dining with him.

One thing you have to admit about the pirates, they are surely funneling the goods this way. Those la'nna la'n Arsuiders aren't getting half the Lewinkob they used to, Hennkinsikee's sending most of its silks out overland through Dil Jorpashil and down the Sharroud. Got some good stuff starting to come in. What? Drought? Don't say that. If the Sharroud gets too low and the traders switch to all-the-way overland, I'm going to lose a fortune. What's Amortis doing, what's wrong with her, don't we tithe enough for her? La'nna la'n priests are sucking me dry as it is.

This thing about the pirates, Rakil thought, *it's peculiar. What's going on? Confusion to all their livers! Tsa! It's going to be a bitch getting my own back.*

Outside the shop, a leather guard tapped his stick on the shoulder of a beggar, a country woman layered in shawls and veiled; she'd been sitting on the walk, rocking back and forth and wailing softly, the begging bowl by her knee and a small silent child cuddled in the curve of her arm, half-wrapped in one of the shawls. She ignored him until he began prodding at her and growling. She labored onto her feet and trudged off, carrying the child and the bowl.

The guard swaggered off.

Five minutes later, the woman was back, rocking and wailing, nursing the child as she did so.

Rakil scowled at the gritty dregs in the thick mug. Either he forgot about Purb and started scratching around for some way of supporting himself, or he spent the last of his coin on a Diviner. This wasn't a good city to go broke in, nor one to try remedying that with scams. Amortis was a jealous god; she had a penchant for drastic retribution if an angry Phrasi caught her ear. Baik a baik, there's still old Vaqar. He twisted his mouth, the name a bad taste on his tongue. Like sucking slime, begging favors from that hetch.

Vaqar knew everything that happened in Bandrabahr and a lot that happened in the backland. He knew what barges were due in, what they'd likely be carrying, who the masters were, their weaknesses and caving points; he knew what to pay whom, what sweeteners were needed to smooth a visitor's path. He was a go-between from the time he was able to run about alone, growing more eccentric as he got older, creepier and more vicious, sitting in his pile of pillows, fingering bits of paper with crabbed cryptic notations like a miser counting his gold. He confined his operations to a few favored clients and occasionally to a new one if he had a story to tell. Or information the old man could use. He might talk to Rakil, if only to hear tales of Kaerubulan.

Rakil had left Vaqar to last because the old maggot made him queasy; whenever he followed Purb into that stinking, cramped room, he had to clamp down on his tongue to keep from vomiting and after he left he headed straight for a bathhouse.

No choice, he told himself. *He's my last source. Bem, man, the longer you sit here, the less you know.*

Rakil got to his feet and went out, dropping a farthin

in the beggar woman's bowl for the luck of her blessing.

Vaqar lived in a musty loft looking out over the harbor. Half a dozen rickety staircases crawled up the outside of the building and Rakil had no idea how many other exits there were to the spider's nest. He went cautiously up the stairs he'd taken before with Purb, pulled the bell chain and waited.

The door opened and a small M'darjin boy stood in the narrow gap, his chocolate eyes wary, his blue-black face closed. "Chih?"

"Vaqar. He knows me. Tell him Rakil."

Vaqar had aged enormously in the decade since Rakil had last seen him. His hands shook, his head bobbled on his long skinny neck, a few wisps of yellow-white hair clung to a scalp spotted with irregular brown splotches. He sipped noisily at the coffee in the mug the boy helped him hold, then blinked his faded brown eyes. "So the Flea took a solo hop this time." The voice might quaver weakly, but the eyes were as shrewd as Rakil remembered, hooded and evil. "Foolish. Look where he landed himself. You said he was on the *Tochshidayan?* Taur-ya, could be he's down with the clams. A man got in yesterday, he was picked up clinging to a spar, one of the crew. Says the ship was scuttled after her cargo was taken off, didn't say anything about Purb." He shrugged. "Knowing the Flea, he whispered in the leader's ear about the riches he could bring flowing into his hands, if you follow me. But your coin will have walked, Raki, you'll never see those pieces again."

"Then the Flea will have to find their brothers for me. Who's an honest Diviner these days? If that's not a contradiction in terms."

"Pay your way first, little slave. The Shifter Land.

All you know. I'll give you a list of those who might talk to you. If they don't, come back and see me. Wet your throat, I want a full tale." He waved a palsied hand at the pot, settled back on his cushions while the boy fetched more tea.

Tavva Lars peered into the water pot, went pale and covered the pot with his hand. "Go. Get out of here," he said. His voice was shaking but very quiet. "Take your money, I don't want you claiming I cheated you."

"What're you saying?" Rakil gathered up the pile of coins and dropped them in his belt pouch. "Why? What's wrong? You want more money?"

"No. Get out of here and don't come back."

Rakil thought of protesting, but there wasn't much he could do. Trying to force a Diviner to work was as futile as herding cats.

Haks aMunir poured ink into a silver dish and bent over it.

She stiffened, looked up, her green eyes full of dread. "No. I won't read for you. Go."

Rakil picked up his money and left.

When he approached the third on Vaqar's list, he found the word had gone before him and he couldn't get through the door. He tried the others and found none who'd talk to him.

"They wouldn't even tell me why," he said.

Vaqar lifted a hand. "Aree aree, I do know that." His hand fluttered back to its pillow. He ran his tongue across his gums, bulging his lips out. "And why?" A lifted finger silenced Rakil. "Listen, sweet slave, let me tell you some things. You've been off in that no-god place, so you don't know what's been happening. Crops been failing in the Burmin, it's turned dryer than the Tark. Listen, listen, you irritate me when you fidget like

that. Take it as it comes or take yourself off. Hunh. Fish
out the Sharroud, they're diseased, warped, you'd have
to be dead before you'd be willing to eat the things.
Week before you got here, must've been a dust storm
up in the Tark, river was thick enough to trot on and so
red it might've been blood. Like the Land was bleeding.
And why all this? 'Twasn't easy to dig it out, but I did.
Uh-huh, I did. Didn't tell no one till now. Nothing I or
anybody could do about it. Amortis is draining us. And
why? Accordin t' these eyemen I tickled into talkin',
she looks like she lay down in a horde of fleas and
didn't get up till they sucked the blood and meat from
her bones. Don't know what happened. Don't care. Going to hunker down till she's plump and sassy again.
Phras'll be a husk, yes, but she'll be back to what she
was and those who last it out, they'll be all right. Closest I could get to what happened to you. She's put a pall
on you and I suspect it'll be a couple years before it's
off." He fell silent and sat staring thoughtfully at Rakil,
his horny lids drawn tight across his eyes.

Rakil looked down; his stomach was knotting, bile
climbing his throat. *Tungjii Luck, if you get me out of
this, I'll oil your belly every year the rest of my life.*

"Mmm-aaah, you're bound up in this thing. Don't
know how, but you pay your debts and that's enough. I
want it known I salved your way, Rakil. You'll do that,
won't you? Witness for me?"

Rakil couldn't force himself to speak, but he nodded.

Vaqar draped his long limp hands on his front. "So,
here's the best I can do. Go see Tak WakKerrcarr up at
Warakapura. The worst he'd do is tell you to get lost,
but he don't like Amortis so you've a chance of waking
his interest. Sorcerer Prime, can't do better'n that." The
tip of his tongue fluttered between his lips as he lifted
his eyes to gaze at the ceiling. When he spoke, his
voice was a moan as if the words hurt him as he forced
them past his lips. "I took passage on a riverboat north

for you and ... have ... paid ... the ... cost. Jattu's *Galalu Gaum*, Karida Wharf. Go. Go. Jattu leaves tonight."

Rakil leaned on the rail and scowled at the farmlands visible from the river, seeing instead of neat green fields, a desolation with immense swirling dust devils that ran like dancers' legs across the plains. Worse than Vaqar said, he thought, grimaced with distaste at the debt he owed that antique slime. "Purb," he murmured, "You owe me one hell of an interest and I mean to collect it. Out of your hide if I have to."

As the riverboat slid across the border between Phras and the Fringe, Rakil felt as if a sheet of glass had been lowered between the two lands, the hot sucking winds of the arid Tark giving way to a mild dampness that smelled of Spring, Warakapura's endless Spring.

The other deck passengers began uncurling from their gloomy, bad-tempered knots. There were threads of tentative laughter, some fitful chatter, broken phrases, a word or two, that gradually began to smooth out into actual conversation, though the topics they touched on were far from cheerful ... *rumors of trouble in Dil Jorpashil ... the restlessness of the Land God Sarimbara ... the great Serpent thrashing about ... the earth shifting and sliding ... the aqueducts breached in so many places water pressure's dangerously low ... ghosts turned hostile and menacing, battening on the living like vampires ... people reporting evil dreams every night ...* not cheerful, but lively discussions developing where there'd been a prickly, uncomfortable silence before.

Listening avidly, picking up all the information he could, Rakil relaxed with them.

At first.

Then he noticed the smell that floated in the slow-moving, heavy air. It was a subtle thing, a touch of over-ripeness, of staleness—as if the forces that maintained the Spring here had grown tired. He breathed it in and he grew tired.

Anger had driven him here, a need to avenge betrayal. And fear, the fear of a man who'd lost his life savings and faced an uncertain future. The struggle he had following Purb, the constant scrounging for money, the heat and stress from Bandrabahr north had ground that anger deep in him, but now . . . now it all seemed futile. What good was this bitter chase doing him? He might as well stay on the boat till it got to Dil Jorpashil. Dil Jorpashil was an important center of land and river trade, a busy, bustling city, so it wouldn't be hard finding work. One thing Purb had done, he'd trained him well. *I'm good at what I do,* he thought. *People know it.*

In the delicate lavender shadows of an oversweet twilight, the riverboat nudged against the landing at Warakapura.

Rakil rubbed at the back of his neck, got slowly to his feet, and wandered off the ship with the rest of the passengers. He was hungry, but so nearly broke he couldn't afford a piece of toast, not in this place. There were trees everywhere in the grounds of the Waystop, sporting flowers and fruit at all stages of ripeness; some of it must be edible.

Drifts of mist from the hot-water fountains meandered through the gardens, droplets of water condensing on the saber leaves of the peach and apricot trees, the bladed leaves of the cherries. Rakil gathered fruit and ate until his stomach turned on him, then he dipped a kerchief in the steaming water of one of these fountains, scrubbed his face and hands, wrung the cloth out and tied it round his head.

The path Vaqar had described led round the north

wing of the huge rambling inn. He frowned at it, turned
back to look toward the riverboat. It was taking on water and supplies and wasn't going to leave until early tomorrow morning.

"I'm here," he said aloud. "I've got time. Why not
finish it?"

The narrow path ran alongside a stream that climbed
through cedars and pines to a large house built of logs
and stone, a house that fit so naturally into the moun-
tainside and the trees that he was on it before he knew
what he was looking at.

He hesitated, then followed the path around a corner
and found the front door.

They were lying side by side in the big bed, a lean
old man with gray-streaked black hair and leathery skin
pulled over long, elegant bones, a woman carved from
ivory with silky white hair and regular features, faint
crow's-feet at the corners of her eyes, deep lines running from her nostrils around a generous mouth.

At first he thought they were dead, then he heard the
soft susurrus of slow slow oh so slow breathing, saw
the faint shift of the sheet pulled over them. "Baik a
baik, forgive me, but . . ." he said.

No response.

Warily he moved closer until he was standing beside
the bed on the woman's side. After another moment of
hesitation, he bent over her, touched her cheek. "Can I
help? What's wrong?"

Her mouth moved, pursing and stretching.

He started to take his hand away, meaning to shake
her awake.

He couldn't break the touch; that cream velvet skin
was a trap like flypaper.

His stomach knotted and his throat closed up as her
eyes opened and fixed on him; they were bright green,

the color of spring leaves, and there was no comprehension in them.

She was sucking the life from him through his fingertips.

He tried to cry out, to break through the animal blankness of that green gaze.

He couldn't make a sound. There was no noise in the room except the rasp of his breathing.

A faint flush crept into the ivory face, awareness into her eyes. Moving clumsily, she swung her arm, knocked him loose.

He fell to his knees and crouched beside the bed, trembling, too weak to move. He hadn't felt this bad since he was a boy and caught the flux.

With a soft grunt of effort, she pushed up, swung her legs over the edge of the bed and paused, gathering herself, then she stood, bent to touch the man, shifting stiffly as if her body had forgotten how to move.

Rakil edged away from her, snail slow, his weakness muting his fear, helping him, in a way, to concentrate on getting out of here. *Mistake,* he thought, *this was a mistake that could kill me. Vaqar, you slime, I'll . . . Gods, curséd meat, get going!*

She straightened, frowning, left the room without noticing Rakil, walking with difficulty as if she were wading against a strong current.

Rakil fell over, lay stretched out on the floor, gathering will and the meager energies he had left.

Time passed. He wasn't sure how long.

Shaking like a palsied ancient, he forced himself onto his elbows and knees and started crawling, inching along, heading for a door that seemed to recede before him.

Long before he reached it, the woman came back. She looked younger and more vital, animation and anxiety in her handsome face. There was mud on her feet and rivulets of water draining from her long white hair;

cuddled between her breasts she carried a fist-sized blue jewel with a star fluttering in its heart.

She ignored Rakil and bent over the man, holding the great sapphire against his brow.

His body softened and acquired a sheen, but that was all. His eyes remained shut, his breathing deepened but stayed slow, slow, oh so slow.

"Tsah!" She moved the jewel to the man's chest and left it there as she turned to scowl at Rakil. "Who're you and what are you doing here?"

Rakil ignored her and tried to speed up his crawl.

She put her foot against his side and tipped him over. "Stay there." She strode round the bed, her vigor and impatience making him feel more tired than ever. A white fleecy robe was tossed over the back of a chair; she pulled it on, tied the belt, ran a comb through her hair. A moment later she was sitting on the bed, frowning at him. "Well?"

"You've killed me." His voice quavered and shook; speaking drained him.

"Not yet. Not quite." One corner of her wide mouth twisted up in a half-smile, her eyes laughed at him. "It's not very intelligent to lay hands on the Drinker of Souls."

He blinked, licked dry lips. "I didn't know."

"In truth, you've done me a favor, so relax, little man." She glanced at the sleeper, returned to her contemplation of Rakil, the laughter wiped from her eyes. "But I will know why you're here."

Voice dragging, hiding nothing (mostly because he was too exhausted to bother dredging up lies), Rakil told her of Purb and Purb's betrayal, of the long chase and the pirate infestation in the Gulf, of Purb's no-show in Bandrabahr, of the Diviners' terror, of Phras' tribulations, of Vaqar and his conditioned help, told her all the gossip he'd gathered in without much thinking about it, watching with remote satisfaction as the warmth in her eyes changed to a cold anger.

"Pawn!" she spat when he was finished. "Oh, no, not you so much, Rakil. Me. We'll see about that. My name's Brann, by the way. Forget about the other thing." She came from the bed and knelt beside him. "First ..."

He flinched away as she reached for him, but she was too quick and too strong. Her hand slapped against his face; once again her skin clung to his, but this time strength flowed back into him.

"You'll do." She got to her feet and clapped her hands. "Graybao." It was as if she addressed someone just behind him.

He sat up and looked around, surprised when he saw nothing.

The air rippled, twisted and solidified into a shadowy, veiled figure. "Momorishshsh?"

"Take this man to the kitchen and fix a meal for him, then prepare a room where he can rest, find clean clothing for him and travel gear. Give him whatever he needs or asks for as long as it does not contradict your constraints. Rakil."

"Ia sim?"

"Follow Graybao; you heard what I told her(?), ask if you need anything. Go anywhere you want, but don't leave Warakapura. I have to think. I'll call you when I decide what I'm going to do."

"Wake up. Up, man."

He shuddered out of the nightmare gripping him and blinked at a face lit from below by an oil lamp. *Brann. What* ...

"She said bring you. She won't answer me alone."

"Wha. . . ."

"Sibyl." Brann's mouth twitched with impatience. "I can't farsee, so I went to one who could. I'll be in the kitchen. Hurry, I don't know how long she'll consent to wait." She set the lamp on the bedtable and went out.

They climbed up the breast of the mountain, wound through pillars of lava and prickly holly bushes until they reached a u-shaped opening, narrow and low, that they had to crouch to enter.

A big woman wrapped in shawls sat in a massive stone chair; she had an ancient wrinkled face, black as the obsidian walls of the cave. She was leaning back, waiting for them, her once-beautiful hands curled over the worn finials of the chair's arms, the black opal in her thumbring glimmering blue and green and crimson in the light of the willo hovering over her head.

"So here you are," she said; there was a purr in her deep voice, amusement twinkling in her black eyes.

"Are you going to answer me now? And no forced rhymes, you don't have to play that game with me. Well, Sibyl?"

"I will answer as I am allowed."

"Hmp. How long have we slept, Tak and I?"

"Fourteen years."

"Why?"

"So you wouldn't interfere."

"With what?"

The Sibyl lifted a hand, let it fall, said nothing.

"Tsah! Settsimaksimin, where is he?"

"Jal Virri."

"What's the fastest way I can get a message to him?"

"You can't."

"Why?"

"He sleeps, sealed within crystal."

"Tsah! Would Slya come if I called? You know she has a fondness for me."

"She sleeps, much of her force drained from her."

"She's a god. How did that happen?"

The Sibyl lifted a hand, let it fall, said nothing.

"Waking Tak, that's bound up in this man's search, isn't it."

"Yes."

"Where is Purb the Flea?"

"Gallindar."

"Can you be more specific?"

"Take Tak and the Talisman Massulit and find Kori's daughter."

"Am I right in assuming she's in Gallindar?"

"At the moment."

"And if she goes elsewhere?"

"The Talisman will show you."

"How?"

"Ask it."

"What price will I pay for the answer?"

"In this case and this alone, none."

Brann was silent for several breaths. "That scares me more," she said finally, "than BinYAHtii's taste for blood. I'd rather pay and owe no favors."

The Sibyl lifted a hand, let it fall, said nothing.

"How do I go? It would be easiest by river, but Amortis would like nothing better than to get her hands on me and wring me dry."

"Amortis won't touch you. That I can promise you."

"Who guarantees that?"

"One with the power to do it. I cannot say more."

"What else can you tell me?"

"Going to Bandrabahr is a waste of time, there are no ships sailing west from there except a few who hug the South Coast."

"Why?"

"Pirate wolf packs in the Shakkar Gulf and warnings in Diviner's bowls. Shipmasters are after profit not war."

Brann ran her hand through her hair. "Tcha! That means hauling Tak overland. What's the Fringe like these days?"

"Kick into an anthill and watch them scurry."

"Gods!" Brann touched Rakil's arm. "You have any questions?"

"Ia sim, I do. What if I say forget the whole thing, the prize isn't worth the chase?"

"Two weeks ago you might have. That choice is no longer yours. You will go to Gallindar with the Drinker of Souls. I am permitted to tell you this, you will find one of your sisters there."

"Sister?"

The Sibyl lifted a hand, let it fall, said nothing.

Rakil drew his hand across his mouth. "Baik a baik, since I must. It was pirates took Purb?"

The Sibyl's face went blank as if her spirit had gone elsewhere. She blinked twice. "Yes," she said, then the chair was empty and the willo winked out, plunging them into darkness.

Brann's fingers closed on his arm. "Relax, I know the way well enough. Come."

They sat in the kitchen drinking tea that Graybao had made for them.

Brann wrinkled her nose. "They didn't even give me time to get bored."

Rakil blew on his tea, sipped at it. "They?"

"Some piggon god and his lackeys. I swear, I wish they were all like Red Slya, asleep most of the time." She raked her fingers through her hair. "I'd better go get packed and see if I can organize some way to haul Tak around."

"Anything I can do?"

"No. Just stay out of my way and keep your head down. The fewer rumors floating about, the better, so I'd prefer you didn't go down to the inn, but that's up to you."

* * *

Three days later, before the sun was up, they rode away from Warakapura, Brann, Rakil, the shadowy Graybao on a nervous pony, Tak WakKerrcarr in a closed litter between two horses. With Graybao scouting before them, Rakil tending the packmules and the spare horses, they moved into the rough grass and scrublands of the Fringe, heading west for Gallindar.

Chapter 13
The Green Man of Gallindar Acts

On the south coast of the Lower Millyss, the early Foréachs built a Summer Palace for the months when heat and humidity made Cumabyar uninhabitable except for everyone who had to live there and the traders off the ships. It was a confection of white lacy arches and colonnades, with jewel-colored tiles in complicated patterns on every wall and floor, a cool, airy place of green walks and marble fountains, of perfect flowers replaced the moment they began to droop, of music from harp and flute players tucked into discreet niches. A place of private courts and secluded rooms, secret passages and hidden listening posts.

Cluinn darra Turry i Dur, second son of the Turry Foréach sent his sailboard skimming around the orange buoy; the bay stretched to the horizon, empty and peaceful, the slow surge of the waves a brilliant, shimmering blue under a cloudless sky. He was a slender man with well-developed shoulders and arms, long black hair pulled back and tied at the nape of his neck; his eyes were blue as the sea, his face just irregular enough to avoid the curse of beauty. His strength and extraordinary control of his body was evident in the way he wrenched the board about, skimming close to the series of markers so he could wring more speed from the sail.

The wind quit.

The triangular sail sagged in its frame and the board

lost way until it wallowed between the waves. He swore, dropped into the water and began swimming for the large raft a short distance from the course, pushing the board ahead of him.

Cluinn poured iced lemonade into a glass, stretched on a slat longchair in the shade of a striped awning and sat frowning at a distant shore where the Summer Palace rose like a cloud into the empty sky. There wasn't a breath of air moving; the raft rose and dipped at long intervals, water slapping at its sides, small sounds that with the clink of ice in his glass were the only things breaking the silence. . . .

Until the raft bucked as a man grabbed the side and swung himself up.

Cluinn dropped his glass, snatched the knife that was slotted into the table and jumped toward the intruder.

Who moved with liquid grace to the far side of the raft, gestured with his forefinger, and smiled as the knife flipped into the sea. He lifted the hand, held it vertical, palm out.

Cluinn stopped as if he'd slammed into a wall.

He blinked, straightened, the red rage draining from his face as his inherited affinity with the Green Man broke through his rage and fear. "You," he said.

"The blood is strong in you," the visitor said.

"Not strong enough apparently, Wayyan Dun."

"There's anger in you, Turry's son."

"Noooo." He dragged out the word, irony thick on his tongue. "Now why should you think that?"

Wayyan Dun said nothing, just looked at him from the greenstone ovals that were his eyes.

"My dear brother is the hero. The Happy Man. The Heir. I rejoice for him that his tie to you is so much stronger than mine."

"Is it so strong in him, so little in you?"

"The testing was fair. The priests say it often enough. Your priests."

Wayyan Dun dropped to a squat, fixed his stone eyes on the young man. "Your brother's affinity is a degree stronger," he said gravely. "That is the truth of it, but you are so nearly his match, the choice is not all that certain."

Cluinn looked at him a moment, his face a mask, then he walked across the raft to the table, filled another glass from the jug, stretched out on the longchair. He lifted the glass to Wayyan Dun, the ice cubes clinking busily, then took a long swallow. "Why now?" he said finally.

"Should Glanne happen to falter for one reason or another, someone should be ready to take hold and keep the Land steady."

Cluinn sipped at the lemonade, eyes half shut. "The Foréach does not welcome extra hands in the bowl of state. He's apt to chop them off." He set the glass on his chest, clasped both hands around it; his face changed to a mask of youthful fervor. "I'd do the same, were I him. Treason, Wayyan Dun. To tolerate that would be to invite a knife in the back." Eyes shadowed by long curling lashes, he smiled sweetly.

"Caution is a trait to be prized in a ruler. So many things can happen without warning."

Cluinn shut his eyes completely, his mind racing as he struggled to understand the god's implied offer. Was it a trap or an opportunity? Why now? A threat to the Green Man? Why me? Why not Glanne the Hero? His mouth trembled with amusement he quickly suppressed because it was too revealing. Glanne the Blockhead. A great battering ram, but worse than useless if one wanted tact or subtlety. We'll see. Oh ba, there'll have to be a little more god unclosed before I unclose myself.

He eased his eyes open a crack. Wayyan Dun's body

shimmered around the edges and when the raft tilted as a wave surged under it and the sun came hot and hard past the edge of the awning, the grain of a deck plank showed through his foot. Cluinn had only seen the Green Man's walkabout simulacrum once before, at the Heir choosing, but he remembered it well enough, remembered its solidity and power. Trouble. Good. He relaxed and let his mouth spread in a smile he meant to be subtly enticing without committing him to anything.

Wayyan Dun returned the smile. " 'Twas your mother who made the judges dance."

The sly attack hit home. Cluinn pressed his lips together, felt the familiar grinding knot below his ribs. The bits of ice unmelted yet rattled against the glass as his hands closed tight, then loosened as he caught at the control slipping from him. "I know that," he said and was pleased to hear his voice lazy and unconcerned.

"Glanne has a problem with his women."

"No, he doesn't. He gets what pleasure he needs from them. They don't last long, but that's their concern, not his."

"A young woman will be coming ashore in Cumabyar within the week, when the wind rises and the ship she's on can make port."

"Who is she?"

"A Sorcerie only half-trained, but dangerous in her ignorance. A pretty child with pewter hair, one eye blue, the other green."

Cluinn jerked up, the glass rolling off his chest, falling with a thump to the planks. "The Honeymaid?"

"No, but your mother might think so, if she saw her. After your brother finished with her."

"Sad, if it happened."

"Ba. Your mother's a pious woman. She'd be very disappointed in Glanne."

"But a Sorcerie?"

"Boddach Reesh."

"The wizard? He's sitting in the Flichtyr playing with his bugs."

"He can quench her fire, don't doubt that, and I've bound him to you. Whatever you ask, he'll do. Or not do. Your shadow, Cluinn darra Turry i Dur. For a time. When the girl is dead, then do as you will and what you desire will be given to you. By Midsummer's Eve, it will be given."

Cluinn wiped absently at the wet splotch on his hairless chest. There was no way to hold a god to his promise. In the end he did what he wanted. But . . . he was afraid of that girl . . . ba'mach! be like a god, Cluinn darra, promise, but keep your fingers crossed.

"Glanne likes his women fleshy and older than him. Why should his fancy light on a slippish girl? As I assume she is."

"That is not your worry, Turry's son. Arrange for him to see her, then let things take their course."

"Shouldn't be too hard. He doesn't like water and the hunting round here's less than exciting. He's been restless for weeks now, he's even ready to defy our mother. Leopards, ba. Swamp leopards in the Flichtyr. We'll stop in the Taygath for a night or two. You can let me know where to find the girl. . . ." He lay back, spinning the plot in his busy, busy mind.

When he looked up again, Wayyan Dun was gone.

Chapter 14
Faan in Cumabyar

The Chained God Unchained grunted and shifted his vast, bulging body into an easier position; the godstuff kept sliding under his mass, squashing and oozing away. He disliked losing his sleek form, but it would be worth the temporary sacrifice when he got Perran-a-Perran into the circle of his arms and squeezed the juice from him. He squinted down at the Green Man, nodded his glittering head. "I congratulate you, sweeting, it's a clever trap. Nicely indirect. Like the work of someone else we know. But I warn you, you're going to have to keep poking her back in it, that pesky little gnat. She has a habit of finding holes and climbing out of them." He tapped his knee, frowned at Chaggar. "You get busy down there, make sure that twisty viper does what he's told. And be careful. If you lose hold of her, I'll take back what I gave you, and a bit more to drive the lesson home."

The wharves of Cumabyar were like all the rest Faan had seen: large lumpy godons, stacks of bales, crates and barrels, grain sacks and huge winejars, lines of ladesmen loading and unloading ships, beggars crouching in cracks and crannies or crawling about picking up scattered grains, vegetable leaves and other bits lost off the continuous shift of cargo, and over all this the sour smell of rot and fermentation, of filthy water and dead drowned things. While Faan waited for Desantro to finish a whispered exchange with Torkel, Ailiki the mahsar celebrated her release from the confines of the ship by trotting busily about, nosing at bales, leaping on barrels, batting at flying insects, pouncing on the tiny rodents that scooted like gray shadows when she poked into the crannies where they were gnawing and eating at the goods piled on the wharf.

Faan and Desantro stepped from an alley into a noisy, open market with three-sided hutches woven from leaves and strips of bamboo or open sheds with bamboo sunshades casting stippled shadows over the goods on the tables. Wherever there was a bit of open space there were musicmakers: bands of children, single youths, women with guitars or drums, men with flutes or fiddles, blocks of wood or pairs of bones, anything that could make a happy noise; some sang in chorus, some alone, some made music without song, music with a powerful beat that set the body swaying, the feet tapping. It was a pleasant cacophony, combining with the heat and the humidity, the wandering stinks and fragrances of the goods for sale, the brilliant colors, with the play of light and shadow, with all the lazy ambience to hammer the blood to a fizz and knock dismals from the gloomiest head.

Faan flung her arms up, stretched extravagantly. Like the mahsar, she was wearied to death by the cramped existence on board the ship, weeks of it, with more weeks to come. Sweating and sticky, relaxed by the heat, she laughed, dug out a handful of coppers and tossed one into each of the collecting bowls of every band she passed. Ailiki kept close to her, brushing against her, singing the odd little song she made when she was contented.

* * *

"Desa, look at this." Faan held up a bit of batik print, a scarf, green and blue to match her eyes, cotton so fine she could see the shape of her hand through it. For weeks now all she'd had to wear were the drab, wrinkled tunics and trousers Humarie had provided, clean and comfortable, but never more than coverings for the flesh. She was starved for color and this bright market, these fluttering lengths of cloth hanging from their clips to entice buyers to the booth, they gave her solace.

Desantro left the cobbler she was chatting with, came, and looked at the material. She rubbed a fold between her fingers, wrinkled her nose. "It'll fade and fall apart the first time you wash it."

"Never!" the merchant said indignantly. "The dye's fast."

"So you say. What are you asking for this little marvel of flimsy?"

"Flimsy hah! This design is created by the great Maess Anel, the cloth woven on the looms of Thay Dohn in the Upper Millyss, whose weavers have won the Palm year after year. It is a work of art, O byrna amach, it should be cherished as such and worth a hundred times the minuscule sum I'm asking. Five arga, any silver coins will do."

"No doubt they will. What's this woven of, gold? Even Lewinkob silks are not so dear."

"Lewinkob, phah! I spit on Lewinkob. Overrated bug farmers."

Desantro let the cloth fall in a puddle of blue and green. "I'll tell you what, it is a pretty thing, so I'll give you twenty coppers for it because I have a generous heart."

"O weh o weh, it's an insult. I weep. . . ."

The bargaining went on, Faan watching, amused because she was forgotten by both of them. The Fire was sleeping again, she was relaxed, almost happy, the only jar in her life the hitch in their chase of Rakil, an uneasiness that pushed at her, made her want to hurry up, hurry, hurry, hurry, back to Jal Virri. Midsummer's Eve was coming fast and they'd lost ground in their search. The wind had died on Cuiller the day after the attack of the pirates and he wouldn't let Faan try calling another. He'd been really hot about it; he didn't like Sorcerers and made that plain every hour of every day on the crawling progress toward Cumabyar. She wrinkled her nose. It was too nice a day to waste on Cuiller's bigotry.

Desantro argued the merchant down to a single silver for the scarf, a price that satisfied both of them; she made him wrap it in brown paper, then the two of them went on exploring the market until they were too weary to walk any more and started back to the ship.

Faan looked at the place where the *Mollinya* had been, at the meager pile of gear, then at the beggar boy who was sitting next it. Her hands closed to fists, heat rose in her.

"Torkel," the boy said hastily. "He paid me to watch your stuff till you got back." He blinked up at Faan, nodded. "He said about your eyes, so. . . ." He got to his feet, took a copper from her with coltish grace, then went sauntering off.

Faan sighed. "He must've left the minute we were out of sight." She bent and picked up the little mahsar, cuddled her against her breasts, drawing comfort from the soft purr.

Desantro stooped, began gathering their gear. "You were right, Fa." She twisted her head around, looking up at Faan. "Burning those wolves meant trouble. Maybe we should've let them fight."

Faan caught hold of a strap, thrust her arm through it and wiggled till her pack was settled in the curve of her back. "Nu, he left our things."

Desantro snorted. "It's the least he could do." She

got the rest of the gear stowed about her and rose to her feet. "What now?"

"We find a room for the night."

Faan came rushing from the third inn she'd tried, muttering under her breath about thieves and extortionists. She looked round for Desantro, caught a glimpse of her through the traffic that rumbled and clopped along the cracked gray paving; the street was even busier than the inns, filled with ladesmen toting burdens bigger than they were, oxcarts, hand carts and the occasional palakeen carried on the shoulders of huge blankfaced men who trotted along wearing little more than sweat and leather loin covers. Desantro was flirting with a painter who was spreading a thick white coat over a section of a wall on the far side of the street. The wall was ten feet high, its street face separated into sections by linenfold pilasters. The space between these had pictures painted by what looked to be at least half a dozen different hands. Some of the sections were new and bright, others faded. It was one of those faded sections the man was painting out.

Faan wiped at her face, grimaced at the smear of gritty sweat on her sleeve. For some reason the city was choked with travelers, with foreigners, traders and folk from the uplands; the first inn was full, no room for a roach, the exasperated host told her. The second had a room left but wanted a silver a head a night, then, as an afterthought, offered her the room for a mere thirty percent of what she charged her customers; Faan's anger flared, the Fire stirred in her flesh and the host changed his tune fast. No room, he said. I was teasing you, O byrna amach, pardon an old man's lack of taste.

The third host was a harried woman who shook her head the minute she saw Faan. All I've got is an attic with straw on the floor and that's for men only, she said, then rushed away on some errand more urgent than unwanted female clients.

Desantro stood with her hands clasped behind her, her face glowing with the heat, her brown eyes alive with interest, her strong, solid body radiating sensuality and sex. The man was grinning at her, laying the paint on with an easy skill that minimized drips and left no streaking. He had high cheekbones and a jutting nose in a face like an axeblade, long straight black hair he tied at the nape of his neck with a thin leather thong. The thong had heavy ceramic beads threaded onto the ends and held there with knots, three beads on each side, glazed in brilliant red and blue triangles. His body was a wedge with broad shoulders and absurdly narrow buttocks; he wore a paint-spotted smock and kneepants, his feet were thrust into worn leather sandals with no backs. When he finished the section he was working on, he knelt beside a small cart loaded with paintpots and rags and began cleaning the brush, still talking, looking up at Desantro, teeth flashing under a shaggy black mustache.

Desantro glanced at the inn, leaned closer to the man. A moment later she straightened and started across the street, dodging and darting to escape being run down. The painter followed her, pulling the cart and strolling along with complete assurance that everyone would go round him, which they did. She reached Faan, glanced from the inn's facade to her face. "Nothing?"

"I'm starting to think we'll sleep with the beggars and their fleas."

Desantro flipped a hand at the painter. "This is Mathen. He's got the answer, maybe."

Mathen gave a jerk of his head, the beads clacking, small, sharp sounds that knifed through the much louder street noise. "Ye come the wrong time, O byrna amach." His voice was rich and musical, with a strong rhythm to the words, a lilt imported into tradespeech from the Gallinase. "By Chaggar's bite, the inns round here will be filled to rafters till t' rinnanfeoyr's run down, ah, grasswar, what that is, and t' Foréach he gets it together to clean out the pirate nests."

Desantro nodded. "Mathen knows a place that has a pair of rooms free; it isn't fancy, but it's clean. If we want, he'll take us there."

Faan ran her hand over her short silvery hair; she wasn't in a mood to trust anyone right now, but there wasn't much choice. "How far is it?" she said.

Mathen spread his hands. "Half the hour, could be, to the north of here, on Cuma's edge. An drasda, 'twill be cooler and quieter. 'Tis my cousin's place, I tell you up front, but none the worse for that." He met Faan's eyes, then looked quickly away, a frown like cloudshadow darkening his face, vanishing a moment later. "And the price?"

"A silver the week for the two of ye, which includes two rooms, your clothes washed, boots cleaned, bath-house and breakfast, dinner ye'll have to find for y'self."

"Mf. Go ahead, we'll follow."

The city was crammed with color, every wall painted with scenes or portraits, many of which were in the process of being changed; they saw at least fifty other painters working, covering over old sections with the thick white base, laying down new color where the white was dry. There was a lot of patter between the painters, jokes and challenges, put-downs and comments which mixed with the street noise and musicians fiddling and banging away. There were clumps of women laughing and chattering, moving both ways along the shell walks, ambling along in no hurry to get where they were going; they wore long loose cotton robes, mostly white or beige, heavily embroidered about the hems and cuffs, elaborately wound turbans or head cloths held on by twisted silk scarves whose fine frail ends fluttered in the bit of wind.

At first Faan leaned on Desantro's arm as Abey-hamal's Gift jabbed this new language into her head, but the worst of the ache was gone by the time they'd left the Market Acra and moved into the Cincheh Acra where small merchants and the more prosperous arti-sans had their homes. Ailiki went trotting ahead of them, nosing into the myriad of exotic smells; she ran up trees, jumped onto walls and scurried along them, swung down again, wove in and out of the legs of the other people on the street, stopped, sat up, looked around, her black eyes shining, her tail curled around her back legs. When Faan came up with her, she trotted along beside the three of them a while, then went back to her ecstatic exploration.

The walkways grew narrower and narrower, the shell layers thinner until they were walking on cracked mud, then in the street itself as walls were built farther and farther out until the walkways were gone completely. The traffic was all on foot except for the rare handcart trundling along, wooden wheels squealing like dying pigs. Except for those wheels, the noise grew more muted as the paintings grew cruder and more crumbly.

The heat was oppressive; the sluggish breeze that had stirred in the more open Acras was blocked here. Sweat lay on the skin collecting grit from the air, drip-ping into eyes, pooling inside elbows. Ailiki slowed to an amble, walking in a wincing prance as the heat of the paving struck up through her pads. Desantro began panting, her face red, her feet catching in the mud.

Mathen touched her cheek, frowned. "You said you come from the South. There's heat there in plenty."

"Not like this," Desantro gasped. "It was dry heat, not this muck. I can feel mold growing inside me. Tchah! A little more and I'll choke on it."

"Chag's balls, since I'm living here year end to year

end, I am forgetting other folk need a day or three growing used to livin and movin in Cumby the steamer." He looked around, then nodded. "I know. We'll get you cooled off in half a trice, Desa m'gratha. Come 'long." He led them down a side way, a crack not wide or straight enough to qualify as an alley.

A few pants later they emerged beneath the arches of an aqueduct. A boy sat cross-legged beside a bucket placed to catch water from a drip. He'd smoothed out a patch of mud in front of him and was drawing on it, scraping out his sketches with a bit of broken board and drawing some more.

Mathen stopped them a few steps off, then went to look at the boy's latest drawing. "You haven't quite got the fractions right, Loo." He bent over, took the stick and made a few quick adjustments. "You see?"

"Tapach, Math." Loo smoothed the lines away with the scraper, wrapped his arms about his skinny legs and blinked at the others, his hazel eyes bright with curiosity.

Mathen squatted beside him. "Spare a minute under the drip? Could save a life, we have maybe a heatstroke working over there."

"Atha Sheeken will have my hide if this bain't full come t' eve." He nodded at the bucket which was filling by infinitesimal increments, it being a large bucket and a small leak.

"Your Atha would peel his Ma for the price of her hide, on that I'll be agreeing with ye. Three drops or four, they surely wouldn't be missed and you will save an anna's life, a traveling anna going to dwell in Cewley's Inn."

Loo grinned, a wide glowing smile that stretched across his bony face, a gold eyetooth glinting at one side of it. He came to his feet with an easy grace, shifted the bucket, and swept through an extravagant bow, an invitation to share his drip.

*   *   *

Desantro squatted beneath the leak, her head turned back so the drips landed on her brow and trickled down her face. Her panting slowed and the tremble went out of her arms.

Glancing surreptitiously and repeatedly at Faan and the little beast sitting on her feet, Loo strolled restlessly about in the shade of the arch, his bare feet squishing in the mud, scraping on the sparse tough grass. He ended up beside Mathen, leaned against him, and whispered something.

Mathen shrugged. He moved to Desantro, brushed her neck with his fingertips. "Can ye be walking now? Best we be moving on." He pulled a kerchief from his pocket, held it under the drip for a moment. "Y' can carry a bit of wet with ye to temper the heat."

Desantro caught hold of his arm and pulled herself up. "I thank the both of ye."

The boy grinned again, the gold tooth shining. His eyes flickered to Faan and away again as he settled himself beside the bucket once more and began scraping his mudflat smooth.

They walked a little distance in the steamy shade of the aqueduct, but it ran east/west since it brought water from high in the Dhia Asatas and they soon had to turn north again and plunge into the Sathoir Acra, a place of shabby tenements and narrow walkways where the air had stagnated for so long it had acquired a certain solidity. Ghosts drifted everywhere, small and large, male and female, fresh or frayed to a thready wisp, their high whining hums louder than the mosquito swarms that spurted up like gritty brown smoke at the slightest brush of sleeve or hand.

Faan slapped impatiently at a ghost that was clinging to her and gibbering nonsense at her: *save us, holy one, give us peace, oh magistra, you are the desired one, the foretold one, the four-souled one who looks from the eyes of twin bodies merged, daughter of fire and belovéd of the Great Gods....* More ghosts joined him, male and female, some so old they couldn't shape words but only moaned at her. She wasn't used to ghosts hanging around like this. Proper Lands laid their earth souls once the sky soul was gone. Even the poor had that right most everywhere, usually because the more affluent got annoyed at the screeches.

The mahsar complaining querulously as she trotted to keep up, Faan touched the painter's arm, felt the twitch of a muscle though he didn't try to move away from her. "What is all this blather the ghosts are saying and why did that boy keep staring at me?"

"Ghosts?" Mathen's mustache twitched and his brows rose.

Desantro chuckled. "Fa's a Sorcerie, Mathen. Bespeaking ghosts comes with the package."

"Aaaahhhhah." It was a musical arc of a sound with comprehension folded into surprise. "Even closer a fit to the old tale."

"Tell!" she said and pinched the painter's arm.

"In times of great trouble the Wonder Weaver comes," Mathen sang to her, his creamy baritone blending with the ghost gibber, the mosquito whine. *"When the gods are sick and men grow wild, the Honeymaid soothes and charms."*

She blinked at him, startled by the second name, having been called Honeychild so long and so often while she lived at the Beehouse. But he couldn't know that . . . there was no way he could know that . . . even Navarre didn't . . . even Desantro . . . well, she might . . . and she might have told him, but what was the point? "Why me?" she said. "If it's as old as all that, I wasn't even born."

"An drasd', it's your eyes, byrna. One green and one blue. We've never seen that here in Gallindar. *Emerald and sapphire,*" he sang, "*gems of sky and earth, they*

*are the Honeymaid's eyes. Cool as Winter Ice she is and
hot she burns like a sundragon's soul.* And it's that little
beast that runs beside you. Ah-la, it's hard to twist a
song to fit my clumsy tradespeak, but y' see why Loo
was so entranced."

"Vema, him and all these ghosts can go. . . ." She
broke off as Desantro cleared her throat; she was annoyed at the older woman's interference, annoyed at
herself because she'd needed that reminder. "We're
only staying until we can get a ship to take us on.
We've got business elsewhere. So whatever it is you're
talking about, forget it, it means nothing."

Mathen whistled a snatch of tune, shrugged. "An
drasda, so ye say and so it may be, sweet Sorcerie. I'll
tell y' this, the two of ye, keep your magic in your
pocket. Green Chaggar sleeps and the Ardafeoyr burns
and the Foréach and all his kin will be scrabbling to
keep their feet, each seeking advantage o'er t'other. Ye
are power and they'll use y' if they can and this I'll say
and then no more, they've had a thousand years and a
thousand yet again to learn the ways of puppetry." He
took them round a corner and past an open space thick
with weed and fungus, then round a patch of palms and
along a canalbank to a small, rather shabby inn.

"And here we are." He cupped his hands about his
mouth. "Cewley, hoy Cewley, I've clients for ye, come
and greet them."

Cewley came strolling from the shabby garden on
the shady side of the house, lazily waving a fan woven
from palm leaves, a tall woman with a vague, friendly
face and a slovenly charm. She was thin to the point of
gauntness, but her cheeks were plump and she had a
lively pair of dimples that added spice to her smiles.

"Veäna, cousin." Her voice was music itself, a rich
and easy contralto that took the local lilt and made a
magic with it. "I hope your friends will not be wanting
to eat any time soon. Gimech has got at the cooking

wine and drunk himself limp and long away." She
smiled at them, dimples dancing. "The first meal of his
ye eat ye will forgive the man his little foibles. Did I
not know better, I would swear by Chaggar's Holy
Sweat it is magic's soul he has. But, aaahhahh. . . ." An
arc of sigh like Mathen's, in a higher voice. "Ye'll be
wanting a bath and a rest till the heat is over. Come in,
come in, my daughter Nual will take ye'r money and
show ye to ye'r rooms."

Fattening for half, the Wounded Moon was a faint
glow above the palms. Faan and Desantro sat on the
balcony outside their rooms watching the water ripple
in the canal. Ailiki was curled in a furry knot at Faan's
feet, her sides lifting in time with the small snores as
she slept.

"When the moon's at half, it'll be Midsummer. The
end of all this, hunh! I don't see how. We'll be somewhere out on the Tha on Midsummer's Eve, nowhere
important. What do you think, Des?"

Desantro wrinkled her nose. "The way our luck is
running, I wouldn't want to guess. Isn't Navarre supposed to be with you come the Eve? What about that
fortunetelling Pool or whatever it was? What you saw
in it, I mean?"

"Dreits said half what it showed were lies. I'd rather
trust him than it. And Tungjii's Promise over both."

"Nu, I won't be sad to be leaving here. It's too hot
even to think."

"Tsa! What about Mathen? He's a nice man, you going to wave him off like you did Yohaen Pok?"

Desantro pushed onto her feet. "I'm going to see if
I can get some sleep while it's fairly cool." A pause.
"Tell you the truth, Fa, I don't know what I want, but
I'm not going to think about it until I meet with Rakil
and know for sure he's all right. You better get some
sleep, too, the Fire's getting itchy again. Look at your

hands, you'll see what I mean." She went in through the jalousied long windows; a moment later Faan heard the door slam between the two rooms.

She looked down. Her flesh was shining a reddish gold, a faint glow that grew stronger as she watched. "Potz. I NEED a teacher."

Moving to the end of the balcony, she leaned on the top rail and frowned at the dark water in the canal as it came curving past the palm grove, thinking about her mother, the dome, the gods and their fiddling in her life, urgency, anger, and misery churning uncomfortably in her.

The broken crescent of the moon rippled on the wind-ruffled surface, the warm wind played in her hair, tickling her cheek with the tips of the strands, the palm fronds swayed with a hypnotic rattle. Her agitation smoothed out under the gentle pressure of the night; she yawned, straightened, and was about to go in, when she heard a rich baritone singing the joys of the hunt, startling a smile out of her at the contrast between the peace around her and that hymn to killing; she leaned on the rail again as the nose of a narrow barge came past the palm grove.

The singer stood in the bow beside the lantern, lounging against the bulwark, facing back along the barge, miming the pull of the bow, the release, his audience two other figures who were sitting on the deck, little more than shadowy lumps. His hair shone like copper in the lantern light, his face was ruggedly handsome, his body sleek and powerful.

As the barge went past, he looked up, saw her, and stopped singing. He stared at her until the corner of the inn came between them.

Faan shivered and went inside.

Chapter 15
Rendezvous

The conifer rustled and shuddered behind Kitya; she shivered as she felt fingers fumbling at her mind. "Get away from me," she shouted. "I won't listen."

Serroi set her cup down, leaned toward Kitya, the little fire between them lighting her eyes until they were orange glows in her shadowed face. "Talk to me," she said. "Tell me about your world."

Kitya gloomed at the fire. "What about my world?"

"I don't ... ah!" The Dancers were rising above the tree, the three moons in line, the largest leading. "The Wounded Moon. When the Wounded Moon was whole, you said. What happened to it?"

"Oh, it's just a story the attoys told to their apprentices when they were bored with studying the lineage chants."

"If it's something that can calm fidgety fledglings, it'll do to pass the time."

"I suppose. It's long enough." Kitya rubbed the heels of her hands across her eyes. "Let me think, it's been a while since...."

···

In the long ago, the dream time, when the Wounded Moon was whole, Neyak Kokmeletat was the Nato'ah Cham of the Nightfields. She was richer than rich, her kuneag herds outnumbered the grains of sand and were fat and lively, with silky black fleece that fluttered in the darkwinds, their eyes the stars sprayed across the Night. She had a daughter called Egra, her only child and the heart of her heart, the song in her bones.

All went well for twelve years. Egra was a lively child, bright and curious, gifted in eye and hand, welcome as honey to kuneag and the kigmeen who herded them and the drovers who worked them both.

In the second month of her thirteenth year, Egra changed.

She grew listless and pale. Every day she weakened, until she lay in her furs day and night without rising, her face to the leather wall of the toopa, sighing from time to time.

She lay there and would not speak though her mother pleaded with her to answer.

•••

The small fire flickered as the wind strengthened. "Wait a moment," Serroi said. "I'll get more wood."

Kitya smoothed the wisps of black hair that escaped from her travel knot and tickled her brow; behind her the rugged conifer whispered and teased at her. She seemed to see—just for an instant—a tall dark man with pleading eyes; a ruby like a teardrop with a fine gold ring through the tail hung from his left nostril, the gaud ill-suited to the cool austerity of his face. He smiled at her and the ruby lifted and rolled, glowing at the touch of the firelight.

Then Serroi was back and the image vanished. The meie set half a dozen sticks on the fire and piled as many more on the stone beside her. "Go on," she said.

•••

Neyak Kokmeletat went to the Chouk'ah of the Elder Women.

My daughter is thus and so, she told them. How did it come upon her and what may I do?

The Elder Women murmured together, then the Towsha Elder spoke: Her Womantime is on her, but she is refusing the Change. We will cast an a'to'a to read the reason. Return to us at Moondark.

Neyak Kokmeletat sat beside her daughter, grieving as the child grew weaker and paler. And still would not speak.

Moondark came.

We are filled with shame, the Chouk'ah of the Elder Women told her, we are filled with sorrow. The a'to'a brought forth only a shadow, a shape we knew not. We have asked our hearts, we have cast the butter and read the omens. An evil hangs over your daughter, but we have no name for it.

Neyak Kokmeletat gave them her blessing for what they had done and went to see the E'het of the Attoys.

Search your songs, survey your lore, she said to them and laid an offering of silver before them. My daughter is suffering thus and so. How did it come upon her and what may I do?

The E'het Kan of the Attoys said to Neyak Kokmeletat: We will search the songs, survey the lore. Return to us at Moonbright and we will tell what we have found.

The heart of Neyak Kokmeletat was ground between stones as she watched her daughter fade. She sang to Egra: I will be torn to pieces if it will save you, you nestle in my heart like a newborn kitten, you sink your tiny claws into my being. Egra, Egraling, tell me what bears on you and I will take it away. Tell me what frights you and I will drive it from you.

But Egra said nothing, just stared at the wall and sank deeper into herself.

•••

As Kitya drew breath and brushed away a spark from the fire that had landed on her knee, words came whispering from the tree: "Serroi, daughter . . ."

Serroi's head came snapping up. "No!" she cried. "I will not listen."

"Remember when my hand caressed your curls, little one, remember the nights by the fire?"

"No, I refuse to hear you. Kat, go on. Tell your tale and let that ghost waste his words on the wind."

•••

Moonbright came.

Our songs are silent, the E'het Kan of the Attoys said to Neyak Kokmeletat. Our lore gives us no answers, Nato'ah Cham of the Nightfields. But it has not failed us wholly. We say to you go to the Sha'to'ah of the Heshlik Water, pay Her price and Ask the Question. If there is an Answer the Sha'to'ah will have it.

Neyak Kokmeletat sat beside the Heshlik Water, calling to the Sha'to'ah, saying, My daughter is suffering thus and so. How did it come upon her and what may I do? Ask what you want and I will pay. Whatever you want, I will pay it, even unto my life, if you can take the Shadow from my daughter, my heart's heart, my Egraling.

A Darkness moved beneath the waters, a mist of Fear and Sorrow floated on the waves. A voice that was many voices and one voice came up from the deeps: Bring your daughter to me, Nato'ah Cham of the Nightfields.

Neyak Kokmeletat bowed her brow to the ground, rose from the reeds of the Heshlik Water, and hastened to her toopa. She caused quilts to be wrapped about the dreaming Egra, placed her on a litter and strapped the litter to Raven and Ebony, the twin ponies who shared the yearday of her daughter and went with her every place she went until the Shadow came upon her.

Her hand on Raven's halter, she walked with small and quiet steps, mourning in her heart that from the quilts there was no sound except the slow and painful breathing of the child.

•••

The whispers kept coming, teasing round them, insinuating between words each time Kitya drew a breath.

"I have changed, Serroi, I have had to change. The magic has drained from this world. I am only a man. A man in hell. Set me free, Serroi, my daughter, my student, my love. . . ."

Serroi's hands closed into fists. She shook her head and would not listen.

•••

Neyak Kokmeletat laid her daughter beside the Heshlik Water. It is done, she said. The Shadow has grown darker and more terrible in the doing, but it is done. Tell me what I need to know.

A Darkness moved beneath the waters, a mist came flowing along the waves. The voice that was no voice and many whispered in the reeds: Speak, O Neyak's Daughter, sing your Sorrows into me.

Egra lifted herself, Neyak's Daughter emerged from the billowing quilts. *I am filled,* she sang, *I am empty.*
I am filled, I am empty.
Hate me as I detest myself.
I am the odor of carrion
and the birds that feast thereon.
I am rot on a summer day when the sun is white
with heat.

You cry to me: speak.
What should I say?
There is no joy in me
no comfort.
To whom should I speak?
Who is strong enough to bear my evil?
My friends do not love me, they do not love at all.
They only try to take what I do not wish to give.
To whom can I speak?
The gentle men have perished.
They are eaten by their evil shadows.
To whom can I speak?
The bold-faced liars are everywhere.
My friends are no friends.
There is no faith in them.
With wretchedness I am laden
With sorrow I am borne down.
Wickedness spites the Land.
There is no end to it.

She sighed a great sigh and let her head hang down;
the wind blew her nightdark hair and pushed the tears
from her golden eyes.

There is one who comforts me.
He is silent and patient.
There is no need for speaking.
His odor surrounds me.
It is sweet as the milkbreath
of a newborn calf.
It is honey on my tongue.
Death is my true friend.
He sits before me today
and comforts me.
My evil cannot touch him.
Death sits before me today
like a stream of cool water
when the rains will not come.
Death sits before me

like a father
Who spends his substance without thought
other than his Daughter's need.

Weary with her song, Egra Neyak's Daughter fell back among her quilts and lay there pale and anguished, tears slipping from her golden eyes.

Neyak Kokmeletat tore the hair from her head, rent the clothing on her body. "Ah weh ah weh," she cried, "why has this Sorrow come upon my Egra, my Egraling who ran on slippers of moonsilver and laughter among the kuneag? Who was the heart's delight of the herders? Who played from morn to night with the furry children of the faithful kigmeen?"

The whisper in the mist came to her ears with the smell of rot and ooze riding on the words. "There is a balance, O Nato'ah Cham of the Nightfields, for every joy, a sorrow. I say to you, your time is done. There is no gift that will bring your Egra back to you or that childish laughter to her heart."

Out of the depths of her grief, Neyak Kokmeletat cried, If that is what must be, if I must see her no more, hear her voice never again, then so be it. If the Sorrow be mine, only let her live. Lift the Shadow from her and let her live.

•••

"Let me live, Serroi, let me live . . ."

The wind grew stronger, prowling about them like wolves around a limping deer.

•••

The Sha'to'ah of the Heshlik Water spoke: "It is not I that can do this. Find the one who can wound the moon and catch her blood in a silver cup. When Egra Neyak's Daughter drinks the Moon's Blood, the Shadow will pass from her.

Neyak Kokmeletat went to her herdsmen. "Who among you," she said to them, "can wound the Moon for me?"

"I am the one," shouted Char'ok the Bold. "Who is there among us who draws a stronger bow than mine? What will be my prize for doing this? Will your daughter be my prize?"

"Half the kuneag," Neyak Kokmeletat told him, "half the Nightfields and the bride of your choice. If that be my daughter, so be it."

The fine cedar arrow of Char'ok the Bold flew high and high, outraced the wind and brushed a star, but it did not touch the Moon.

•••

"Touch me, little one, touch me and give me peace, I am in torment, my disciple, my daughter, a touch of your cool hand will give me peace."

•••

Neyak Kokmeletat wrapped herself in layer upon layer of fine black silk and came to the Court of the Sun.

She bowed low, brow brushing the brightly figured carpet before the feet of the Dragon who was the Sun.

The Sundragon spoke: "O Nato'ah Cham of the Nightfields, why have you come here wrapped in veils of darkness?"

"I am wrapped in grief and sorrow, O Firebreather. A Shadow hangs over my daughter, Death sits before her, whispering sweet lies, courting her with songs of oblivion."

"And what is that to us, Nato'ah Cham of the Nightfields?"

"To that one who wounds the Moon and brings me seven drops of her blood in a silver cup, I will give the whole of my herds and my fields, I will serve that one all the days of my life."

Kappannah Murrain came boldly forward. "Lift your veils," he said to Neyak Kokmeletat. "Let us see the worth of your service."

Neyak Kokmeletat unwound her veils and let them fall about her feet. She was pale as moonlight, her hair rippled from her crown to curl about her ankles, softer than silk and black as moondark; her eyes were sable promises, her mouth fire to heat the blood.

Kappannah Murrain smiled his pleasure. "My silver arrows of pestilence never miss their mark. I will do this thing and you will serve me, Nato'ah Cham of the Nightfields, my Nightfields you will be."

Kappannah Murrain's slim silver arrow flew high and higher, it brushed a star that shattered and fell as dust, it brushed the Moon.

The Moon flushed dark and shuddered, but no blood fell.

Neyak Kokmeletat walked the face of the world, seeking here and seeking there. Her robes grew tattered, her feet were covered with dust. She took a knife and cut away her hair and left the long black strands for the birds to weave into nests. There were many who tried for the riches she promised them, but no one came closer than Kappannah Murrain.

•••

"Let me walk the face of the world, Serroi, give me a chance to repair the harm I did before, I confess it, I mourn what I have done, let me atone, my daughter. . . ."

"Go on, Kat, go on quickly."

•••

Her feet bleeding, her hands shaking with cold, her lips cracked from the breath that blew in clouds from her mouth, Neyak Kokmeletat crouched by a mountain tarn and wept for her daughter, mourned her failures, and did not know how she could go on.

A youth came from the trees and spoke to her. "Why are you here, Nagh'a, in rags like this, where are your furs, Nagh'a, to keep out the cold? Why do you grieve, Nagh'a, how can I serve you?"

•••

Translucent, but clear as an image in a mirror, the tall man stalked the darkness around them. He stopped, reached toward Serroi, sighed and drew his hand back when she winced away. He moved closer to Kitya. His voice was stronger when he spoke to her, a magnificent voice, rich and caressing. "Listen to me, visitor, hear me. You are not set against me like her, you have an honest heart and will not condemn me, listen to me, all I ask is what you gave her. Set me free, daughter of the plains. Could you endure being planted in one spot for year upon year, unable to move, to speak? Feel what I have felt. Free me. . . ."

The anguish in the voice churned her insides, she glanced uncertainly at Serroi, saw the meie's stony face.

"No, Kat, don't listen to him. He could convince a hare to skin and roast itself for him. Go on with the story and when you finish, I'll tell one and the night will pass. I promise, it will pass."

...

He listened to her story and led her to his toopa; it was small but neat and the fire welcomed her as much as his words.

"Rest here, Nagh'a, and at moonrise I will do what you need."

Neyak Kokmeletat said to him: "If you bring me seven drops of the Moon's Blood in a silver cup, I will give you my herds and my Nightfields and my daughter as your Bride."

"I have what I need, Nagh'a. I will do this thing for pity's sake and naught else."

He took a golden arrow fletched with eagle feathers and he took his horn bow he'd made with his own hands and he stood upon the Mountain and looked upon the Moon. "Isayana Mother," he breathed into the chill and empty air, "Bless my arm, let my aim be true."

The arrow rose high and higher, gleaming in the Moon's silver light, high and higher in a strong, true arc. It struck the Moon's left shoulder, tore loose a wad of flesh and carried it back to the youth.

He wrung seven drops of the Moon's blood from the Moon's flesh, seven drops in a silver cup, then burned the flesh that no one could constrain the moon through it.

Egra Neyak's Daughter drank the blood, rose smiling and joyful from her quilts. She danced with Isayana's son and went to live with him in his toopa on the Mountain.

Neyak Kokmeletat spoke no more to her daughter, but she could look upon them from the Nightfields and share in their joy and it was enough.

...

"And so the Wound was in the Moon and we see her like that now, a piece gone from her shoulder, crescent, half and. . . ."

The howl of the wind suddenly rose to a shriek, it tore at them, threatened to snatch them off the cliff.

Navarre appeared, stumbled toward the tree, his hands outstretched.

"Nooo," Serroi cried and leapt between the Magus and the shuddering tree.

Kitya flung herself at him, wrapped her arms about him. "Navarre," she screamed, "don't touch it."

"Kat?" A grin spread across his battered face, "I. . . ."

His foot came down on a crack and he fell into it, Kitya clinging to him. The last thing she saw was Serroi smiling with triumph, her arms outstretched, the ghost of the Sorcerer rising above her.

Chapter 16
Captive

The Chained God Unchained glanced into Gallindar, saw the wars growing more vicious, the Girl walking unwitting into the trap he'd engineered. "You may survive this, too, Sorcerie, but you'll have the sass beat out of you."

Hungry again, he contemplated the Witch of Lewinkob, grunted onto his feet and lumbered over so he could get a better angle at her. He was eating the table clean, the choice growing limited. It didn't matter, soon he would be more massive than the world below and there'd be only one left strong enough to hurt him. Only one. And not that gnat girl. No indeed.

Faan woke feeling good, filled with energy. She stretched and yawned, lay in the crumpled sheets scratching idly at the soft round of Ailiki's skull. "Aili my Liki, tomorrow we're going to be on some crowded, reeking ship, bored out of our skins and ready to eat nails." She yawned again, kicked off the top sheet and sat up. "Let's enjoy today, mh?"

She dressed in the cleanest tunic and trousers, kicked the others into a pile for the maid to wash, twisted the length of material she'd bought the day before into a turban. She looked into the bubbly mirror, smiled at the way the blue and green patterns brightened her bi-colored eyes. "Some better, nu? Ah, my Liki, no money and no time, or I'd live in that market for a week and hunt up a tailor. Gods, I'd love some new clothes. Anything besides black and brown."

Ailiki sat on her hind legs, crossed her forepaws and grinned at Faan, her dark eyes glittering in her small flat face.

"You!" Faan swooped down, scratched between the mahsar's tulip ears, then danced to the door between the rooms and banged on it. "Desa, Desa, don't waste the day snoring."

There was a muted mutter from the other room. Faan giggled and went round the bed collecting the things she thought she'd need for the day; her hands glowed intermittently, but the fire was pale and she ignored it, refusing to think what it might mean.

The door opened and Desantro leaned in, yawning, her hair falling into her eyes. "Fa, you mind going alone? Mathen wants to use me as a model when he paints the panel."

"I can't think of anything more boring." Faan wrinkled her nose. "You want to trust the bargaining to me this time?"

"Just don't scare the Master too bad, Fa. Remember what happened with Cuiller."

"T'uh, I'm not silly, course I won't."

Desantro smiled at her and withdrew, pulled the door shut after her.

When Faan left the inn, she walked past women clustered along the canal doing piles and piles of laundry in water that foamed with soap but looked clean enough otherwise. They were laughing as they worked, babies in slings on their backs who rose and dipped as their mothers scrubbed and rinsed the mounds of clothing piled in baskets beside them. *Enough to make the little*

*rats seasick. Potz, I jeggin well am not going to get my-
self into that mess, kid hanging on me. . . .*

"Gonna gonna kick and scratch," she sang under her
breath and walked faster. With their laughter, the
worksongs that one would start and the others take up,
the women in their worn white dresses and white turbans were a pleasant picture, but babies made Faan remember things she didn't want to think about,
especially Midsummer's Eve and the disappointment
she felt about that, nothing going to happen except another excruciatingly dull day aboard ship. "Gonna
gonna set me free . . ." She turned down one of the
streets heading in the direction of the waterfront.

It was a street of artisans.

In a coppershop, workmen tapping at pots and trays
sang a hammer song. Morning sunlight streaming
through the lattice that roofed the alcove where they
worked drew capering red glints from the copper, while
shadows from the small leaves of the vine that crept
across the lattice danced across their faces and their
busy hands. Faan watched a while, tapping her foot to
the music, then walked on.

In a leather shop, a man was laying silver into black
leather on a saddle that seemed more like a sculpture
than anything a mortal man could ride. His hands
moved with a precision that Faan watched with delight,
it was almost a dance, a tiny finger dance.

At a pottery a man was carving patterns into glazed
ware not yet fired; at another table a woman was
readying cloisonne with gold wire and powders; at a
long bench a line of apprentices male and female were
applying glaze to cups and plates fired to bisque, at another more young folk were taking them from molds.
Outside the door some children played on drums and
pipes, making a simple but lively noise. Faan dropped a
copper in the begging bowl as she moved past.

Dye shed and chandler's shop, cutler's and cobbler's shops, work songs and street music, bright and lively, reminding her of home.

Faan danced along the walk, swinging to the music, missing her friends. It would have been so fine if Ma'teesee and Dossan strutted along the street with her, arms linked, giggling together. But there was only Ailiki, running along, sometimes beside her, sometimes ahead, nosing into whatever caught her transitory interest.

Faan turned into a wider street, heard a noise behind her, and pressed against the wall as a band of horsemen came riding along at a fast walk. Their black hair was drawn high on their heads, bound round and round with copper wire with sprays of waxed hair fanning from between the turns like a bottle brush. Their torsos were bare except for carved leather straps with wide silver studs set a hand's width apart along them. They had wide leather belts studded with arrowpoints and half a dozen thin curved daggers; their voluminous trousers flowed back from sturdy legs, rippling along their horses' flanks. Their high-nosed, fierce faces and powerful bodies were laced to one degree or other—the older, the more skin was involved—with an intricate tracery of tattooed blue lines. Every one of them had studs and jeweled rings climbing up their ears; the leader who was visibly the oldest, with threads of white and gray peppering his wild mane, wore a ring through his left nostril, the diamond hanging from it glittering with every breath he took.

Contempt for citydwellers and sedentaries visible in every line of their wild bodies they rode with no attempt to accommodate themselves to the traffic around them; anyone in their way had to jump aside or get trampled.

A woman near Faan was jostled hard enough to

knock her bundles out of her arms and throw her to her knees.

Faan pushed through the milling crowd, helped her to her feet, then bent to pick up her belongings.

"Yacchod!" The woman glared at the swishing tails of the last rank of horses, the swaying arrogant backs of the riders. "Wayyan Dun set the sucking ghosts on you."

Green man. Must be Chaggar's pet name. Sucking ghosts? That's not anything I ever want to meet. "Who are they?" she asked the woman. "I'm a stranger here and not one to lack courtesy, but it seems to me that lot pay no mind to city rules."

"The Taythel and his yacchod?" The woman nodded as she took her bundles from Faan and contrived to settle them so she could move without dropping everything again. "Ye be right, byrna amach, they have no more manners than the bogg they herd, those riders." She smiled suddenly, satisfaction on her worn face. " 'Tis most likely the Foréach has called them from the Ardafeoyr to answer for the border villages they have pillaged in their shachal rinnanfeoyr. 'Tis their tails he'll twist, howl how they may, the spogs, and much they do deserve it." She looked fully at Faan for the first time, saw the bicolored eyes and turned pale. Before Faan could react, she pushed into the angry, muttering crowd and vanished down a side street.

"Potz!" Faan snapped her fingers, caught Ailiki as she leaped in answer, then strolled on, scratching absently at the soft round of the mahsar's head. "If there's anything I don't need, my Liki, it's idiots like that."

Some of the pleasure squeezed from her morning, she moved along the street, picking up snatches of talk from the clotting crowd, men and women gathering in knots to castigate the behavior of the Grasslanders, gloom over the war and what it was doing to trade and prices in the city, how the place was getting overrun with refugees fleeing the border towns to escape the horrors there, more cautious complaints about the slowness of the "authorities" (the word was whispered and she noticed after a while that no one said Foréach or Turrys or mentioned the Family) to react to the problem. They gloomed about the weight of the northrons on the public purse, taxes had gone up already and were bound to go higher, and where were they going to get the money with trade dropped off to a trickle, those pirates, they were worse than the yacchods.

Ailiki wriggled, scraping her hands along Faan's arm. She let the mahsar jump down and watched her run about. *You're right, my Liki, it's none of my problem. We're out of here fast as sail can take us.*

In the Market quarter Faan grinned as she saw Desantro across the street, looking bored and sweaty as she posed for Mathen who was laying down color in broad, swift strokes. Already he'd caught a vigorous hint of Desantro in those simple lines. Faan watched a while longer, fascinated by the portrait that grew before her and the skill of the man who made it, then she walked on, sauntering into the Grand Market, the brilliant, often clashing colors a feast to the eyes, the beggar bands surrounding her with sound and rhythm, not exactly like the music she'd danced to on the Jang, but enough to send her feet tap-tapping and her blood bubbling.

By the time she reached the lines of godons that curled around the bay, she was relaxed, hot, a little tired, and happy. Ailiki trotting before her, she ambled down the alley and emerged, blinking, into brilliant near-noon sunlight.

For a moment she couldn't understand what she was seeing.

The wharves were empty, the whole waterfront was silent and still.

The half dozen ships tied up there yesterday morning, busy loading and unloading, they were gone. It was as if during the night a fire had burned them to ash and a hard wind had carried off the ash until there was not even a smell left.

She looked around for someone to ask what happened, but there was no one there, not even beggar boys like the one who'd guarded her and Desantro's gear.

"Oh potz! What a fiasco. Jeggin gods, I bet that's it, sticking their stupid noses in my business."

She slid her hands down her sides, straightened her shoulders. "Aili, come on, let's go find Desa and see what she thinks."

When the mahsar reached her, she turned. . . .

And stopped as a man stepped from an alley three wharves on, the sun glinting on his bright, copper hair.

Chapter 17
The Ingathering Begins

While the guttering, straining Wrystrike whirled him on and on, Navarre held tight to Kitya and threw every bit of strength he had left to willing himself back to his own world, to Faan who needed him. He clutched at that need as if it could reach into this no-space and hook him out and Kitya with him.

Kitya strained against him, her fingers digging into his back; he could feel her will melding to his with a strength she hadn't had before—or he hadn't noticed. "Kat," he cried and saw the sounds of the little word go spinning away, silver beetles caught in a black and silver maelstrom.

She moved against him and he felt a tenderness as vast and all-encompassing as this place he'd plunged through again and again while the Wrystrike played its games with him. He freed a hand and touched her face—and felt the tenderness flow from him into her, blood to blood. She looked up at him and smiled, then laid her head against his chest, on the torn and mud-smeared cloth.

The Wrystrike wrenched them apart as if their fondness angered it, flung them down with the last of its force into the middle of a bandit attack and dissolved with a labored squeak.

Kitya sprang to her feet, snatched a jagged rock, and flung it at a howling mass of rags and hair that leapt at her from a clump of brush and caught him in the middle of his beard as an arrow thudded home into the side of his neck.

There were three fighters holding off an indefinite number of attackers scattered through the grass and brush on the low hills around them—a white-haired woman on a lanky blue roan who rode as if she were part of her horse and used the powerful horn bow as if Tungjii himmerself kissed each arrow and sent it home; a long lean man with a familiar look to him that puzzled Navarre—he had a sling and a pouch of lead balls which he used sparingly but effectively as he loped about, guarding the woman's back, helping her protect the small herd of horses and pack mules milling around a covered litter both defenders seemed to value. The third was a shadowy, uncertain form huddled on a black and white pony who stayed close beside the litter and flung out knots of smoke that froze whatever they touched.

It was a bad place to fight off an attack, the low point in the middle of five hills, no cover, no clear escape path. The attackers were Fringe bandits (Tavvas, folk called them when they weren't using more forceful language, grass rats), ragged and vicious, cunning rather than intelligent, never attacking except when the numbers were theirs. They must have rejoiced when they saw these well-supplied travelers moving through their lands without any guards, must have thought it would be over fast; when they found they were wrong, they were too stubborn and greedy to give it up and try for easier prey.

"Good work, fighter," the white-haired woman yelled to Kitya. "Watch it!" She loosed a second arrow and skewered a Tavva creeping up from the side. "Move in tighter. Guard your back."

The man whistled to get Kitya's attention, tossed her a spare sling, then went back to his prowling, the sling whirling slowly as he moved, speeding up with sudden force when he saw a mark, slowing again once the shot was off. The place where they were standing had once been a streambed, so there were plenty of pebbles about. Kitya scooped up a handful and began looking for targets of her own.

The sun was resting on the hills to the west, bleeding vermillion and gold into the clouds boiling around it. The shadows were long and confusing; the brown rags of the Tavvas, their dirt smeared faces and dark hair, made them nearly impossible to see in the growing dark.

Navarre rubbed his hands together, ignoring the swirl of battle around him. Though the Wrystrike was temporarily disabled, freeing him from his usual limitations, he had almost no energy left, but if he didn't do something and do it quickly, Kitya and he were going to end up dead with the rest of these people, their bodies picked over by flea-ridden hands for any value there might be on them.

He closed his eyes and fought for focus.

The shadow figure on the pony cried out. "Momor-ishsh, noyn! Prilbap!"

He ignored the creature, his visualization of the timelines around him growing in complexity, silvery flows that shimmered and shifted.

He tangled his fingers in them and tugged.

The land rippled and heaved around the Tavvas, knots of air slammed into them, the earth melted beneath their feet or threw up sudden walls that fell on them.

He freed a hand, collected heat from the red red sun and shaped it into bombs, lobbing them at the bluish glows that marked the points where the Tavvas lay or knelt, touching them off as they merged with the glows.

The Tavvas who weren't killed outright by the blasts that blew holes out of the hillsides shrieked and ran into the brush, the noises of their flight dying into a wide silence.

Kitya caught him as he fell to his knees.

The white-haired woman swung off her mount and knelt beside him. She touched him briefly and he felt strength flow into him, warm and intensely satisfying.

Kitya walked to the lean man, gave him back his sling. "Okanakura bless, it came in handy." She glanced over her shoulder, smiled as she saw the pallor leaving Navarre's face, along with much of the strain, then turned back to the man. "Your name's Rakil, isn't it. From Whenapoyr."

His eyes wary, he busied himself tucking away the spare sling. "Do I know you?"

"Neka, but I've met your sisters and you're very like them."

He retreated to the horses, began fussing with the saddle on a lanky sorrel. Over his shoulder he said, "My sisters?"

"Mm. Your younger sister Tariko is in Savvalis; we," she nodded at Navarre who beginning to stir under the white-haired woman's fingers, "lived there for a while. She's married to a civil servant and they have two children. Very happy, from all accounts. Odd isn't it, you were so close and never knew it."

His hands stilled for a moment, then went back to checking the straps. "So close? How do you know that?"

"Your elder sister Desantro came with a friend to Savvalis; she wanted to know where you were. I made a kech and pointed you."

"Where is she?"

"We got separated on Kaerubulan, it's not a good place for magic and the people who make it."

"Ia sim. She alive?"

"I don't know. As I said, we were separated. For what it's worth, a Diviner told us you and her are going to meet before Midsummer's Eve, so she's probably all right."

Navarre opened his eyes and smiled up at the woman. "I could get to like that."

She shook her white head, amusement in her green eyes. "Not a hope, dreaming man. I got out of the business of nursemaid two score years ago. Will you be able to ride?" She looked from him to the horses. "Without a saddle, it'll be. We haven't any spares."

He pushed up, flexed his arms. "I can do what I must."

"Good. I want to be somewhere else when the sun goes down and there's not much time for that."

The eerie servant evanesced like smoke, came back a moment later and whispered in the woman's ear, then flowed back onto the pony and sat waiting.

Navarre and Kitya on the spare horses, the woman holding the lead rope of one of the litter bearers, the man handling the mules, they set out, following the servant on a winding course through the hills and the gathering dusk.

The old Waystop was crude but defensible, an eight-foot wall of cracked rock, with the well in the middle of the circle, a rotting gate off its hinges, summerberry vines crawling over the stone, their fruits dark and succulent, marking the season as clearly as any man-created calendar. With the sun a nailparing of crimson on the brow of the hills, they scrambled to get the fire laid and the camp set up, the horses and mules fed and watered, then crowded inside a rope corral strung between iron loops set into the stone. The servant vanished, brought great armloads of grass for the beasts, then for the beds. Rakil went to gather what wood he could find among the small twisty trees on the hillside, the white-haired woman and Navarre worked over the litter, getting it off the horses and into a protected section of the circle.

Kitya glanced up from the bundles of grass she was spreading, saw Navarre leave the woman and stroll out the gate. Worried about what he might do, she followed him.

"V'ret, let it go. We can manage."

He flicked a clot of hardened mud off his sleeve. "Perhaps we could, but why should we, love? Look, the Wrystrike's winded for the moment, I can feel it brooding, but until it recharges, I'm free."

She reached up, drew the narrow tips of her long fingers along the stubble on his cheek. "Nu, I thought that's it. It's not what we need, but what you want to do."

He caught her hand, held it against his face. "You read me too well, Kitkat. Tell me true, would you really mind having clean clothes, blankets, a saddle, soap, food, your knives and a brush for your hair?"

"Saaa, V'ret, you'll need a muletrain bigger than theirs and a month to fetch all that."

Leaving a burst of laughter behind, the uneasy memory of a wild note in his voice, a wilder look in his eyes, he shimmered and vanished.

A breath later he was back, blankets knotted into sacks hanging before and behind him. He shrugged out of them, straightened, and stretched until his joints cracked. "Aaaah," he breathed, a sound so full of joy that Kitya had to smile despite the anxiety he'd given her.

"So fast," she said.

He grinned. "I'm a Magus, Kitcha; time hops to my call when I lay my whip on its sides."

"You're drunk as you used to get with that Varney."

"Not drunk, Kitkat, just happy." He sighed and the euphoria trickled out of him with his breath. "Don't worry, I won't do it again. With Meggzatevoc and the Wrystrike worrying at my heels, I pushed the last bit of that more than I liked."

She touched his arm, felt the tremble in the muscle. "Nu, you're here, that's good enough. So what did you bring?"

"Your riding clothes. In here." He set his hand on the bundle she'd held before him. "And the green dress, the one I like the best. Just in case, you know. As for the rest, I did the best I could." He shook his head. "I never paid attention to you, Kat, and I'm sorry about that."

"Hmm. I hope you brought your razors. You look such a scruff someone's bound to shoot you for a Tavva."

He caught hold of her, pulled her against him. "Will you kiss me if I'm clean-face, dama?"

"When there's no audience, valdiev. I don't perform in public."

He laughed again, let her go, and went to see about hot water for a shave.

Cradling her mug in her hands, Kitya looked across the fire at Navarre, her body heating as she thought of the blankets and the darkness where they were. Navarre moved his head, their eyes met and she stopped breathing for a moment. When she roused, the white-haired woman was talking to her. "What? I was thinking, I didn't hear you."

"You told Rakil his sister was traveling with a friend. Describe her, please."

Kitya raised her thin brows. "You assume it was a woman?"

"I assume, ia sim."

"Why?"

"Describe her, please."

Kitya glanced at Navarre. He spread his hands, meaning you might as well tell her. "Why not," she said after a moment. "A girl rather than a woman, sixteen, seventeen, something like that. Tall. Thin. Long black hair. Skin like old cream, darker than you, lighter than me. An odd thing, her eyes were different colors, one blue, the other green, I'd not seen that before."

"I have," the woman said. "Once. When I attended her Namegiving. Faan Korispais Piyolss. You and we coming together, it was inevitable, I suppose. Gods!" She drew back until her face was once more in the shadows. "Magus!" Her voice was sharp. When he looked across at her, brows raised, she said, more quietly, "Talk to me, tell me what this is about."

Out in the darkness a wolf howled and another and another until there was a chorus of them, the drawn out sounds carried on a strengthening wind that snatched at the summerberry vines and sent their stiff, serrated leaves scraping at the stone. The Wounded Moon was a fattening crescent, riding in and out of coursing clouds, her pale white shine mingling with the reds and golds of the fire.

"I've been thinking," Navarre said. "About where I saw you before this. Took a while to dredge up that memory. Kukurul. With Settsimaksimin. It was a long time ago, almost thirty years, I think. Brann. Tja, that was the name. You haven't changed; if anything, you look younger."

The shadows shifted on her face; Kitya thought she smiled. "Oh, indeed, Magus, I have changed, and greatly. It just hasn't left marks on my flesh. Brann is the name given me by my father. I have another, you might as well know it. Drinker of Souls." The shadows shifted again, suggesting a scowl. "And an attribute, plaything for the gods, puppet jerked about on strings. What is this about, Magus?"

"Navarre."

"The Wrystrike?"

"Unhappily, tja. Before we go further, tell me about that." He nodded at the litter intermittently visible in the shifting fire and moonlight.

"Why?"

"We've given you Faan. Favor for favor, Drinker of Souls."

She was silent a moment, then she nodded. "Since we seem to be joined in this business, will-we nill-we, and it's absurd to hover over him like a motherhen over her single chick. That's Tak WakKerrcarr."

"The Prime?" Navarre set more sticks on the fire, narrowing his eyes as the wind brought the smoke to sting them.

"No less. My lover, for the few years I was left awake to enjoy him."

Rakil looked up from the boots he was oiling; his teeth glinted in a brief grin, then he refolded the rag and busied himself with the boots again.

"Awake?" Navarre raised a brow.

Brann grimaced. "We were bespelled. Tak being what he is, I suspect it'd take a god to do it. If I ever find out. . . ." Her eyes narrowed and her face went stony hard and still for a moment, then she tucked her anger away. "Rakil came along and woke me, but Tak still sleeps and I can do nothing about that. Navarre, will you read him for me? But don't. . . ."

"Don't worry, I won't try anything I'm not sure of." He frowned. "Why did you leave Warakapura? This trek across the Fringe . . . there's nothing out here. I may be limited in applications, but my learning is as thorough as any."

"Ask the Sibyl, I'm only doing what she said. You know—or guess—a good deal more than I. Tell me what this is about. It's the third time I've asked. I'd appreciate an answer."

"I could say I don't know and that'd be true. I could also say it's about your friend's daughter, Faan. That's only a guess, but likely enough."

"Faan. You're not the first to mention her."

"The Sibyl?"

"Ia sim. So?"

"First time I saw her, I knew she was trouble. Between Megg and the Wrystrike, I was rather thoroughly shut down, but it didn't take much magesight to notice what was coiling round her. Web of a drunken spider. Fate lines and forces converging on her. I tried to ease her off, but it didn't work." He hesitated, rubbing his palms on his knees, the lines in his face deepening as he made up his mind. "You've got Massulit with you, haven't you. You don't need to answer, you've got it concealed somehow. I can't sense it, but I don't need to. Faan saw it. . . ."

Rakil set the boots aside, wiped his hands off, and dropped the rag; he wrapped his arms around his legs and frowned over his knees at Navarre.

Kitya glanced at him; she was predisposed to trust him, it was his likeness to Desantro that did it, but she was afraid of letting down her guard with anyone right now. *Mama said it's the ones you trust who hurt you most.*

Brann stirred impatiently as Navarre continued to brood at the fire. "Go on."

He smoothed his hand across his clean-shaven chin. "In the gardens of Ash Dievon in the city Savvalis," he said finally, "there's a place called Qelqellalit's Pool. A Power dwells there who will answer a querent's question with an image. Faan looked into the pool and saw me standing beside her on a tor across a selat from Jal Virri, in my hand a great blue jewel with a star at its heart. When she told me about the vision and the jewel, I knew it at once. What else could it be but Massulit?"

"Why on the tor?"

"It's complicated."

"What have we more of than time, Navarre?"

"True." He gazed at his hands, rubbed his fingers together, then gave her a brief sketch of Faan's history. ". . . so Abeyhamal set the dome in place to keep the child's mother and friends from interfering in her war, especially since one of those friends was a Sorcerer Prime . . ."

"Settsimaksimin."

"Tja. But once the war was over and she had what she wanted, she went about her business and didn't bother herself about the dome."

Brann sighed. "Nothing new in that."

He nodded. "So when Faan set out looking for her mother, you can guess what she found. Little Sorcerie, she burns so hot she scares me to the marrow of my bones, but she couldn't scratch that crystal."

"A fire-caller? She comes by it honestly, her mother was a demon handler when she was barely more than a student. Friend of mine. More exactly, friend of a friend. Go on."

"Nu, she can be captured, tormented, used, but she can't be killed or deflected for long from her journey back to the tor. The people she needs—look at us, moving toward her like iron to a magnet. Who's doing it? I don't know. Why's it happening? I don't know. Can we do anything about it?" He shrugged.

"I see." She got to her feet. "I'll stand first watch. The rest of you sort out the night between you."

Chapter 18
Disappearances

DESANTRO

Desantro squinted her eyes against the sweat rolling from her hair, sighed and straightened her face as Mathen clucked his tongue at her. *Faan had it right. This is boooring. By now she's at the wharves. If she hasn't stopped to fool about the Market. Bet she has. Taouk! We haven't money to waste on eensy fiddles some hoks are bound to cozen her into buying....* "How much longer, Math?"

He smiled at her, teeth glinting beneath the fringe of mustache; she remembered how it tickled and teased her when ... she wrenched her mind away from last night, her worries were now and needed dealing with.

"Faan ..." she started.

"Mamabéag, your chick will do just fine. Keep still only a little bit longer, then I've got what I need."

Kiy'h! You, too, ihou? Just because I've got some doubts and good reason for them?

Faan's little jab at her had festered more than she'd realized. She really didn't believe the girl was capable of teasing a shipmaster along so he'd give them a good rate and, above all, take them on as passengers. Faan wasn't stupid, she was just riding too close to the edge, to apt to show fire at a minor insult. *And if she does, nu, there goes the passage. Wants her mama. Hmp. Don't we all? Now and then, anyway. Good kid,*

*but she's starting to scare me some. The fire's getting
stronger. It's enough to make a statue nervous. Poor
baby. Life is potz, hot and steaming. Like me now.
Gods, finish that will you, Math? I'm worried about her.
She doesn't need to know I'm there, but I'll feel better
if I can see what's happening.*

Mathen swished a brush in a can of cleaner, began
wiping it with a rag. "A chaerta, Des, 'tis far enough
now, I can go on from here without your lovely self.
Mamabéag, go find your chickling and relax your
innerds." He took a small brush from the jar, got to his
feet. "I'll still be seeing ye at the Eskerichal for lunch?"

"Ba, unless the sky falls in."

She hurried through the Market into the nearest alley
between godons, stopped in the mouth of it, astonished
by what she was seeing.

The wharves were empty, no ships, no ladesmen, not
even any beggars nosing among the few broken bales
left behind.

Faan stood near the water's edge, her body tense as
she stared at a man a short distance off, a handsome
man wearing a yacchod's wide trousers with an embroidered vest laced loosely about his torso, leaving
most of his chest and arms bare, the sun turning his
copper hair molten and sliding like a caress along
smooth skin tanned a golden brown.

"Come to me, little one, come to me, sweeting, I'll
make you a princess with silk and jewels and all the
perfumes in the world," he crooned to Faan, his rich
baritone seductive as a witch's spell. His arms lifted
into curves meant to clasp her, his shapely, well-tended
hands beckoned to her.

Fire rippled along Faan's arms, small blue flamelets
that danced a finger's width above her sleeves. "I will
not," she said. "Go away." She slid a hand under one of
the flamelets, held it dancing above her palm, ready to

throw. "I mean it, I'll burn you bald if you come closer."

"Come to me, sitabéag, come to me, dulcerie, I'll show you sweeter heat than those fires of yours."

Desantro eased out of the alley, slid along in the shadow under the godon's eaves and crouched behind a broken crate; she chewed on her lip wondering what she should do. Go back and get Mathen? He knew the rules round here and the people. . . .

A man stepped from the alley at the end of that godon, close enough Desantro could have touched him; he flung an egg that crashed at Faan's feet and sent a yellow mist gushing up around her, blowing out the flamelets; Faan coughed and her legs shook, then collapsed under her and she spiraled into a heap on the planks. He went with small, mincing steps across the wharf toward her, touched her with his toe, then beckoned to the other.

The eggman was short and wiry, embroidered all over with blue tattoos; leather thongs dyed bright colors were braided into his gray hair; his jerkin was woven from more thongs and sewn with bits of wood, all different kinds, and pierced stones, mostly water polished pebbles and amber beads; he wore more amber beads in long ropes thrown round his neck and carved amber drops hanging from his ears and nose. His boots were carved leather with inch and a half heels and high tops; from the way he walked, he wasn't all that used to wearing anything on his feet. His face was lined, his eyes a muddy blue, half-hidden under wrinkled, warty lids; his thin-lipped wide mouth was pinched into a cynical, down-curled smile as he looked from Faan to the man who was strolling toward them.

"You have not gone and taken the fight out of her, have you, wizard? I did tell you and did say it strong, I do not want that, wizard. I shall be annoyed if you have forgot yourself."

"I have done nothing but tie her talent, Glanne arcosh Turry i Dur, this tigret has her hands and teeth and no doubt she'll use them. If you wish, I'll turn her loose and watch you burn."

"Nay nay, I'm not such a fool as that. A chaerta, pick her up and let's go."

The Chained God Unchained dropped the husk of the Witch, wiped his hand across his mouth as he watched her sinking deep among the clustering earth elementals, little more than an outline of what she'd been. "Sour eating," he grumbled. He glanced into Gallindar, chattered his teeth in a moment of applause as he saw the Fleagirl collapse, then burped and lurched to his feet. Kyatawat sang to him with its fluttering, flittery powers, the ponderous and malice-filled Wieldys, all different flavors waiting there, just for him, where he could winnow a hand through air and catch a palmful of Wees as appetizers. The plot was on track, the girl was not yet dead, but if Glanne's history was any pointer, she would be soon.

Desantro crouched behind the broken crate and watched them leave. She didn't know what to do—a wizard and a man of power in the land, how could she touch them? Especially when Faan had been taken out as easily as a toothless baby.

She dithered a moment longer, then ran down the wharf to the alley they'd disappeared into, eased her head round the corner of the godon in time to see them pass out into the Market—without a gesture at concealing what they were doing. "Gods! He's a high one for sure." She wrinkled her nose but went down the alley after them.

When she reached the end, she slowed and strolled out as if she were sightseeing on a pretty day. A softness touched her leg and she looked down. Faan's pet was moving beside her, brushing against her as if the creature sought reassurance. Desantro bent and held her arms in a loose circle. Ailiki jumped into them, resting against her breast, trembling but silent.

It wasn't hard to track the men through the Market. The big copper-haired man walked in a bubble of silence where seller and buyer alike concentrated on their business, not-seeing, not-hearing, scarcely breathing. When the lordling and the wizard went out through the broad gate into the city, the noise behind them expanded enormously as if the Market had passed through and out of the eye of a storm.

Once she was in the street, she set Ailiki down, gave her a scratch behind the ear. "It's too hot, hinnahey. Your feet'll have to do you." She slipped after the men unnoticed, followed them through the streets, the lordling striding along as if he owned ground and air alike, the wizard hobbling after him, bent over under Faan's weight. No one saw them because no one looked at them and that odd invisibility covered Desantro as well.

They crossed through the whole of the city and passed into the hills beyond where the grand houses were, closed behind high walls like the Sirmalas of the Maulapam in Bairroa Pili; the lords of this land lived here and at any other time folk like her would be chased from this place with dogs. If that Gallinder Mal weren't unknowingly running interference for her, she couldn't have gotten half this far. Maybe by the back alleys where the servants came and went, but not out here.

She stopped in the shadow of a flowering tree, petals from the great purple blooms blowing against her, and watched the red man go striding through a lacy gate, the delicacy of the carving doing nothing to conceal the strength of the barrier. Ailiki ran after them, but stopped abruptly even though the gate was open and the guards were ignoring the little creature.

She rose on her hind legs, her black paw hands scrabbling against an invisible barrier, then she abandoned the attempt, found a patch of shadow and curled up in it, her head laid on her forepaws. *You're right, hinny, I stop here, too. He's home and there's no way I get in after him. At least, not now. Potz! If* Navarre *were here.... Hmp, IF and a copper bit will buy a cup of tea. Math, deee-yo, he's the one, he'll know who that is and what's happening to Fa. Nu, I don't need telling about that last.* She shivered and started making her way cautiously back to the Market Acra.

The Eskerichal was a Riverside building surrounded by orchards and date groves with vine-shaded arcades built around a many-tiered, high-leaping fountain that provided a background for the harpist who tinkled away for the edification of the diners. Mathen was a friend of one of the waiters who was an apprentice portraitist without enough clients yet to support him, so they got a choice table overlooking the river and far enough away from the harp so they could talk without shouting, in a section of the arcades with only three other tables in use. The waiter brought them tea and crusty rolls, then a platter heaped high with shrimps fried in delicate batter, steamed crabs, goma tails in their bright red plating, and small fish no longer than her hand with silver speckled dark grey skin and flaky white flesh.

Mathen swept his cup in a salute, his eyes glittering with excitement. "Ye brought me luck, Des. Mas Tavree liked the painting so much he commissioned me to do his wife and daughters."

"I'm glad." She made a face at him. "All that sweating and sore muscles was worth something after all."

They ate in companionable silence, surrounded by

the pleasant, peaceful sounds that slipped through the burbling of the harp. Shouts came up from boats in the river, the orange trees outside the arch rustled and creaked in a slow breeze that was heavy with damp, while the latticework alcove was filled with the small sounds of cutlery and clinking china.

Desantro was hungry and the food was superb; she pushed thoughts of Faan from her mind and set about enjoying Mathen's celebration.

"Did Faan find ye a ship?"

Desantro sighed, crossed her knife and fork on her plate. "Nay," she said. She took her hands from the table and clasped them in her lap. "I saw a peculiar man on the wharves, someone called him wizard. He'd come about to my ear . . ."

She went on to describe him, having started with the wizard because she still wasn't sure just how she was going to handle telling Mathen what happened, for she had a feeling that the painter would be out of there at first mention of the copper-haired man.

Mathen stroked his thumb across his mustache. "If your eye is as good as it seems, then Boddach Reesh has come to town." He stirred honey into his tea, set the spoon on its holder. "That is an odd thing, my Desa. The sorréals say it again and again, the man loathes people and loves bugs and spends his days in the Flitchtyr swamps, playing with his loves. It makes me wonder if the rinnanfeoyr has come into the Flichtyr. D'droch, Des, these are troubled times. Is it sure and is it certain your chicklet is truly not the Honeymaid, come to us for the righting of wrongs?"

Desantro thought about that a moment, wondering if she should encourage the idea so he'd be more willing to help, then she shrugged; too much she didn't know. "Ask the gods, not me."

"No ship to take you? I don't understand that, I don't

at all. It seems to me the shipmasters should welcome a sorcerer, the pirates being so bad this year. If she fiddled it right, or ye did," he smiled at her, touched her hand, "canny callee, a master might even pay ye to travel on his ship."

"That might be true if there were any ships in port."

"What?"

"The bay's as empty as a dancefloor the morning after."

"Diachra, m'diachra! It's starving that means, my grath. And farewell to my portraits once old Tavree smells this out, and that's now, I'm fearing. It's riots, dulcerie, fires and death." He looked cautiously around. There were a few more diners in the alcove, but they seemed preoccupied with their own meals and conversations. "Will you be wanting more, Desantro?" he asked with a stiffer formality than he'd used before.

"Nay, Mathen. I've had a sufficiency. More would be too much." Uncomfortable, she gave back the same formality; there was a sinking in her stomach. He wasn't going to help. She could feel him pulling away from her.

A path led from the back of the Eskerichal down to a jetty reaching out into the river through a tangle of cypress trees, reeds and water bushes. It was quiet now, deserted.

"Your lunch came up from here, Des." He took her arm and walked her to the end of the jetty. "Ye wouldna believe how busy the dawn hours are, boats putting in and slipping away again, but there'll be nothing along again till the evening so we can talk here with no ears to listen."

They sat at the end of the jetty looking out over the broad, silt laden river. A small splash caught Desantro's ear and she looked down. An oddity was climbing from the water onto a cypress knee, a little brown man not much taller than her hand was long, with a tangle of weed about his loins, pointed ears and bright black eyes. He perched on the knee and sat looking at her with interest and expectation.

On the long journey from Zam Fadogurum, during the nights when there was nothing else to do but watch the waves tip over, Faan and Desantro had traded stories from their lives to help the time pass faster. A Riverman came up again and again in Faan's tales; he was a pivot point in half the crises of her short life. "Look, there," Desantro said aloud.

"What?" Mathen roused from his reverie. "What was that?"

"There, see?" But as she pointed, the Riverman jumped from the knee and vanished into the murky water.

"A bricha leaping, that's all," Mathen said, annoyance at the interruption sharpening his voice.

Desantro grimaced, but let it drop.

Back in the grip of his worries, Mathen rubbed his hands up and down his thighs. "Empty bay," he muttered. "Empty it is and who can remember when not a single ship was in? And what is Turry Foréach doing about it? Nothing and less than nothing. He paddles in the waters of Mocheery Bay with his callybéagies swimming naked like little fish between his legs. And the Green Man sleeps. . . ." He straightened, twisted around to fix his eyes on Desantro's face. "Boddach Reesh, ye say?"

"Not I, you're the one who named him. A wizard is all I said."

"And how did ye know that? Can ye tell a wizard by the seeing of him?"

"Faan's the magicker, not me. Someone called him wizard and . . ." she hesitated.

"Something happened. The Honeymaid?"

"Whatever. Fa was taken, carried away. I need help, Math. I need to get her out of there."

"I know a strongarm or three who wouldn't cost too much. Where's there? And who is it that has her?"

"It was a copper-haired man who told the wizard what to do. The wizard called him. . . ." She hesitated again. "Glanne something."

"Diachra, m'diachra! The Heir himself. Nay, Des, there's nothing anyone can do for ye. With the best will in the world, nothing and nothing and nothing. Count the lass lost, think of her as dead, for it will not be long till that is true enough. Mourn and dismiss her, my gratha, my sitabéag."

She could hear the cooling in his voice, though his words were as caressing as before. *I was right. He's running like his tail's on fire. Hah! wirrikur, I won't let you bolt without some blood to pay for what you've had.* "Nay, Math. The wizard might have his claws in Fa now, but there's no one yet been able to keep her penned. Help me get to her, Painter. If she blows, she'd burn this city to the ground."

He swallowed, shaded his eyes with his hand, more to hide them than keep the sun away. "Help? I'm only a painter, Des. What can I do against the Turrys?"

"I don't know. If I knew, I'd do it. This is your homeplace, Math. There must be something."

Chewing on the ends of his mustache, his face darkening with anger at being forced like this, he turned his shoulder to her and scowled at the thick brown water flowing with massive force past the end of the jetty. It seemed to spark a memory in him because he straightened with a jerk. "The Blind Man. Ba, that's it. I'll take ye to the Blind Man."

"Who's that?"

"He knows things."

"Diviner or what?"

Mathen bounced onto his feet, reached out to pull her

up beside him. "What," he said. "Diviner, ba, he is that, but more and more, beyond my telling. We will go along by Cewley's Inn and clear out your things, for if ye're to go against the Turrys, ye will not be wanting to destroy the folk who've been kind to ye, my bratha di gratha, then it's off to see the Blind Man. If he will, he can be telling ye more than any other man in all of Cumabyar and in all of Gallindar besides. . . ." He babbled on and on, but she stopped listening.

"Follow the path," the Gate Hag said. She pointed to a narrow gap in the thick stand of young cypresses with ghosts hanging in their rough green foliage like bits of cloud, their indecipherable murmurs a faint background buzz. "Blind Man, he will be the yard beyond, waiting to answer what ye ask him." Desantro waited while the ancient woman limped away, heading for her seat in the Porter's Hutch at the mouth of the alley that led back here.

Apart from the ghost noise, it was very quiet here. Desantro resettled the straps of the bags, the gear from the rooms that Mathen had more or less forced her to clear out and plunged into the odorous shadow under the trees.

I'm going to strangle that wirrikur. I'm going to set my hands around his neck and squeeze. She dropped the bags on one of the few dry tussocks of grass in the sea of mud and squatted beside it, inspecting the Blind Man, cold dread growing in her.

He was fat and pale and hairless, with the face of an idiot baby. Streaks of white scarred the pale blue ringing odd-sized pupils that moved erratically whenever he blinked. One lid sagged lower than the other, the difference exaggerated by his lack of eyebrows. His only clothing was a bulky loincloth streaked with the mud he was planted in. His house was behind the ooze, a lean-

ing hovel, walls weathered gray and covered with lichen, so tottery it seemed to her that a hard gust of
wind would blow it to a pile of splinters.

He thrust his hands into the mud, squeezed and
kneaded it. "What do you want?" he said.

Desantro was surprised by the beauty of his voice, a
musical baritone, full and flexible. She closed her eyes
so she could listen to him and not see him. It would be
easier to feel confidence in him that way. "My friend's
in trouble. She was carried off and I want to get her free
from the man who took her. And I'll need a place where
I can lie up safe while I'm trying to figure out how."

"And how do you plan to pay for my services?"

"I have money," she said, adding warily, "a little."
She ran her tongue over dry lips. "Mathen did say your
fees are reasonable and you won't take money for what
you can't do."

"Don't want money," he said. "Want you."

Desantro scratched at her nose. *Little tik, must be the
only way he gets any kumering. Why not. It'll save my
coin, Faan had most of ours with her. Shut your eyes,
Des, and make him talk to you, it's a grand voice he
has.* "A chaerta," she said, "if you include a visit to a
bathhouse in that plan."

"Fastidious for a beggar."

"I'm no beggar. Forget it. I'll see what I can do on
my own." She got to her feet and reached for the straps
of the gear bags. If she let him muscle her now, there
was no guarantee he'd make any real effort to give her
the help she needed. She had no idea what she'd do or
where she'd go if he let her walk away, but walk she
would.

He must have heard that in her voice, because he
called out hastily, "Sit, sit, byrna amach. No beggar,
that's true. Ba, 'tis true. Sit now and tell me your troubles."

She lowered herself to the wiry grass, sat cross-legged, leaning forward a little, with her hands on her knees. "Nu then, how do I go about this?"

"You saw your friend taken."

It wasn't a question, but she nodded, then remembered and said, "Ba, I saw it."

"You saw who took her?"

"Ba. And heard his name and followed him home."

"And you came to me. Why?"

"Mathen. Ask your Gatekeeper sometime how fast he dumped me and left."

"G' durb. The name?"

"Glanne something. Copper-haired man."

"Ahhh. The Heir himself, was it? Amazing the Painter didn't drop you in the river when he heard that name."

Briefly amused by the Blind Man's percipience, Desantro grinned. "I'm sure he thought of it."

"Nim dwair. You wouldn't be knowing what it's like here." His voice was really singing now, flowing like water into her ears; she closed her eyes and bathed in the sound, a faint drift of hope entering with the words. "All Turrys are tied to Chaggar the Landgod, the Heir more than most, a fact that is ground into every Gallindari from the moment he pops from the womb. The Green Man himself, old Wayyan Dun, has his hand round them, whatever they do, and who can fight a god?"

She opened her eyes. "Who's talking about a fight? I just want to slip my friend loose and get out of here."

He drove his hands deeper into the mud, working it, clawing his finger through it as if it gave him direction or something like that. "A web," he sang to her. "A web of danger and . . . and . . . I can't tease it out . . . tell me the whole of it, byrna amach, every little thing."

"Nu, Faan, that's my friend, she was standing on the wharf looking at this man, the Heir, Glanne whatever it was, and. . . ."

"Nay, begin when Faan your friend put her foot down on Gallindar's land for the very first time."

Desantro wriggled on the grass, wondering just how much she should tell, then decided if she wanted effective advice, she'd better do what he asked. She'd forgotten her disappointment; there was something about the man that jumped over his ugliness and gave her hope, more hope the more she listened to him.

"Cuiller," she began, "he was master of the ship we had passage on, he took off on us because Faan scared the potz out of him when she burned six pirates to the waterline, she's going to be some hot sorcerer once she gets her training. You'd think he'd be happy with that, but he wasn't. Anyway. . . ." She settled into the tale, eyes closed, trying to dredge up every wisp of memory.

He interrupted her only once—when she described the wizard. "Boddach Reesh. Wayyan Dun will be deeper in this than I could read in the mud, or that man would not come near the city. Even for the Foréach."

"That's more or less what Mathen said. What I want to know is, if he never shows up round here, how come everyone knows so much about him?"

"He is the Grand Wizard of Gallindar, byrna amach. The sorréals sing of him in the contests of the Catharreins each Spring and Fall and mothers call upon his name when their children misbehave. After Wayyan Dun, he is the Power of our land." He moved his hands in the mud. "You've told me her name and her gift, but nothing of her appearance. Describe your friend, byrna amach."

She did, but when she'd finished, he only nodded and said, "Go on."

". . . and so I sit here, wondering what you can tell me and if it will be any help at all."

The Blind Man's arms hung loose beside thighs bulging with rings of fat; his hands worked and worked in the mud. The life drained from his pudgy face, his bulbous mouth drooped open, his skin turned gray. Waves moved across the face of the mud, slapped against his legs with squelching sounds that set her stomach churning. She expected the smell to be as revolting as the appearance of the muck, but it wasn't, it was only wet dirt after all, no filth or corruption in it.

The churning went on and on, then subsided as he pulled his hands free and slapped them down on his thighs.

"Honeymaid," he sang to her, his voice soft and crooning. "Gods' weapon made flesh, poor child, over and over used and discarded when the need is gone. Wayyan Dun is sick and so the Land is sick and the Heir is sicker, in head not body. You are right to worry about her. Before he's had her long, she'll be yearning for death. . . ."

"Not Faan," Desantro broke in. "The rest may be right, but that's not. Other folk have tried to contain her and in the end it doesn't work. Even your Grand Wizard will burn unless he's quick enough to leap far and fast when his hold is broken."

The Blind Man dropped his hands in the mud again, squeezing it and kneading it. She'd cracked his concentration, but she wasn't sorry for it. He had to know what Faan was like, or he could make mistakes in his reading that would ruin all of them.

"Wild Magic," he sang suddenly. "That's the key. Call it to you, contain it within you. Take it to the Honeymaid." He shivered, pulled his hands loose again, laid them on his thighs.

"How? I've got no gift. I'm just an ordinary woman, I can't even see the Wildings. Faan can, I can't."

His arm muscles twitched, his eyelids fluttered, his head nodding unsteadily. "The Riverman. Go ask him." He forced his mouth into a smile that made her feel like gagging. "Not now," he said and held out his mucky hands. "Help me up. 'Tis time you paid, O Edaféada."

The ceiling was so low it brushed her hair; in the light from the lowering sun that came through broken shutters and splits in the wall where boards had warped apart, Desantro saw trails of dry, gray mud crossing and criss-crossing the sagging floor and in one corner coarse bedding laid down on rags that crept from beneath the covers, the dried bones of dead clothing.

The Blind Man stopped in the corner opposite the door where the deepest shadows were. "Undress," he said. "And lie down."

Because she could hear in his voice that he expected her to protest or try to ease out of the bargain, she laughed. "I was a slave, didn't you know that? I've had worse on worse." She kicked out of her sandals and began pulling loose her shirt ties. "Talk to me, Blind Man, sing to me. Your voice makes bubbles in my blood."

She pulled off the shirt, dropped it on the blanket, began working on the trousers' lacings, turning as she did so to see what was keeping him.

He was crouching in the corner, his head down so she couldn't see his face.

"Nu, does it offend you I mean to take pleasure from you? Let me tell you, Blind Man, the more I get, the more I give." She stepped out of the trousers, dropped them beside the shirt. "Come here, come to me," she murmured, in almost the same coaxing, cooing tone she'd used to encourage plants to grow.

"Nay," he said suddenly, his voice harsh. He surged onto his feet, bulges bobbling as he moved. "Follow me."

"If we're going back outside, I'll get dressed first."

"No need. Just come."

* * *

"Take my hand. This is my world, so I've put no light in it, only texture and scent."

After the first few turns where the darkness was absolute, soft and black, tucked around them like a thick wool blanket, light appeared that grew gradually stronger, a shimmering nacreous light that danced along the walls of the cavern waking faint rainbows in the washes of crystalline lime. *I'm the first he's brought here or he'd know that.* She reached out carefully, slid her fingers along the nearest wall, silken smooth to the touch—and eerie because her fingers left tracks on the stone and when she pulled her hand back, she brought away ovals of light on her fingertips.

The corridor opened suddenly into a great domed chamber with white stone trees whose leaves were thin-sliced jade, whose fruits were every sort of gem there was, garnet and amethyst, topaz, chrysophrase and tourmaline, peridot, opal, cornelian, jasper, olivine and citrine, sapphire and onyx, and everywhere among the colored stones, teardrops of diamond that caught the magic light and broke it into bright, blinding spears. Flowers grew among the trees, black roses with heavy bittersweet perfumes, night blooming jasmine and stranger blossoms that she'd never seen before. A stream came tumbling down the far wall to end in a lake smooth and black as a polished obsidian mirror.

When they reached the floor of the chamber, he led her through the trees on a grassy path, the grass soft and slippery under her feet; it made her shiver to walk on it, a sort of foreplay. She smiled at the thought and was pleased with herself that she'd planned to give more than she promised. *I said to him, what I get, I give back. And now it seems, what he gets, he gives back tenfold, or a hundred. . . .*

He led her into a pavilion hung with silks and brocades, broideries and corduroys, with quilts laid down over fleeces so clean and soft she slid her feet across

them and sighed with pleasure, then did it again, and
yet again as he echoed her movements, laughing with
her.

"Come," he said. "You wanted a bathhouse, come
see mine."

He led her out the other side of the pavilion and into
an enclosure sketched in white stone lace that had a
deep pool in the middle of it with water from a
warmspring flowing through it, bubbles like glitter scattered through the liquid.

He caught up fistfuls of petal pellets from the alabas-
ter jars placed about the rim and dropped them into the
water. As they opened, trails of delicate perfume rose to
coil round Desantro. He reached out with a confidence
that belied his blindness, slid his hand along the alabas-
ter rail of a spiral ramp. Still not speaking, he went
down the ramp, waded into the center of the bath and
held out his hands to call her to him.

Later, in those sumptuous quilts, he turned to her shy
as a boy with his first love and she taught him a love
song and loved him all the night long.

FAAN
In the Cummiltag, the Turry Palace

Glanne arcosh Turry i Dur and the Wizard Boddach
Reesh stood in a room without windows, watching
while the mute maids dressed the sleeping girl in white
silk and lace and laid her on the bed. One of them went
out, came back with manacles wrapped in soft, sueded
leather dyed white; the maids stretched her arms out
and chained her wrists to the bedposts, then bowed and
left the room.

Glanne arcosh moved to the bedside, touched the
short silvery gray hair that framed the sleeping face. "A

lovely little beast," he murmured. "Tigret you said, ba, true, a silver tigret."

"I warn you again, Glanne arcosh Turry I Dur, this one is dangerous in ways I'm not allowed to speak about. Let her go. You have plenty of women to choose from."

Glanne scowled at him. "It's this one I want and have her I will."

Boddach Reesh bowed, a flash of anger in his eyes. "You are the Heir, Arcosh i Dur. You speak and I obey."

Chapter 19
Grass

Rakil eased himself in the saddle, straightened his back, moved his shoulders. He was weary from the endless riding, even wearier of the company that had descended on them. The Magus might have saved them—Rakil had his own notion about that, figuring once the Tavvas got close enough for Brann to get her hands on them, she'd have scared them so much they'd still be running—but since then that purbog and the snake woman had eaten their food, ridden the spare horses so they had to move slower, stop more frequently to rest the beasts, feed them more grain, even spend part of the day walking, all because they couldn't switch mounts like they'd been dong. And all this time Purb was sitting out there somewhere in Gallindar spending Rakil's money to buy his life another day, another week, leaking coin like a bucket with a hole in it. Anger ate at Rakil's stomach; his food repeated on him, he was getting headaches that would have floored a god.

His head was throbbing now, his eyes blurred and there was a ringing in his ears; he rode beside Brann and watched her turning again and again to scrutinize the Magus as he rode close beside the litter. She wasn't paying attention to the surroundings like she had been before they were attacked, she just watched that curséd Magus pretending he was working on WakKerrcarr and left their protection to the collection of fogs and fiddles she called Graybao. Bad business. This was spooky country. The Fringe she called it. Fringe. Like it was some kind of decoration. After they lost sight of the river there was someone or something prowling about the camp all night, every night, waiting for a chance at the horses or at them. Brann caught two of them after a week of this and left their husks in the brush; that and the attack had kept the prowlers off for a while, but they were back last night. If Brann didn't wake up, the Tavvas were going to start making runs at the horses again.

For the past three days the Magus had stayed beside the dreaming Tak WakKerrcarr, day and night, eating what was handed him, letting that snake woman tend him, wrap blankets around him, as if he were really doing something.

Rakil rubbed at his temple. Chirkin magickers. 'S one thing the jellies had right, keep 'em out. Wish I was back in Tempatoug. . . . He thought about Humarie and a vise closed on his middle, pain like fire rushing through him; his head hurt even more . . . Humarie . . . gods, I can't go back . . . even if I squeeze my money out of Purb . . . it's his fault, stupid old vunkhar, why did he have to blow it? He had a good thing there . . . Humarie. . . .

At the second feed stop on the fourth day after the attack, the Magus seemed to shake himself and come alive. Graybao was off somewhere and Brann was busy inspecting the horses, Kitya helping her, dealing with sores and other problems. Rakil went round after them, putting on feedbags, doling out water, muttering to himself about scutwork and slackers.

The Magus stretched, rubbed at the back of his neck and wandered away from the horses. He found a small rocky hummock with a tuft of grass on the top, lowered himself onto it, and sat waiting for Brann to finish what she was doing and come talk to him.

Rakil kept an eye on him and when Brann started toward the Magus, he eased around behind the hummock and squatted beside a clump of brush where he could hear but not be seen.

"Sa, Navarre. what do you say?"

The Magus smoothed his hand over his hair, seemed surprised to feel his braid hanging down his back. He pulled his hand down, frowned at his fingers. "It is the most complex weaving I have ever seen," he said; he was speaking slowly as if he chose his words with great care. "Last night I followed his timeline to see if I could catch the creation of the web. Fourteen years . . . wasn't easy . . . you were there, asleep . . . WakKerrcarr seemed to be sleeping . . . there was a . . . roughness . . . that's not the right word, but . . . I couldn't read it . . . as if he were . . . linking . . . with a . . . force . . . outside him . . . the web was not there, then it was . . . whole and complete . . . so that was no help. I've tried everything I know, traced every line I could separate from the others, I can stretch them, pull them loose, but I can't find a free end, not even a false end. I could keep on, but the Wrystrike is strong again and the result would almost certainly not be worth the danger. To tell you true, even if I went on, I doubt I'd get anywhere. WakKerrcarr is the only one I know capable of undoing such dense spell weaving."

"You're saying you think he did it himself?" She moved impatiently. "Why not a god?"

"WakKerrcarr is WakKerrcarr. If anyone knows that, you do. A god might destroy him, but not without a great effort and a lot more noise than I saw. Neka, if WakKerrcarr didn't do it alone, he helped. There's not a smell of a threat. It's as if the web is protecting him." He dropped his hands, fingertips resting lightly on his thighs. "It's certainly concealing him. From magesight, I mean. I close my eyes and he's simply not there."

"Ahhh, I think I'm beginning to understand."

"If anyone can."

"We're delivering him to this girl of yours."

"Not mine. Never mine."

"Whatever."

He got wearily to his feet. " 'You'll find the way, Honeychild,' " he said. " 'You'll gather it bit by bit as you pass along the path of discovery.' " He started for the horses.

Brann caught up. "What was that?"

"Tungjii told her that. Faan. He," he nodded at the litter, "he's a bit and I'm a bit and you're a bit, Rakil. . . ." he looked around, nodded at Rakil as he emerged from the brush, fiddling with his belt to make them think that's why he'd gone there. "He's a bit. All the bits she's gathering on her way back to the womb."

"You don't like her much."

"I don't dislike her. She's headstrong, ignorant, abrasive and thoughtless. On the other hand, she has a generous spirit, she's so full of life that even her glooms are stimulating, and she can surprise you into laughing when you don't really feel like it." He pulled himself into the saddle, sat looking down at Brann. "She's too turbulent, that's all."

"She's young."

"Tja, but I doubt she'll grow out of it." He smiled suddenly, his eyes sinking in webs of wrinkles. "I can see her a bent old woman, banging her staff and yelling at someone for walking on her shadow." He touched his heel to the horse's side and moved up to join the snake woman who was riding on the lanky gray Rakil privately called Boneshaker and avoided when he could.

Better her than me, he thought. His head was feeling better, not that there was any reason for that. He couldn't see that the situation had changed. He watched Brann, nodded. She was tending to business again.

*We'll get on with it now. Ia sim, she wants to get there
more than me.*

The Ardafeoyr was a great triangle of rolling grass-
lands tucked in between the Dhia Asatas and the Assatu
Spur called the Baryim Fiacla, dry, hammered by the
sun, kept alive by springs fed from a deep aquifer
where the Green Man lay sleeping for years on end and
by the river Tenyasa which looped in extravagant slow
bends through the grass.

When Rakil followed the litter from the foothills, a
grassfire flickered on the horizon and a pall of gray
smoke covered most of the sky.

Insubstantial gray cloak fluttering like a patch of
smoke torn from that cover, Graybao came over the
knoll directly ahead of them, bending low on the pony's
neck to avoid the limbs of the crooked, stunted trees
growing on its crown.

Brann touched the forward litter horse, stopping it,
then rode to meet her(?). Rakil watched her lean down
and listen intently, then wave Graybao off and come
riding back.

"There's a problem. Graybao has sniffed out a
number of yacchod war parties, all within a day's ride
of here." She spared a smile for Rakil. "If you thought
the Tavvas were bad, they're only thieves, these are out
for blood." The wind blew around them, heavy with
burning smells, breathing an endless sough ough that
was already beginning to get on Rakil's nerves.
"Navarre, will you be able to farsee for us? I have a
strong dislike for plunging into things blindly."

The Magus stroked a spatulate forefinger across the
muscle ticking beside his eye. "At intervals," he said.
"A mirror stirs up the Curse, but doesn't quite prod it
into acting." He frowned. "You sure you want to try? If
they have witches or shamen with them. . . ."

"I'm sure. At least, that it's worth taking the chance. Graybao has gone to search out a spring for us. I've asked for a little-used one, small and out of the way." She made a face. "From what I know of the Grasslanders, some family will be claiming it. Let's hope one of them doesn't come along and show his resentment of trespassers."

The spring was little more than a seep collected in a basin of fired brick that was beginning to crumble. Beside the basin Rakil saw a pile of wet, rotten debris. Graybao had done a rough cleaning before coming back to report and the basin was half-full of clear water. Brann smiled. "Last year's leaves. Good," she said. "We should be safe from disturbance for a few days."

"Days?" Rakil glanced at the packmules. "We're running low on grain and food." He was city-bred, never been more than a short walk from food, water, and shelter; once these supplies were gone, though, he hadn't a clue where they were going to get more and thinking about that put knots in his belly. As far as he was concerned, once he had Purb's neck in his hands and had wrung payment out of him, he was going back to Kukurul and stay where the only bugs he had to worry about were a few fleas and roaches, where someone else would cook his food and clean his clothes, where he wouldn't be bored to the point of ossification.

"When we reach a river landing, we won't have to worry about supplies," Brann said impatiently. "This is the beginning of the prime trading season."

"With a war going on?"

"Did that ever stop Purb? I doubt it. War or no war, there'll be trade barges on the river. People have to eat. And arm themselves."

"You've got the say, I'm along for the ride, that's all."

Brann looked thoughtfully past him at Navarre and

Kitya standing beside the mules, inspecting the small barren hollow, the sparse grass, pale hardpan and dusty grey stones baking under a sun whose heat was barely lessened by the veil of smoke it had to pass through. "According to the Sibyl I need you," she said dryly, "so keep your hair on, Rakil; I'll take good care of you. We'll leave as soon as I'm sure what we're riding into. It's a fool who outruns her data." The litter horses were moving restlessly, making the wood and canvas structure creak in an irritating, irregular rhythm. "Tsah! This is wasting time, let's get the camp set up." Over her shoulder, as an afterthought, she said, "If you're so anxious to know about Purb, why don't you ask Kitya to point him for you?"

"I don't know if I can." Kitya pressed her thumb against her mouth and looked vaguely around as if she sought something that wasn't there. "The Shawar said I'd be stronger . . . still, no homeplace . . . not really . . . no proper herbs. . . .

Rakil waited impatiently for her to make up her mind; the camp was as quiet as the circling biters would let it be, the air heavy with heat and particulate from the dozen fires to the west of them. Navarre had contrived a patch of shadow for himself with a few sticks and a blanket. He was stretched out in the shade, a wet scarf wrapped about his head, covering his eyes, trying to sleep and build the strength he needed for the mirror. Brann was leaning into the litter, giving WakKerrcarr a sponge bath, murmuring to him though he probably couldn't hear her. Graybao materialized for an instant, then was gone again in one of her(?) scouting prowls. *Tungjii kiss the creature, sharpen her(?) nose.* Even the mules were half asleep, browsing now and then on the tender ends of the scrub or tonguing loose mouthfuls of the sun-dried grass.

He touched Kitya's arm. "There's nothing happening now, who can be sure about later?"

She blinked at him. "Vema, I'll try it. No promises. I have to find some herbs first and a bit of bone. Do you have anything I can use as a tie? If Purb has touched it, that'll be even better."

"I've a cloak of his, I can unravel some thread from it. And there are some earstuds he wore. Gilded bronze. Does metal matter?"

"Iron's stubborn and angry, silver augments, bronze leans into you. The studs will do just fine, so get them ready. And . . . while I'm hunting for what I need, would you find a bit of ground that's smooth and flattish, sweep it off and lay a fire for me. Mh. Away from here, at least two hummocks between it and Navarre. Otherwise, for sure I can't do it."

Rakil sat in the meager shade of one of the low twisty trees that grew on the hillocks, frowning as he watched Kitya redo what he'd already done, moving her hands and knees over the carefully swept dirt, brushing at it with her fingertips, picking off the smallest fragments of leaf or bird dung, even worm castings. She was graceful as the serpent her faint scaling suggested, the same sinuous strength, a curious combination of opposites, soft and hard, fierce and tender—he licked dry lips, understanding finally something of the attraction she had for the Magus.

She reassembled the sticks for the fire, worked over them until they were burning steadily, then sat on her heels and gazed gravely up at him. "Come down now, Rakil. Sit across the fire from me and think of Purb. Try not to let anger slide in, remember the better times. If you can. It'll help and I need all the help I can get since there's no blood bond between you."

* * *

Kitya dropped two fuzzy gray-green leaves into the fire, releasing a pungent, not-quite-unpleasant odor, passed the wingbone of a bird through the smoke and chanted some words filled with vowels and clicks.

> *Illeeyuga nah'meh ham'meh*
> *Purb pak't Flea ak'nona inalayyah*
> *Owha okanoah ana okah*
> *Rakil ah'ke'a ya ka'ayan*
> *Keech koh kai kanayayeh.*

She reached down beside her knee, lifted with slow care a twist of paper that held a reddish-brown dust she'd scraped from the top of a dry mushroom, tipped the dust into the fire. It burned with an eerie green as she chanted some more.

> *Naga ney a whana hey*
> *Ahey kuna Rakil a'ya'goa*
> *Keech kaneeyeh owha koa*
> *Illeeyuga Purb onga 'yowey.*

She circled the fire with her arms, held out her hands, palm up. Rakil dropped the earstuds in her right hand and the coil of thread picked from Purb's cloak in the other.

Still chanting, she looped the cord about the studs, bound them to the bone with intricate knots she tied so fast he couldn't follow the motions of her fingers. Then she tied a black feather, a white one, and several mottled brown ones to the bone.

> *Owka owka otouka owka*
> *Neeya illeeya*
> *kechkech kaneh eeya*
> *EEEE YAAAH!*

She tied more knots, drew out a long loop of thread, whipped more thread about the loop, making a cord strong enough to hold it by, all the time passing the kech again and again through the diminishing trails of smoke. She broke off the remainder of the thread, dropped it into the fire, then waited.

When it had burned to a fine line of gray ash, she beckoned to him, but as he reached for the kech, stopped him just before he touched it. Remembering what she'd told him, he bent over the fire, drew in a lungful of the smoke, held it until he was nearly choking, then let it trickle out again. This time, when he reached for the thread, she let him take it and chanted a short couplet.

Ohla esshon a-oka
Neeya anna a-noka

She cracked her hands together.

Rakil swung the kech away from the fire, held it as far from him as he could, hanging free at the end of the cord. "Pa-Purb," he cried, his voice hoarse from the smoke.

For a moment the kech swayed aimlessly with the shaking of his hand, then it plunged about like a bird at the end of a leash, finally whipped around and froze, pointing south and a little west. They were heading in the right direction and the strength of the tug was a measure of how close they were.

Sweat beads popped out on his face. "Tuzra," he said.

The strain went off the cord, the kech went dead.

"Pa-Purb," he said.

Once again the wing bone plunged about and tugged at his fingers, pointing the same way it had before.

"Tuzra."

Hands shaking, he tucked the kech into the tiny tubu-

lar container Kitya had woven from blades of grass.
"K'berk. It's been a long chase."

Kitya nodded. "I felt that." Talking as she worked,
she bent down and began scraping sand into a rampart
about the coals. "Remember, don't activate it around
Navarre. All you'll have left will be garbage." She
pushed a section of the rampart onto the fire and began
scraping the rest of it inward. "And for a little extra
surety, keep it next to your skin as much as you can."

He got to his feet, tucked the kechtube into his shirt
so it rested just above his belt. His mouth was so dry he
could almost feel his teeth cracking and the taste of the
smoke lingered on his tongue, the smell of it in his
nose. "K'berk," he said again, and left her on that glaring, oven-hot patch of sand, using a handful of dried
weeds to brush away the marks they'd left.

The Wounded Moon was a pale blur in the mix of
cloud and smoke, summer clouds as dry as the smoke,
promising nothing but heat, melting with the dawn so
they didn't even give a measure of protection from the
sun. Rakil sat in the shadows at the rim of the light
from the dying fire, a small fire built in a hollow
Navarre had dug into the slope beside the seep.

Graybao materialized beside Rakil suddenly, a
ragged patch of gray focused on the Magus, her(?) curiosity so strong it was like a perfume. This was the
third time she(?)'d done that, so he didn't flinch and
swear as he had before, just glared at her(?), then went
back to waiting for the Magus to make up his mind
what he was going to do.

The snake woman sat beside Brann, her head on her
knees. The Magus had spent the last ten minutes telling
her what a fool she was to fiddle round with unneces-
sary magic here, did she think the yacchods didn't have
noses who'd sniff that out? And lots more complaints
like that. Whipping the woman after she was down and

miseried to death. Brann tried to explain, but he told her it wasn't her business and keep out. Rakil would've enjoyed that if he liked the Magus more or trusted him. Drinker of Souls, phah! Interfering bitch who got her kicks sticking her nose in men's business. He touched the small bulge above his belt, the kech in its tube. Snake woman . . . Kitya . . . she was the best of the lot. Leave her alone, porbut. If you're going to do your thing, get on with it, but shut your pichrin' mouth. . . .

He touched the tube again, stroked his thumb over the small round. He's close . . . so close . . . a few days. . . .

Navarre dropped to the sand and sat with his legs loosely crossed, his knees almost touching Brann's; he let his head hang, then snapped it back, sucked in long breaths, exploded them out, over and over and over until he was swaying dizzily, his eyes ringed with white.

He spread his hands and a film delicate as a soap bubble shimmered between them.

"Ask," he said. His voice seemed to come from a great distance, bringing echoes with it.

Brann leaned forward so she could look into the film. "Show me the safest route to the Tenyasa."

IMAGE:	Overhead view of the grasslands. A black dot quivered a moment at the edge of the map, then extruded a line from one side. The line leapt almost directly north, paused at a small blue dot.
NAVARRE:	First Camp, Spring Faiyad
IMAGE:	The line crept slowly this time, moving west for about half the distance of the first leg, pausing beside a large, irregular blue circle.
NAVARRE:	Chaggar's Pool, truce ground, rest and resupply.

IMAGE:	The line plunged south and west, paused again.
NAVARRE:	Third camp. Dry.
IMAGE:	The line raced straight west and merged with the wider blue line of the river as it swayed in a deep bend to the east.

The echoes gone from his voice, replaced by weariness, Navarre said, "There's a takull brake, thickets of béalberries on both sides of the river, good concealment, no locals to make trouble."

"Or give us any help." Brann scowled at the map. "We need a barge. We can leave the mules behind, but we have to have horses for the litter, at least that."

Once more the Magus bent over the mirror, his head almost touching hers. "Ask," he said.

Rakil shifted uneasily on his patch of hillside. The wind had died, silence was a blanket over the hollow, pressing down on it, pressing down on him until he could hardly breathe. More than that, the air around him had a thick greasy feel that churned his stomach. If this was what the chirkin Magus meant when he said Wrystrike, then he'd better pull his horns in before he got them ground into the hardpan.

Rakil caught a shimmer of gray in the corner of his eye. Graybao was back a fourth time, leaning forward, her(?) insubstantial form trembling with excitement. It's got her(?), too. Chir! There's nobody on watch. He checked his belt to make sure the sling was tucked through the loops, then got quietly to his feet and walked into the darkness.

The smother dropped away as he left the hollow and moved through the dry hummocks, trying to walk as quietly as Graybao but making considerably more noise than he liked to think about. He stepped on stones that turned under his foot and nearly threw him, snagged his toes on roots that for some reason crooked up out of the ground; twigs broke and grass rustled.

He slowed up and that seemed to help and as his eyes adapted to the dark, he began enjoying the walk.

Wind that was almost cool moved across his face, taking with it the tension and anger that'd built in him since the Magus started his tirade, then his magicking. *The snake woman's kind of magic is more my style,* he thought. *It's a human sort of doings.*

He glanced toward the camp and went into a brief panic when he couldn't see the light from the fire; he took another step, started breathing again as a faint glow touched the branches of a tree. He changed direction and began making his way in a slow circle, watching for that glow as the trees obscured, then revealed it. Getting lost out here would be a humiliation that would half kill him. Chir! Every one of them had some kind of magic but him. He was a passenger, only reason Brann hung onto him was what the Sibyl said. He stopped, stared up at the hazy moon. *And the Sibyl said nothing, just answered yes to a question that Brann put all the work into. And said to me what was obvious, I was going into Gallindar with Brann. The doubletalk you got when you were read for free, a hook to bring you back with gold to cross the palm.*

Once when Purb was tapped out (a combination of bad judgment and bad luck even worse than the Shifter mess), with moneylenders breathing blood down his neck, he installed Rakil in a street booth with a deck of cards, Rahman Baroman the Wonder Boy, and got himself up as the pseudo-Rahman's flunky and shill. Rakil learned all the tricks there were that year, all the ways to coax the silver from a money sac and tips from silly women who took a fancy to a smooth-skinned youth. All in all, it wasn't a year that did much for his self-esteem or his view of humankind. And this smelled a lot like that.

He blundered on in his ragged circle, the watch-walking an excuse to stay away from the fire; he'd never surprise anyone this way, he knew it well enough, but there was a certain satisfaction in doing something—even badly—that someone else should have taken care of.

Graybao appeared so suddenly he swore and jumped back, swore again as he found himself in a thorn bush. "What is it?" he said as he began detaching himself from the thorns.

She(?) gestured toward the fugitive light, then drifted off, back to doing the rounds.

Must be finished, he thought. *Hope Brann learned what she needed. Gods! If we have to do it again.* . . .

The Chained God Unchained felt the tickle of the Wrystrike, let the shriveled husk of the Wieldy Hugwuhpady drop into its holdland, and bent from the godrealm to inspect the source of the tickle. "Power damnéd, can't I get rid of any of them?" Huffing and puffing with annoyance and satiety, he slapped half a dozen of the nearest war bands into riding at the seep, then reached into Kyatawat again, snagged the Wieldy Dubdukawudy and began eating him without pleasure or anticipation. Seeing Navarre come back nearly untouched from the dozen universes he'd passed through, seeing Kitya, seeing Rakil, all of them heading straight for that girl, it was enough to take any god's appetite away.

As Rakil came into the shrinking circle of light, Kitya lifted her head. "My pum's tingling like it's got the mange. We have to get out of here. Now." She was on her feet, a spring uncoiled, running for the pile of gear.

The Magus rubbed his hand across his face. "We lost, Brann. Somebody sniffed us." He set his hands on his thighs and levered himself up.

Rakil was about to ask what was going on, but Graybao whistled in like a hiss on the end of Navarre's s, a streak of gray smoke that went vertical without gaining much definition. She(?) uttered a quavering shriek that brought Kitya around, staring, a saddle in her hands. Navarre straightened. Brann turned to look at her(?).

Graybao spoke, her voice the whiny rustle of hot wind in high grass. "Sssix directionsss, sssix bandsss, riding hhhere, blood in eyesss, hhhhate. We go?"

"We go."

"Brann!"

She turned, frowning. Navarre had crossed the hollow to stand beside the litter. "These yacchod, they'll be trackers," he said, "used to running down stray boggs. You want to know how good herdsmen can be at that, ask Kitya sometime about her folk. And they have to have someone with farsight . . . or, I suppose, farsmell, with them. I've an idea for that last, tell you later if it works. You'd better find some means of blowing away our traces, otherwise it's no use running."

"I'll do that. Kitya, Rakil, get the mules packed and the horses saddled. I'll be with you a minute. Graybao, you're our best hope for. . . ."

Her voice faded as she bent her head close to the servant's sketch of a face. Rakil shrugged and went to join Kitya.

"Kat, come here."

Kitya straightened, pushed sweaty straggles of hair out of her eyes. "V'ret, we've still got. . . ."

"Just for a moment. I need you to try something."

She sighed. "Sorry, Rakil, be back soon as I can."

He shook the saddle, swore under his breath as it shifted loosely. "Ia sim. When I see you. Suck it in, you porbut, haven't got time for this hoytch." He unbuckled the cinchstrap, lifted the saddle, then slammed it down again and hauled on the strap, getting it tight enough to suit him before the beast could blow up again. The small victory flushed out his irritation; he grinned, scratched the gelding under his chin, then went on to the next beast, his ears cocked so he could hear what was happening with the Magus.

"Kat, I've hooked into the web around WakKerrcarr and teased it out until it should cover us, if we keep close enough."

Rakil glanced at them in time to see Kitya nod; she was listening with her whole body. *Someday I'm going to have a woman like that, gentler though, softer. Like Humarie. . . .*

"You've got a touch of magesight, I've never asked you how far it reaches."

"About ten handtigs . . . that's about here to where I made the kech."

He frowned. "You don't need to go that far. Just over the hill there," he pointed, "so you can't see us, then you try if you can feel us. You understand?"

She snorted. "I'm not an idiot, V'ret."

He stroked his forefinger along her face. "But I am, it seems. Ah! there isn't time. I need to know if I've done what I think I've done. So on your way, Kat."

Over her shoulder, she said, "Count on it, V'ret, when we're out of this, you and I will talk."

She came trotting back a moment later. "Nothing there," she said. "That's all?"

"All I need."

"Then let's get out of here."

* * *

They rode north from the seep, following the route laid down by the mirror, Brann leading with Kitya holding the guide reins for the forward litter horse. Navarre was in the litter, lying beside WakKerrcarr, holding the web around them to hide them from the magesight. Rakil rode behind the litter, leading the mules, the spare horses linked to them; despite the urgency around him, he was more relaxed than he had been. With Graybao as a wind behind them, blowing away hoofprints and other debris, fluffing up crushed grass, doing what she(?) could to erase any signs that folk had passed here, with the Magus in there blocking sha-noses, they might, just might, have a chance of sneaking free of this trap.

He snickered under his breath. Sneaking? It was absurd. Four riders, nearly a dozen horses, three mules, two semi-corpses in a litter and a flying fog. He sobered quickly. It'd be even more absurd sitting and waiting to get slaughtered. Six warbands? Gods!

He thought about slipping away, losing himself in the grass and letting this circus attract attention away from him. The problem with that was he'd likely get lost in truth and either die of thirst or end up in the middle of one of those warbands and get chopped for his trouble. Later, though, once they got to the river. . . .

Now that he had the kech, he didn't need Brann to find Purb for him. It was a pleasant thought. Since she'd nearly drained the life out of him, he'd walked on tiptoe around her, smiling like a good little slave. One of Purb's early lessons. You don't ruffle feathers on someone who can hurt you. Now that he could get free of her, he acknowledged how much he hated her for making him cringe again, turning him into the helpless baby he'd been when Purb bought him. He wasn't a boy any longer, he was a man. On top of all that, she attracted trouble like dead meat brought flies. The farther he could get from her, the faster, the better he'd like it.

Not yet though.

They rode into the night in a whirl of little sounds that traveled with them, Graybao the wind whispering behind them, rattles of pebbles, snapping twigs, grass rustles, the creaking of the litter, the saddles, the mule packs, the clinks from the bridles and other metal objects knocking together. Rakil coughed as a gust that was part Graybao and part nightwind slapped dust and leaf fragments against the back of his head and swirled them around into his eyes and nose.

It was a peculiar flight, a creep into the dark with a long stop every two hours to feed, water, and rest the horses and mules. At each stop, Brann came quietly to Kitya and Rakil, laid her hands on them and drank from them, then leaned into the litter and transferred the energy to Navarre.

Then they moved on.

At the third stop Graybao reported that two of the warbands were almost at the seep, two more were farther out but close to crashing into each other.

At the forth stop Graybao came chuckling like wind over standpipes. She(?) announced that the bands at the seep were walking around each like strange cats. It appeared they were nominally on the same side in the war, but not all that happy about it. The other two were enemies and were too busy killing each other to bother about intruders in the grass.

Brann rubbed at the crease between her brows. "You're beyond the web when you search like that, what if the shamen or whatever they've got smell you out?"

A shadowy hand smoothed the front of her(?) robe,

her(?) stance oozed smugness. "Thhhat lot, thhhey're barely sssparkusss, not a conflagration like our Chhhezin thhhere." Shedding fragments of fog that melted into the moonlight, she(?) waved toward the litter. "If one doesss not wisssh to be sssseen, only hhhim could sssee one. Them? Hhhardly. Nor man nor mage can follow usss."

At the seventh stop Graybao came in more soberly. "A new band hasss reached the sssseep, it'sss attacking the othersss. The two thhhat were fighting hhhave broken off, hhheading away, back to their own dissstrictsss, about hhhalf of them are dead, the othersss wounded. Thhhere isss a difficulty ariisssing, thhhough, more bandsss are coming thisss way. Thhhey're far yet, but thhhey come."

They reached Spring Faiyad when pink was streaking the east.

Rakil looked around from the mules where he was unhooking the ropes and taking the packs down as Navarre came from the litter, shaking with exhaustion despite the energy Brann had fed him. The Magus moved to a blanket Kitya had laid down for him, walking like an old old man.

So he's finally earning his food. It's about time. Sa, that means the web's collapsed. Chir! Uneasy, stomach churning, Rakil went back to work, fussing now about the chance some warband could come riding in any minute. This wasn't a seep, it was a well with drinking troughs and a sod corral in good repair and there were fresh hoofprints in the mud.

Kitya hurried to Navarre, took his arm. "V'ret. . . ."

"Nu nu, Kat, I'm all right. Better than I look. The Strike can't reach me in there. The weight's gone off me; I've had it so long I didn't realize how heavy it was. It's coming back now. Coming back. . . ."

"Nu, V'ret, sit down and rest and I'll bring you some soup. You'll feel better when you've got food in your k'nar."

After the horses and mules were stripped and herded into the corral, Rakil took soup and bread from Brann, then went to sit with his back braced against the sod, watching the others and worrying about what was happening out in the grass.

Navarre drained his mug, set it on the blanket beside him, drew his hand across his mouth, wincing as his palm rasped on the stubble darkening his face.

Kitya caught hold of his hand as he lowered it. "Lie down, V'ret, I'll shave you."

He smiled at her, tightened his fingers about hers, rubbed his thumb across her palm. "Later, Kitkat. If I lie down now, I'd be asleep before the water was hot."

Brann looked up. "Graybao said the grass round here is starting to swarm with yacchod. It can't be the war, that doesn't make sense. So what's drawing them?"

Navarre was watching Kitya who was at the well, tipping water into a fire-blackened pot. He moved his shoulders, hauled his knees up, rested his arms on them. "A frightened god," he said.

"What?"

"Frightened of Faan."

"She isn't anywhere near here."

"Doesn't matter. You're a bit and I'm a bit and Kat's a bit, remember? He kills us and Faan's weakened somehow."

"I know gods can be stupid, but. . . ."

"Kat, come here. Tell Brann what the Shawar said about the enemy."

With her usual unstudied grace, Kitya dropped onto the blanket beside him. "Mm. Let me see." She laid a long, narrow hand across her eyes. " 'Your god wants change to end, he wants no surprises, he wants to extirpate every possible danger to his existence.' That's what one of them said. Another one said, 'In the end the only way to achieve total safety is to destroy everything that lives. He does not know it, but that is where he aims.' "

Brann looked startled, then angry. "I know him," she said. "I know who it has to be."

The Magus woke up at that. "Don't say his name or you'll call him. We've had enough attention from that source."

"Bem, you're right. I'll just say I've had experience with that one I'd rather not repeat. A lot of people ended up hurt or dead and he got what he wanted." She walked to the litter, stood frowning out at the grass. "I didn't have any choice then. . . ." She stroked her hand along the wood frame of the litter. "And I don't now. . . ." She turned to him, her mouth twisted in a half smile. "Though this time I'm just a bit in the background. Poor Faan. If he's organized this mess we're in, I wonder what he arranged for her? Spring Faiyan . . . I said safest way to the river, that should mean the warbands won't find us here. Magus?"

Navarre was stretched out on the blanket, his eyes closed, while Kitya was working soap into a lather on his face. He cracked an eye. "Maybe. It's the wrong direction. They'll expect us to be going south."

Kitya finished with the lathering. "Those that are left after they finish killing each other. Be quiet now. I don't want to slice off your nose or some bit equally important."

"A minute, Kat. Brann, Graybao's still on watch?"

"Mm. Why?"

"How long can she(?) go without rest?"

"She(?)'s been resting for fourteen years. Believe me, she(?)'s enjoying herself. In any case, we've broken the backtrail enough by now, she(?) can gather energy tonight, once we're moving again."

He closed his eye, let his head fall back. "One of these days, when we're out of this, I'd like to know her(?) history."

They slept undisturbed through the heavy, punishing heat of the day and at sundown they started west, heading for Chaggar's Pond, riding with the same slow care and wariness.

Chapter 20
Prisoner and Plotter

FAAN

Faan woke in a room without windows.

Her wrists were locked into manacles padded with soft white leather. Her legs were free and she wasn't uncomfortable, but she was as helpless as a bird with clipped wings. For several frantic moments she twisted and kicked, but the core under the soft leather wrappings on the manacles and the short chains bolted to the bedposts were fine steel, the posts themselves were gilded and chased, but they, too, were steel.

She gave up the struggle for the moment and lay panting in a tangle of white silk sheets. *Nayo nayo, girl, don't be a fool. You can't break yourself loose. Use your head. It's all you've got left.*

She straightened out, lifted as much of herself as she could so she could see more than the ceiling.

The bed was wide and longer than most, meant for a man wider and taller than most. She was lying in white silk sheets with a pillow in a silk sham under her head. Her hair was combed, she was clean and not naked as she'd expected when she woke and realized where she was, but wearing a shift, white silk and fine lace, that slid sensuously about her body with every small move.

Across the room a tall white candle burned on a gold stand, the steady flame blurred by the perfumed mist the candle was giving off, a clean, piny fragrance that surprised her, it seemed unsuitable to the purposes of this room.

The floor was covered with white fur, so clean it looked like threads of ice.

Three of the walls were unadorned, smooth white tiles fitted so tightly together that the surface was almost seamless. She glanced at the fourth wall, looked hastily away, clamping her teeth on her tongue as she fought to control the nausea that threatened to choke her.

Memories. . . .

Rape and a whipping and the dead she left behind. . . .

Jea and Dawa sitting on the stairs, talking about clients to avoid, what happened to another Salagaum last week, saying I took one look at his toys and told him nayo nay that wasn't my thing. . . .

Zembee, one of Mama Kubaza's girls, what her face and body looked like after the pain freak got her. . . .

Mamay Reyna lying in stench, bones broken and thrusting through skin mottled with bruises, smeared with blood, fingers crushed, tongue torn out, eyes gouged out and thrown like smashed grapes onto his chest. . . .

"Nayo!" she shouted at the emptiness around her. "I won't remember. Abeyhamal made him whole. I paid the price and SHE did it! He's whole . . . he. . . ."

Sobbing, gasping, she wrenched at the manacles round her wrists and called fire. *CALLED*. **CALLED.**

Nothing.

Since Valdamaz, fireworms had crawled through her sinews, getting stronger and stronger, threatening to bore out through skin and bone, consume her and everything around her.

They were gone.

She went still. "I'm empty."

An idea struck her, startled a laugh out of her. "I've been wormed. Like a pet dog."

She was still giggling when the door opened and the copper-haired man walked into the room.

The Chained God Unchained glanced into the room. "Hysteria. Sweet, sweet." He thought about watching longer, then shrugged and went back to his eating.

DESANTRO

Desantro looked at the bit of paper with characters she couldn't read scrawled across it. "What should I wear? What's he going to expect to see?"

The Blind Man chuckled. "Desa, ah Desa, how would I know?"

"Hunh! Like you know everything else. Nu nu, I suppose it isn't that important. Long as I'm neat and cringe a lot."

"A little more than you did with me, sitabéag, but not a lot. He's a prickly man, Wayyan Grual is, but he wants workers not culpoggas."

She set the paper on the table beside the hairbrush he'd found for her, touched his arm. "Fadha fadhin, tell me, this won't get back to you?"

"Nothing you do will bring hurt to me, that I swear 'tis true."

"A chaerta, Riverman first, then Grual. Let's see if I remember. Along the canal to the High Aqueduct, follow the arches to the Shaddegair at the backside of the Cummiltag Wall, ask for Grual and give him your note. You SURE you want me to use your name?"

"Name?"

"Whatever." Despite bringing her to his secret place,

he hadn't told her his name, didn't now; that bothered her, but she could accept his lingering mistrust. He had plenty of reason for it. "I remember too well Mathen's face when he heard what happened and understood what I meant to do."

"There are advantages to being what I am, sitabéag." He smiled and stroked her arm. "They aren't immediately apparent, but ah my grua, ah my durlchéan, even Chaggar will let me be."

The morning was warm, perfumed with the touch of overripeness that belonged to the days near Midsummer's Eve. The wind that almost always blew along the streets of Cumabyar was busy this morning, a playful wind, tugging at scarves, teasing hair, lifting dry leaves and other small debris, then casting its burden against the painted walls. The paintings reminded Desantro of Mathen and she felt a twinge at the memory of how abruptly he dumped her, only a twinge that went quickly away. It was too easy to understand why he did it. She was a stranger, meant to be a night's pleasure and a day's romance, a link that would break at the slightest pressure. He had family here who could get hurt, friends; why should he prefer her to them?

It was cooler by the river, the wind brisker, making the cypresses murmur and bend, the reeds bow low; when it began to tease her hair into a bird's nest of tangles, she took out the scarf she'd asked the Blind Man to find for her and wound it around her head, tucking the ends in so they wouldn't tickle her neck. She hated things on her head, she always had, but observation had shown her that women covered their heads in public. Sometimes it was only a gesture, a delicate, translucent veil, but there was always something. She hadn't meant to put it on quite this soon, but that didn't matter. She grinned. *What a potz you were, Des, asking the Blind*

Man what to wear. Good thing he took it right. But then he's a surprising man all round. Man . . . mmmmm. . . .

There was a loud splash, then several drops of water hit her face. She turned.

Riverman had climbed one of the bitts along the side of the jetty and settled himself atop it, his tiny heels tucked into cracks in the wood. "Yah," he said, his voice like a mosquito's whine; he sat staring at her, digging thoughtfully into the weed around his loins.

Desantro stared back, uncertain how to feel. Despite her experiences with Faan, she still wasn't used to these oddities of magic that popped up everywhere. She searched for words to lead up to what she needed from him, found none and said abruptly, "I have a friend."

"Honeymaid," Riverman squeaked at her.

"She says that's nonsense."

"What does she know?" He shrugged. "'Tis true."

"Whatever. She was carried off. I need to break her free. One told me you might help."

"HE cho scared a her, HE sweating rivers, lakes, will be oceans soon enough. Over and over HE push this man and that, this thing and that, try to kill her, try and try. Din't work, yah? Keeps trying. Got Chaggar on it now. Cho, troubles and troubles."

She tapped her fingers on her knee. "Who is this HE?"

Riverman scratched uneasily at his weed, cracked a waterflea between tiny thumbnails and flicked the debris into the turgid water by the jetty. "Can't say. Littl'un. Get tromped should I talk too much. Do what I can. That is true, ba, true."

"Hmm. One said to me, collect the Wild Magic, get it to my friend. One said to me, Riverman will call it for you. Or tell you how to call it."

"Ba, ba. 'Tis easy. Honeymaid, she draw the Wildings, bees to bloom, ba ba. You go inside the Wall?"

"I will be trying."

"Yah hah, you will do. Come to River each morn and stand where you sit now. Wildings will nest aneath you skin. You take 'm inside, Honeymaid will call 'm. Cho?"

"That's all?"

"Why fuss up a simple thing?" He jumped to his feet, sketched a salute at her, then dived into the thick dark water, the rings of his passing blown away by the wind almost before his heels had vanished.

Desantro blinked, glanced at the sun. There was time to get something to eat, but the thought of food nauseated her. She rose, brushed off her trousers, retied the scarf and started for the canal.

Tucked deep within the massive wall, the Shaddegair was a shabby wooden door with a hatch in it. *Lowlives Hole, that's what it means, even if it doesn't say that. Nu, knock . . . diyo, that's it, k'thump k'thump. So, answer will you? If it's that hard to hear, you should have a bell.*

Something brushed her ankle. She looked down. Ailiki was pressing close against her, half hiding behind her leg. "Nu, furface," she murmured, "still trying to get in? Tsa, be patient, we'll see what we'll see."

The hatch slid back and a sullen face looked out. "What you want?"

"Wayyan Grual. I have a note for him."

The guard thought that over, then the slide squeaked shut and she heard fumbling thumps on the far side of the planks. Ailiki pressed harder against her leg.

The gate swung open a short distance. Desantro walked through the narrow gap easily enough though there was something like cobwebs that resisted her briefly. She pushed and it let her through. Behind her, she heard an angry squeal. She looked over her shoulder. The mahsar was beating at the air with her forepaws, wailing her outrage and her grief.

The guard ignored the beast, swung the gate shut and thunked the bar home. "Gawl," he yelled. "Get out here." He turned to Desantro. "Gawl, he'll take you to the Kuic's office."

The Gardener Kuic (who did the work though a Turry cousin had the title of Garden Koil) was a short, wiry man with a neatly trimmed beard and mustache, silver-gray and less than a thumb's width long. He looked at the paper on the desk in front of him, then at Desantro. "Do you know what this says?"

"Nay. I don't read Galladash."

"Hmm." With slow, meticulous movements, he rolled the paper into a spill, held it to the dishlamp flame and watched it char to black ash. He scraped the ash into a bin beside the desk, brushed his hands together, and got to his feet. "Come with me."

They passed numbers of workers hauling away fresh plants from the sheds, bringing back those whose blooms had faded. Grual nodded to several, ignored the rest. Desantro felt them watching her, but she thought it wiser not to notice.

The workshed Grual took her to was a long, open building with a thatched roof and a bench running down the middle, a whitemetal sheet covering the wood and potted plants scattered along it. At one end there was a bronze pump with a flared mouth that gaped like a gargoyle over a deep basin. Tools hung on hooks on the sections of wall between the wide, unglazed windows. Two women were working at a table near the other end, transplanting seedlings from flats to small redclay pots. They stopped talking when Grual came in, kept their eyes on their work as long as he and Desantro were in the shed.

Wayyan Grual set a short, tapered finger on the rim of a pot that held a scraggly, overgrown plant that looked a little like the mafua bushes that popped up everywhere in Zam Fadogurum. "Tell me about this."

Desantro bent over the plant, examined the axils, the leaves, the growing points at the end of the branches, scraped away the soil near the main stem, crushed one of the leaves between thumb and forefinger, sniffed at it. She sighed with pleasure at the feel of leaf and soil; it'd been far too long since she'd done work she truly loved. "It's a healthy plant gone leggy. I'd say all it needs is pruning, though it's late in the season for that, or would be if I were where I worked before. I haven't been here long enough to understand the growing patterns."

"We have more than one season, there's water for it and sun." He smiled. "You're right, though, it was left on its own longer than it should be. Prune it. Let me see how you'd do it."

Wayyan Grual took her along the bench and tested her again and again, and was pleased and smiling when he finished. "It was no lie, you do know plants," he said as he led her to the basin and waited while she pumped water so she could wash her hands.

Desantro sniffed. "Unless you're bone from ear to ear," she scrubbed at her nails, using a battered brush with half its bristles missing, "anything you do for twenty years, you'll know well enough."

Grual handed her a towel that was worn thin and soft with many washings. "I know some who'd learn nothing if they did a job twice that long."

She could hear the curiosity in his voice; he wanted to ask why the Blind Man was cadging work for her, but whatever made him read the note and burn it was strong enough to strangle his questions unborn. And squeeze a courtesy out of him that he didn't show many others—that was evident in the way his workers acted round him. *Tungjii kiss you sweet, Blind Man. I don't know what I'd do without you.*

Wayyan Grual settled himself behind the desk, folded his delicate hands. "Your skills are considerable, byrna amach. And you understand what questions to ask to fill in what you don't know of local conditions. I'm going to set you to work under Megglen Bris in the Currtle Garden where the Turry Daughters walk. I won't bother giving you instructions as to how you should conduct yourself if a Daughter should happen to pass by you. Watch Bris and do what she does. Questions?"

"Nay. I learned my trade in palace grounds."

"Ahaaahhhah." It was the arc of breathy sound she'd first heard from Mathen's mouth, then again and again throughout the city. "One silver a month and you find your own lodging." He unlaced his fingers, tapped his thumbs on the desk top. "If you were Gallindaree, you could have a room with the maids, but as a foreigner you must be clear of the Cummiltag an hour before sundown each day. Is that acceptable?"

"Most generous. When do I begin?"

"You will present yourself at the Shaddegair tomorrow morning one hour after sunup and at the same time every day after that with the exception of certain feast days. Bris will let you know which they are."

It was dismissal. Desantro bowed and left.

Bustling about the kitchen at the back of the hovel where the Blind Man ate most of his meals, Desantro laid out the food she'd brought from cookshops in the Market while the Blind Man brewed tea to his taste. ". . . and when I said I learned in a palace, he lit up like a festival lamp, the heechin little snob." She chuckled, pulled a chair to the table and sat down. "Weetha witha, I've gotten lazy in my travels, mi grayth. I'll have to be getting up before the sun, walking an hour to the River for the Wildings, then all the way back to the canal and up along it to the Shaddegair, another hour. And all that before a whole day's work and then I have an hour coming home. Diachra, m' diachra! Soft and lazy."

The Blind Man laid the chicken leg on his plate, wrinkled his brow. "The River walk I can do nothing to shorten, but near dawn and dusk the canal boats come and go, you could ride a draft ox and save your wind for better things." He added his chuckle to hers. "If you wish," he added. "I would not presume."

"Presume away, mi grayth. I've sunk my scruples about using you, turn about is fair enough." She leaned across the table and ran her forefinger from knuckle to knuckle on the back of his left hand. "Friend?"

He prisoned her hand in his. "Friend."

Desantro stood at the end of the jetty waiting for something, she didn't know what.

A patch of mist came flowing along the River, caught the sun and sparkled. Soapbubbles, clear and fragile, hundreds of them dancing toward her.

They swung into a funnel shape, blew round her in a brightness that made her blink—and in an instant had sunk into her flesh.

She felt nothing, saw nothing more.

After a moment longer, she left.

FAAN

Shaking, weeping, lying in the stink of his and her body wastes, Faan heard the door shut. She got her head turned in time and vomited until she was bringing up only spoonfuls of yellow bile.

The mute maids came in, lifted her and pulled away the soiled sheets. While one held her off the mattress, the other scrubbed at the stains on the ticking until the worst of the stench was gone. Then the pair of them cut the remains of the shift off her and washed her clean with all the tender care they'd give an old table or a chair they weren't quite ready to throw out. They wrapped her in a huge soft white towel and went out carrying the soiled coverings.

Aching, depleted, Faan lay on the damp ticking, eyes closed, trying not to relive the past two hours. The memories came despite her efforts, but weariness . . . emptiness . . . they had a value now, insulating her from the worst effects.

She'd fought him, feet and teeth, twisting and turning to get away from his hands and the little whips that tickled then cut and the other *things* he used on her, but he laughed at her, a flush came into his cheeks and life into his eyes—so she stopped fighting, lay passive, letting him do what he wanted with the flesh, trying to retreat into herself and not feel what was happening to her. He laughed again. She understood then that he knew more tricks than she could imagine and enjoyed countering them. And he would always be able to go farther than she could endure because in the end he was going to kill her anyway so there was no "stop" in him.

She fought again because she had to. To refrain would in some terrible way be a kind of consent and she could not bear the thought of that.

It was a brief session, ending in a passionless rape that left her feeling as filthy inside as she was on the outside.

Passionless—that was what truly frightened her. Anger, lust, she expected those, she could deal with them, but there was nothing there . . . nothing . . . nothing nothing nothing there but the splendid facade . . . the inside of the man had been eaten away. . . .

The mute maids came back with clean sheets, cotton this time, old and mended. She saw that and sighed with relief because that meant he wasn't coming back, then she was angry at herself for feeling that relief.

As easily as they'd stripped it, they made the bed under her, slid a clean cotton shift over her head and tied the shoulder straps in neat knots. They clicked another length of chain onto her right hand manacle to give her a little more freedom to move and locked it around the post again. They removed the left hand manacle and let it dangle between the bed and the wall. One of them held up a chamber pot, set it beside the bed, then she went out, leaving the second mute maid to move about the room, dusting and straightening and doing a final clean.

She returned with a bed tray, sandwiches and a pot of tea. As she set it down over Faan's legs, for the first time she looked directly at Faan and saw the bicolored eyes.

Eyes opened wide, pupils dilating, she made a warding gesture that Faan hadn't seen before, called her companion to see. They gazed enigmatically at Faan, looked at each other a long moment, then sank back into their usual lethargy and left the room, the lock clanking loudly as they turned the key.

Faan touched the tray. "Food. Potz. I can't. . . ." She thought about refusing to eat, but she knew she'd just be forcefed; there was no point in bringing that on herself. Besides, if she was ever to get out of here, she'd need all the strength she could gather.

He came about the same time on the next day and it was worse.

On the third day he didn't come.

She tensed every time the door opened, was furious, shouting her rage when it was only the mute maids replacing the candle in the corner so she wasn't in complete darkness, later bringing her lunch, at intervals checking the water in the jug by the bed, emptying the chamber pot and doing all the fussy little jobs to keep the room sweet.

The hours passed. She stretched and tensed, pitting muscle against muscle, played small games with herself, names and places, anything to keep her mind from memories new and old. The only way she had of judging time was when the maids came, took away the old tray, brought her a new one and even that wasn't sure, they could be playing tricks on her. At his orders. Messing with her mind. He wasn't content with her body, he meant to break her mind as well.

She tensed as the candle flickered. She hadn't looked at it for hours . . . or at least, for a long time. There was only about an inch and a half left.

She cringed.

And fought against thinking about darkness again, as if he could read her thoughts wherever he was and find a weakness in her he could use to break her faster.

Mind and body.

If they let it go out, I'll scream. And he'll know. . . .

She stared at the candle, willing it to burn more slowly—and as she stared, a glitter seemed to rise from the perfume mist about the flame and drift toward her.

Honey chickee, sad we be to see thee here so sunk in miseree.

The tiny voices were as familiar as her own and more welcome—until she wondered if they were real or only phantoms conjured out of her fear . . . fear escalating into terror. She stared at them, her mouth open, her eyes stretched so wide they hurt.

Hon nee ba bee litt lee chickee, it is we ee, trul lee we ee. Tis no dream. We're what we seem.

They gathered about her, drifting before her, shimmering bubble people, darting in streams to brush against her face, to slide through her hair.

How did you get here? There's a wizard. . . .

Clever littlees, ba, we be. Slip and slide, wait and hide, off he go, thennnn we show.

"He's gone?" Chains clinking, she brought her hands round, tried to call fire. As before, nothing happened. *Why am I still . . . dead!*

Honey chickee, don't you fret, 'tis a curtaigh set, 'tis in his place and wards this space.

But you're here. Can you do anything about it?

Slip and slide, steal inside, sweet and neat, who can tell? Not wizard's spell. They jiggled in the air, upset and unhappy because they couldn't help her. She could feel their sorrow as if that agitated motion was their means of weeping. *Honey chickee, wait and see, more and more and more we be, time will come we break his drum, curtaigh shatter, set you free.*

More of you? How did you get here, then? And can't the . . . rest . . . of you just slide into this . . . this place . . . like you did into this room?

Sorrow sorrow, honey baybee, Green Man's walls keep out us smalls. Pickaback we come inside, huddled 'neath Desantro's hide. Tomorrow more and more each day, in the end that man will pay.

Desantro! How did she know. . . .

Desantro see and follow thee, find a man and make a plan. Rest now, chickee, sleep and heal, dream the pain is all unreal.

The Wildings clustered on her arms and melted into her.

She wasn't alone. She wasn't abandoned. She had friends who'd risk a lot for her.

That, more than anything else, eased her hurting mind. For a brief time she imagined she could feel the bubble people wriggling about, getting comfortable in blood and bone, then a gentle lassitude spread through her. She stretched out on the bed, pulled a sheet over her, and drifted into a healing sleep.

Chapter 21
More Trouble

They reached Chaggar's Pool about an hour after dawn; it was actually a lake, so wide Rakil couldn't see the ends of it, gray water under a gray sky, dotted with boats, the small figures in them setting out nets, hauling them in or simply waiting, water ruffled by the wind that blew smoke he couldn't see into his eyes and twisted his hair into knots.

And the land round it was crowded. There were small gray tents erected in close clumps everywhere he looked, thousands of them. And there were children everywhere, playing or searching through the grass beyond the tents, bringing in dried boggpats, handfuls of grass for the shaggy, blatting chorta tethered among the tents. There were women everywhere, clustered about tiny boggpat fires, talking, spinning, drinking glasses of weak tea. And a few old men.

He touched his weary horse into a faster walk and caught up with Brann. "You're thinking about going into that?"

"They saw us as soon as we saw them, better we pass the ward stones than try to circle out here. Besides, it's Truce Ground."

"Truce, seems I've heard stories of 'accidents' when times are hot, truce or no."

"You've got another way?"

"I'm just along for the ride, it isn't me who's got strings on power, ask the Magus."

She gazed at him a moment, her eyes blank, then she snapped her fingers and Graybao materialized beside the roan. "Bring my black cloak, the one with the cowl." When she(?)'d gone, Brann said, "Rakil, no doubt someone will be oozing around, asking you about me and that." She flipped a hand at the litter. "A mercy-errand would be best. Hmm. You can tell whoever it is he's a rich man and my husband, he's had a curse put on him and I'm taking him to the Grand Wizard to see if I can get it peeled loose. You're a guard and horsehandler. Navarre is his younger brother and Kitya . . . hmm, she's harder to fit in . . . let's say she's a curateur, direction finder, and cook." She took the cloak from Graybao, wrapped it around her and pulled the cowl down so it concealed her face. "Krish! What it is to be a proper and respectable lady." She chuckled. "I never was, not even when I was a baby. My mum used to scold me for running wild. You'd better get back to the mules, Rakil. I'll see that Kitya has the story and she can pass it to Navarre when he emerges."

The Ardammiosh, Director of the Wayyada Mionnage that served the Ground, was a tall, thin woman enveloped in layers of heavy white cotton; there were dark circles under her eyes and her bony hands trembled with fatigue that came from trying to stretch supplies and services too far to too many people. "You are welcome to stay within Bounds for the three days of the Stranger's Grace, but I can give you no food or tea, no supplies at all. I ask your pardon for this, it is not our custom to stint visitors, but you have seen how we are pressed. Take as much water as you wish, though I warn you to boil it for health's sake, even what you use for washing." She turned her head, spoke to the young mionn waiting in a corner of the room. "Rüissy, show the Mena Plavra and her people to the place we've kept for visitors." She turned back to Brann. "It is some distance from the water, but it's better that you keep apart from the refugees. I don't say safer, but accidents happen and these are not good times for anyone."

Brann bowed and took Rakil's arm, pinching it when she read in his face the "I told you so" he was thinking. "I do understand, of course I do. We will be gone as soon as we have rested a little, bathed, and tended our stock."

Eyes followed them as they wound through the groups of women and children, clans and villages clumping together, watching each other with suspicion—and watching these newcomers, their wealth and their beasts, with anger and hunger.

It wasn't only eyes that followed them. Some of the older boys came from the camps and drifted behind them, saying nothing, just watching.

Rakil was careful not to look at them. *Grass version of street trash, that's all you are. Not old enough to kick a piglet. Chirkin little hanorfs, keep back or you'll get your ishers lopped. Brann, I hope you know what you're doing. If we have to hurt one of that lot, this place's going to blow higher than Old Pikeface's Hair.* He smiled with satisfaction as he saw Brann lean toward the girl who was leading them, her hand moving in a minimal gesture to point out the boys. *So you are awake. Baik a baik, that'll work for a while, but. . . .*

Graybao had scoured the countryside out beyond the reach of the refugees and brought in several armloads of dry boggpats, so they had a fire for the soup Rakil was getting very tired of and a mug of tea apiece, and fire to boil some water, hardly enough for shaving, let alone a bath.

Brann drained her mug, looked ruefully at the scatter of leaves in the bottom, then set it down. "I'd planned to stay here a while. We all need rest, especially the litter horses and the last hour before we saw the place I was thinking of nothing much but hot baths and rare meat. Ah well, so much for dreams."

Navarre was lying stretched out on a blanket, his head in Kitya's lap. He pried his eyes open, sighed. "When do we go? Tonight?"

"Not tonight. I'm drained, so I'll be taking a walk later."

"If they find out what you're doing. . . ."

"Ah Magus, I've had centuries to practice. A touch here, a touch there, what's to notice?"

"Remember what the Shawar said. We have an enemy and he's not limited to his senses."

"Then let's hope he's busy elsewhere, or disinclined to disturb us while we're here."

Rakil watched her walk away and began thinking once again about taking off on his own. According to the Magus' mirror, it was only two days from here to the river and if he went straight instead of doglegging it, he could make it in a lot less, maybe even one, especially if he took two horses and traded off and didn't pamper them like Brann insisted on doing.

He got to his feet and went to stand his watch with the herd; go or not-go, if those 'norfs from the camps got off with a horse or a mule, that lessened his own chances of surviving this. They had butchers' gleams in their ferrety eyes.

Graybao was gliding silently from horse to mule to horse, turning her(?) hidden eyes outward from time to time, staring at length at a scraggly bush here or pile of rocks there. Rakil nodded to her(?), set up a pile of clods as a target and took out his sling. *Lesson, you 'norfs. Watch and see what'll happen to your chirkin' heads, you come antsying around here*. When he went with Kitya to fill the water skins, he'd scooped up a pouchful of water-smoothed pebbles. He tucked one of

them in the pocket, got the sling up to speed and re-
leased it.

The pebble hit the top clod, exploded it to powder.

He grinned, popped in another pebble, and blew out
another clod. One by one, with immensely satisfying
precision, he took out the clods until there was only a
scatter of dust left where the pile had been. He dusted
off his hands, tucked the sling through a belt loop, and
went strolling around the outside of the wide rope corral
they'd set up to keep the beasts from wandering off.

Some time later he saw a shadowy figure leave the
camp and head toward the lake. Brann on prowl. He
shuddered, rubbed at his neck. *Drinker of Souls, gods,
what am I into?* He stretched and yawned, ambled into
camp to get Kitya to help him shift the corral so the
horses and mules would have fresh grass to graze on.

Kitya's scream hauled Rakil from an uneasy sleep,
the anger in it grating in his ears. Behind him he heard
Navarre grunt and roll out of his blankets. Half naked
and still half asleep, Rakil scrambled up, carrying sling
and pouch with him, ran toward the corral.

Fires blazed up in a wide arc beyond the herd,
torches that shadows waved as they leapt howling from
the darkness out beyond the corral. He knew what they
were about, trying to stampede the horses and cut out
one or more of them before anyone could stop them.

Kitya howled back, loosed a stone, and sent one of
the attackers sprawling. Rakil joined her and started
hunting targets of his own.

He missed the first one. There was a heaviness in the
air, a familiar pressure that threw his aim off temporarily. Navarre was pushing WakKerrcarr's web out to
cover them . . . no, to cover the herd. When Rakil took
an instant to look over his shoulder, he saw the beasts
shimmer and disappear. He swore under his breath and
went back to stinging the would-be raiders.

The attack faltered as the herd vanished.

The torches from those downed by the pebbles touched off the dry grass. The fires began to spread. The attackers fled, yelling "Fire!" as they ran.

Graybao came swooping down from wherever she(?)'d been, hovered over the fires a moment, then blew away. She(?) returned a moment later with a water skin and blankets which she dropped to Kitya and Rakil. She emptied the skin on the most vigorous flames, went back for more while they started beating at the fire.

The heaviness expanded enormously for a brief instant, gallons of lakewater arrived, dousing them and everything about them, snuffing the fires and turning the embers to black mush.

Then the web snapped back, the horses were there again, shying nervously but not as spooked as Rakil expected. After some snorting and a few curvets and capers, they went back to grazing, ignoring the flare of Wrystrike fire that leapt to the sky a half mile away, then went racing south, dying as it moved.

The Ardammiosh came storming out to them, an angry, muttering crowd close behind her. "What have you done," she demanded in a loud voice. The crowd echoed her. "What were those fires? Why are those boys dead?" She gestured at shadowy bodies like wet rags tossed on the charred earth.

Brann caught the cloak more tightly about her body, drew back so the cowl left her face in deep shadow. Navarre stood at her left, his hand on her shoulder, his face drawn with fatigue. Rakil stood at her right, a sling dangling from his hand. "We have harmed no one," she told the Ardammiosh, "we've simply made it clear we will not be harassed or victimized."

"What are you saying?"

"These 'boys' came at us masked and waving

torches, trying to steal the horses." Her voice rang out, deep and rich, singing the words to the listening crowd. "Blame them for the fires, it wasn't our doing. If my sjodai had not strained himself and tossed part of the lake on the flames, you'd be looking at dead and burned enough to cry shame at those who lie there or hide among them behind you." She moved her hand slightly, the pale sheen of it stark against the dull black of the cloak. "If we'd wanted to kill them, we'd have used bolts not pebbles. If any are dead, not merely knocked silly for the moment, then we are sorry, but we accept no blame for it. My husband's life is in my hands and I will keep it safe."

"If that is true. . . ."

"If!" Brann drew herself up, indignation vibrating in the visible parts of her body. "Can you give me any acceptable reason why we would endanger ourselves and the beasts we so urgently need? Can you give me any acceptable reason why we'd do it now after traveling so far across so many miles of plain and mountain? Turn it about. Why would the boys do this? You yourself have said there's hunger in the camps and refused to share your supplies with us."

"I am shamed." The Ardammiosh spread her hands and bowed her head. "I ask your pardon, O Mena Plavra."

"It is given. As you have said, these are difficult times."

"Ba, Mena Plavra. It is clear your people can protect you, but I will leave two mionna as witnesses. For your sake and ours, I must ask that you do not stay another night. You have the right, I will not drive you off, but as a favor, O Mena Plavra, be on your way as soon as you can."

"As you ask, so it will be. Sundown will see us gone."

* * *

Navarre collapsed on his blanket. "All you smell out there isn't burned grass, that's the Wrystrike steaming. It's the web, you know, it keeps the Strike away. Ahhh, mabra bramzin, that took it out of me."

Kitya laughed, dropped beside him. "When I looked back and saw those horses fade, saaa! Brann, you get charged up?"

"If I took this cloak off, I'd shine like the moon. Listen, I'll walk watch, Kitya, Rakil, Navarre, get as much rest as you can. We'll leave sometime after noon tomorrow. I meant to wait till dark, but I'd rather catch any plotters before they're ready for us."

Rakil's nose twitched; he looked up from the feet he was scrubbing with a corner of a towel. "Hmm. I doubt that."

"Bem. Any suggestions, then?"

Rakil shrugged, yawned. "No point in talking about it. We'll go and see." He squeezed out the towel, hung it on the end of the litter, and went back to his blankets.

As he rolled into them and tucked the ends about his feet, he yawned again and lay with his eyes almost shut, watching the others move about, listening to them talk. Nothing important, just chat. The black cloak swung past him, Brann moving so lightly he couldn't hear her footsteps. He tucked that image away as something to beware when his chance came. *I'll stay till the river, then I'm gone.* He wiggled his hand under the pack beside his head, touched the tube with the kech in it. *Sleep lightly, Purb, and look over your shoulder. I'm coming and I will have my coin.*

Tickled and niggled at by another burst of magic, the Chained God Unchained let the half-drained Wieldy go and frowned, the lines sinking deep in living metal strained by the bulges it was supposed to confine. "Power damnéd be, the cherk is getting stronger.

Wrystrike or not. Add him to that girl and
hmpf!" He shifted his ponderous body, caught
more chaos stuff to stuff behind his back and
ease the weight on his spine. "I know this
business, I played this game and won. I'll win
again." Perran-a-Perran, a touch here, a touch
there, marching his pawns and keeping his
fingers hid, his aim concealed. "I'll make you
show yourself," he muttered. "I'll pull you from
the shadows so I can see you and get a line
on you. Yessss."

He peered into Gallindar, scowled at the
bloody mess he'd created; the warbands he'd
sent after Drinker of Souls and the Magus
were fighting each other, too intent on slaughter to bother about the strangers creeping
through their grass. "Saaa! I see your finger
there, my enemy." He watched the company
move from the Truce Ground and head south
through the grass. By coincidence or not, they
were moving through a nearly empty section,
a section he'd helped clear out. "Me! You're
using ME!" That made him even angrier. He
drummed his fingers on his gilded thigh, narrowed his eyes and inspected the ground
ahead of them. Tall grass, some of it so high
it rose above the heads of the riders. Dry
grass. Tinder dry. "Ahhh! That's it. Fire. The
Magus plays with fire, let's give him a bellyful
of it. Fire to the right of them, fire to the left of
them, fire ahead, and fire behind. Let's see
them escape from that!" He sank back on his
cushion, smiling with anticipation. "Ride at
peace, you curséd gnats. Nothing will happen
till sundown when the shadows are long and
the light dim, then. . . . ahhhh, then. . . ."

Chapter 22
Changes

FAAN

Day merged with day and the man left Faan alone. When she thought about it—which she tried not to, or at least not often—she wondered if he had others penned like her; that made her queasy, sorry for them and at the same time desperately glad they were there. If they existed. Maybe he'd got all he wanted for a while. Listening on the stairs to Reyna and the other Salagaum when they didn't know she was there and talked about their clients had taught her that men varied a lot in what they wanted and how much of it. Or maybe it was part of his game, letting her hope a little, relax a little, so her terror would be sharper when he came back.

She didn't really care. She was too bored, too furious at him and life in general for trapping her into this place to waste much time on wondering about what the man was doing. And too afraid. For many reasons, she was terrified. Midsummer's Eve was getting closer with every breath she took. Tungjii's Promise, what good was it if she couldn't be on Jal Virri? If she didn't have the jewel and Navarre, or whatever it was going to take to free her mother? It was too late already for Jal Virri, but there was still a thread of hope. *Find Rakil before the Eve. Diyo.* She had to get out of here, had to get on with finding him, had to do the last things in this long ritual dance whose purpose she didn't know, probably would never know, except that somehow it was part of what she had to do to reach her mother. *Mother. Mamay. I NEED you. I NEED NEED NEED.* . . .

With only one chain on her wrist, she could move around a lot more. That tiny additional freedom seemed to bring the walls in on her, make her feel her imprisonment more intensely. There were times when she stood by the bed and beat her hand over and over against the metal post.

Even the Wildings couldn't amuse her for long. They were just there, filling the unvarying twilight of the room with their dancing sparkles, filling her mind with their absurd little rhymes, more of them every day as Desantro walked them past the barrier Wall. *Desantro. Tungjii bless her for her loyalty and her stubbornness.* The Wildings fled to the ceiling and hid behind the tiles when the mute maids came in for the meals, to change the candles, to take away the chamber pot; once the women were gone, the bubbles dropped down around Faan, clustered about her when she grieved, brushed so very gently against her when she fell into one of her fits of anger. *Wild Magic, bléssed be it for the comfort it gives me.*

Sometime in that respite—she no longer knew if it were day or night outside the room, she judged time by candles and counted a new day every fourth candle— she jerked at the manacle on her right wrist—and her hand *changed* to something like molasses taffy; it stretched into a tentacle and slid from the steel ring. She gaped at the thing, gulped as it flowed back into an ordinary hand, the hand she'd known all her life. "What is. . . ."

Hon ee chick ee, Shifff tee hee hee be ee nice, show us twice, hit the floor, show us more, hee ee hee hee.

Shifter? Faan looked at her hand and watched it change as she willed it wide and flat, then collapsed it into a tentacle again, rubbery and apparently boneless. Hastily, made uneasy by this melting away of what had been the single constant in her life, she returned the hand to its proper state.

She sat with her fingers laced and frowned at them without really seeing them, brooding about this new . . . what? instinct? She must have, without understanding how, picked up this thing from the Shifters of Kaerubulan. It had to be them, there was no other way. She didn't have the learning of the Magus, the eyes of the Sibyl, but she was reasonably sure that this was something new. She'd run as a white hind in the Mezh, but that was different, the pouring of her essence into a new form shaped by forces outside her. She'd had no choice, no way of saying what the form would be. It just happened. This. . . . She closed her hand into a fist, flattened it on her thigh. This was as conscious and controlled as learning to dance. It was a dance, a dance of the flesh. *As if I absorbed it just by being around them. Or maybe when my magic killed the guards, it sucked this . . . this whatever it is out of them.* She shuddered. It was an ugly thought, and one all too likely to be true. *Or it could be Abeyhamal's Gift . . . it kept trying to make me SHIFT . . . I can't use my Talent outside my skin, the Wizard stops it one way or another. Diyo, that's it, it turned inside and it's using what the Gift got from the Shifters. Diyo, that IS what happened. It must be. . . .*

She brooded some more while the Wildings fluttered about her, brushed against her, clung to her hair, played on hands that kept changing as if the hands were learning their own possibilities while her mind was elsewhere.

I want to kill him. I want him dead.

Chick ee bay bee, no and no, that is not the way to go. If he's dead, then so are you, make him hurt and weep instead, his blood is shed, your chance is fled, you give in, the god he wins.

What god? Everybody talks about a god, nobody will tell me which.

Honey chikee, we ee litt lee, canna say the name today, better so you don't yet know.

K'lann! It's MY life you're fooling with.

The Wildings pulled away from her; for a moment they flittered nervously about in the shadowy dusk up near the ceiling, then melted into the stone so she couldn't scold them any longer.

Faan sighed, then began trying out her new ability, playing with her body as if she were a child thumping clay about.

Honey chikee hit the sack, marching maids are coming back.

For an instant Faan was on the edge of panic, afraid she couldn't remember how to return to her original form. Then her body spoke and the panic went away. The body knew its prime shape, she could trust that. Her lingering unease vanished with that realization; she sighed and untangled herself, got her wrist back in the cuff and was lying passive as the door opened and the mute maids came in, the same two. Always the same two. She watched stone-faced as they pulled in the cart and began cleaning the room.

DESANTRO

Desantro sat on the edge of the bath looking fondly down at the Blind Man as he used the nail brush on her toenails, his fingers sliding with sensuous delicacy along the tips of her toes.

"You should clip them, Des, they're getting too long."

"Later." Her voice shivered with the waves of pleasure that were rippling up through her body.

He set the brush on the edge beside her and began

massaging her feet. He didn't speak again for a long time, so long she began to wonder why.

"Is there something wrong?" she said.

"My name is Cyram." He took his hands away and turned his back to her.

She didn't know what to say or do. In the end she simply answered as if it were a gift he'd put in her hand, "Thank you."

"Stay with me. When this is over, stay with me."

"Oh." She twisted her hands together. "You don't know. . . ."

"I know what I feel in you, I know your laughter, I've heard you fuss and grouch in the morning when your temper's hot to touch and your tongue too quick for kindness. I know your gentleness and your strength. Desa, nothing you can tell me can be worse than I've heard from others." He kept his back to her so she couldn't see his face as he couldn't see hers at any time and used his voice to weave a magic round her. "How many men have said they loved you . . . and vanished the next morning? How many have you told the same . . . and vanished yourself? So I won't say those easy words, but I'll spend our lives giving them meaning."

Her eyes burned from tears she'd stopped shedding so many years before, when weeping was as futile as words; there was a lump in her throat and her tongue felt too clumsy for speech. She strained hand against hand and fought for control. "Cy, Cyram, it isn't that. Mi taihra, mi tau, I bore half a dozen children when I was a slave, but they don't know me, they never had a chance to know me, they were taken from me when they'd survived the first month. It's as if they were only dreams I had, not blood and bone and breath. So I NEED to find my brother. I NEED to have a family, blood that will know and remember me into the years after I'm dead. Tariko my sister and Rakil my brother, they're all I've got, all I ever will have now. You see, the last time, it was difficult, I nearly died. The General who owned me wouldn't let his Chambermassal call Kassian Zazukar, that's a woman priest who knew about birthings, he made him fetch an Aboso, a doctor priest almost as arrogant as him. The Aboso bungled things, the baby died and I can't have more children. All in all, that suited the General well enough, he wouldn't be pleased if he had to trade trained hands for a blob of stinking flesh that would need years of feeding and tending before it earned its way. There have been times since that I've been sure he paid the Aboso to do what he did so he wouldn't have the problem forced on him another time. Do you see? That's what you have to know. No children ever. No son, no daughter. Do you see? That's why I can't give you any kind of answer until my brother knows that I am still alive and well enough, until my brother knows my history and can pass it on. Do you see?"

He turned slowly in the water, held out his hands. When she leaned down and took them, he smiled. "Desa, o sitabéag o dulcerie, have you looked at me lately? Would I be wanting to pass this form to a child of mine who'd grow up cursing me as I cursed my father? Not that I ever knew him. My mother died of me and the mionns who raised me would not say a word of either. The other children were never so reticent. They circled round me and sang it to me, over and over they sang it to me, that my mother was a whore, my father was a sailor on a trading ship who came and went and never knew what he left behind. The mionns were kind enough, but I could feel their fingers hating to touch me. The children were not kind. They touched me with fist and stone, with nails and teeth. In all my life, you are the first to come to me without loathing, to touch me without that hidden tremble in your hands, though even you I had to buy like all the rest."

She slid into the water and wrapped her arms about

him, her own sorrows forgotten for the moment. "Only in the beginning, mi tau, only in the beginning."

FAAN

The mute maids motioned her onto her feet; they threw the old covers on the floor and dressed the bed again in silk sheets lavishly embroidered in white silk threads, pulled embroidered white shams onto fresh pillows.

After the first jolt, Faan stood frozen, her breath coming in short, quick gasps. In spite of how she thought she'd prepared herself to face this, the shock was everything he would have wished.

She stood passive as they untied the shoulderstraps of the wrinkled sweaty nightgown she wore and pulled it down, tapping her knees one by one so she would step out of the circle of cloth. Then they washed her with meticulous care, buffed her fingernails and toenails, stroked perfume over the hotspots on her body, finally tied on a white silk shift.

Faan lay down as their taps demanded, closed her eyes while they shortened the chain on her right arm and locked down her left again. *Nayo nay nayo nay nayo nayyyyy. . . .*

She heard the slip slip of their feet as they walked away, the click of the door as they went out. *I'm not ready for this, I don't know what I should do. . . .*

The Wildings came and brushed across her, whispered in her mind: *bite him, honey, scratch him, babee, strangle him a little, a bittle, a tittle, then we'll flee, you and we.*

With a kettle-whistle they swirled around and plunged into her, tickling along inside her skin, warm and funny. When the man came in, she was smiling.

She looked at him and giggled. "Antsy prantsy an't he fancy?"

That startled him so much he tripped over his own

feet, scrambled to right himself, his arms flailing, his meticulously combed hair falling into his eyes.

Bouncing on the bed, she laughed at him, mocking him. "Dance, clown," she shouted and clanked the chains against the posts. "Mug and jig for me, you've bored me to tears before this. Do you think you could fall on your face? I'd enjoy that."

He straightened and stood with his head back, gazing into the shadows that drifted about the ceiling. His chest rose and fell inside the leather vest, quickly at first, then slowing as he sucked in long breaths and let them trickle out between stiff lips. He lowered his head and smiled at her. Still without speaking he walked to the tool wall and stood braced, his hands clasped behind him as he contemplaced the instruments hanging there, deliberately postponing his choice to increase her nervousness and regain the control that had slipped briefly from his hands.

The Wildings bubbled anxiously inside her. *Now, babee, now, honey, attack attack behind his back, squeeze his neck, then let's trek. Do it do it do it do do do do it!*

Faan considered the thickness of that neck, the strength she remembered, ice forming in the pit of her stomach.

He reached out, ran his fingers along an odd shaped rod with something like a spoon at the tip. She didn't know what it was used for and shuddered at the thought of finding out.

He tapped a nail against it, producing a faint chink, the only sound in the room other than the rasp of their breathing, then pulled his hand back and took a side step to stand before a new section. He was not wholly calm yet, a muscle was jumping beside the one eye she could see and tendons bulged in his neck.

It gave her time to get ready. *Don't rush it, take a lesson from him. Control. Calm. Wind up. Then explode.*

She elongated her hands, squeezed them through the

manacles, shortened and thickened her legs, altered her feet and changed her toes into horny blades, curved and powerful as eagle talons, thickened her shoulders, making the muscles denser and more powerful, turned her arms into tentacles as puissant as her new legs, changed her teeth into a cat's curved fangs. Silently she curled up until she was crouching on the end of the bed.

With a wild shriek, she sprang, landed on him, sank her teeth into the back of his head, her talons into his buttocks, wrapped her tentacles about his neck and squeezed.

He screamed, then fought, whirling to slam her against the wall, doing it again and again as he clawed with one hand at the thick-skinned tentacles that were strangling him and with the other reached for the instrument wall, fumbling for anything he could use as a weapon against her.

She squeezed harder, gnawed on the back of his head and ripped her talons from his legs, contorted her body so she could slap her feet against the wall and thrust, flinging both of them away from it, knocking him off his feet to land on his face in the thick white fur, smashing his head against her face and nearly jolting loose her grip on his neck.

She tightened her arms, laughed in her throat as his struggles grew feebler and finally stopped altogether.

Honey chickee, let him be, if he's dead, then so are we.

Vema vema, I hear.... Gagging at the taste of his blood in her mouth, Faan shifted her fangs to teeth and lifted her head. "Ah gods!" She eased her tentacled arms from about his neck and rolled off him, her body sliding with practiced ease into its prime shape.

She jumped to her feet and ran shakily to the bed table, gulped a mouthful of water from the jug, spat it out, gulped more, spat again, then splashed what was left over her face and neck, washing away the blood that stained her skin. Fingers trembling, she snatched loose the ties, stepped from the shift and kicked it away. "Jeggin silk. Nothing to. . . ."

She looked down; her feet and legs were soaked in blood high as her knees. "What am I going to do, a mess like this, no clothes. . . ."

The Wildings giggled, clustered along her legs, flushing pink as they sucked in the blood, then glittering as they 'changed' it to their grossamer substance. They spun up around her, wove together into a long white robe with a cowl she could pull over her head.

Chickee hur ree, last a while then gone like smile. Find some dimwit, snatch his outfit, tail on fire, skip this byre.

Vema, I hear you. Wizard?

Boddach snoring, finds this boring.

Good. May his dreams be sweet. Door's locked. Where'd that gurk put the key? I was stupid I didn't notice.

To unlock it, search his pocket.

Wrinkling her nose with distaste, Faan crouched beside the man and gingerly poked her fingers into a trouser pocket.

He stirred.

Without pausing to think what she should do, she made a fist, the flesh dense and hard, slammed it into the back of his head, knocking him insensible again. She grimaced, wiped her hand on a clean spot on his trousers, then probed for the key, found it and stood.

When I open the door, will that stir up the Wizard?

Open door, wizard snore.

Nu, that's good. So let's get going.

DESANTRO

A sparkle dropped to bounce urgently in front of Desantro's face as she pressed the dirt down about the last of the plants she was assigned to transfer. It was late, near sundown, the shadows long, the air steaming still from the day's heat. The Currtle Garden was empty, Megglen Bris had wandered off somewhere, the Daughters were in their suites titivating for the evening meal, so Desantro was enjoying herself, humming a song from her almost forgotten childhood. She ignored the Wilding bubble until she was finished, then sat on her heels wiping her hands on the rag from the cart. "Nu, what is it?"

Honey's sliding, stop your biding. Follow me, come and see. "Nu, hold on a minute." She collected her tools and the pots, stacked them on the cart, and began pushing it toward the back gate that the workers had to use. "The timing's good, I was ready to quit anyway. Stop your jigging, I'm going to do what I always do this time of day. A fuss isn't something any of us want, do we? Nu, you found me, so bring Faan to meet me, hmm? We can go out together, lose ourself in the mob that leaves, hmm?"

Dressed in loose trousers and a shirt with the sleeves rolled up because they were inches too long, following a single sparkle, the other Wildings nestled inside her, Faan came round a corner, stopped as she saw Desantro. The girl's face was pale and drawn, there was a darkness in the bicolored eyes that laid a sick cold lump in the bottom of Desantro's belly.

She unwound the scarf from her neck, tossed it to Faan. "Wrap this round your head, your hair's too strange with your face, it'll catch the eye and we don't want that. And um talking about eyes, you better keep looking down. Um, is there something behind you I should know about?"

Faan shook her head. "Not for a while, he's still out. When he wakes, though. . . ." She shrugged. "I think he's someone important."

"You don't know?" Desantro clicked her tongue.

"The Heir to all this, that's who. Now hush, no talking till we're outside the Shaddegair." She grinned. "You'll find someone waiting for you there."

"Your brother?" There was a flash of hope in Faan's bicolored eyes.

"Ahh now, you wait and see."

Ailiki leapt into Faan's arms, pressed against her, trembling and whimpering. "Has she been out here all this time?'

"Since you were taken."

"Ailiki my Liki, my little one." Faan shifted the mahsar, stroked her hand over the soft fur, turned to Desantro. "Where are we going?"

"Friend of mine said I could bring you to his place. Said there even Chaggar can't touch you."

"Mathen?"

"Oh, him. Pah! He ran for cover when I told him who took you, I saw it, you wouldn't know that, you were flat out, anyway, it's someone else. He's important to me, Fa. Don't go by what he looks like, it's . . . oh, never mind, just know he's a good person and give him his dignity."

"You tell that to me?"

"Diyo, you. So just be quiet and move, we've got to get you under cover. Fast."

Chapter 23
The River

RAKIL

The tall grass hummed with the night gleaners, the mix of insects and tiny rodents barely larger than a thumbnail that combined to make the sourceless sound that hovered over the Ardafeoyr when it was at peace, when the herds of bogg and the solitary prowlers that preyed on them were elsewhere, when the riders of the grass, the yacchodor, took their tramping horses, their quarrels, their songs, their ruler's arrogance to other parts of the land.

The litter creaked rhythmically, the sound timed to the plod of the horses' hooves, mingling with the creaks and jingles from the riding gear. There was a steady tearing sound as the mules snatched mouthfuls from the grass as they moved, which mixed with the rumbles from the stomachs of the horses, the whuff huff of their breathing.

The Wounded Moon was nearly whole, its color-leaching white light obscuring the stars, so Kitya went first, for holding line was her gift and here in the long grass visibility was the length of the horse ahead of you and every direction looked much the same. Brann rode beside the litter, leading Graybao's pony. She(?) was out on her hourly swoop through a wide circle about them, checking to see if there were warbands close enough to threaten them. Rakil rode beside the front mule, the lead rope half hitched loosely through the bronze ring beside his knee; with Navarre riding rearguard two horselengths behind the mules he was nervous and unhappy, feeling trapped. It was one thing when the Magus was really working to protect them. Back there, though, all he had were his hands and Rakil didn't think much of those.

Two days. Nights, rather. What's left of tonight and tomorrow night. Once we hit the river. . . . He ran his thumb along the kechtube under his shirt. *Find a village . . . a fishboat . . . anything with a sail . . . I won't need protection if this lot aren't with me. . . .*

He went on brooding over his plans, hampered not at all by a lack of information about the land and the city he was aiming for. Purb hadn't been interested in Cumabyar or its legal products. The pearls smuggled out of the Falagash Islands, they were something else, but it was easier trading with smugglers in Jedeti or Kanzeer where the Flea had acquaintances with ties to the local powers. Rakil wasn't worried about his ignorance. One city was much like another; there were always cracks and crannies a knowledgeable man could slip into and do what he had to do.

Graybao plunged past Kitya, hovered in midair in front of Brann. "Fire!" she(?) wailed, swept a ragged, gray arm through a wide arc. "All round. Every ssside. Moving in, don't matter thhhe wind." She(?) dropped to the ground, stood waiting.

Navarre touched his horse into a quicker walk, circling around Rakil to join Brann. "I don't smell it, how far off is it?"

Graybao turned her shadowy eyes on Brann; at her nod, she(?) said, "One hhhour, perhhhapsss, if thhhe rate ssstaysss sssteady."

"A complete ring?"

"It isss sssooo."

"How long has it been burning, could you tell?"

"Only a few minutesss, thhhe burn wasss only ssso wide." She(?) lifted one translucent hand, measuring about five feet from the ground.

Brann combed her fingers through her hair. "Katarm! Navarre, the Tenyasa's miles off, could you snatch water from it like you did from the lake, enough to wash us a way out?"

"Tja, but there's an easier way. And it's more certain. Whoever started that fire can touch off another no matter how much water I hoist. And it's more my sort of thing. Magus work." He smiled, slid from the saddle. "I'll be riding in the litter. Keep close together, the smaller the area I have to timeshift, the better."

Brann frowned. "Timeshift?"

"Tja. I mean to take us behind time, maintaining position and proceed from there. We'll pass the fire ring a half hour before it was lit." Kitya started to speak, but he held up a hand. "I can do it without harm to us within the shield of WakKerrcarr's Web."

"What happens outside it?" Brann waved a hand at the grass swaying above them in a wind that couldn't reach them. "I remember the flare last night. How many do we kill to save ourselves?"

"There's a cost for everything, Drinker of Souls. You, if anyone, ought to know that." He passed his hand across his face, the palm scraping over the stubble on his chin. "There'll be fire from the Strike, but there's already fire there, it'll just be worse."

Kitya nodded. "Which they've done to themselves. Nu, nakana-la, my mother says take care of your own and let them that are hitting you do the same."

Rakil scowled. "Never mind them out there, what happens to us when you snap the web back?"

"Anything happen to you last night?" He shrugged, put his hand on the frame of the litter. "Like I said, keep tight; if you slip from under the web, you'll be ash before you know what happens."

* * *

The air was thick and sour, with a sizzle to it near the curve of the dome drawn over them. The horses were skittish, ears back, heads jerking—almost as skittish as their riders.

Rakil hunched his shoulders, chewed on his tongue, cursing silently all magic makers, gods, and bitchy women who sucked up trouble like mother's milk. He unhooked the skin from its half-ring, squeezed out a mouthful of water, slung it back, settling it against his leg; in this clueless waste the small weight was reassuring. Life was in that skin. Life and maybe escape.

An hour passed. The Magus kept the lid clamped tight.

Another hour.

And another.

There was a great squeal that ran across the dome of the sky, a sheet of flame that seemed to reach at them, only to turn aside at the last moment and go rushing off across the grass, burning it, burning the earth beneath it, leaving behind a vast black scar.

Whirling winds howled round them, scouring every exposed inch of skin, tearing at the litter until it swayed and rocked; the forward litter horse squealed, but Brann slapped her hand against its neck and it stood rooted to the ground, anchoring the other horse with the litter between them.

Rakil was too busy with the mules and his own mount to have much attention left for what was happening around him, but he caught a glimpse of an immense black funnel heading straight for them. "Haich chorro!" He slapped the water skin behind his knee to make sure it was still there, jerked the lead rope loose, smacked the wall-eyed pinto he was riding into a full-out run and headed for the horizon.

KITYA

Kitya forced her mount around, took him as close to the
rear litter horse as she could without crushing a leg; she
leaned over, caught hold of his harness, using the obdu-
rate, unruffled gray and her voice to steady him, keep
him from trying to break from the poles and bolt, her
mind busy the while, thinking more of Navarre than the
perilous situation they found themselves in. *He guessed
wrong, I wonder if that was the Strike working on his
head, or just his usual vanity. Dear V'ret, he will do it,
cautious as a coney one minute, running wild the next.
Mama said to stay away from men like that, they'd get
you killed faster than the brash ones. Toowi tawi, he
has his points, my Magus, and I expect we'll live
through this one, too.*

The funnel cloud roared down on them, danced aside
at the last moment—Kitya swore later she felt it cursing
with frustration as it tried to get at them—and went
rushing southward, tearing up grass and everything else
in its path.

The mules were gone and all the supplies. Rakil was
gone with his horse and whatever he had on him.
Navarre was sunk in a fever of exhaustion, too drained
to do more than sleep and sweat.

Brann stood with her hands on her hips, inspecting
the damage. "Graybao?"

"Momorisssh?"

"You think you could find the mules?"

She(?) didn't bother answering, just sublimated into
the smoky air and was gone.

Kitya was rubbing down the rear litter horse with a
wad of grass; she looked around. "What about Rakil?"

"He's been antsy for days." Brann's mouth twitched
into a humorless halfsmile. "Since you made the kech
for him. It's no accident he's among the missing. Let

him take care of himself, I'm sure he's quite capable of it. As for us, I've gone over what the Sibyl said and I don't think we need him any more."

"Nu, I suppose you're right. And it's only a day to the river and he's got water." She went back to tending the horse. After a minute, she said, "Did you like him?"

Brann used her belt knife to cut grass, wadded it into a pad and went to the forehorse; she began rubbing him down, crooning to him. "Ah, honey, that's a good horse, does that feel good? I thought so." Over her shoulder, she said, "I don't know him, Kat, not really. He doesn't let himself be known."

"Poor Desantro. He's kin, so she's stuck with him."

They worked in silence for half an hour, checking the gear, tending the horses and Graybao's pony, giving each a pint of water from the skins they kept tied to their saddles, staking them out to graze a while.

Brann unlaced the curtains on the litter, pulled them back so the sleepers could get some air. "Doesn't seem to be much change in either one of them. Let's just hope our ... um ... enemy is busy somewhere else. None of us could light a match right now."

Kitya nodded, dropped onto a saddle, and sat with her knees pulled up, her arms wrapped around them. "It's going to be a thirsty finish if Graybao doesn't bring back those mules."

Brann didn't answer. She reached into the litter, stroked her fingers along Taks' face, her eyes abstracted.

Dawn was pinking the east when Graybao appeared, leading the three mules and two of the spare horses.

Kitya stood. "Did you see anything of Rakil?"

Graybao snorted. "Hhhhim? Hhhhahhh! Hhhe hhheading for thhhe river fassst as hhhe can pusssh poor damn hhhorse." She(?) turned to Brann. "Isss a ssspring two mile sssouthhh of hhhere. Fire and ssstorm empty thhhe land, will be sssafe a while."

They roped the horses to the mules; Kitya took the lead rope and sang encouragement to her charges as Brann started the litter after Graybao. "Mika cho'a peshra zrunik," she crooned to them, "ne sha'ne kook peshril zrun'kak. Mika cho'a. . . ." Over and over she sang the words as her mother had taught her, enticing them after her, calming their fears as they moved into the charred slash the raging Wrystrike left behind. There was the stink of magic as well as the bitter bite of the ash and that made them nervous until they moved out of it.

The sky was empty, the rising sun leaching the blue from it, turning it to a hammering white grill. There was no air moving, not even a hint of a wind. The dust the hooves kicked up stayed there, dropping back to earth in infinitesimal stages. Except for the thudding of those hooves, the creak and jingles from the gear and Kitya's droning song, the silence was thick around them, oppressive.

The funnel storm had caught the edge of the spring, ripping several of the low, twisty trees from the ground and tossing them into the basin, breaking it, letting the water out, knocking down the woven cover. When Brann saw the damage, she swore, then swung down. "Well, Kat, we go to work. Graybao, make sure the stock doesn't wander off and keep watch as best you can. Kat, let's get the packs off the mules and see if we can rig some sort of harness, so we can haul those trees out." She unlaced the curtains, leaned into the litter, emerged swearing some more. "He's still out. We could've used his muscles. Ah weh, we do what we have to do."

* * *

"Look at this, Brann, it's as good as we'll get." One of the downed trees had a branch that divided into two smaller branches, each of them curving out in reasonably similar arcs. "Cut a couple of blankets into strips for padding, ravel a section of rope to tie it all together and we've got a fair collar. Bring me the hatchet, I'll cut this loose and start shaping it a bit more, you can deal with the blankets."

"Che'unga are'gay," Kitya crooned to the mule. "Ta'muzra are'gay, ong'ek che'un 'gay, aree are' are'gay," she sang, caressing him with hand and voice as he threw himself against the collar, dug in, and hauled at the last of the trees. "Mika cho'a, che'ung, che'ungaaaa. . . ."

"Ease up a minute, Kitkat, there's a stub of a branch caught, I think I can shift it."

Kitya broke off her song, patted the mule into standing easy, looked over her shoulder at Navarre who was stooped above the tree, tugging at it, trying to rock it around so he could free the snag. "So you woke up finally," she said.

"As you see . . . ah!" The tree turned faster than he'd expected and another branch stub caught him in the knee. He hobbled a few steps back. "Go," he said.

Kitya examined the collar, checked a spot that seemed to be chafing, rubbed at the mule's hair, smoothing it flat. "Puk ya puk ya, Mika cho'a," she crooned to the mule, stroking her hand along his neck. "Puk ya, che'unga. Ong'ek ahhh ong'ek, thum na alo. Alo, are'gay."

The mule threw himself against the collar and dug in again, driving forward step by step until the tree came rolling loose and he snorted and did a little dance that came within a hair of one of her feet; she laughed with him and slapped his neck. "Are'gay, ong'ek."

Favoring his bruised knee, Navarre hobbled across to

her as she cut the ropes and eased the collar over the mule's head. "Why do you always use your home-speech, Kat? I've noticed it before and meant to ask."

"But you forgot, ah-kun? Something came up, ah-hun?" She clicked her tongue. "It reaches places where I do more than speak, V'ret. Brann," she called, "tree's out, you can start with the stones now." Her hand on the mule's neck, she began walking him to join the little herd grazing at the edge of the spring grove.

Navarre limped beside her. "Sorry about the fire-storm, Kitkat, it was more ... um ... frenzied than I expected."

"Wrystrike throwing a tantrum, hai-yah?"

"Something like that. Where's Rakil?"

"Took off. I suppose he figured we were trouble he didn't need any more."

"The kech?"

"That, too."

She dumped a handful of grain in the nosebag, strapped it on, and turned the mule over to Graybao. "You hungry, V'ret?"

"Edgy," he said. "I don't know why."

"Nu, you'd better eat anyway. It's all that sleep, you'll feel better doing something."

He caught her shoulders, pulled her to him, rubbed his hand up and down the nape of her neck. "Ahhhh Kat, when this is over...."

She rested against him for a moment, then set her hands on his chest and pushed. "Tja, but till then, you bring me some firewood, hmm?"

He laughed and let her go. "Midsummer's Eve," he said. "Mark it down."

They stayed the day at the spring, the grass noises gradually strengthening as the wind rose. It blew tenta-tively at first, like a man dipping a toe in a lake to test how cold the water was, then with more assurance. The day gleaners darted from shadow to shadow, gnawing at roots, snatching up seeds and fruits knocked down by the storm. A tiny ruskdeer came tittupping warily through the trees, snatched a mouthful of water, jerked its head up, its curved horns glinting like polished jet in the sunlight filtering through the leaves. It snatched another mouthful and went skittering away.

Brann was curled up inside the litter with the curtains tied back so she could get air while she slept. Her head was on Tak's shoulder, one arm was laid protectively across him. Graybao was sitting in the shade of a clump of trees atop the nearest knoll, watching the horses. Kitya slept a few hours with her hand in Navarre's; she didn't like the heat, it made her pant and gave her bad dreams.

She shuddered awake shortly before sundown, staggered to the basin. Stripping, she scooped up water in one of the horse buckets, dumped it over her head, did it again, shuddering at the shock of it. The spring was small but its sources were deep and chill and the basin had a closely woven roof of split withes which kept it in shadow all day. The storm had torn the cover down, but Brann had contrived new supports when she built the basin back and it was just a little tottery now. Kitya took the pins from her hair, shook out the knot, ran her fingers through it, sighing with pleasure as the grass wind moved over her wet body and she was cool again for a little while.

Then she dressed and went to wake the others.

RAKIL

The horse threw up its head and whickered, then quickened the plodding walk which was all it had been capable of a moment before. Rakil tightened his grip on the reins and trotted along beside the beast. *It's either the river or a warband. Tungjii Luck, if it's water, I'll oil you with the best for a dozen years.*

The moon was down, but the stars burned like white fire; the long grass had quit a few miles back, giving way to patches of bare earth and varieties of scrub. The land was more eroded, crossed by dry washes, dipping into hollows, rising into brush crowned hillocks. He came over one of those hillocks and saw a band of darkness ahead, the river brakes, he was sure of it. "Whoa, horse, chirk! stand still, will you. . . ."

He settled into the saddle. "Baik a baik, it's water for us both, but not you till you cool down a little, I want you in shape to sell if I have to."

Getting through the tangle of saplings and berryvines took him the rest of the night. Tired, bleeding from dozens of scratches, he slid from the horse's back, half-hitched the reins to a tree behind a thicket of smaller saplings—the tree itself was hardly bigger around than his arm, but it was enough for the moment. Groaning with the soreness in every muscle, he lowered himself to the ground and started pulling off his boots.

"Cromp shadda. Shadda. Shadda. Cromp kidda. Kidda. . . ."

He froze, listened, rolled behind a bush. He couldn't understand the words, but he knew the rhythm; it was a leadsman's chant. A glance over his shoulder assured him the horse was out of sight from the river—if the beast would just keep his mouth shut the men in the boat wouldn't notice them.

A long, heavy barge came gliding round the bend, its sails reefed to minimum, just enough left to give it some way. There were two men at the tiller; from the tension visible in their bodies, this had to be a tricky stretch of river. The leadsman was leaning over the bow, casting his line with mechanical regularity, chanting the numbers in a shrill cadence that cut easily through the noise of the river.

Rakil grimaced. *Brann was right, she'll get her barge.* He closed his eyes, dropped his head on his crossed arms. *No business of mine now, just keeping out of her way is all the connection I mean to have with that one. Chir!*

When the barge had vanished round the next bend, he finished dragging off his boots and waded into the river. He drank, splashed water over his face, scrubbed at his battered arms until most of the sting was gone, then straightened suddenly as he heard the sound of singing coming along the water. *Gods! It isn't even full dawn yet.*

He plunged back to the bank, threw himself up it and into the shadow under the trees before the second boat appeared, a lateen-rigged twelve-footer crewed by three men in a good mood, with dozens of ropes hanging over the sides to the baskets holding their catch, keeping it alive and fresh for the markets to the south. A good day even before day began.

He watched them with envious eyes as they disappeared around the second bend. A smaller boat would be better, but he'd take what he could get. *Chirkin bad timing, this. Have to wait till dark before I try finding the village they're from.* He rubbed a hand across his face. *Shave . . . hnh! cold water, no fire for me, not now, no fire, no food. . . .* The horse whickered again, pulled against the reins, wanting water. "Chir! Have to get rid of you. There'll probably be horses around and you'll be announcing yourself the minute you get wind of them." He got to his feet. "Gods! I'm tired. Baik a baik, old beast, hold your oats till I get the tack off, then you're on your own. And I go expropriate me a boat."

At sundown the villagers retired behind high, thick earthen walls with guard dogs and their handler prowling the tops, but they didn't bother guarding their boats. What they feared came out of the grass, not the river.

Rakil showed his teeth in a predator's grin. *Too bad for them.* The village was across the river but that was no problem, he'd come upstream a good way from them; all he had to do was swim over and he was on his way south. He was a good swimmer, thank Purb for that. Old Flea had used him more than a time or two, swimming goods ashore he didn't want the local authorities to know about.

He waited a while longer, then stripped down, stuffed his clothing and other belongings into the saddlebags, tied them and the water skin onto his back and slid into the water.

He knew more about riptides and undertows than he did about rivers and the current was more powerful than he expected, but in the beginning he wasn't worried, just swam harder, angling across toward the line of boats; if he missed the first, the second would do, or the third.

He reached the middle and the river took hold of him, fought him as he tried to hold the angle, sweeping him along, threatening to suck him under. Gods! it was strong. And it was a long time since he'd done this much swimming. *Relax into it, man, let it do the work. Mutay mutay, that's the way, seduce the chirkin beast. . . .*

Foot by foot he won closer to the other side, closer and closer until he was out of the main thrust of the current and could sharpen the angle. The moonshadows of the boats slid past, then slid over him and finally he was close enough to catch hold of the rudderpost of one boat; his hand slipped, but he'd slowed himself enough to get a better hold on the next and hang there gasping, his legs so heavy he couldn't have walked even if he'd pulled himself from the water.

Up on the wall one of the guard dogs barked, but the handler scolded it and sent it on.

Rakil pressed his free hand over his mouth, stifling a gasp of laughter. One of Purb's dicta: People see what they expect to see and wouldn't believe the truth if you beat them over the head with it.

A rat bumped into him, squeaked, and paddled rapidly away. "Mutay mutay," he muttered, "get moving, man, before you ossify here."

He pushed himself into the littered water between this boat and one he'd caught onto first, paddling as silently as he could, feeling along the side until the water was so shallow his feet touched the bottom. The boats were tied to posts set into the bank, the mooring cable short enough to keep the bows dug into the mud.

The handler and the dogs came by again. He waited until they had time to get round to the other side, then hauled himself up, rolled over the rail and lay still, pressed against the stanchions, until he learned whether the noise he'd made had been noticed or not.

Two more rounds without any disturbance.

He sat up and looked around; he'd lucked into a ten-footer with a single mast and a well-built sail locker. "Tungjii," he murmured, "I owe you a big one."

Twenty minutes later, he was in the middle of the river, heading south.

KITYA

They left the spring at sundown and reached the Tenyasa around an hour before dawn. The river was a dark mirror with silver streaks where the starlight touched the current lines, undisturbed at the moment by any traffic.

They stripped the mules, packs, saddles, and halters,

and turned them out to graze as they wanted, did the same with the horses except for the two harnessed to the litter, then they set up camp and waited.

A day passed. There were fishing boats moving along the river, but nothing large enough to take the litter and its horses.

A second day passed.

No barges.

On the third day Kitya climbed one of the sturdier trees and sat in a crotch watching the water run. "I'd never thought I'd say it," she murmured to herself. "I am boooored." She giggled and scratched her nose. "After all that's happened the past few weeks, you'd think I'd welcome a little rest, but no, I want to get going, I'm bored bored bored here. Come on, you barges, you know you're going to be coming along sooner or later, why not make it sooner?" She kicked her feet, then leaned forward along the branch as she saw a small dark speck slide into view around the next bend up. "Ch'! another fishing boat." She straightened up, leaned against the trunk and thought about Serroi for a moment, wondering what the little woman was up to now. "Ahhhh, I'll never know, will I? Life. Find a friend, lose a friend." She kicked a bare foot, wiggled her toes. "Barge, barge, come on, barge."

As if in answer to her call a broad blunt nose edged around the bend. "Hai-yah! We're in business." She swung her legs over the limb, pushed off, caught at it to check her fall, dropped lightly onto the roots and took off running. It felt good to run, excitement bubbled in her blood, the wait was over, Midsummer's Eve was less than a week away and Navarre had promised that was it, that was the end.

Navarre stood on the riverbank, facing north, waiting for the barge to get close enough, Massulit cradled against his chest. Brann stood beside him, her hand on the shoulder of the forward litter horse. Kitya stroked the neck of the patient hindhorse, whispering her song beside his ear so she wouldn't distract Navarre; the Magus was tense, she could tell by the set of his shoulders and the way he held his head. There were people here, it wasn't like out in the grass, he didn't say much about it, but having people dead or maimed because of something he did made him sick, it was why he jumped so hard on Faan that time. He did what he had to ... he didn't want to have to ... that was why those were such good years in Valdamaz. She slid a sigh into her song. *Good years. Nu, we've good years coming, if I have anything to say about it.*

Massulit glowed.

The glow expanded, a sphere of shimmery blue that raced outward, upward, sinking into the ground.

It sped through the barge and stopped.

Everything stopped.

The Magus gestured. River water flew into an arch between the bank and the barge and froze solid, a gleaming silver bridge.

Brann tapped the shoulder of the litter horse, then flattened her hand on him to keep him steady as she urged him onto the bridge. Kitya sang a little louder to her charge; his ears were twitching, his head was up, but he took a step, then another, then moved steadily across the arch and onto the barge.

The Magus turned to face the barge. He stepped onto the bridge and walked slowly toward them, moving as if he waded through deep water with the weight of the world on his shoulders, the blue glow shrinking as he moved, erasing the bridge behind him.

He stepped onto the deck. His eyes were sunk deep in dark circles, his face was drawn, almost skeletal. Kitya shuddered at the melancholy she read there, the pain. He turned, looked outward. He straightened his shoulders, braced himself and drew the blueness back into the Talisman.

Wind screamed from the sky, the barge heeled over, righted again as a sheet of fire headed for it then skimmed past without touching them. The fire landed in the trees on the bank, consumed them in an instant, then raced away across the scrublands destroying everything in its path.

The Magus turned again, faced the startled, angry captain. "We will be traveling with you to Cumabyar," he said. "You've seen, so beware. Anything you do against us will be returned a hundredfold."

"Ba ba, so get ye'selves out the way. How long ye held us up here any.... D'droch! There's the *Fitcher* comin' up on us. Pras, Ughy, roll out three hands sail, hop it, want it set five mins past. Ernéach, I want to hear ye singing the leads, now, not breakfast tomorrow. Weetha witha, rest a y', get this mess trim so we c'n make up the longin' between us and *Fitcher,* look a her, she's gonna be up our backside ye next breath...."

Gradually the massive barge gained speed and more space opened between it and the one following. The bargemaster eyed it warily for nearly an hour, then he relaxed enough to get hot again and come charging at Navarre.

"Lissen a me, fool." He thrust his purpling face at Navarre, set bony fists on his wide hips. "We got one score mine barges coming long river, that's four hands full if ye need y' fingers for countin', and 'f ye got the sense 'f a mudcat, ye c'n see the river she's low. We mess up the spacin', then we got...." He stopped to search for a strong enough word but found none. "We got a mess. Tungjii Luck was blowin' kisses at ye, man, 'cause we pick up a gust earlier and stretch the longin', orwise ye'd be sitting on a holed out hulk ridin' the mud."

Navarre raised a brow. "Nay," he said.

The bargemaster blinked at him, opened his mouth, closed it again. He swallowed. "Na ay." His voice broke in the middle of the word, which annoyed him so he shouted it again, "NAY?"

"Nay. I would not allow that to happen."

"Oh." The bargemaster stared at him, the tip of his tongue running over his thin lips. Once again he opened his mouth, closed it without saying anything. He pushed past the horses and made his way to the bow and stood there, his shoulders hunched, his hands clasped behind him.

Kitya touched Navarre's arm. "Come, V'ret, put that thing away and let me work on your shoulders, you're so tight, you're thrumming like a harp."

"Before I fall down, hmm?"

"Nu, it wouldn't do your image much good."

He chuckled, tossed Massulit into the air, caught it and tucked it into the front of his shirt. He looked down at the bulge, shook his head. "I look like a half'n half that time's been hard on. If we move atop that middle bin, we'll be out of the way."

Four days later they went ashore at a landing outside Cumabyar. Mollified by a broad silver coin Brann proffered as payment for transport down river and promise of more, the bargemaster found a house for them on the outskirts of the city, four rooms with leaky roofs and a backyard hardly larger than a closet enclosed in crumbling walls.

Chapter 24
Convergences

Grunting with the effort, the Chained God Unchained got to his feet, stood with legs braced, dusting his hands off, the Hunger that had become a habit gnawing at him still. There was nothing left worth dredging for in Kyatawat, he'd sucked every Wieldy dry and the Wees were so skittish he couldn't catch them any more. The war in Eyoktyr called to him; Lair Iolair the Land God was roused and angry, he could smell her musk and it was starting to excite him.

He glanced into Gallindar, saw Faan trotting beside Desantro, the mahsar in her arms. His curses sharper than ice blades, hot and gold as the light that glittered on the vast curves of his body, he lifted a fist, tried to smash it down on her.

His fist rebounded from an invisible shield that intervened without warning or any sign of where it came from.

He roared with rage. "Chaggar, get after that girl! Gaaaah, can't you do anything right?" Scowling, he watched the Green Man shiver, then crouch, making a simulacrum which he sent trotting toward the Cummiltag.

The sight of the scuttling godlet was good as a gulp of seltzer, settling his rumbling belly.

"All right" he told himself. "My time's not yet and this is not the place." Grumbling under his breath, he stumped over to Eyoktyr and reached for Lair Iolair.

FAAN

As Desantro led her from the thicket of young cypresses, trees thick with clusters of ghosts flushed pink by the setting sun, ghosts that moaned softly as they stared at her, Faan gazed with dismay at the plump, ugly creature sitting in the wallow, working its hands in the gelatinous mud. *HIS hands. I have to remember that.* She met Desantro's anxious eyes, nodded, meaning I'll do what you said. She took a deep breath and walked toward him.

He lifted his head, turned his face toward her. Even the diminished light left to the day was cruel, accenting every seam and scar, the white-laced irids, the sag of his plump mouth, every unfortunate aspect of his form.

Ailiki jumped from Faan's arms and hopped gingerly from tussock to tussock until she was at the edge of the deepest muck. She sat up, crossed her black forepaws over her white ruff and contemplated him a second before tilting into one last leap, landing in his lap to nestle against him, purring loudly.

Faan was startled into laughter.

The Blind Man smiled, wiped a finger on his loincloth and scratched the mahsar along her spine. "One who is becoming," he said.

Faan blinked at the beauty of that voice. "She's the one thing I've managed to keep."

"The one who has stayed," the Blind Man corrected gently.

"Ba, that's better said." She ran a tongue across her lips. "You understand what's involved here?"

"Better than you, Honeymaid. Nay, there is no use denying what even the earth of Gallindar knows for truth." He tapped his finger on Ailiki's head. "Jump, fasfas, or you'll tumble in the muck." When the mahsar was clear, he stood, gray mud coating his haunches and his hands. "Come," he said and trudged to the tottery hovel that stood behind the muck. "You will be safe here, Honeymaid."

CLUINN DARRA TURRY I DUR

Glanne lay sprawled on the white fur carpet, the back of his head lacerated by . . . it looked something had chewed on it . . . and his legs, his buttocks . . . clawed . . . at least he was still breathing. Cluinn whirled, caught hold of the wizard, shook him. "You LET this happen, you. . . ."

Boddach Reesh touched Cluinn's wrist; pain shot through his body and he was flung against the white tile wall.

Reesh was by the door when Cluinn's eyes cleared. "You'd best make up your mind what you do want, little brother," the wizard said, his voice like dry leaves fluttering.

Cluinn looked at the sprawled, mutilated figure. "My brooother," he said, drawing out the syllables, surprise and wonder in his voice. "I thought . . . I thought it would be disgrace. That is what Wayyan Dun said . . . nay, implied . . . I did not know that I would have to see him . . . I did not know that I would feel so. . . ." He straightened. "Heal him."

"Nay, little brother. My hands are tied on this. I am forbidden to alter what the Honeymaid has done." The lines in his worn face deepened and his eyes turned dark as the sludgy pools of his swamp. "Ba. She is this time's Honeymaid. Wayyan Dun lied to you." He crouched, his flesh growing denser, his aspect turned fierce and frightening. "I'm for home. You Turrys leave me out of your plots, they're none of my business and they disgust me." He shouted a word that Cluinn's mind wouldn't hold and vanished.

Cluinn stared a moment at his brother's body, then he strode to the door. The mute maids stood in the shadowy court outside, the sunset flaring over their heads, arms crossed, hugging themselves, eyes huge with fear. He tapped the older one on the shoulder. "You. Fetch the Carach, see he knows Glanne's hurt, see he brings whatever he'll need." As she went hurrying out through the open gate, he turned to the other. "You. Clean the room, there should be nothing compromising left when the Carach gets here. You understand?"

She nodded and scuttled past him. He glanced at the door, but he didn't go back in. When Glanne was whole, huge and dominating, laughing at his little brother, charging through life without a care for what he was doing to others, it was easy to hate him, to grow sick with jealousy and want him humbled, hurt, forced for once to take second place. Wayyan Dun hadn't even hinted at death, only held the promise that Cluinn would *have* and Glanne *be without*. Seeing Glanne like that, bleeding, torn, his breath loud and labored, Cluinn was sick with anger at the god and . . . and at the girl.

Girl? Thing. That's what she is. Sucking Ghost given flesh. I'll get her! She'll pay. Malheasta! She'll pay.

He paced the gritty flags, glaring whenever the mute maid flitted past him, carrying away the aids hanging on the tool wall.

Following close behind his lantern bearer, followed by his nurses and his aides, the Carach came bustling into the darkened court, a little bald man with enormous coppery mustaches and a dithery, arch manner that

Cluinn found especially irritating this day. "The waghin was urgent, O Prionsar. What IS the difficulty?"

"The Heir has been injured, he's in there. You see he's taken care of." Cluinn brushed the hair from his eyes, smiled as he saw the Carach wince and draw back when he got a good look at Cluinn's face. "His life is in your hands," he said, beginning to relish the new power in his own hands; with the Heir taken out, he was Heir Presumptive. It didn't lessen his anger at the girl or his sickness at his brother's injuries, but pleasure coiled in his stomach and he felt himself recovering his composure. He nodded briskly. "Your hands," he repeated to underline the point. "I must inform the Foréach and my mother the Réachta, so I'll not be there to oversee your work. I hope I shall not be needed. Go, no more fooling around here, Carach. Go! My brother needs you."

He watched the little man hurry off, then left the court, moving through the thickening dark, driven to a trot by the fury of the anger building in him, heading for the guard barracks and the office of the Kuic Gara, the chief of the Cummiltag guard force. If he was asleep or eating or whoring, too bad, he was going to have to get up off his haunches and start the hunt for the girl. With those eyes and that hair, she shouldn't be too hard to find.

FAAN

The scream tore through Desantro's pleasant drifting dream; she jerked up and sat gasping and dazed, blinking into the darkness, the bed moving under her as Cyram stood. She reached out and uncovered the night lamp. "What is it?"

He was holding the cassock he'd tossed over the chair before they went to bed. "Go back to sleep, Des.

It's just Faan. I expected this. She was too composed. I know Glanne and his tastes, she'll have had a very very bad time the past few days."

Desantro slid out of bed. "Nay, Cyram, I couldn't sleep. I'll go with you. She might want a woman's hand."

The Wildings swirling above her in agitations of glimmering foam, moaning and crying out in their tiny voices, Faan writhed in a tangle of sheets, her face the only thing about her that Desantro recognized, her body a horror of shifting, twitching flesh and rubbery bone. Burning flesh. Red flames and blue flames leapt over her appendages, struggling to break free but not quite escaping the hold she kept on them despite her nightmare. Ailiki pressed her body against Faan's side; her dark eyes were full of fear and sorrow, but she stayed where she was despite the danger.

By the time they reached her, Faan's screams had stopped but Desantro found the girl's whimpering and gasps more disturbing. She set her hand on Cyram's arm, stopped him, told him what she could see and he could not. "She's changing. As if she's a shifter, she's making tentacles and pods and things that I couldn't name, it's sickening, Cy, horrible."

"That explains the mechanics of her escape," the Blind Man said calmly. "What else?" He nodded as she told him about the Wild Magic and Ailiki. "When I'm settled, m' grua," he said, "gird your courage high and find a limb for me to hold, mm?"

"There's fire, too."

"Then you'll be snatching fast and careful, eh my sitabéag, my dulcerie?"

Cyram the Blind Man sat beside Faan, cradling in his strong hands a limb that shifted shape a thousand times; fires burned round his fingers but did not touch him.

"*Screanhai*," he sang softly to her, his voice reaching out to caress and surround her,

> *Screanahai, I feel your heart leaping*
> *Circin scafrai, I hear your sad cheeping*
> *Caisachercai, stop your sad weeping*
> *Caochan-mo holds you secure*
>
> *Saradagad, I feel your heart yearning*
> *Scallbéag scriai, I see your fires burning*
> *Sobbra diachra, stop your soul's churning*
> *Caochan-mo holds you secure*

Desantro rubbed her hands along her thighs. *This is Faan. Not a monster. Faan, child, sad little one, I know how she hurts, I've held her before when memories got too much for her. Shape doesn't matter, it's the soul that matters, Cyram has showed me that a thousand ways . . . ah, what pain she's in. . . .*

She captured what she thought was a wrist, a hand, held it gently between hers, just held it, letting the Blind Man's voice weave a spell that had nothing to do with magic.

A few minutes later the body was Faan again, the whimpering stopped, and the girl opened her eyes. "What. . . ."

Cyram rubbed her hand, but said nothing.

Desantro bent closer. "You were dreaming, Fa. Burning and changing."

The Blind Man set Faan's hand on the blanket beside his knee. "Tell us what happened. Tell us all of it. Purge yourself, child. See? Your little friend the mahsar is curled against your side, she didn't leave you, she exhausted herself trying to get to you. See the light that swims over you? The Wildings are here, they weep for you, listen to them. Desantro is here. She labored for you. We all did. What happened wasn't your fault, get rid of it. We can hear anything, we're your friends, we love you, it doesn't matter what happened, believe me, it doesn't matter. . . ."

Faan closed her eyes, tears sliding from under the lashes. After a moment, she began talking.

KITYA

Kitya stood in the middle of the bare yard, hands on hips, scowling at the cloudless sky, turning in a slow circle as she did so. It was early in the morning, but the day was already hot and white, the sun like a hammer. Her hair was loose from the knot she usually wore it in; the fine black strands stood out from her head, moving as if blown by an erratic wind, though there was no wind, the air in the yard was as still as stagnant water.

Brann looked out the kitchen door, came over to her. "So?"

Kitya blinked, smoothed her hair down, grimacing as it clung to her hands, wrapped itself around her fingers. "Have you ever stood in a place where two or three streams meet and felt the currents knitting around your legs, tearing apart, colliding, sometimes all these things at once?"

"No, can't say I have. It sounds complicated."

"Simple compared to what's coiling round this city." She brushed at her eyes, moved her shoulders. "Nu, I've decided. A child's trick might work when something more difficult will not."

"Will telling it compromise you?"

Kitya chuckled. "Neka, never would. I'm going to make me a find-it pebble, set it on my tongue, and go wandering to see if I can chase Fa down that way. Depends on if she's loose or in a trap somewhere."

Brann sighed. "Tak hasn't stirred; if I didn't see him breathe every hour or so, I'd think he was dead. For him to wake, Faan must have to touch him, or at least come close. I don't want to push you, Kat, but if you could hurry. . . ."

Kitya put on a long dress of heavy white cotton, wound a length of white cloth into a turban and pulled the end across her face, attaching it to the twists of cloth with a pin Navarre had bought for her late yesterday. She'd seen several women dressed like that and it served to hide the more obvious aspects of her foreignness.

She popped the pebble in her mouth and left.

At the end of the unpaved street that led to the house, she turned in a slow circle, trying to sort out the one direction that had a tarter taste than the others. It was difficult, the change was so slight.

Panting from the heat, she hurried along the intersecting street, stopping at every corner to hold the pebble against her palate and slide her tongue across its lower surface. As far as she could tell, there was no change.

At the fifth corner, she frowned, then turned into a lane that wound toward the bay; she'd barely taken two steps when the tartness increased measurably. She tucked the pebble in her cheek and went quickly along the weedy, cluttered lane, clinging to the line of shadow on the north side where the tenements were taller and blocked some of the punishing sun; she was bred for northern climes and didn't deal well with heat, especially this clinging humid type that bled its damp into her lungs and made her breathing labored.

The tartness grew stronger and stronger until her mouth was puckered with it . . . then it started to fade. She swore under her breath and turned back.

Moving back and forth, dizzy with the heat and the labor of breathing, sickened by the increasingly foul taste in her mouth, Kitya kept walking, getting closer and closer to Faan with every turn she made. . . .

Until she tottered into a shell-paved street lined on both sides with neat, smallish houses, large courts attached to them, high walls and hidden gardens. There were people in the street, more than a hundred of them, all poor, workers, women and men who'd left their jobs to squat and stare at a house that shimmered through layer upon layer of ghosts. The watchers were packed in neat curved rows; shoulder to shoulder they waited without speaking or doing anything but stare at the house. As Kitya stood on the corner, astonished by all this, at some signal she couldn't read, a section of the squatters stood; several of them walked away, still without saying a word. The ones who stayed moved forward, leaving their own spots vacant. Several others appeared a moment later, took the vacated places and began their own vigils. They were packed so tightly, layer upon layer of them, that she hadn't a hope of getting through them. She didn't have to. Faan was in there. They knew it and she knew it.

She looked carefully around, setting the place firmly in memory, spat the pebble out, and started back to report to the others.

CLUINN DARRA TURRY I DUR

Glancing nervously at the Prionsar standing silent in the corner of the office, the Kuic Gara took the list of outside workers from the Housekeeper, ran his finger along it. There was a red check beside each name. It was midmorning and this was the fifth Koil he'd interviewed, with a lack of success that was making him increasingly nervous. Turrys expected results and everything he'd done so far had brought him nothing. No intruders anywhere, no one missing so far. Either the workers were

Gallindari and hadn't gone beyond the Wall for days, or
they were innocently at work, without a stain on their
characters. This interview was going the same way.
"Every one of them came in this morning? You know
that of your own observation?"

A Turry Outborn with more pride than good sense,
the Housekeeper scowled at him. "Certainly not. That is
the business of my Kuics, what are they for, otherwise?
I will say this, they are competent, all of them and if
they mark a woman present, she is."

"Call them here and hold them ready to answer my
questions."

"And the work?"

"If they are so competent, that should be settled by
now. The workers presumably can handle what has to
be done, otherwise why were they hired? Bring the
Kuics here and wait. Any more insolence on your part
will be treated as rebellion against your Foréach." He
smiled sourly at the sudden beading of sweat on her
face. "As you go out, call the Garden Koil, tell him to
get in here."

Cluinn stood in the shadows at the back of the room,
arms folded, eyes on the floor. According to the
Carach's messenger, Glanne was stable, neither failing
nor improving; a reassuring postscript added that this
was good news, time was the best of healers. The edge
was off his impatience, his anger had cooled to ice now
that the search was well started, agents in the streets
with the girl's description, the Kuic Gara winnowing
through the work force to find the one who brought in
whatever it was that nullified the wizard's spell.

The Garden Koil was one of Cluinn's many half-
uncles, a white-haired ancient, half-blind and hard of
hearing, but not a stupid man for all that.

The Kuic ran his fingers along the list of names, not-
ing the checks by each—halting by a name with no

check beside it. "Desantro. Foreigner. Assigned to the Currtle Garden. She didn't come in this morning? Why?"

"I assumed you'd want to know, so I brought the Kuic with me. Name Wayyan Grual. Shall I call him in?"

Wayyan Grual smoothed a thumb along his jawline, stroking his short silver-gray beard. "Ba," he said slowly, "she came to me a few days ago on recommendation. A good worker, a great deal more skilled than most we haven't trained ourselves. She spent her days in the worksheds and the Currtle Garden, did nothing out of the ordinary. Either Megglen Bris or the shed steward Sorv Harrag can account for almost every moment of her time inside the walls and can attest she never went near the Closed Courts. I spoke to them when I made the list; they're willing to swear to what I've just told you. Do you wish them summoned for questioning?

The Kuic Gara glanced at Cluinn but the Prionsar said nothing, just kept staring at the floor. "Ba, have them brought to the anteroom. We'll talk with them when we're finished with you. What more do you know about her?"

"Very little. I tested her knowledge and was pleased by it. She did mention that she learned her craft within palace walls, she did not say where that palace was."

Cluinn looked up. "On recommendation," he said. "Whose?"

Wayyan Grual's hands shook; hastily he laced his fingers together to conceal the tremble. He touched his tongue to his lips. "Is there any need for that? It is not possible she had a part in . . . in whatever this is about."

The Kuic Gara slapped his hand on the desk. "Answer, ahmdan!"

Wayyan Grual started, bit his lip so hard it began

bleeding. "There's nothing wrong, O Gara-gai. It was only the Blind Man, the mud reader, you know, the one in the Acra Athuilinn. She brought a note from him. I threw it away. It was of no importance. He's read for me, done me a favor, that's why I saw her, why I gave her the test. It isn't why I hired her. I hired her because she was good, not because of that letter. Ask Megglen Bris. She was impressed, too." His voice trailed off; he sat hunched over, a terrified little man, waiting for the crunch.

RAKIL

The tavern was dark and crowded. Rakil sat at a small table shoved against the wall and sipped at a stoup of cheap red wine; he'd found out his first day that the beer in this land was both expensive and slop only a desperate man would drink.

For the past four days he'd been nosing about, trying to find someone to slide him down the coast. No luck. He kept hearing the risk was too big, the profits too low; he didn't believe either, he knew smugglers who'd sail in a hurricane if they thought there was a cargo in it. Another day almost shot. These Gallindari were a bunch of dithering cambo-lyors, still looking him over. It was driving him hakalouk; if they didn't get a move on, he was going to end up chewing his elbows.

He drank more wine and swore under his breath, next place he climbed down, they'd have to have some good brew or he was out of there. One thing you could say for the jellies, they knew their beer. He sighed, thinking of Karascapa Tavern, the noise, the color, the smell of it at Midsummer when the best of the ales were broached. Spiced wine, poker hot, that was fine for winter, but come the sun, it was beer that was best. Midsummer's Eve, tomorrow night, Humarie would be getting ready for ... Purb the Flea, his fault I'm not there now, may he return as a flea in truth and get smashed as soon as he was out of the egg.

A man came through the crowd and stopped at Rakil's table, a one-eyed man with his gray hair pulled through a glazed ring and a heavy china earring dangling from one ear. He flourished a roll of paper and a stick of charcoal. "Ye portr'et, doon amach?" As Rakil started to wave him away, he leaned closer, muttered, "Ye lookin f'r a slide west?"

Rakil pulled the wine pot to the edge of the table, curled his hands about it. "Might be. How much?"

"Two gillas and m' drawin' with it.

Rakil took two of the broad coppers from his purse, set them on the table, kept his fore and middle fingers pressed down on them and waited.

The picture surprised him when the man finished and passed it to him; it was an elegant drawing, as good as any he'd seen. The scruffy old man had caught a strong likeness with a few crisp lines and some patches of shadow, and beyond that had produced a rhythm that turned the whole into a lively dance for the eyes.

The old man smiled at his surprise, tapped his patch. "The hands remember," he said, "but the eye, nay, color is gone, depth is gone." He folded his hands on the table, fingertips touching the coins. "There's a man who knows a man who might be willing to slide if you come to terms."

"And where do I find this man who knows a man?"

"In the Grand Market, seek among the bootseller booths for the Sign of the Trefoil, then look for Skel Fewlwad, you can tell him by his red hair and the thumb that's missing off his left hand." He stood, bowed, walked away without looking back.

The sun was low in the west, nearly touching the shakes on the godon roofs, glaring into Rakil's eyes as he turned into Market Street. Despite the heat and the lateness, the streets were thronged near the Market, with street musicians, players and people hawking off trays to earn enough to feed themselves and their families, clustering around anyone who might possibly buy from them, anyone with a foreign look. He elbowed his way along, ignoring the tugs at his sleeves and the curses at his back, his purse tucked inside his shirt with one arm crossed over it.

Inside the gate there was more order but nearly as much desperation, shouts from the merchants, clamor from the musician-beggars at their traditional patches of claimed earth. Frowning at the noise, Rakil showed a copper skel to a beggar boy, bent down to shout in his ear. "Lead me to the bootmakers' stalls, hm?"

"Through here, doon amach. Possmo cul, Serkas." He slapped his arm at the merchant yelling at him to get away, then trotted along one of the aisles between the booths, looking over his shoulder and beckoning Rakil to follow.

"Rakil? Is that you? Is your name Rakil?" It was a woman's voice, low and throaty, not one he'd heard before.

Rakil snapped his fingers to halt the guide, turned to confront the woman, wondering who she was and what she wanted.

She was standing before a spice merchant's display, almost within arm's reach, surrounded by the pungent smells from the pots open behind her, a stocky woman somewhat older than he was, with a freckled face and exuberantly curling light brown hair. She looked familiar, but it was a moment before he realized it was his own face he was seeing, the one reflected in the mirror when he shaved. "Desantro?"

"It is you. Gods, it is you." She flung herself at him, hugged him so hard his ribs creaked.

"Quasquas, Desa, let me breathe. How long has it been?"

She loosened her grip, moved back a step to stand with her hands flattened against his chest, her eyes fixed on his face. "Too long to count the years. You're looking well, Raki. Is Purb here? Do you have to. . . ."

He looked around nervously. "This is no place to be talking about that."

"Vema, I've just about finished my buying. Come home with me, there're people I want you to meet."

"Aaah, I can't, Desa, not yet, there's a man I've got to see."

"Sa sa, then later. Supper. I'll buy. You know a place, or shall I. . . ."

"The Dobbey Yun, Saddlemaker's Street. You know it?"

"I can find it. An hour?"

"Baik a baik." He started to turn away, then caught her in a hug of his own. "Tsa! it's good to see you, Des."

CLUINN DARRA TURRY I DUR

"But . . ." Cluinn ground his teeth; his mother always did this to him. She never gave him credit for anything he tried, never! And worse, his father listened to her. Trusted her. He leaned into the window, watching the sun go down on his hopes, the darkness come sliding in to cover that sucking vampire who drained his brother.

"That's always been your worst fault, Cluinn. Jumping to conclusions." The Réachta Maissora Turry Gaoth Turry stabbed her needle through the cloth with a vigor that expressed her exasperation with her second son. She was a tall woman, her thick, long braids as determinedly copper as they'd been when she was an unfledged girl, her face lined now, a thin face with the jutting cheekbones all the Turrys had; she was a cousin who'd married a cousin before he was named Heir and who'd congratulated herself on her foresight every day since. "Nay. You've done well enough so far, ahaaahah."

That surprised arc of sound was an insult that knifed through Cluinn more painfully than any curse.

The Foréach grunted, looked up from the list he was running his thumb down. "Well enough," he rumbled, flipped the page over and started down the next list.

"There are only three people missing," Cluinn said patiently. "It wouldn't take an hour to bring them in and start the questioning."

"Precipitate as ever. Never act before you have ordered your facts." Maissora Turry Gaoth sighed, set the tambour frame on her knee. "The Kuic Gara assures us that by tomorrow noon we'll know everything there is to know about poor Glanne's unfortunate liaison and then, if there's still need, we'll have those low sorts brought in. Such people know nothing, Cluinn, they don't have the achinn to plan something like this, at best you'd only get a few hints, at worst you'd frighten off the real plotters. You didn't consult the Arddwar. Why?"

"What would he have to do with this? This is a secular matter, nothing to do with the god."

"Jump jump, just like a little flea—with about as many brains. Anything that touches the Heir, Cluinn, anything, that also touches the god."

The Foréach looked up again. "Feyra feyra, Cluinn. Your Mother's got it on the head again. Touches Heir, touches Wayyan Dun. You go see the Arddwar, tomorrow's soon enough for those gnats that keep biting you. They aren't going anywhere, I've closed the port and set the Gara Airn'aic guarding the roads and the waters. Nay nay, they're not going anywhere."

* * *

Cast by the watch torches, Cluinn's shadow jagged ahead of him as he paced along the top of the Cummiltag Wall, staring down into the dark blot that was the city. He'd pried surveillance out of the Kuic Gara, a pair of men for each of the houses, to keep an eye on them during the night and follow anyone who tried to steal away. It was all he could do till the rest of this foolishness was played out. *Where are you, Chaggar? You promised me your help. You promised!*

Chapter 25
Focus

Faan kicked the sheets back, wiggled on the pallet, stretched, then rolled up till she was sitting, her arms wrapped around her legs. She felt good, rested, and hungry, filled with energy in a way she'd hadn't been for days.

Ailiki sat on her hind legs, her black forepaws crossed over her white ruff; her mouth was open, her dark eyes twinkling with silent laughter.

"Hah!" Faan scrambled onto her knees and jumped up, looking around for the shirt and trousers she'd worn from the Cummiltag.

There was a pile of neatly folded clothing beside the pallet, green silk underthings, a bright blue silk blouse and a darker blue skirt, long, slim, made from a heavy cotton, copiously embroidered in a hundred more shades of blue. A blue and green scarf fell off as she shook out the skirt, a scarf like the one she'd been wearing the day she was taken. For an instant her happiness faltered; Ailiki pressed against her leg, warmth flowing into her. "Nayo, I won't! I don't have to think about it." She bent, touched the mahsar's head, laughed and began getting dressed.

She danced in circles a moment, watching the skirt swing out from her legs, then she dropped onto the pallet and buckled on sandals dyed a dark blue to match the skirt, picked up the last of the objects put there for her to find, a box made from a dark, tight-grained wood, polished until it was smoother than the silk in her blouse. The tiny hinges were bronze and set into the wood so that only the loops showed. She used her thumbs to push up the top, then gasped with pleasure.

There was a necklace inside, disks of turquoise in a heavy silver chain, a pair of earrings to match.

Faan leaned over the dark still water at the end of the ivory pier, using it as a mirror while she combed her hair, sighing at the gray curls that clung to her skull, mourning again the long black strands that Reyna had brushed and brushed. She thought about him with a gentle sadness, the pain of losing him washed away by the nightmare of the last days.

She heard a step behind her, turned her head. "'Morning, Desa."

"Stand up, let's see you. Ah, the things do fit, I was a little worried about the skirt."

"It's beautiful, all of it. How did you know. . . ."

"I picked up your gear from Cewely's, but Blind Man said you'd NEED something bright and pretty once you came out of that place. I remembered that scarf you liked so I bought stuff like it. You look good, Fa, real good. You hungry?"

Laughing, Faan tucked the comb into a pocket in the skirt and reached out her hand. "I could eat a horse with room left over." She winked at the mahsar. "Ailiki, too, I don't doubt. Lead us to it."

The intensity of the light streaming through the small dusty windows set high up on the walls of the crude kitchen made Faan blink in surprise. "I hadn't realized it was so late."

"Nu, Blind Man said to let you sleep as long as you needed; he said there was nothing important you had to do this morning and you needed rest. You needed it bad, he said. And it's not all that late, it's still over an hour till noon." While she talked, Desantro took the kettle from the fire, steam streaming from the spout, and poured it through tea in a woven wood strainer into a silky pot. "Das'n Vuor," she said. "The real thing. He likes things that feel good, you know. I've never touched anything so precious." She set the pot on the table beside Faan's hand, brought over a drinking bowl. "This didn't lose its handle, it's not supposed to have one. It belongs to a set that's older than my grandfather's grandfather would be, were he still alive. Think of it, something that fragile. The pot's got Callim's Mark on the bottom, the mark of the maker. Blind Man showed me, said everyone who knew pots knew his name. From some island on the far side of the world, he said. Dead two hundred years, he said, but still folk know his name. Isn't that amazing, Fa? I wish I were a maker like that. . . ." She sighed and broke an egg into a frypan. "Scrambled good enough?"

"Fine." Faan pushed Ailiki aside and drew a finger along the curve of the pot; it was almost like stroking something alive. "Two hundred years, sa sa. Where is the Blind Man . . . has he got a name? I feel funny calling him that."

"His name's his business. If he wants you to know, he'll tell you. He's outside, sitting in his muck. I don't know why, he told Catycamm the Hag to send folk away if they came to talk to him. Not that they could get through that mob in the street. Nu, I suppose he wants to keep an eye. . . ." She chuckled. "Nay, that's wrong, isn't it. He wants to keep a hand on things so they don't blow up in our faces." She tilted the egg onto a plate with two slices of buttered toast, brought it to Faan, then fetched another drinking bowl and settled herself across the table, dropping into silence as she sipped at the hot tea.

"You look. . . ."

"Happy?" Desantro ran her thumb across the bowl's black glaze, then she nodded. "I am."

"You're going to stay with him?"

"This time, you mean. Diyo, I am. I finally am."

"Then there's something good come of this."

"More than just that, Fa." She set the bowl down, flattened her hands on the table and leaned toward Faan, her eyes shining with excitement. "Day before last, I was in the Grand Market, buying some things, when who should come walking along like he owned the place? Rakil, Fa, Rakil himself."

"Your brother? Really your brother?"

"Deee-yo." Desantro jumped up, began pacing back and forth in front of the cookstove. "You were right, Fa, the mirror was right. You said match freckle for freckle and that's the truth. Took him only a minute to recognize me though he hasn't seen me for twenty years— and I knew him even faster when I saw him in the round. He had to meet someone so he couldn't talk right then, and I had to be back here, of course. But we got together later, for supper."

Despite Desantro's enthusiasm, Faan could hear the echoes of her disappointment in her brother's lukewarm response; surely after twenty years of separation, he could have put off any business he had for a few hours if he couldn't manage a whole day. She had a feeling that she was going to feel as tepid about Rakil as she did about Tariko. Vema, that didn't matter, they weren't her kin. She reached out, scratched the mahsar between her ears. *You're better than the lot of them, sister mine.*

"We talked for hours, Fa. He's going to meet me again, noon, same place, Blind Man says I should bring him here and I will, didn't the Diviner say we two would set eyes on him before Midsummer?" She stopped by the table, hands on hips, a light dusting of perspiration shining on her face. "You know what today is, Fa? Tonight rather? It's Midsummer's Eve. Right on schedule, hmh?"

"I knew it was soon. Not quite this soon. I kind've lost track of time in that. . . ." She closed her hands tight about the drinking bowl, its hoarded warmth vaguely comforting. Ailiki felt her trouble, crept to her, and pressed against her arm. "I thought we'd be in the Myk'tat Tukery by now, but maybe that wasn't what Tungjii meant after all."

"Nu, all he said was when you found my kin, you'd find your key. He didn't say when you were going to use it. Or how."

"Nay, that he did not. Your sister brought me Navarre, though we seem to've misplaced him for the moment, so I suppose Rakil here means the Talisman should be around somewhere."

"Nu . . ." Desantro pushed back her chair and stood. "While I'm cleaning up here and getting ready to meet Rakil, why don't you go talk to the Blind Man? Blind he may be, but he's got the clearest sight of anyone I know."

Kitya smoothed back the wisps of hair escaping from her high knot to tickle her face, shifted her feet, her boots scraping on the gritty setts of the courtyard. It was nearly noon and the sun was hammering at them, but Navarre wouldn't give the signal to start. He stood with his hand in the litter, resting on Massulit, waiting for the right moment. She couldn't see the Talisman, but its glow crept between the unlaced curtains, painted blue highlights on his face and loose white tunic.

Graybao shimmering beside her, intermittently only a patch of smoke, Brann stood with her hand on the lead horse's neck, waiting, as they all were waiting, for Navarre to say it was time to move.

* * *

Rakil scowled at his cup because it wasn't politic to scowl at his sister. He'd forgotten how bossy she was, how sure she was that she alone knew what was best for everyone. "I've got a smuggler willing to take me downcoast and Kitya's kech to lead me from there. I don't want more complications, Des. That's what those people mean. I don't want to go anywhere near Drinker of Souls again and she's in Cumabyar by now, heading straight for your friend Faan."

"Nu, Raki, I don't want to find you just to lose you again. Talk to the Blind Man. Please?"

"Lose me? I'm not a baby, Des, not your baby brother now, I don't need you protecting me."

"It isn't for you, Rakihi, it's for me, my peace. Please?"

"I can't stay, the ship's leaving with the darktide and I'm going to be on her."

Desantro glowed at him, having got her way. "Come on, then. The sooner we get there, the longer I'll have you."

The Kuic Gara's pale blue eyes switched nervously between Maissora Turry Gaoth and her son. He resented her presence here when he should have been reporting either to the Prionsar whose reactions he could predict and deal with or to the Foréach. He didn't understand the Réachta and he was afraid of her; he didn't know what she wanted so how could he give it to her?

From the window bench where he sat, his legs drawn up, his arms draped over his knees, Cluinn watched him, angry and amused, knowing everything passing through the Kuic's head. Hadn't he felt it all himself a hundred times before?

The Kuic Gara wet his lips, opened the folder in his hand and began droning on in a report that as far as Cluinn could tell said nothing that they hadn't known yesterday. There was a bitter taste in the Prionsar's mouth, a foreboding of failure.

The grand doors sprang open and the simulacrum of Wayyan Dun strode into the room. "WHY DO YOU LINGER?" His voice struck at the walls, breaking hooks and sending ornaments crashing to the floor; it hammered at the Réachta, tore her sewing away from her, knocked the Kuic Gara onto his knees, then onto his face. It didn't touch Cluinn.

Wayyan Dun crossed to the Prionsar, set his large green hand on Cluinn's shoulder. "THE HEIR SPOKE TRUTH BEFORE AND YOU DID NOT LISTEN, YOU DID NOT ACT."

"The Heir?" Maissora Turry's voice was full of indignation. "The Heir is injured and unconscious, he said nothing."

"THAT SICKNESS YOU CALL YOUR SON IS NO LONGER MY CHOSEN; THIS IS HE." He hauled Cluinn from the window bench, stood with a massive arm around the young man's shoulders. "THIS IS HE WHO WITHOUT QUESTION HAS DONE MY WILL. I MYSELF PROCLAIM HIM HEIR AND FORÉACH TO BE. COME, MY MAEC, MY BRATH, THE GIRL IS AT THE BLIND MAN'S HOUSE. CALL YOUR GUARDS AND GO. I WILL AWAIT YOU THERE."

The simulacrum faded to a green shimmer, then vanished.

Cluinn drew in a long breath, closed his eyes a moment. Then he turned to the Kuic Gara who was trembling and still on his knees. "You heard Wayyan Dun. I want twenty men and twenty to stand in reserve. We will leave for the Blind Man's House in fifteen minutes, you and I and the guard." Ignoring his mother, he stalked from the room, the Kuic Gara hastening after him.

"Now," Navarre said. "We start now."

* * *

"Best not go out, Honeymaid. That lot would be tearing ye apart."

Faan started, looked around. The Gate Hag had crept from her hutch and was standing in the shadow of the tulip tree by her doorstep; the tree was shivering in a wind Faan could neither feel nor hear, a wind that sent the rose-tipped petals fluttering down around her stooped form.

"What do they want?"

"Nothing. It's what you want that they've come for."

"Then they can sit till they ossify. Potzheads. Colthu, Old Woman, when Desantro brings her brother back, let them in fast, huh? And none of them out there."

The Gate Hag cackled. "Worry your head about what you're to do, bébé, and let an old woman take care of what has been her business for more years than you've been breathin'."

Faan settled on a tussock of grass, grunted as Ailiki jumped against her stomach, then settled in her lap. She stroked the mahsar and watched the Blind Man work his mud. "What do you see in that?"

He drew his hands free and rested them on his thighs. "All things are in the Mother."

Faan snorted. "Save that for your paying clients."

He smiled. "See. That's not the right word, Honeymaid."

"Do me a favor. Call me Fa. Honeymaid gives me knots in the belly."

"A chaerta, Fa. In the mud there is only now, all past and all present are there in that now; it is my Gift to untangle them. In the mud are the patterns of all things; it is my Gift that I can read them."

"What are my patterns telling you? If you feel like answering me. There's no profit in it. You've housed me, fed me, clothed me, all I have you already own."

He ignored her acerbic comment, dropped his hands in the mud again and left them there, still as hibernating turtles. "I have been trying to do that very thing, young Faan; all the morning I have been running the tangles of your life, but the knot is beyond me. I can tell you nothing."

"Gods!"

"No doubt."

Rakil looked from the Blind Man to Faan, opened his mouth to speak, but before he could get the words out, there was a noise behind him. He wheeled, swore under his breath as he saw the litter emerge from the trees, swaying and creaking from the slaps of the low hanging branches. Brann walked beside the lead horse. She nodded at him, briefly, no smile, and headed for Faan.

Kitya grinned and waved at Desantro; she was walking with Navarre beside the litter. "Sveik, Des. We took the long way round."

"Nu, it's Midsummer's Eve. Whatever way, you got here."

Rakil looked down at her. "I told you, Des,' he muttered, "I didn't want to see these people."

"Now you're here, Rakihi, does it matter that much? They're not interested in you, it's Faan they're for."

"But that woman brings trouble with her. Come with me, Des. If you feel you have to, you can come back later when the mess is over."

"Kao kao, Rakihi. Look, the mess is already started."

Faan got to her feet as the strange woman came toward her, leading that litter, anxiety glittering in green eyes that somehow seemed familiar, something she'd seen in a dream, perhaps. Ailiki crouched at her ankle, watching the woman, sending waves of warmth up through Faan. "I know Navarre and Kitya, but who are you?"

"My name is Brann, I am also called Drinker of Souls. And I do know you, Faan Korispais Piyolss, I was present at your Nameday. And I know that little creature beside you. Greetings, Ailiki, it's been a long time. Navarre."

Navarre reached into the litter, brought out the jewel Faan had seen in Qelqellalit's Pool, the sapphire orb that was bigger than his fist, cool and shimmery like distant water. The star in its heart pulsed and called to her. "Take it," he said. "Hold it, Sorcerie. It's what you came here to get."

Cluinn darra Turry i Dur, Heir by the proclamation of the Land God Himself, marched a conqueror through the streets of HIS city, twenty guards behind him, crisp and disciplined.

When they reached the Blind Man's street, though, the marching stopped. The street was choked with people and Cluinn's forces couldn't move—until Chaggar himself came striding along the way, the Green Man himself, a broad giant with a rakish, rat-eaten look, half the leaves of his garment turned brown and breaking with every shift and change of the semi-translucent body, the wind of his passage laden with the odors of hot grass, leaves, pollen, and rot, a melange of green things living and dead. As he came nearer, shadowy eye-blotches fixed on the house where the Blind Man lived, he grew taller and taller until his head was lost in sundazzle, his immense green feet bringing darkness to whatever he stepped on, though no harm, he wouldn't harm his own. But he terrified them and they scattered before him, opening the way for Cluinn and the guard.

Faan took the sapphire warily, holding it away from her as if she feared it would bite. There was a low thrum rising from the heart of the earth as the blue glow of the Talisman crept slowly out from its center until she was bathed in it.

Screams and yells of rage came from beyond the trees, crashing noises, sounds of feet, the figure of the Green Man appeared, caught in sunglare, striding in ominous silence toward the house.

As soon as she touched the jewel, the litter swayed and groaned, Tak WakKerrcarr rose to his knees, swung down and walked with long strides to stand looking down at Faan. "What is it you want, Sorcerie? Think before you answer."

From the heart of the Blue she looked up at him. "I don't have to think," she said. "I want my mother."

Cluinn burst from the trees at the head of his guard, his sword out. He saw Faan, roared something incoherent and ran at her.

Chaggar reached down an immense hand like painted light and dragged it through Faan, immersing her in its green but otherwise not affecting her. He cried out words too huge for her ears to comprehend.

The mud glowed a thick wild blue and rippled into waves tossed about like ocean waves in a storm. Cyram the Blind Man sat unmoved in the middle of it; Desantro knelt beside him, her hand on his shoulder.

Three appeared, standing close together.

A tall burly man in a rumpled white robe, with long gray hair falling past massive shoulders, skin like polished mahogany, yellow eyes that burned as he looked around. He saw Tak WakKerrcarr, nodded a greeting at him.

A second man, shorter and thinner, with sleepy amber eyes and a spiky thatch of copper hair. He stood looking around, saying nothing, as calm as the two Sorcerer Primes who stood contemplating each other with the prickly distaste of two alpha wolves who didn't quite want to offer challenge.

The third was a woman with long hair the grayish brown of last year's fallen leaves and pale translucent skin. Her hazel eyes opened wide as she saw Faan. "Who?"

"Mother?"

Kori Piyolss glanced from Faan to the mahsar and back. "Faan? How. . . ."

"God-work," Faan said, her voice echoing through the haze, eerie in her own ears. "You've been asleep for nearly fifteen years."

Chaggar clawed at Faan again and again, a cat trying to catch a ghost mouse it couldn't believe wasn't there.

Tak WakKerrcarr snapped his fingers and Massulit whipped from Faan's hand to slap against his palm. He closed his fingers round it and lifted it high; Settsimaksimin moved to stand shoulder to shoulder with Tak, lifting his arm, holding it pressed against Tak's, wrapping his long fingers about Tak's hand. The blue light spread out from them, lifting over them into a huge glimmering dome that encompassed the bending form of the Land God.

Chaggar shrank until he was merely a giant, a giant of green jade, hard and tough as that toughest of stones. He knelt in the muck beside the Blind Man, bleeding green into the blue glow of the mud waves racing across the pool, adding enormous force to the engine building under the dome.

* * *

Faan held Ailiki in her arms and burned. She and the mahsar were forms of blue fire, then blue and green fire after Chaggar changed sides.

Holding hands, Navarre and Kitya came to stand blank-eyed beside her, Kitya burning green, Navarre burning blue.

Cluinn moaned, dropped his sword; he took a step to one side, another and another. The guards falling into line behind him, he circled the muck in a stamping, sidling dance. By the time he reached the place where he had been, the Gate Hag was there with the people from the street.

Their voices held to their deepest notes, a basso thrum throbbing to the pulse of the blue glimmer, round and round they followed him, guards and watchers, chanting as they moved: YMACH UNCÉANG YMACH DÉAMHAN YMACH UNCÉANG YMACH DÉAMHAN. . . . Over and over. YMACH UNCÉANG YMACH DÉAMHAN.

A tentacle of fire, mixed blue and green, whipped into godspace and coiled round the Chained God Unchained. It snapped the immense golden form into mortalspace, brought him crashing

into the bay outside Cumabyar. He roared his fury and struck back, gold light pouring from his form, eating at the blue, eating at the green. BinYAHtii throbbed, its field oozing out like a hungry red mist, sucking up everything it touched, nibbling at the edges of the tentacle that held the Chained God Unchained, fraying it relentlessly though it couldn't attack it directly. The Talisman Massulit fought it off.

* * *

Faan dredged her soul for all the bitterness, anger, hate, loss, anguish, all the harvest of her short life, flung it into the fire. Kitya patterned the pain with the force generated by the circling dancer, the power of the mud, the Other Thing that was there, the Thing with No Name and she gave the weave to Navarre who funneled it through himself into the Wrystrike.

Howling with all the frustration built from its attempts to fulfill its nature, the attempts that Navarre had diverted again and again, the Wrystrike whirled out around and behind the God, hitting him between his shoulder blades, just above the heart, if he had had a heart, spearing into him, doing what it was crafted to do, destroying. . . .

BinYAHtii exploded.
It rained red dust into the Bay, turning the waters into a scarlet acid that seethed and boiled and ate away everything in it down to bedrock.

All the Power the Chained God Unchained had eaten from the gods, powers, chthonics and demiurges rushed in a great roaring stream from the hole the Wrystrike punched into his substance, burning the Curse to less than ash as it leapt away from the convulsing god.

The Chained God Unchained dissolved.
The Living Metal sublimated into the forces that had created it. They danced in jags of light across the seething crimson water, darted finally into the earth and were absorbed there, spreading through the world, feeding the hungry godhusks that the Chained God Unchained had flung aside when he was finished with them.
The components of his original form fell into the

Bay, rotting vegetation, plastic and metal so old it fell to dust before it even touched the water.

BLESSED BE YOU ALL.

The immense voice broke the straining stillness that held them all.

A sweetness that was as piercing and powerful as the most intense of orgasms touched them, Faan, Navarre, Kitya, Brann, the Primes and all the rest. With a collective sigh they fell where they stood and lay unconscious around the Blind Man's mud.

Desantro stood. "Nu," she said, "that was something else." She frowned at the scattered bodies. "They're not dead, are they?"

The Blind Man chuckled. "After this, we'll have to be satisfied with smaller pleasures, m' grath. Nay, they are not even close to dead, only out for a while." He got to his feet. "Come, dulcerie, we shall have to be moving out all but those that belong here for the while. We'll put them in the street and let them wake there."

Desantro put her toe under Cluinn's ribs, lifted him a little, let him fall back. "This one meant to kill Faan, maybe we should tie him up till he has a chance to reconsider."

"Outside, sitabéag. I don't want him in my house. Besides, he won't hurt anyone. He won't be allowed."

"Some god? Cy, I wouldn't leave a god to pick up boggpats."

"No god. Me."

"Oh." She caught his hand, squeezed it. "You I trust. His shoulders are there, ba, right there, I'll get his feet."

She looked at the row of sleepers stretched out on the sparse clumps of grass. "Faan, her Mama, Ailiki,

the Sorcerer and that other one, What's-her-name ...
um ... Brann and her Sorcerer, that weird servant of
hers, Navarre, Kitya, my brother. An even dozen of
them, Cy. What are we going to do with them all?"

"Wait," he said. "They'll wake in the order they're
meant to wake, Des. Would you put some tea on for us?
I'm thirsty and I hear in your voice that you are, too."

Graybao sat up. "Nay, gentlesss, that isss my work,
ressst and I will ssserve you."

Desantro blinked at her. "Nu. . . ." she said dubi-
ously.

The Blind Man spoke, laughter bubbling in his voice,
"Nay, Desa, let be. Come, rest beside me."

Rakil jerked upright, looked hastily about, blinking
in the blinding sunlight. He saw Desantro sitting in the
mud beside the Blind Man, sipping at a cup of tea.
"What? Des? What happened?"

"We killed a god."

"I'm not in the mood for games. What time is it?"
He jumped up. "I have to get ready, the ship. . . ."

The Blind Man lifted his head. "There are no ships
left in the harbor, there'll be none coming in or leaving
for a week at least."

"That woman. . . ." His teeth chattered, he was so angry. He started for Brann. "That norou maldize, I knew
she was. . . ."

"Stay," the Blind Man said, and Rakil stopped as if
he'd run into a wall. "Listen to me, Desantro's Brother,
there's no need for this. The man you want is dead.
Purb the Flea went to the bottom of the Notoea Tha before you reached Bandrabahr."

"The kech. . . ." He put his hand on the small tube,
intact beneath his shirt. "Guffrakin. . . ."

"One who needed you here to play your part in his
game, he brought the kech to life and made it point and

put the words in Guffrakin's mouth. I name no names but swear on my mud that what I say is truth."

"Then your mud can have this." Rakil plucked the tube from inside his shirt and threw it down. "And I. . . ."

"Wait. Desa, the pouch, give it to your brother." As Desantro stood and came to Rakil, dripping droplets of the gray mud much to his disgust, the Blind Man added, "This is courtesy of the Turry Heir though he doesn't know it yet. I wouldn't spend any of it anywhere in Gallindar, but it should keep you well elsewhere. There will be ships returning in a week or so, the Bay will have cleared, you can go where you wish, Desantro's Brother, though you'll always be welcome here."

Rakil looked round, didn't try to hide his grimace of distaste. "Thanks," he said. "I might take you up on that. Des, I'll write when I settle somewhere, Kukurul probably. Take care."

She watched him leave, sighed, and went back to the Blind Man. "More tea?"

"If you will. Does it hurt you, dulcerie?"

"Twenty years," she said. "Ties grow weak, m' grath. Regret? Ba. Hurt? Nay. I told you what I needed most from him and that I've got. He'll tell the tale to his children, if he ever has any, and to Tariko's. It's too good a story to leave behind. I'll be remembered by my blood."

Navarre and Kitya woke. He touched his head, stared wildly around.

"What is it, V'ret, what's wrong?"

"Nothing," the Blind Man said. "He is just realizing that the Wrystrike is gone, destroyed. He's a free man now."

"Oh."

Navarre got to his feet, held out his hands. "Let's go home, Kat."

DAW

Jo Clayton

The Wild Magic Series:

☐ **WILD MAGIC: Book 1** UE2496—$4.99

Faan was a mortal, kidnapped by the mightiest of goddesses, and trapped in a war between gods. Could she learn to master her own powers before the rival gods destroyed her?

☐ **WILDFIRE: Book 2** UE2514—$4.99

Faan embarks on a difficult and daring search to find her mother, refusing to remain a pawn in the deadly games being played between gods and wizards.

☐ **THE MAGIC WARS: Book 3** UE2547—$4.99

When universes meet and the wild magic is unchained, will Faan and her comrades survive the chaos of a sorcerous war?

The Drinker of Souls Series:

☐ **DRINKER OF SOULS: Book 1** UE2433—$4.50

She was Brann, the Drinker of Souls, from whom all but the very brave and the very foolish fled in fear.

☐ **A GATHERING OF STONES: Book 3** UE2346—$3.95

Trapped by the Chained God's power, can Brann and her allies find the magic talismans to set the god—and themselves-free?

EPILOGUE

Midsummer's Day was bright and fair—and quieter than usual as the city recovered from the death of a god and began repairing the ravages from the battle. No one knew exactly what had happened, but they all knew Chaggar was awake and tending to business and the rinnanfeoyr was over.

Desantro brought Cyram the Blind Man his afternoon tea, stood looking around the big empty yard.

"You know, Cy, you've really left this place to the weeds and wind. I could make it bloom with more beauty than the Cummiltag will ever know. If you don't mind."

He chuckled, set the drinking bowl on the tray. "Don't disturb my mud, my sitabéag, my dulcerie. That's all I ask."

half the afternoon and a lot of hot air arguing about the best place. The horses?"

"Desa and I got the harness off them and she took them to the other side of the trees so they could graze."

"So we're rid of the Chained God."

"If a god can be killed, he's dead."

"May I beg a cup from that pot? I'm dry enough to drink your mud."

Kori Piyolss sat up.

Faan stirred, sat up, dislodging Ailiki from her ribs. The mahsar complained querulously, then settled herself in Faan's lap and began grooming herself.

"So you're my daughter. And I've missed your growing up."

"And you're my mother and I don't know you. Gods!"

"You burn hot, daughter."

"Not at the moment, Tungjii Bless. Will you teach me?"

"I'll help you, child, but I won't be your teacher." Kori smiled uncertainly; the smile turned to a grin as Faan giggled. "I'm not such an idiot as that. Maksim can teach you, he's good with fire. And he needs a challenge for his soul's sake." The smile became a burst of laughter. "I have a feeling, Fa, you'll singe his hide before you're through and boil the fat off his bones."

"Is he my father?"

"Nay, child, your father was a fancy of mine. I'll tell you about him later." She held out her hands.

Hesitantly Faan took them, gasped as force flowed between them, the conduit opened by their shared blood. She lifted her head, her eyes glowed. "Mamay," she said.

"Home?"

"The Smithy outside Savvalis. It's home enough for now. We've got a lot of talking to do."

"Tja, we do." From the circle of his arms, Kitya smiled at Desantro. "Tungjii kiss you sweet, Desa, you and your friend."

Navarre's arms tightened about her, then they were gone.

The two Sorcerers woke together and Simms the Witch a moment later.

Tak used his staff to lever himself up, held out his hand to Settsimaksimin, grunted as he hauled him onto his feet. "You keep putting on weight, Maks, you're going to end up immobile."

"At least I don't go round crawling with every bug in a hundred mile circle."

"Want a beer? You and your friend?"

Maksim rubbed his hand across his mouth. "Sounds good to me. Blind Man, tell them," he wave a large, shapely hand at the sleeping women, "where we've gone, hmm?" He linked arms with Simms and Tak and the three of them strolled into the trees.

Brann woke, sat up. She got to her feet, groaning as every muscle she owned protested. When she was on her feet, she looked around. Desantro and the Blind Man were sitting in the mud sipping tea. Graybao was a gray mist, refilling the pot with hot water. Faan and Kori were lying a little way off, still out.

"Where. . . ."

"They went for beer," the Blind Man said. "They'll be back soon, the beer in Cumabyar is a sin against all drinking men."

"If that's so, they'll be even longer. Those are Sorcerer Primes, my friend. If they want beer and can't find it here, they'll go to where it is—after spending